Dark Secrets

by

V. A. Risby

ISBN-13: 978-0692055038
ISBN-10: 0692055037

For Kaitlyn
who is my inspiration
in everything I do.
Without her input this
story would have never been told.

Dark Secrets

Book 1

The Dark Series

1

The crunch of dead leaves was lost over the sound of his pounding, bare feet and rapidly beating heart as he ran, his hands up in front of him to ward off the sting of branches and leaves that nipped and bit at the delicate flesh of his face. For just a moment, he darted a glance back at the dark-headed girl with the tear-stained face, running at his heels. But it was only for a moment. The low rumble of thunder seemed to come from around them.

Quickly, he jerked his gray-eyed gaze back ahead; the small form of an animal darted in front of him. He fought to keep pace with it. He knew he couldn't lose sight of it, though ever so often it appeared as if it glanced back to see if he was still there.

The fear raced along his spine as he glanced behind him again. Not to the girl, but further back. The jagged streak of lightening cut through the night sky, illuminating the dark, dense forest. The fine, downy hair raised along his arms as he made out the large black shape, lumbering behind them.

It was getting closer.

He forced himself to pump his legs harder, ignoring the pain that sliced through his feet as the sharp sting of fallen limbs tore into his soles.

"Come on!"

The yell seemed to echo from every direction, urging them to move faster.

He heard the whimper, didn't know if it came from him or the girl. He didn't care. He just kept running, the terror threatening to choke him, freeze his small muscles. He couldn't give into it. If he did, that thing would get him. He couldn't let it.

A glance back showed it was getting closer.

Fire seemed to burn through him from his exertion. They weren't going to make it. He knew it. Ahead of them, the small animal gave a cry of distress. He glanced to it and saw it had stopped. He was forced to as well or he'd run it over. He didn't understand why until another flash of lightening brightened the sky. There, before them, another large, black shape was emerging from the dark depth of the woods.

They were surrounded.

A choked sob emanated from the small girl. Then the rain started, coming in torrents.

The panic, the fear, they were making it hard to breathe as the heat coursed through him. He raised his hands, each pointed in the direction of one of the dark, shadowy figures. He closed his eyes and—

With a start, Sawyer Randal jerked awake, his head lifting from where it had been resting on the cool glass of the SUV window. Rapidly blinking his gray eyes, he fought to push the sleep away. As he straightened to a sitting position, he adjusted the dark sunglasses he still wore.

"Good dream?"

He glanced over to his left. In the opposite bucket seat, the identical gaze of his twin sister met his. She had one brown brow raised in question.

He thought to tell her no, but his forehead furrowed as he tried to recall what had woken him. He knew he'd dreamed, but it was gone, just as some dreams were prone to do. Instead, he answered her with a shrug of his broad shoulders.

Seeming to understand no answer would be forth coming, she said, "We just crossed the city limit. She glanced out her own window at the tree-lined streets. "Welcome to Willow Oak."

Sawyer glanced back out his own window. He saw a house with a well-manicured lawn and perfectly shaped shrubs. It was perfect, like in those cheesy Christmas movies his mother liked to watch on some cable television channel. Definitely wasn't the life he was used to back in Chicago.

They were all quiet, taking in the surroundings as they passed house after house, well-kept yard, after well-kept yard until his father turned onto a winding, tree-lined driveway, paved in what appeared to be smooth stone.

The vehicle pulled to a stop before the gray-gabled Victorian home.

For a moment, none of them moved. He felt as if once he stepped out everything was going to change. But that was a ridiculous thought. His hand went to the handle; he pushed open the door. It seemed to be what everyone needed to break them out of their own suspended animation. The doors swung open, the other three passengers climbing out of the SUV.

"What in the world are we doing here?"

Sawyer surveyed his surroundings as soon as his feet touched the stone driveway. He pulled off his dark sunglasses and turned to look at his twin sister Kira. Even though she had voiced the question aloud, she didn't glance at any of them. Instead, she was focused on the house before her.

Sawyer wondered the same thing. At first impression, the town of Willow Oak appeared nondescript. He didn't understand why their junior year of high school had to be spent here, and why they had been uprooted by their parents and forced across the country.

It had been a complete surprise when their father had come home one day and announced his promotion and transfer.

Dragged from their home in Chicago, where there was always something for them to do, they now found themselves thrust into a small, rural town in upstate Maine.

Such an isolated, desolate location didn't scream out the next step in a supposedly flourishing business career.

As Sawyer stared up at the old Victorian house—another supposed benefit of Gary Randal's new job—he cast a speculative glance over at his sister to see how she was fairing with their new reality.

This time Kira's gray-eyed gaze darted over to meet his. They shared a look of understanding. Having been nearly inseparable for most of their lives, they typically seemed to know what the other was thinking.

Around the age of seven, they had been abandoned by their biological parents. Taken into foster care, they had been in the system for almost two years before Gary and Diana Randal had adopted them. They'd only ended up in Chicago because one set of foster parents had moved, taking them with them before dumping them in the strange city. That's where their parents had found them. And they had lived there ever since. It was their home.

Leaving the only home they remembered did not set well with the twins, more so moving from the bustling city life to a town that wasn't to be found on any maps. Google Earth provided no help either.

Before the move, an internet search revealed the town didn't even have a website.

What type of town didn't have a website?

If not for the letter they'd received in the mail—what town even did that?—welcoming them all to "Magical Willow Oak," there would be no proof that the place even existed.

"This is the home base for your international company?" Sawyer felt the need to ask his father, hoping for some form of clarification. He hadn't even seen another vehicle since they'd crossed the city limit sign. The houses they had passed—all Victorian he had noted—hadn't had any in the driveway either, if they'd even had a driveway. Street-side parking was something they were used to so that didn't seem very odd in itself. The fact that no vehicles were parked on the street, though, was another matter entirely.

Gary appeared every bit as skeptical as his son felt, which only furthered Sawyer's unease.

"Yes, though I will now have to travel overseas a bit, or at least that's what I was told."

Kira glanced around, before turning to look behind them back to the drive. "I can't believe this town even has an airport."

Gary ran a hand through his already disheveled peppered hair. "It must be on the opposite side of town."

Once again, Sawyer glanced to his sister. He read the look in her silver eyes accurately: *Where are we?*

Their mother must have been feeling the same way as she placed a comforting arm across Kira's shoulders. "The house has a lot of that...charm and character those people always seem to be looking for in those home buying shows." No matter the words, she didn't appear convinced either. In fact, she looked as cynical as they did.

"You'll see," Gary told them, looking between the house and his family. "It will all be great. New town, new people, new lives. We can all be whole new people here."

Again, Diana gave Kira a one-armed hug. "I happen to like the people we are."

Sawyer glanced away with a roll of his eyes, but he couldn't help the grin that tugged at the corners of his lips. It was such a corny thing to say, so much like his mother.

They were lucky that it was the Randals that had adopted them all those years ago. They'd never once doubted how much they were now loved. That was apparently something their biological parents hadn't felt for them.

Cold and shivering, huddled with his sister under a rickety porch at an abandoned house. That was his first memory. They were seven, or at least around that age. Neither of them knew for certain.

He didn't remember what had happened before or even how or why they were alone. But he knew he had been terrified. That feeling had always stuck with him.

Kira didn't recall the events either, just the scared feeling.

He found that odd.

He would think one of them would remember what had happened, or at least something that had led them to that moment. But it was as if the events before they were found had been erased. They didn't even know which one of them was older, let alone their birthdate. The only thing either of them could recollect was their first name, and that they were twins. That was it.

At first, he had worried about it, nearly obsessed over it—what else was he supposed to do, as he waited in overcrowded foster homes—but not any longer. It didn't matter anymore. He'd moved on. And that was because of his mother and father. In fact, it had been years since he had thought anything about it at all. Yet, for some reason, it was now playing heavily on his mind. He almost felt as if he was that small child again, terrified, cowered under that porch, having no clue of who he really was or where he had come from.

With a shake of his head, Sawyer dispelled the wayward thought. He didn't know why it had hit him now. It must be the newness of their surroundings that was bringing up the long ago feelings; he'd thought he'd outgrown it.

Yet, as he surveyed the place he now found himself, it felt almost like a memory. He'd never had one of those before. But that didn't make any sense; it wasn't even possible. But the feeling of déjà vu wouldn't abate.

He and Kira were found in Philadelphia. No way could two barefoot, small children make it from wherever they were in upstate Maine to Philadelphia.

Shaking his head, he tried to forget the thought. He'd let it all go. It didn't matter any longer. It was a lifetime ago.

Now, apparently, his future was in a tiny little New England town. With a rueful shake of his head, he continued to survey this new house. High school graduation and college were sounding pretty good if it could get him back to an urban environment, Chicago or maybe even New York City.

Wherever it was, it had to be bigger than this little place. He thrived on the noise and congestion of a large city.

"Well, let's go see our new home." Gary gave them a reassuring smile then started up the stone steps that led to the wrap-around front porch.

Sawyer exchanged another look with his sister then had no choice but to follow her and their mother. As he stepped on the wooden porch, it hit him. A dull hiss—not quite a buzz—sounded in his ears, making his head seen heavy, and him feel as if he couldn't breathe. Automatically, his hand swept out, his fingers tightening on the white painted wood porch railing.

Hot and fast, an image flashed in his mind. His marble-gray eyes closed as he focused on the sudden pictures in his mind. A man, tall, dark hair stood at his side. They both looked over a porch railing—the same railing he now clung to. The man's body was rigid, tense; a muscle ticked in his jaw as he stared down at another man who was standing in the yard, his lips lifted in a smirk. Their clothing was odd; it seemed very old fashioned.

As suddenly as it came, the memory fled, leaving Sawyer panting, trying to catch his breath. His head dropped down, his chin all but touching his chest as a wave of intense pain shot through his head. It felt as though his brain was on fire. His stomach rolled with a wave of nausea.

"Honey? Are you all right?" His mother's gentle hand lightly touched his cheek.

"Sawyer?" Kira's concerned voice came from his back.

He couldn't force himself to offer any reassurance. All his energy was focused on not being sick.

"Let's get you inside so you can sit." His father's hand rested under his elbow, offering the aid he needed. His legs felt like rubber and didn't want to support his body.

Taking a deep, measured breath, Sawyer slowly lifted his head. The nearly blinding pain was receding. He blew out air in a hiss. He rotated his neck from side to side until he heard the satisfying crack. The pain had reduced to a dull ache. Finally, he managed, "I'm ok." His eyes opened and met the concerned gaze of his mother. "I don't know what it was but...I'm ok now."

She didn't appear convinced at all. Her brow furrowed as she studied him.

"Let's still get you inside so you can sit." His father quickly crossed to the door and taking a set of keys from his pocket that was clearly labeled, he inserted an old brass key in the standard handle lock. No dead bolt for this town.

Sawyer didn't even realize he had held his breath until his father turned the handle and the door opened. Nothing rushed out at them; nothing cataclysmic happened. He didn't exactly understand why, but he had been waiting for it, waiting for something. They were met by silence.

His sister cast him another worried glance, which he answered with what he hoped was a bolstering grin. She nodded, slightly, and then moved behind their father, peaking around his side to see into the dark interior of the house.

Gary looked back to his wife and son then stepped forward to flick the light switch by the door, bathing the interior in a warm, dusty glow. Then he turned toward them and strode purposefully forward. "Come on. Let's get you inside."

"I'm fine now. Really," Sawyer tried to reassure.

"Just humor us," his mother said, her tone still infused with concern.

He nodded. For her, he relented and slowly moved forward, flanked on either side by his parents. He felt weak, and he didn't like that. As they approached the door, Kira stepped back to allow them room.

Sawyer glanced inside and braced himself. The feeling that something was coming was back.

Nothing happened.

No more weird flashes, no more sudden, nearly debilitating pain. It was just a house. White sheets shrouded furniture. The floor was visible, dark hardwood running the expanse of what he could see. It even carried up the staircase that was wide enough for at least two people—if not three—to use at the same time. The staircase was off to the right of the front door. It led to a wide landing and then curved into more stairs that led to the second floor.

A large crystal chandelier hung in the center of the foyer. It looked as if candles, not light bulbs were in it. But that made no sense as his dad had flicked the switch on the wall. On either side was a curved archway. The one to the right led to a hallway. He could make out a door then eventually another arch that opened into some sort of room. The left arch led directly into a room with sheets covering many objects.

His father must have come to the same conclusion as he led him left. His mother and Kira quickly moved ahead of them. They each went to different pieces and yanked off the white sheets covering them, revealing impressive antique furniture. The white upholstery gleamed against the dark wood frames.

His father led him toward the two-seater that Sawyer was afraid even to sit on; it looked too expensive and delicate.

"I'm all right. Whatever it was, it's passed." He tried to reassure them as he was still met with three concerned gazes.

His mother's look was nothing short of skeptical. "I'd really rather you sit for a moment. Just to make sure."

It was true; he felt perfectly fine now, but he couldn't deny her simple request. Nodding, he gingerly lowered himself. He leaned back a bit, trying to find a comfortable position. After the three of them exchanged another fretful look, they cautiously moved toward other parts of the room.

"Thank goodness the walls are a light color," his mother said as she surveyed the dark flooring.

Kira pulled off another covering, revealing the mantel of a dark fireplace. On it set an antique, white clock, with a round top etched in gold. As Sawyer watched, his sister's brow furrowed. She reached out a hesitant hand and lightly touched the piece, her fingertips dancing over the glass face.

As she studied it, her words came in a thoughtful, hushed tone. "I feel like I've seen this before."

Abruptly, she turned on her heel and approached one of the few remaining blanketed pieces of furniture. She whipped off its shroud to reveal a rich, dark wood piece. It had two seats beside each other, though each faced the opposite direction. Her fingers skimmed over the solid wood. "This used to set over here, and I'd get in trouble for having my muddy feet in the opposite seat."

The words came out without thought, seeming to shock her as she turned to them, her eyes wide and confused. "How would I..."

She couldn't seem to finish as she glanced back from the clock to the chair.

Their parents exchanged an equally perplexed look. "A dream, perhaps," their mother suggested, though she didn't look convinced.

Sawyer studied his sister. Her gray eyes appeared almost glassy. Then she shook herself, seeming to break the near trance it appeared she was caught in. Her gaze met his for a moment, and then quickly moved away, surveying the room again.

Getting to his feet, Sawyer did his own quick once-over of the room.

"We should explore," their mother said, hooking her arm through Kira's. "We'll want to know where to direct the movers once they arrive." She came forward and gently laid her hand against his cheek.

He answered her unasked question. "I'm fine. I'm not sick. I promise."

The smile reached her eyes this time, her relief apparent. "I'm glad. You were so pale. You had me worried."

He gave her a quick hug. His grin sought to reassure her. "Come on. Let's see what kind of place we have."

As a unit, they moved from the vaulted ceiling living room, which had glass doors leading out to the wrap-around porch. Stairs on the side of it led to a covered patio that emptied into what appeared to be a garden. They went back into the living room and exited through a rounded arch near the back. It spilled into the dining room. Gary pulled the sheet from what ended up being a white sideboard with gold etching. Sawyer yanked off another linen, revealing the matching dining table; twelve high-backed chairs surrounded it.

"That is beautiful," Kira's voice whispered, her tone filled with awe. "It's like something in a fairytale castle."

Diana ran her hand along the hard plane of the tabletop. "It is," she said in response to her daughter's comment. "I don't know what we're going to do with all of our things. These are too beautiful to get rid of."

Sawyer looked around, surveying the room, thinking back to the other. This furniture wasn't his style, definitely too formal for his tastes, especially if this was supposed to be his home. He liked the sleek appearance of the more modern designs.

"Maybe this is all of it and the other rooms are empty." Gary offered that idea though he didn't appear very convinced of it.

Sawyer figured the best way to find out was to see. He led the way into the next room, which was the kitchen.

The kitchen seemed completely different from the rest of the house. Sleek and modern with stainless steel appliances, even a gas stove. White cabinets and sparkling quartz countertops completed the updated look. When Sawyer turned, he found his father had already pulled off the sheet draping the center island, complete with matching quartz. It was better than their kitchen in Chicago.

"This is amazing," their mother breathed out. "It's a dream kitchen. I've always wanted something like this." Hesitantly, her fingers skimmed the quartz. "So much counter space."

The kitchen opened into a family room, complete with more antiques. A door with a stain-glass panel led to a home office. In the hallway Sawyer had noticed off the foyer earlier, they found a lavishly decorated half bath and two hall closets. One looked large enough to fit four people but strangely had no rods to hang anything.

With a glance to each other, they ascended the stairs— they *were* wide enough for two people. The top of the stairs opened onto a landing. More sheets shrouded wing-backed chairs. It appeared to be a reading nook. The first door they went into revealed another room with a vaulted ceiling. They found an antique dark wooden bed, minus the mattress, a sofa, and two more chairs. The room contained a walk-in closet and then opened up into a large master bathroom.

Turning in a circle, Kira took it all in. Then she turned to her parents, her smile wide. "I call this room."

Their father laughed. "Nice try, honey."

Grinning, she led them back out, finding two more large bedrooms, complete with their own bathrooms. They were comparable in size. Kira took the light blue walled bedroom, while Sawyer claimed the one with the red walls. Another office and a large spare room rounded off the second floor.

As they descended the stairs, Diana fretted. "We are going to have to make some decisions. Our furniture and these pieces won't all fit. Something will have to go into storage."

"I actually like this furniture," Kira said as she went back into the family room. She flopped down on one of the sofas. "It doesn't look it, but it's actually really comfortable."

Sawyer shook his head. "I want my things. This." He threw out a hand to encompass the house as a whole. "Yeah, this isn't me."

"Once the movers get here, we'll go through everything and make decisions," Gary announced as he took a seat in one of the chairs.

"I'm torn but—"

The knock cut through Diana's words, bringing them to an abrupt halt. It sounded like a thunderclap in the house, seeming to echo. Sawyer glanced to his sister, his brow creased in thought. There was no way the sound should have been that loud at the back of the house.

Quickly, Gary was on his feet. "I didn't expect the movers for a few more hours."

They followed him from the room. Sawyer stepped into the foyer as his father opened the door. It wasn't the men who had taken their belongings in their large white truck. Instead, a man and woman stood there both appeared in their early to mid-forties. The man was tall, his hair gray. The woman was petite, her complexion pale, which was even more startling with her flame red hair. They were dressed rather formally, he in dress pants and a long-sleeved buttoned shirt, her in a long green skirt and white silk blouse.

"Michail," Gary said, reaching out to shake the other man's hand.

The newcomer smiled. It eased the hard lines around his face. "Gary, I'm glad you all made it safely." Then his dark green-eyed gaze came to Kira. He studied her for a long moment.

When Sawyer shifted closer to her, that penetrating gaze came to him. He didn't glance away; instead, he returned the open appraisal. He felt as if the older man was trying to take his measure.

Suddenly, the older man's grin grew.

"Michail," Gary said, drawing the man's attention, "this is my wife, Diana and our children, Sawyer and Kira." He then turned to his family. "This is Michail Hopewell, my boss."

He shook their hands in turn, giving them another broad grin. "This is my wife, Constance."

The redhead smiled. "I'm so glad to finally meet you. Michail speaks very highly of your husband."

"Oh, yes." Diana stepped forward, took the other woman's hand, and shook it lightly. "Gary has only had wonderful things to say about your husband." Then she stepped to the side. "Won't you please come in?"

Diana led them to the living room. "We were just discussing the furnishings. Some of us are in love with what is already in the house." Then she cast a pointed glance in Sawyer's direction, though she softened it with a smile. "Though others are craving their old belongings."

"I think we have the old backwards," Sawyer said under his breath.

As Constance took a seat on the sofa Sawyer had been on earlier, she glanced around the room. "We aired the house out and had cleaners come before you arrived. No one has lived here in almost ten years, but the house has been recently decorated."

"Well, it's beautiful. Whoever did it tied it all together beautifully. The rooms are light and airy even with the heavy, antique furniture."

Constance's hazel-eyed gaze darted back and forth between Kira and Sawyer. "A few of the pieces from the previous owners remain. They were here in this town for as long as I can remember. Their daughter-in-law...she was my best friend all through childhood." She fell silent for just a moment, as she seemed lost in a memory before she shook it off. Her smile was bright when she continued. "We did have the kitchen completely redone for you. We thought it would be better as it was as authentic as the rest of the furnishings."

Straightening from his place by the door, Sawyer studied the two strangers. He could see it there, in their eyes; they were holding something back. But what? And why? There was nothing suspicious about any of this, and yet, he was on edge, waiting. A sense of foreboding crept up his spine.

Once again, he glanced to his sister to see if she was getting the same feeling of unease. Instead, she wasn't paying attention to any of them. She was standing before the fireplace, once again, her fingertips tracing the detailing of the clock atop the mantel. Her brow was knitted in concentration.

With purposeful strides, he crossed to her, ignoring the adults who were still conversing. He stepped to her side; his gaze focused on her instead of the timepiece that she apparently found fascinating. He glanced down to her, her five and half-feet putting her under his six.

He tilted his head toward her. "What is it?" Something was bothering her.

She worried her lower lip with her teeth. Finally, she released it and then turned to him. Her voice was low when she spoke. "I feel…it's as if I've been here before. I can't shake that feeling. It makes no sense.

But he was nodding in agreement before she finished speaking. "That's…earlier when I first stepped on that porch…it was as if I was seeing myself standing there but I was young. It seemed so real, but that's not possible."

She cast a furtive glance around them, seeming to get the impression they were being watched. "We couldn't have been here before." She shook her head at the thought and dismissed it. "That wouldn't even be possible. This is our first time here."

He opened his mouth to—he didn't know what exactly. Part of him wanted to refute her claims, yet he realized she had to be correct. It wasn't possible. Granted Pennsylvania wasn't too far from Maine, but for two children all alone, it might as well have been the entire country. Something, though, still nagged at the back of his mind. He turned, stared passed the arched opening to the banister of the staircase in the foyer.

Suddenly, another image hit him, almost knocking him to his knees. He could all but feel himself sliding down that wood banister. At the bottom was the same man he'd pictured on the covered porch earlier. This time he was smiling, his dark hair mused, his hands stretched out, waiting to catch him as he sailed with glee.

Gasping, his hands reached out, searching for anything to keep him upright.

"Sawyer!"

He heard his twin shout his name. Her voice seemed to come from far away, but it couldn't have been as then one of her arms wrapped around his waist, trying to support him.

Once again, the pain sliced through his head, burning, cutting, making him want to scream from its intensity. It seared, sent his stomach rolling. He was going to be sick.

Stronger arms came to him, carefully easing him forward and then down onto a sofa. He opened his mouth to tell them he was all right, but no sound would come. He belatedly realized his eyes were closed, shutting out the offending light glimmering in through the large windows. Everything inside him hurt.

A cool cloth was pressed against his forehead. He felt his mother's gentle hands on his face. He could make out muffled voices, but he couldn't understand what they were saying. Forcing himself to take a slow, measured breath, he had to be calm. He had to make sense of what all these images were, and why they were coming to him now. But more than anything, he had to fight against the nearly unbearable pain.

"We need to get him to a doctor."

That was his mother. He could make out the worried, nearly frantic tone of her voice.

Sawyer started to shake his head in protest, but the movement sent his stomach to lurching, rolling violently again. He stayed still to say one word, "No." The thought of going anywhere made him want to hurl.

"I agree with your mother. Something is wrong."

"Just…give me a moment." He didn't want to talk. He wanted to be left alone if only for a moment.

They must have sensed that as they fell silent though his mother remained by his side. He didn't know how long he lay there, but he felt the tension slowly seep from him. Only when the pounding in his head eased did he brace himself on an arm to rise into a sitting position.

Hesitantly, he opened his eyes, afraid that if his gaze caught on something else that it would trigger another painful response. The first thing he saw was his mother's concerned eyes staring at him, seeming to watch for any signs of distress. He tried to give her a reassuring grin, but he was sure it came out strained.

"Honey?"

"Sawyer?"

The questions came at him from his mother and sister. He knew what they were asking. Uncertainly, he glanced toward the staircase again since he could still see it from his vantage point. He was met with nothing this time, which was a blessed relief but also a cause for more confusion.

When he spoke, his voice seemed hoarse, raspy to his own ears. "I remembered sliding down that banister to some man. That was what happened on the porch. It was like a flash of a memory." He glanced up, met his father's worried and confused gaze.

"What is going on?" Gary asked aloud to no one. "After all this time, you're getting your memory back now?"

There was a hesitant clearing of a throat. Sawyer turned his head slightly, his gaze colliding with the dark green one of Michail Hopewell.

The man looked regretful. "I…"

He glanced to his wife, and Sawyer noted her glassy eyes. He saw the hint of unshed tears in the depths.

Taking a deep breath, Michail told them, though his attention was focused solely on Sawyer. "I can explain it all to you. If you'll let me."

2

Kira glanced to her brother then back to the man. He was essentially a stranger, so how could he know what was happening to her brother? The answer was he couldn't. It wasn't possible.

A sliver of fear, of awareness, crept down the base of her spine. She took an involuntary step back.

"How would you know, Michail?" Gary asked. His brow furrowed in confusion.

Another step and Kira felt the back of her legs bump the sofa upon which her brother was sitting.

Their father's boss and his wife's gaze were focused on them, seeming to search for something almost like recognition. Feeling as if she could no longer support herself, Kira sunk down on the sofa next to her brother.

"I think…perhaps we should all sit," Constance said. Her voice seemed as if she was forcibly keeping it light and cheerful. It didn't work.

Glancing to her parents, Kira watched as they exchanged a perplexed look before their mother took the seat on the other side of Sawyer. Their father settled in one of the chairs near them.

Another hesitant look, then the Hopewells took a seat opposite their position.

When they didn't say anything for a moment, Kira darted a quick look to her brother. His jaw was rigid, his body tense, as he waited. Instinctively, she knew he felt it, too. Impending dread slid down her, taking up residence in the pit of her stomach. Whatever they were going to say, she didn't know if she wanted to hear it—no, that wasn't right. She *knew* she didn't want to. It wasn't going to be good.

She opened her mouth to tell him that, to tell him to keep whatever he thought he knew to himself, but she found the words wouldn't come, her tongue like sandpaper in her mouth. Instead, she sat there, staring at him.

"There was a time I wondered if we would ever get the chance to tell you. And now. . . ." He shrugged his shoulders, his gaze, though, never leaving her and Sawyer. He looked at them as though he was afraid he would never see them again, as if they were going to get up and run.

Ever get the chance?

What in the world did that mean? This man only knew her father from work. She hadn't ever met him before; she'd remember if she had.

Suddenly, it hit her. Drawing in a ragged breath, she blindly reached for her brother's hand.

She didn't remember them, but she didn't recall anything from her earlier life. Were they saying…?

Her eyes widened, horrified at the thought of what was coming. Her hand tightened around her brother's, and she glanced to him. He had the same, wild, perplexed, nearly crazed look that she figured she mirrored. He squeezed back, the pressure almost painful, but she didn't care. She needed it, needed something to keep her grounded as she felt as if she was spiraling.

"Michail," Gary said, "you're not making any sense."

Michail quickly looked to his wife. She nodded and gave him a weak, sad smile. Sucking in a deep breath, he took them all in. "I'm not trying to be cryptic. I'm really not. It's just…I don't know exactly where to begin. There's so much that I need to explain, to tell you. You'll have so many questions. And I know I need to do it. I *have* to do it because if I don't…" He shook his head. "You might not get the truth from someone else." Then abruptly, his gaze hardened. "I *know* you wouldn't get the truth from some people."

The Randals exchanged an even more confused look.

Then to her horror, Kira heard herself ask, "What truth?"

The older man's gaze softened again. "There's a lot to get through, and we'll tell you all of it. I just…I need you to keep an open mind. All right?"

Sawyer nodded his gaze still steady, intense as he waited.

Apparently, Michail took her brother's confirmation as everyone's agreement. Another sigh, then he said, "There's something I have to explain first about this town. Willow Oak…there are other places like it in this country and around the world. Towns that seem no one has ever heard of before."

"There's no town website," Sawyer said, bringing up something that had bugged him about this place from the very beginning, "No map location. Just those directions sent in that letter."

He abruptly snapped his mouth shut, and Kira knew he did that to keep back his derogatory feelings on the subject. He'd already brought it up with her plenty of times.

"Exactly." Michail nodded as if that proved his previous assertion. "That letter, it was addressed to you four and by reading it…that was the only way you were allowed to enter the boundary. Well...it was the only way Gary and Diana could enter."

Sawyer released her hand and sat forward, his elbows on his knees. His gaze darkened and pinned the older man to the spot. "*That* doesn't make any sense."

"It will." Constance's voice was soft, almost soothing. "Just…it will."

Sawyer's eyes narrowed, and Kira knew he wasn't going to let that go. But she wanted this to continue. She wanted to know what in the world was going on with the people who sat before them.

Turning, she cast her brother a look that made him snap his mouth shut. His glare was mutinous, but he remained quiet. Satisfied, she turned to the older couple. "Go on. Please explain."

The man sat back on the sofa and took his wife's hand in his, seeming to gather courage and comfort from it. "It goes back to many years before my time, over three hundred years actually. When this country was in its infancy, well you all know about the European countries' colonization. During this time…other people thought to make a fresh start here. Until then, this was mainly a raw, untamed land. But don't get me wrong, others of our kind were here, just not in the numbers there are today."

Her forehead creased as she pondered his choice of words. Finally, Kira asked, "Our kind?"

Again, Michail and his wife exchanged a troubled look.

Kira forced herself to not stomp her foot in irritation. She was tired of the man being so cryptic. She just wanted it all out and now.

He must have sensed her frustration as abruptly he sat forward, his gaze on them, intense, penetrating. "There are people in this world that have certain…qualities that others do not possess. They have…powers. They have magic."

Kira's eyes widened. She glanced to her family, knowing her perplexed and now leery expression was mirrored on their faces. She had not gotten the impression that her father's boss was crazy or delusional, whatever one wanted to call it, whenever he was mentioned in reference to work. However, there it was. Now they needed to know if he was prone to violence in his delusions. They wouldn't want to say the wrong thing and anger him.

Apparently, her father was of the same mind as when he spoke, his tone was soft, almost tentative. "Michail, are you feeling all right?"

Sawyer's hand tightened around hers; he took their mother's in his free one. Kira felt him tense. She knew he was planning to run if he felt the need arose. She shifted herself slightly to prepare. She would help him if at all possible.

Michail nodded, a small smile coming to his lips. "I know it seems crazy. I would not believe it either. I…" He glanced to his wife then surged to his feet.

Kira jumped, gasping and shrunk back on the sofa, leaning in closer to her brother. He'd been too quick for them to even move. The older man turned away from them and to a chair in the corner that was still covered. Suddenly, the pristine white sheet whipped away from the piece of furniture. It sailed through the air and came to a rest at his feet.

They shot to theirs.

Sawyer started edging her and their mother toward the open archway. Michail touched the chain around his neck then something was in his hand. He casually waved the stick he now held, and what appeared to be a steel door appeared, blocking the exit.

Kira's eyes widened. This could not be real. Icy fear climbed along the base of her spine, making her nerves raw and on edge as she waited, fearful of the unknown, fearful of what his next move would be.

Sawyer released her and grabbed their mother as her knees buckled. Their father was instantly on his feet—his moment of stunned horror forgotten as he went to his wife. He and his son helped ease her back on the sofa.

"I'm sorry." Michail's tone was contrite. He waved the thing in his hand again, and the door disappeared as quickly as it materialized. "I just wanted to explain."

"What…" Kira shook her head, trying to focus and regain her thoughts. "What was…that?"

Wearily, Michail sat down again beside his wife. He seemed as if the weight of the world rested on his shoulders. Carefully, he laid the piece of wood on the table. It wasn't just a stick. She could see that now. It was long and thin, with curious shapes etched all along the sides.

"It's…what we need to try to explain," she said, her gaze beseeching them to listen.

"I'm all right." Diana tried to appease her husband and son's concern. She glanced back to the couple sitting opposite her. "Let's…listen to what they have to say."

Constance nodded. "Thank you. I know this seems impossible, but it's the truth. There's a whole world out there that people do not know exists."

"But how? I don't understand." Gary glanced to his family from his seat on the arm of the sofa. Then his wary eyes focused back in the Hopewells' direction.

"Other places where people…like us…live, they're protected with magic, just like Willow Oak. The same barrier is in place to keep them hidden. Unless a person is, what you would term, supernatural, they may not cross the barrier unless they have been invited, which is the reason for the letter you received."

Gary rubbed his eyes before he sat forward. "This seems insane."

Michail nodded. "I know it's a lot to take in."

"It's unbelievable," Kira muttered.

"It must seem that way." Constance leaned forward and reached out a hand. It hovered over Kira's before she reluctantly pulled back. "However, it is the truth."

Kira glanced to her brother once more. She recognized the same look in his eye as the one she knew she had. She needed the answer to their, so far, unasked question.

Sucking in a deep breath, she asked, "Why us? Why were we invited here? None of us can do magic."

Again, the couple exchanged a look. The only way to describe this one was bittersweet. Michail squeezed his wife's hand once more before he turned to them. "Yes, you can...you and Sawyer...because of your parents."

Kira glanced to her mother and father. Instantly, she shook her head in obvious disbelief. There was no way that either of her parents could have anything to do with this. They were the most mild-mannered, *normal* people she knew.

The skepticism must have shown on her face as Michail added, quietly, "Your birth parents."

Kira couldn't breathe, couldn't think, couldn't move. The words *birth parents* played in a constant loop in her mind.

Could it be?

Even as the thought penetrated her muddled brain, she shook it off. No, this was a lie. It had to be a lie, because for this to be true...

No!

She couldn't even entertain the idea. She and Sawyer had been abandoned. It didn't matter who their parents were or what they were. They had to have been abandoned. Children did not have their only memory of childhood be of them alone, cold, barefoot, and terrified unless something horrible had happened to them. They were old enough to have memories of their biological parents if there were any worth remembering.

They couldn't recall them for a reason. It had to be from some sort of trauma. Why did she want to know about people like that? She didn't.

She opened her mouth to tell him that, to tell him not to say another word, but to her horror, she found no sound would come. She just stared at them, wide-eyed, and waited. For what she didn't know, didn't *want* to know, but she was powerless to say a word.

"You know our birth parents?" Sawyer asked.

The words whipped her head to the side, her attention going straight to her brother. She wanted him to call the question back. She didn't want to know the answer. She didn't want to know any of it. She'd made peace with it long ago. She wanted it left in the past where it belonged.

Her gaze darted toward the door. Perhaps she could make a run for it. Even as the thought hit her, she knew she couldn't. Frozen, she was frozen in fear and with a desperate need to know even though she inwardly cursed herself for wondering. It didn't matter; it *shouldn't* matter.

"Yes." Constance's smile was filled with warmth and understanding, yet that hint of sadness was still there. "Your mother and I grew up together, right here in this town. We were best friends."

"Were?" Kira found herself asking the question without conscious thought. She shook her head. She didn't want an answer from these people, as apparently, they were crazy. They had to be with all that they had said so far.

"Your parents were…killed almost ten years ago." As Michail said the words, he glanced back and forth between them.

"No," Sawyer said, his voice strong, forceful, and brooked no argument. "You don't know what you're talking about." He rose to his feet. "This is insane. We were abandoned. Left to fend for ourselves in Philadelphia. I don't know what is going on here, but you people are insane." He grabbed their mother's hand and pulled her to her feet before his gaze encompassed them all. "Let's go. We have got to get out of this town."

"They didn't leave you," Constance said, her words low, the anguish evident in her tone. "They didn't have a choice."

Those softly spoken words halted Kira. She turned from her position near the door where she had been following her stunned looking family. The woman still seated on the sofa looked miserable, her eyes glassy, but there was something else in them, some hint of familiarity hit Kira then.

Crossing her arms over her chest, she faced them fully. "Then tell us. All of it. Right now. No more procrastination. Lay it all out because from the little bits you're telling us, you both sound insane."

"You have to understand the history of our world," Michail explained.

Kira made a hiss of disgust as her eyes narrowed. He was still dragging this out. "Short version."

He nodded, though she could see the slight narrowing of his own eyes at her tone.

"Three hundred years ago there were two factions in the magical community, those that wanted to live life as they had been which is to say closeted away, living peacefully from those that weren't magical, though oftentimes in the same communities. They just kept their abilities a secret. Another group was tired of 'hiding' as they termed it. They wanted to live in the open, but more than that. They saw those without magic as lower than them. There was infighting, nearly all out war, but in the end, it was decided to stay in secret, away from Non-Magical people.

"It wasn't long after that was decided that the Salem Witch Trials began." He shook his head in loathing. "Magical people, they were shocked at those trials as normal women, men, and even children were being put to death. It was mass hysteria. But then it happened. An actual witch was burned. She'd fallen in love with a man who didn't possess any magical abilities and told him the truth about herself. Needless to say, he didn't take it well.

"After her death, those that had been opposed to remaining in secret used this incident as proof of Non-Magicals' barbarianism. No more did they want to live out in the open and with normal people. They wanted Non-Magical people to be subjugated or killed. As angry as this witch's needless death made people like us, it was still decided to remain as we were, separate. There was much fighting, nearly a war. In the end, those that wanted to keep our abilities secret prevailed. Because of this decision, a powerful curse was cast against every witch and wizard, those living and future generations."

He paused and glanced back and forth between her and Sawyer. His expression was serious, intense; it was as if he wanted them to grasp the gravity, the truthfulness of his words. "The curse said for the cowardliness of those that wished to hide all would be punished. From that moment on, only one heir was possible. Every magical being must remain hidden, only horror stories and nightmares of their existence were allowed in the realm of humans. That world, the Non-Magical world, was now forbidden. But, as with all curses, there was a way to break it."

Constance laid her hand atop her husband's. "Not so much a way to end it as there wasn't anything anyone could do, but it was a prophecy of sorts. You see, it said that there would come a time when 'a set of two will be born, each with a power never known before. Their birth can mark the end to the hidden lives of cowards.'"

Kira glanced to her brother. What in the world did that mean?

Abruptly, she shook her head. It didn't matter; this was crazy. It made absolutely no sense whatsoever.

"When you two were born—the first siblings in three hundred years—it ignited once more the debate to live as we were or to no longer have our powers remain a secret."

Almost against her will, Kira found herself moving forward. "You know this makes no sense. Right?" She shook her head. "Let's say you're correct, that everything you've told us is the truth. What are we,"—she threw her arm out to indicate Sawyer—"supposed to do? So us living here will let everyone run out and tell the world that hey, guess what, those Hollywood movies you've seen of magical creatures are actually true? That sounds insane."

"It does." Michail agreed. "But it is the truth…well to a degree."

She lifted a dark brow in question as Sawyer came to stand beside her. They stared down at the seated couple.

"There have always been two sides. And you two, you both are the most powerful witch and wizard in the last three hundred years. Whichever side of this debate you both land on will be powerful. But either side…there's no guarantee which will win. The guarantee is that this debate will be ignited again. I fear this time it will lead to all-out war."

"There's only one problem with this little fairytale you're trying to sell," Sawyer said, his voice hard like granite.

"And what's that?" Michail asked.

Kira thought she saw the twinkle of amusement in his eyes, so she relished telling him, "My brother and I don't have any powers. We're normal…and sane," she couldn't resist adding.

"And what does this ludicrous story have to do with our birth parents?" Sawyer asked. He caught Kira's hand and started slowly edging her back to where their parents still stood, seemingly rooted to the spot.

"Don't you see?" Michail's voice took on a hint of desperation. "You two are the most powerful witch and wizard in hundreds of years. Your parents, they were content with the way things were…are…but there are those that are not. To have your power on their side…they wanted you both. If they could raise you, mold you into what they wanted, they'd have everything they needed."

Kira shook her head in denial. "No, it sounds like your saying…" Her words broke off.

Slowly, Constance rose to her feet. Hesitantly, she approached them. "No one knows what truly happened that night, but the ones who caused it and you two. But your parents, they died protecting you that night."

Taking a step back, Kira's eyes widened. Her shoulder bumped into her brother's. It spurred him from his bemusement at the admission. "You just said no one knows, so how do you know that."

"You're both alive. Your old home was destroyed in the aftermath. We found...them...and some of the ones who had attacked. Both of you were gone. We feared they had you, but us—and others who are of our same ideals—we never stopped looking. And on the chance you hadn't been taken, we knew we had to find you and keep you safe. It took two years before, Michail found you." She looked back to the man who was still seated on the sofa, her gaze imploring him to speak.

"My first thought was to take you, but I knew you would be safer away from all of this. So measures were taken, spells put in place to hide your presence. Only a select few people in our government knew of your location. I saw to that while I was in office."

"But we're here now," Sawyer reminded them. "You've brought us to this place where apparently, people will kill for us. This is safe? Not to mention, once again, we have no powers."

"That's where you're wrong." Constance took another step closer. "You see, in our world, for witches and wizards, power is bound in children at their births. The impetuous nature and exaggerated emotions of children could account for some disastrous consequences. Magical abilities are bound until the age of seventeen. By that time, the knowledge of right and wrong…well it is hoped that wisdom allows for valid choices and decisions. It is, however, not always the case."

Kira rubbed her temple. The beginning of a powerful headache was focused on the back of her eye. She fought to shake it off. "But again, you brought us to a place where people were murdered because someone wants us."

"You'll be seventeen in a week. Your opinions cannot be swayed by the brainwashing these people would have done. You've been raised in a loving home."

"In a week?" She glanced to Sawyer and found her twin's gaze on her. Their birthday. They'd never known when that was and now…They'd always celebrated on the day they had been adopted, but to know their true birth date was something they had never even hoped for. And now it was in their grasp.

At that comment, Gary stepped forward, slightly edging himself in front of both of them. "For the sake of argument, let's say all of this is true. I know it would be a shock—that's an understatement—for people to find out that everything we've always thought is make-believe is actually a reality. However, why can't it be told? Over time people accept almost anything."

"If only that was what they wanted," Michail said on a sigh. Slowly he rose to his feet. It appeared as if he didn't want to make any sudden moves in case he spooked them. He slowly started pacing. "These people, they feel they have been grievously wronged by our way of life. They want revenge. They want to annihilate most non-magical people. And the rest…they want to enslave. There is no dissuading them."

His gaze turned back, focusing on Kira and Sawyer. "That's what's at stake. And that's a lot to put on your shoulders, but you're almost of age. You had to be back here. We had to tell you, because we didn't want you to suddenly have abilities you knew nothing about. You would be scared and terrified, you and your parents. You had to know."

Turbulent gray eyes glanced to her brother. His nod was barely perceptible. Her hand sought his, squeezing it, answering his unasked question.

He sucked in a deep breath and then met the older man's intense scrutiny. "I guess we all have a lot to talk about."

V. A. Risby

3

He was in shock. There was no other way to describe it. He'd sat there in stunned silence, listening as the Hopewells explained this fantastical world and life to them. He'd heard every word they said, took it all in, and he still didn't believe any of it.

He still hadn't believed it even when the movers had arrived, and their furniture went flying through the air and into the proper rooms.

It was unfathomable.

Magic.

He was freaking magic.

Seriously?

This had to be some grand delusion. Or perhaps he was having a seizure. That might explain it. Something had to be wrong with him as there was no rational explanation for any of it.

Slowly, he approached the mirror that was attached to his sleek, black metal bureau. As Sawyer studied his reflection, he waited. For what, he didn't exactly know, but still he watched his image, waiting to see if he would turn into the sideshow freak that the Hopewells said he was.

"If I understood them correctly, nothing will happen until our birthday next week."

He whipped around from his place of contemplation to find his sister leaning against the doorframe. He relaxed instantly and turned back to his reflection. He'd understood that, too, but surely there would be something before, some change if this insanity was even halfway true.

With a sigh, Kira pushed herself away from the door and joined him, staring back at their images that gazed at them. "I keep telling myself they have to be crazy but then…"

"How did he block the door? How did our furniture go flying around the house?" He met her gaze in the mirror.

"It was real, wasn't it?" Her voice was soft, almost timid. It didn't sound like his sister at all.

"I'm afraid it is."

With a sigh, she tore her attention away from the mirror and paced the length of the bedroom. This time she came to stop in front of the floor to ceiling window on the far side of the room. "Our entire lives have been a lie. Dad's job at a made-up company just so they could keep tabs on us, though now they want him to be some sort of liaison for the normal world and this loony place."

With one last glance, Sawyer went to join her.

They stared in silence at the twinkling lights of the town that spread out as far as he could see. Kira wrapped her arms around her waist. "What are we gonna do?"

He knew what she meant; he just didn't have an answer for her. He wished he could reassure her, give her some hope, give her something concrete to hold on to, but he didn't even know where to start. He tucked his hands in the front pockets of his worn jeans. "I wish I knew." The words were soft as he tried to think of something that made sense. But he realized nothing did. He wondered if anything ever would again.

Glancing away from the window, she stared up at him. "Do you think…I mean…are we going to have to actually go to school with them? I know what the Hopewells said but…" She threw her hands up in the air and turned away, walking across the room again. She whirled back around. "I don't even know."

But he knew. He knew how she felt. Were they supposed to walk into that school and act all normal? Would stuff be flying around? When they got a book would it fly through the air at them? Did they even have normal classes?

"I want out of here."

He agreed with his sister. He wanted to leave, too. He wanted to go back to Chicago and forget any of this had ever happened. They could pretend this was all just some horrible nightmare.

"I wish we could, but I don't know if they would even let us leave after going to so much trouble to get us here." And they had, employing their father for all these years…many things had gone into this charade. He couldn't see them giving it up now.

Kira raised her gray eyes to meet his gaze. "You think they would try to stop us?"

He sighed and then went to sit on the edge of his bed. He'd kept his old, familiar black one. He hadn't wanted the wooden antique that had apparently belonged to his grandparents—grandparents he didn't remember so he felt no attachment to. He'd wanted his modern pieces, his remnants of the life he missed. That life had made sense. That life was the one he wished he was still apart of instead of this insanity. "I think they would. They want us here. That's apparent. And I think if we tried to leave…I think they wouldn't be happy."

With a nod, Kira once again resumed her place at the window. "I keep thinking when I wake up in the morning it will have all been a dream. But I know that's not going to happen. Deep down, I know that." She turned to him. When she spoke, her voice was a whisper. "We weren't abandoned."

His own gaze darted up. He felt an unfamiliar lump lodge in the back of his throat. She was right; they hadn't been discarded like pieces of trash, something he had always thought. Their parents had died protecting them. And this resentment, this near hatred Sawyer had felt toward them for as long as he could remember…he now felt guilty. Every awful, horrible thought he'd had for the people who had brought him into the world, he now regretted, because he *knew* what the Hopewells had said was the truth. He and his sister had been loved, not tossed away at the first opportunity. Their birth parents had actually given up their lives to keep them safe. How could he not let the shame swallow him for every nasty thought he'd had about them as they'd been shuttled from foster home to foster home? It was now eating him alive.

When he spoke, Sawyer's voice was scratchy with raw emotion. "We weren't."

The corner of Kira's lips lifted a bit, though her identical gray-eyed gaze appeared glassy. "Our birth parents loved us." Then she glanced to the open door. "Do you…do you think…" She couldn't seem to bring herself to voice the question aloud.

However, Sawyer knew the direction of her thoughts; he'd thought the same thing. "They're probably scared and in shock, but mom and dad…no way will they leave us. It won't happen." And he believed that. It wasn't a lie designed to make her feel better.

Her tension seemed to seep from her rigid posture, leaving her shoulders hunched. "I didn't think they would.

I just…I just wanted to hear someone else say it." She turned then, her arms wrapping around her waist. "Do you think…will they be all right here? Nothing will happen to them, right?"

He knew she needed reassurance. But the problem was he couldn't give it to her. He didn't know. He didn't know if *any* of them would be all right. This was a strange, foreign place, and Sawyer had no idea how any of them would survive in it. But they'd do their best; they had to. They had to figure out what was going on; they owed that to their birth parents for the sacrifice that they'd made all those years ago.

He glanced to the side, surveyed his new bedroom before he met her nearly identical gaze. He felt it then a sudden sense of determination. "They will be because we'll make sure they are. If the Hopewells are to be believed, we're supposed to be these powerful, magical people. We can take on anyone."

He saw the corner of his sister's lips twitch as she fought back a smile. He knew why; it stilled sounded ludicrous.

She shook away the thought. "I don't feel powerful." She inclined her head toward a lamp sitting on the black desk nestled on the far side of the room. "What's supposed to happen? Can I turn it on?"

"It's not even plugged in. I couldn't find any…" But his words were halted as she raised a hand and gestured toward it.

The black glass exploded, sending shards flying through the air.

Sawyer jumped back, eyes wide as he stared at the spot where his lamp had just set.

That had not just happened.

Slowly, he turned to his sister. She wasn't looking at him. Instead, it appeared as if she was frozen as she stared at the empty spot, her hand still raised. Her mouth opened and closed wordlessly.

"What happened?" The question was shouted before their father entered the room.

Sawyer didn't know what to tell him, couldn't even find the words to tell him anything. He could only stare at his sister—no, her raised hand—in shock.

"Kira? Sawyer?" Their mother asked the question as she appeared in the doorway. At her movement, Sawyer forced himself to look in her direction. She was pale and appeared to have aged ten years in the last few hours.

She approached slowly, almost hesitantly, and that was when he knew. She was afraid, of them. The realization unfurled in his belly and caused a lump to form in his throat. His mother was scared of him.

Gently, she touched Kira's shoulder.

The feather-light touch sent Kira jumping back. Her hands balled into fists as she forced them to remain at her sides, her head shaking back and forth, seeming to try to ward off any more comforting gestures.

"Don't...don't touch me. I don't..." She couldn't get the words passed her trembling lips. As the first tear rolled down her pale cheek, she snapped her mouth closed.

"Kira, I—"

"No!" She cut off the words. Quickly shaking her head, she moved passed her, careful to keep from touching their mother. Gaze downcast, she brushed by their father who still stood in the doorway, cautiously keeping her hands at her sides as she fled the room.

It was silent until they heard the slamming of the door to the room that only earlier Kira had picked for herself.

Sawyer could feel both of his parents' attention was focused on him, but he couldn't meet their gazes, not just yet, as he continued to watch after the space his twin had just vacated.

"What…what happened?"

Taking in a deep breath, Sawyer forced himself to focus on his parents. But he didn't know how to tell them. How could he explain something that he didn't even understand himself?

"We were just talking about how this had to be some joke, something other than the truth." He could see it all again, unfolding right before his eyes as he glanced back to the now empty spot. He shook his head in denial. That could not have just happened. "She just gestured to the lamp and then…" He didn't finish. He thought the glass shards littered around the desk spoke eloquently enough of what had transpired.

He watched them for their reactions. He wanted an inkling of what they were thinking, and he desperately wanted to know if he had been wrong before. Would they leave? Would this be too much? Would he find tomorrow that they had abandoned him and Kira, just as he had always assumed their biological parents had?

The fear clouded both of their eyes. Then his mother seemed to deflate before him. Soundlessly, Gary stepped forward and took her hand in his. She glanced back and forth between her husband and her son. "I had hoped…" Her words trailed off. Then she shook her head and seemed to stand a little straighter. "Even after everything we have recently seen, I still thought they were crazy. I thought they were making this all up." Her scrutiny focused in on the desk. "I guess it was the truth." With one last squeeze to her husband's hand, she moved forward and placed her calm, steady palm against Sawyer's cheek. "So now we find out all we can about this place, about these people, about you and your sister's abilities, and about your…parents."

His sigh was one of relief. His own hand came up, and he pulled her into a nearly crushing hug.

"It will be all right. You'll see everything will be all right."

His mother's words of comfort caused a fear he didn't even realize to drain from his body, leaving him feeling limp.

When she finally pulled back, it was with great reluctance. "I need to go talk to your sister."

He knew that, knew that Kira needed her, but part of him wanted to be selfish, to keep their mother with him just so she could constantly reassure him that everything would indeed be all right. But he couldn't, not right now. Instead, he relaxed his grip on her and allowed her to move away.

He was surprised when his father didn't follow. Instead, with a sigh, Gary Randel came forward and sank onto the edge of the sleek, black bed. His elbows rested on his knees, his face cradled by his hands.

After a brief moment of indecision, Sawyer crossed to him and slowly lowered himself down beside his father. Subconsciously, he mirrored Gary's posture.

"I thought it was all a dream. I keep thinking I'll wake up in that hotel we stayed in last night and all of this…it won't be real."

His father's voice was filled with confusion. Sawyer turned his head and found his father's brown-eyed gaze focused on him, filled with an almost desperate hope. But he could see it slowly receding.

"I want that, too." Sawyer glanced back to the spot where the lamp once set. "I don't want this," he whispered. Then, slowly, he rose to his feet. He concentrated, focused his mind, pictured how the lamp had previously looked, whole, and then waved his hand.

Nothing.

He didn't know if he was disappointed or relieved. He turned to glance at his father over his shoulder and found Gary watching him. A hint of relief was slowly seeping into his eyes. "Do you think…perhaps it was just a tremor in the house?"

Sawyer wanted to reassure him, tell him that what had happened had been a huge coincidence, but the words wouldn't come. He hadn't lied to his father before, and he didn't want to start now. He'd be nothing but honest. "I want to say yes, but I don't believe that."

Slowly, Gary nodded.

Into the silence, Sawyer whispered, "I'm scared." The words slipped passed Sawyer's lips before he could call them back. The involuntary confession had his eyes flaring. He hadn't even known it was the truth, but to his horror, he realized it was.

His father was before him almost instantly. His hands went to his shoulders, tightening just a bit, causing Sawyer to meet his gaze when all he wanted was to look away.

"But we'll get through this. We'll deal with this like we deal with everything, as a family. Eventually, it will all make sense."

Sawyer wanted to believe him, wanted to trust in the blind faith his father seemed to have, but he couldn't, not completely. Something held him back, tugged at him, causing him to worry, triggering a sense of rising panic, building along the base of his spine and slowly spinning out. Yet, he took in a deep breath and pushed it back. He fought for a weak smile.

"Trust me," his father said, his voiced filled with determination.

Sawyer forced himself to nod, but he took no comfort in the words. He couldn't believe them, no matter how hard he wanted to, as the mounting sense of dread took hold.

Nothing would be all right again.

4

"Now what?" Even though she asked that question of her brother, Kira didn't glance toward him. As she sat in the backseat of the family SUV, all she could focus on was the old brick building that loomed in front of her. Two other identical buildings were spread out on the immense green grounds. It seemed like a very large school. And if this was just the high school…

Neither of them had wanted their parents to drive them, but they'd insisted, which was probably a good idea because, left to her own devices, Kira didn't know if she would have even made it to the school. She would have been tempted to run as fast as she could in the opposite direction.

She still felt that way right now, especially as she could see students staring in their direction, the only vehicle in the area. No other kids were being dropped off.

The car ride over had been uncomfortably silent. None of them knew what to say. This was their junior year of high school. The only thing on her mind should have been prom and starting to think about college choices. Instead, she was afraid that if she went inside the school that someone was going to curse her, or she might accidently blow someone up.

Was there even such a thing as curses?

She had no idea. And that was the problem. The only thing she knew of the supernatural—besides the weirdness that the Hopewells had imparted them with—was from movies, books, and television. But then again, no two of those were alike, so who knew what she and Sawyer would be facing once they stepped inside that building.

Would anyone even notice them?

What if someone did cast a spell on them?

Could someone even do that?

Her breath started coming in short, panicked bursts. She felt as if she was suffocating.

"It will be all right," Sawyer reassured from her side, sounding calm and determined even if he did fiddle with the blue and black striped tie of his school uniform.

She glanced toward him. She was still in the grips of her fear. She didn't know if she would ever be able to escape from it. "How can you be so sure?"

"What other choice do I have?"

The words were so simple and logical, and yet Kira took a measure of comfort in them. She could do this. It was happening whether she was prepared or not. It was just up to her if she was going to go into the old, morbid, brick building with her head held high or if she would be a terrified idiot.

She refused to be an idiot.

But she wouldn't be responsible if something came flying at her head.

"It will be fine. I'm sure it will be just like normal."

Slowly, with a feeling of impending dread, Kira nodded at her mother's words, but noted the older woman didn't appear too sure herself; she appeared nervous. Her father tried for a reassuring smile, but it came out more like a grimace. Hesitantly, she pulled on the door handle. Sawyer mirrored her actions but with more self-assurance.

If her brother could do this, so could she.

As her black, buckled oxford feet planted firmly on the dark pavement of the parking lot, she waited. For what she really didn't know. She suspected it was the feeling creeping along her spine that she might be struck down.

But she wasn't.

Nothing happened.

She released the pent-up breath she hadn't realized she had even been holding. She cast a quick glance to Sawyer and saw he seemed to relax marginally, too.

They could do this; go to school with apparent freaks. Though apparently, they were freaks now, too. Just what she always wanted to be, she thought with a roll of her eyes.

"Ready?" Sawyer asked with a glance over his shoulder.

She nodded, not trusting herself to speak, too afraid the words would come out as a scared squeak. The tingling along her spine had turned into a knot of apprehension lodged in the pit of her stomach. She might actually be ill. If that happened, her horrid day would be complete.

Forcing her feet to move, she stepped up beside him and inhaled a deep breath.

"I miss our old school. I miss my friends. I miss Kate and meeting up before class started to catch up on any news after our last text the night before." Kira couldn't help the wistful tone that entered her words.

But Sawyer was nodding his head in agreement before she finished. "I know. Jack, Thomas, and I…we would've had early morning practice on the weights. Our first baseball game of the season is today. I wish I was there."

She missed her old life something terribly. She'd give almost anything to be able to call Kate, her best friend for the past five years, and tell her everything that was going on. It was a need, yet even as it threatened to nearly overwhelm her, Kira knew she couldn't act on it. Forget that there was no way for her to contact Kate as their cellphones didn't work and forget their laptops, how could she explain all of this without sounding as if she were losing her mind?

She couldn't. It wouldn't be possible.

"Come on," Sawyer said, with an incline of his dark-head toward the old building. "Let's get this over with."

Automatically, she fell instep beside him, hoisting her backpack higher up on her shoulder. She tried to be casual as she glanced around. People were staring. She and Sawyer were the focus of attention. She could see heads swiveling in their direction as they moved toward the building.

"It will be okay." Her brother reassured. "Just breathe."

"Easy for you to say," she muttered under her breath. She felt like a sideshow freak. But she did as he suggested, sucked in a deep gulp of air, and with purposeful strides, continued forward with her chin raised in defiance. If people wanted to look at her, well, then, she was going to pretend it didn't bother her in the very least.

Sawyer reached the heavy wooden door a step ahead of her and yanked it open, stepping back to allow her to enter first. She braced herself, waiting for something, some big explosion, something momentous.

She was met with nothing.

Releasing the pent-up breath that she hadn't even realized she held, she glanced to the left and then the right.

It looked like a typical high school, though older than what they were used to in Chicago. She didn't think she would find state of the art equipment or the latest technology, but it appeared…ordinary. Nothing about it screamed magic or even a hint of anything supernatural. They even had lockers. It looked completely normal.

However, she supposed looks could be deceiving.

As her brother stepped up beside her, Kira glanced once more in the opposite direction, and that was when she noticed it, the furtive stares and whispers that ended quickly when they noticed her scrutiny.

Great, she had known it would come, she just didn't think that it would be so soon.

"You always gawk at the new kids. It's like an unwritten code," Sawyer said at her side.

She glanced to him, but he didn't notice as he was busy doing his own perusal of the area. Brave words, but he didn't seem to care for the scrutiny either as his lips pressed in a grim line.

She was tired of standing out in the open in the sea of blue, gray, white, and black school uniforms. She felt exposed. "Let's go to the office." When he looked to her, she gestured toward a marked door further down the hall to her left. He nodded in agreement and fell behind her as she moved forward.

Keeping her head held high, back straight, Kira made her way toward the door labeled *Headmaster's Office*, trying to not think how anyone in her path, quickly moved out of the way. She felt like how Donna Brascoe must have felt as she walked the halls. She had been *the* it girl at their old school. The one that all the girls had wanted to be like; the one all the boys wanted to date. Her power came from a mixture of fear, loathing, with a hint of admiration and lust—from the boys—thrown into the mix.

And as everyone parted in her wake, Kira realized she hated that feeling. She did *not* want to be the Donna Brascoe of this school.

She yanked the old wooden door open with more force than she had intended, causing the frosted glass to rattle in the pane. She cringed when it brought even more unwanted attention in their direction.

She could do this. She just needed to calm down. Deep breath, then another. She made her way inside, Sawyer behind her, shutting the door in his wake.

"Hi." She managed to get the word out with only minimal stammering. It was hard to concentrate with the school receptionist looking at her.

Focus, she told herself. "Kira and Sawyer Randal, we're—"

"Oh!" The older woman's excited exclamation cut off any further words. She stepped down from behind the tall desk, and Kira did a double take. She was a very short, plump woman with warm brown eyes. Her wide grin and sweet face had Kira mentally likening her to a cherub.

"We've been expecting you. So sorry we didn't meet you out front." She took Kira's hands in hers, then quickly released one so she could grab one of Sawyer's. "It's just so good to have you both here."

Kira glanced to her brother. His eyes were wide under the effusive welcome. He looked as stunned as she felt. She didn't know what to say or how to respond; apparently, neither did he, as he remained rooted to his spot.

"That will be enough, Madame Banks."

That cool voice had the overly exuberant woman's smile dropping instantly. Quickly, she released their hands, and her gaze darted nervously over her shoulder.

"Quite right, sir," she said, hastily climbing back up to her tall, oak desk. She cleared her throat once, her tone now holding a calm, professional edge that didn't seem to mesh at all with her warm, exuberant greeting.

"Here are all the papers you'll need. These forms will need your…parents' signatures." She thrust three sets of papers in their direction as she cleared her throat. "And these two." She held two pieces of paper that were half the size of the others. "Are your schedules."

They took the proffered materials, but Kira found her gaze not even glancing at them. Instead, her gray-eyed gaze was scrupulously studying the man behind the older woman. He had to be in his early to mid-fifties with dark black hair that hadn't yet been sprinkled with even a hint of gray. But what arrested her were the dull green eyes that were coolly assessing her and Sawyer. There seemed to be a cold, calculating look in them.

Subconsciously, she took a step closer to her twin. Her movement seemed to break the older man out of his contemplative study, as he seemed to shake himself and step forward. He extended his hand and without conscious thought, she shook it after he dropped Sawyer's.

"Headmaster Crofton," he said by way of introducing himself. "And you both, well no introduction is needed. Sawyer and Kira Sayer or Randal now I'm told. The first siblings in three hundred years." He glanced over his shoulder and gave the small woman sitting behind the desk a quelling look. "You'll have to forgive Madam Banks, but you both are something of celebrities in our world."

"There's nothing to forgive." Sawyer's voice mirrored the same cool tone, and it was then that Kira noted he seemed to be picking up the same unease she was. "It was nice to have a friendly welcome. New school, new town."

He shrugged his broad shoulders. "Whole new life. It's nice to feel accepted."

The older man drew himself up somewhat stiffly. His lips thinned into a tight smile. "Be that as it may, we do abide by a rigid set of standards here. Ones that we expect everyone to adhere to."

Kira looked down at the meager amount of papers in her hands. "Is there a rule book then or something?"

"Yeah," Sawyer seconded. "We wouldn't want to step out of line or anything."

"Horrible way to start off at a new school," Kira added, forcing her own lips not to quirk up at the older man's visible annoyance.

"We'll see about getting you something." He then turned back to the woman who was watching this exchange with rapt attention, which only seemed to further his irritation. "Call for my daughter and Dalen." He glanced back to them. "They will show our new students around campus."

"Yes, sir," she said, reaching for some bizarre looking contraption that set at her side. It looked almost like something one would use to put fluid in a car.

As her quiet voice spoke into it, Kira could hear it echoing in the halls behind them. It seemed a normal mode of address—once one got past what the woman used—and something she wasn't expecting at all. She expected something flashier, something *magical* for lack of a better word. But there was nothing. It was just ordinary. So far, everything had been a letdown.

"We hope you all will get settled soon and become immersed in our community. I understand you have no memory of your previous time here."

An uneasy, icy feeling settled at the base of Kira's spine and slowly spread upward, causing her to tense. Her brother asked the question that was causing her own disquiet.

"How do you know about that?" The suspicion was clear in his tone.

The headmaster chose to ignore it. "The council had a meeting once your location was discovered."

The words were said matter-of-factly as if they should know exactly what he was speaking of.

Kira exchanged a quick glance with her brother before she turned back to the older man. "What council?" Their father's boss had mentioned a government, but nothing really more about it. He'd left out the fact that everyone apparently knew details of their lives, like their lack of memory for one. It brought up the question, what else did this council know about them?

"Willow Oak's governing board, Miss Randal." His tone took on a slightly patronizing timbre as if he shouldn't have to explain such trivial matters to her.

"We weren't aware there was a governing board. Or any board actually." Sawyer's words were clipped as he defended his sister. "Which apparently, you should know since you know of our memory loss."

The headmaster looked down his nose at both of them. "Then I think you should both try and immerse yourselves in our culture. We wouldn't want any misfortune to befall you because you don't understand how things work here."

It was a threat, plain and simple. Kira knew that this man was one who still held the belief that Non-Magical people were beneath Magical ones. In fact, he probably thought most people were beneath him and anyone he deemed worthy like himself. It seemed that was the same in any world, enchanted or not.

And if Michail Hopewell could be believed, their birth parents had not been of the same mind. Their parents had wanted to live a quiet, content life as they were, but that choice had been taken from them by people who thought differently. People like the man that stood before them. He could even be responsible for their murder.

The very thought forced a chill to run down the base of her spine. Subconsciously, she took a step closer to her brother, bumping into his side. Her quick glance to him showed he had thought the same thing.

Before either of them could say any more, the office door swung open, causing a faint tingling of what sounded like a bell to fill the oppressive silence.

"Yes, Father?" a girl questioned as soon as she had stepped inside.

Kira turned slightly to study the two people, but she didn't want to completely ignore the headmaster's disturbing presence. She felt to turn her back on him could be a disastrous mistake. Yet, instinctively she knew she couldn't dismiss anyone that called this man father.

The girl appeared to be around her and Sawyer's age. She was a little shorter than her own five six, with dirty blonde hair that danced in tight ringlets around her shoulders. When her gaze met Kira's, she noted the coolly assessing hazel eyes.

Forcing her observation on, she turned to the boy. He was around Sawyer's six foot, with sandy blond hair that fell in a careless wave and deep, chocolate colored eyes. His build was impressive, looking like a football player—if they even played football here.

Kira's brow knitted at the thought. What did they do here? Did they all behave like normal teenagers or was this going to be another eye-opening experience? Did they drive cars? Go to the movies? Do anything normal?

"Flora, Dalen, I want you to meet Sawyer and Kira Randal." The headmaster's voice was clear and firm as he walked around to stand behind the two newcomers. His hands went to the girl's shoulders. "This is my daughter, Flora. And this," he said, with an inclination of his head, "is Dalen Langley."

They both offered welcoming grins, which Kira returned, but as she watched, she thought she noted a slight narrowing of their eyes. And then Flora's look took on an almost calculated appearance as she glanced in Sawyer's direction.

"Another copy of their schedules, Madam Banks." When he spoke this time, his tone was clipped and put-upon.

The older woman rushed forward to hand him the papers that seemed to come from nowhere. After he took the proffered white slips, the woman then quickly scurried back behind her tall desk.

"Flora and Dalen will show you around our campus. I've already taken the liberty of arranging your schedules in accordance with theirs. That way you'll have a familiar face in your classes." A smile accompanied the words, though it didn't appear to reach his eyes.

The headmaster leaned forward and handed the papers to the other two students. As Flora Crofton glanced at the slip, she glanced over her shoulder at her father, a flicker of annoyance in her eyes to which he answered with a stern nod.

After a moment, she tossed her curls over her shoulder and turned back to them, a wide smile plastered on her face. Her gaze focused on Kira. "It looks like you're stuck with me. We have Astronomy and Meteorology first hour."

As if on cue, the shrill ring of a bell sounded out in the hall.

"We better go." She cast one quick glance in Sawyer's direction, the regret practically oozing from her. Then with a toss of her head, she directed that Kira should follow her out the door.

Kira barely refrained from rolling her eyes as she, too, glanced to Sawyer. Her twin's lips crooked up in an amused smile. And then the shorter girl disappeared through the doorway, leaving Kira no choice but to follow.

She glanced to her left and saw other kids swarming in the hallway, darting into open doorways. When she turned, Flora was already moving off to the right. Kira hurried to catch up to her to hear the other girl saying, "Your class load is full this year, but that's typically the case for fourth years, so much to learn with our powers and all." Then she glanced over her shoulder and gave her first genuinely friendly expression. "Next year should be a bit better."

Kira barely managed to nod; she was too busy glancing back and forth around her to pay much attention. She noted the other students casting furtive glances in her direction as she passed. She ignored them, ignored the feeling of being watched as best she could, and instead tried to take everything in. Another quick glance over her shoulder showed Sawyer disappearing in a room down the hall in the opposite direction.

And then it happened, that embarrassing moment every self-conscious person dreaded, Kira collided with the open door—thankfully, she didn't smack herself in the face—having not turned enough to enter. It was hard enough that it propelled her backwards. She might have been able to catch herself, but she crashed into the student unfortunate enough to be walking in behind her. Her black backpack struck the body following her, producing a groan of pain. Hands went to her back to stop her momentum she supposed. It might have worked if her legs hadn't tangled with the other student's. They went down in a mess of twisted limbs, and in Kira's case, absolute mortification.

To her horror, she found she was actually atop the other student. Quickly, she scrambled to the side, shoving the blue and black plaid skirt down smoothly, so as not to give anyone a show. The roar of the laughter and whistles surrounded her from inside the classroom and from the remaining people still in the hallway.

She tried to block it all out. She could *not* deal with this. If she thought about it, the mortification, she'd be in tears in no time.

Instead, she fought for calm. Taking a deep breath, she raised her gaze to take in the other prone person on the floor. The apology she had been about to offer died in her throat as her gaze landed on eyes the color of frosty, blue ice. They were striking eyes; that exact shade she had never seen before, almost white, the blue was so clear. And then she took in the entire face, the jet-black hair that ended in careless, short waves; the dark, slanting brows; the straight nose leading to lips that were lifted at one corner. The raven hair and tan complexion made the eye color all the more prominent and mesmerizing. And he knew it, if his knowing smirk was any indication.

Every thought left her head. She knew she was gaping at him—later the memory would steal her breath away with humiliation—but she found, to her horror, that she couldn't pull her attention away.

"Oh, dear," she heard from a soft voice from inside the classroom.

Instinctively, Kira knew it wasn't her guide's voice. The sound, though, was enough to end her own bemusement. She glanced away, and in that instant, the boy quickly got to his feet, his movements sure and confident. Then his hands gripped hers, pulling her effortlessly to her own. Before she knew it, she was standing. He reached down to scoop up both of their discarded bags and handed hers to her.

He was taller than she was, around her brother's height. All lean muscle prominently displayed in the tapered cobalt blue jacket and snug white button-down shirt untucked from the black pants that looked like chinos. The blue and black striped tie was loose under his collar.

One of his brows lifted and his lips quirked in what Kira knew was an amused gesture. She didn't know the cause until she realized she was still gawking at him, and that she hadn't made any move to take the proffered bag.

Quickly, she reached for it. Her "I'm so sorry," came out in a stammered gasp.

This time a full grin turned up his lips, along with a cocky gleam in his eyes. The uniform jacket did wonders for the color of his eyes, bringing out the icy blue perfectly. Absently, she wondered if the shade had been chosen as a compliment to him, but she shook the thought off as absurd.

He opened his mouth to say something but was cut off as a petite girl appeared at her side.

"Are you all right?" The question was directed at Kira.

She barely managed to nod before the bell gave its shrill cry.

"Can the rest of us get in?" another voice called from the congested hallway. The annoyed tone cut through everyone's momentary standstill and sent the students in the room who had rose to see what the commotion was all about back to their seats.

Red heat stole up Kira's cheeks as she quickly muttered her apologies once more and turned into the classroom Flora had disappeared into moments before.

Kira spotted her guide quickly, sitting in a seat near the back, surrounded by two other girls, one was glaring at her while Flora and the other were giggling to outright laughing. Their attention was focused on the doorway, and the spectacle she had just made. Stiffening her spine, Kira marched toward the back and plucked her schedule from the other girl's limp fingers.

"Thanks, but I think I can manage from here," she said in a clipped tone. She ignored the shock from the rest of the girls and the sputtered indignation from Flora and instead, turned back to the room at large. Near the front were empty desks, one by the sandy-haired-blonde that had asked if she was all right.

Making up her mind, Kira quickly slid into the empty seat beside her and offered her a sheepish smile.

The other girl's grin was genuine. "Hi. I'm Ella Hopewell."

Before Kira could respond to the other girl's last name, Ella asked once more, "Are you all right?"

Darting a quick glance behind her, Kira found that icy gaze on her, intent and watchful. His lips lifted at one corner in cocky arrogance. And then he winked at her, actually *winked* at her. A funny quiver shot through her belly.

Quickly, she turned back in her seat. She tucked a stray chocolate wave behind her ear and cleared her throat. "Yeah, just completely embarrassed." Then as if almost an afterthought she added, "Kira Randal."

The door slammed with a resounding bang, cutting off any further overtures of friendship as a young woman with long midnight blue hair took her place at the front of the room behind a black podium.

5

He'd ditched Dalen Langley as soon as humanly possible. The other boy liked to talk too much about himself and his hobbies, plus throw in the comments about girls he liked or those he had been "seeing" with too much information. It had been more than Sawyer had wanted to know, especially from a stranger. When Dalen had started in on Kira, Sawyer knew he'd had more than enough. He wanted as far away as humanly possible. He didn't want to hear that about his sister.

Gross.

It hadn't been that hard to navigate his way through his first four bizarre classes, which he noted didn't contain his sister. He was sure that was deliberate on the headmaster's part. Something about that man didn't set well with Sawyer at all. In fact, he gave him a decidedly uncomfortable vibe.

But then again, so had Dalen. Actually, Sawyer didn't know if anyone around here wouldn't unnerve him. He felt like everyone was watching him, students and teachers alike. He walked by them, and they would stare and whisper. It might have been bearable if he was at least with Kira, but this, alone, it was a lot to try to take in and handle with any sort of calm. And calm was not something he was feeling, not anymore.

In a matter of days, his entire world had been turned upside down. He didn't know what was real, and as he surveyed the unfamiliar faces in the classroom he sat, he realized he didn't want to be there, in this town, in this situation, not even a little bit. It all had to be some sort of outlandish dream as he wasn't magic, nor was his twin. And his parents surely hadn't been murdered in some contrived plot. Though if this was some elaborate ruse, he had no idea what the reason for it was.

The shrill cry of the bell woke Sawyer from his stupor. He had no clue what had occurred in the class. Nothing was normal here. He wasn't taking Trig or Chemistry. No, his classes consisted of subjects such as Readings, Omens, and Oracles; Botany; and Magical Creatures.

Slowly, he got to his feet, allowing the other students to proceed him out the door. He tried to ignore the looks cast over more than a few shoulders.

Unhurriedly, he gathered up his book and binder and made his way out to the hallway and into the thinning crowd as most of the others rushed to put their own belongings away and make their way to the cafeteria.

Was it even called a cafeteria here?

After stowing his things in his assigned locker—normal, which made him think this was all some sort of elaborate hoax—he cast a quick glance up and down the hallway, looking for his sister. Not seeing her, he figured she was already inside.

Taking a fortifying breath, he moved in the direction most students were heading. He paused in the doorway to get his bearings and felt the unnerving tingling running along the base of his spine that he was being watched.

Right then and there, he decided he'd had enough. He didn't hide, didn't try to act inconspicuous; instead, his gray-eyed gaze boldly surveyed the area, meeting the stares and looks of people who were openly gawking at him. Most quickly turned away at being caught staring; only a few met his gaze full measure. One of those was Dalen who was already seated at a round table near the rear of the cafeteria. The table only held two other students. They were speaking, while staring in Sawyer's direction.

With a shrug of indifference he didn't feel, Sawyer turned and made his way to one of the food lines. The food actually looked edible even if he didn't completely recognize it. He selected his choices and then turned to find his own place to sit.

More than one inquisitive face met his perusal. He ignored them all and chose a table to himself on the opposite side from the one Dalen occupied.

He was lifting his fork to his mouth, when he noted Kira enter, but he noticed she wasn't with the Flora girl who had been assigned as her guide. Instead, she was with a petite, light-haired brunette. The girl was pretty, and the look she was giving his sister was friendly, not curious, not calculating, just nice. Perhaps not everyone was horrible here.

Kira glanced around the large, open room. He inclined his head in her direction, and she smiled. A few words to her companion, and then they quickly moved off for their own lunch.

Sawyer took a bite of the meat on his tray, keeping part of his attention focused on his sister, the other alert to his surroundings. Then she was at his still empty table, the brunette at her side. They both set their trays down.

"Sawyer, this is Ella Hopewell. Ella, this is my brother Sawyer."

The smile the other girl aimed in his direction felt as if it hit him right in the gut.

He barely managed a "hi" before he had to clear his throat. Focus, he needed to focus. And then the realization of the name hit him. "Hopewell? That's the name of our father's boss." It wasn't a question, but she chose to explain it anyway.

"Yeah, that's my dad." She pushed her shoulder-length, layered hair back, seeming to search for something else. Then she added, "He can be a bit…" She let her words die off as if she didn't know how to explain him exactly. She glanced back and forth between him and Kira. "I can't even imagine what it must have been like to have all of that laid on you and so suddenly."

Sawyer pushed his plate aside, any hunger he had been feeling gone. It was replaced by this need to know, to understand what exactly was going on around them. "So he told you then about us? And I guess everyone knows we have no memory of what happened before."

"Well…yes and no."

That answer confused him even more. He glanced to Kira and saw she was wearing the same perplexed look he was feeling.

"Your memory loss was already hinted at once they found your location. But I didn't need to be told about you."

"If he didn't say anything, then how do you know about us?"

She sucked her bottom lip into her mouth, worrying it with her teeth before she spoke. "I have to assume he told you about the prophecy, correct?"

"Yes," Kira answered, seeming eager to get an explanation, too.

"Well," Ella said, picking up her fork and pushing the noodles around on her plate. "You have to understand that here, in our world, you both are something of celebrities. You always have been, well…only really with the people who didn't know you, so everyone knows *of* you. But it's more than that. Well…at least with me."

He didn't know what to think about that. He didn't like it, but it explained even more the open curiosity about them. And then another thought hit him.

"The first thing we remember is when we were seven. So apparently, we lived here before that. We don't remember anything from that time. But do you? Surely we were in school then." He glanced around the cafeteria. "So do you all know us from before?"

"Some of us do," a voice said from his side.

Quickly, Sawyer glanced up, not having heard the newcomer's approach. The boy was as tall as him, same build with short blond messy hair and very odd eyes. The center almost seemed to glow with an amber light, then as it moved out turning a dark, almost emerald green.

He pulled out a chair and sat down, his tray coming to rest on the table. "I'm Gabe Meyer, and I knew you before. Actually, you and I," he said with an indication toward Sawyer, "were best friends. We practically lived at each other's house."

Sawyer's skeptical gaze collided with Kira's before he turned to the other girl. "What about you? Did we know you before?"

She tucked a wayward tendril of hair behind her ear. "Yeah. You and I…we knew each other, but that's because Kira and I were inseparable."

His sister shook her head. "I just…I don't remember any of this, nothing."

Sawyer leaned back in his chair. "And that right there is why this entire thing is so unbelievable. I mean, come on, someone drops by your house and tells you that you have magical powers—no offense to your dad or anything," Sawyer added. "He seems like a nice enough guy, bit intense though."

Ella smiled at the comment.

"I can see that," Gabe said. He took a healthy bite. After he chewed and swallowed, he offered, "It's just hard for us to understand that as this is all we know. No one had to tell us we would have magic. We just grew up knowing that from the beginning. You knew it before, but now…yeah, it's come from nowhere, so I get where it would be…" He paused as if trying to find the right word. Finally, he settled on "difficult." Though after the word left his mouth, he didn't seem to like it either.

Sawyer nodded in understanding.

"When you say it like that, I suppose it makes sense." Kira let out a held breath as she slowly surveyed the cafeteria. "It's also hard, not only being the new kids at school, but to have everyone staring at you."

Gabe and Ella glanced around and noted that more than quite a few of the other students' attention was focused in their direction.

"You also have to understand that, yeah, it wasn't that bad when you were here before. Everyone knew how important you both would be, but everyone had grown up with you. You were still just you. Now…" He shrugged and glanced away.

Hesitantly, Ella offered, "It's…since what happened…everyone's wondered if you were both still alive. And then when everyone heard you were found and coming back, which most everyone just learned about this week. It was kept very quiet. Sorry, but it's like everyone is waiting."

Abruptly, Sawyer sat forward, leaning closer to them. "That's just it. What are we supposed to do?" He exchanged a glance with his sister, and at her nod, he added, "We don't get it. What is it that everyone is wanting from us?"

"Honestly, I don't really know myself," Ella whispered.

"Look," Gabe said, "all we know is what the prophecy says. What it really means, who knows for sure. It could mean whatever someone wants it to."

"But that's just it. Are we supposed to lead some army and take over the world—or at least the world that's still sane?" The frustration was clearly evident in Sawyer's tone.

"And that's the burning question. What will you and your sister do?" a voice from behind them said.

Sawyer turned in his chair to face the newcomer. Behind him stood Flora, Dalen, and a boy and girl he hadn't seen before. It was the boy who had spoken. He had a dark, brooding look about him; an appearance that girls typically fell for in movies. A quick glance over his shoulder seemed to indicate his sister might be of that mind because as she stared at him, a dull red crept up her cheeks.

Whoever he was didn't matter to Sawyer in the least. He hadn't cared for his condescending tone. "And why exactly would that be of any of your business?"

The two girls at his side bristled; Dalen looked stunned.

The boy's lips lifted in a snide smirk. "I'm Lucien Norwood, and you'll find that everything that goes on in Willow Oak is the business of the Norwoods."

Sawyer leaned back in his chair, seemingly unconcerned; a smile turned up the corners of his lips. "Then I guess you'll have to come to the realization that all of that has changed now that we're here."

"No." Lucien shook his head. "You'll recognize your place soon enough."

"Is that so?" Sawyer asked, slowly rising to his feet. He sensed more than saw his sister and their two other companions jump up also.

It was the blond boy Gabe that spoke. "Norwood, it's their first day. They're not used to your own special brand of self-absorption. Why don't you run along."

A black brow rose in annoyance. "And when are you going to learn to mind your own business, Meyer? I wasn't talking to you."

He shrugged his broad shoulders then chuckled. "Probably around the same time you stop being such a prick."

Red heat suffused the black-haired boy's face. He started to take a step forward, when Kira said, "Okay, look, I don't know you, but I do know that I'm tired of people staring at us like we're some sort of sideshow freaks, so if you could back off that would be great. You're drawing even more attention to us. I'd like to be invisible for, oh, I don't know, fifteen or twenty minutes. You know, enjoy the rest of my lunch without people staring at me."

He turned to face her fully, his smile coming out in full force with not even a hint of the annoyance he'd displayed toward the two boys. "It's the least I can do for the girl who knocked me off my feet earlier. Though..." He paused as his gaze slid over her from head to toe. "I don't think you could ever be invisible." He cut a glance back to Gabe, but this time a disgusted gaze marred Lucien's features. "You and I will finish this later."

He turned then, moving off to the opposite side of the cafeteria, the two girls and Dalen following in his wake.

"Knocked him off his feet?" Sawyer asked of his sister though he didn't glance in her direction.

"Literally ran into him and knocked him down. Took him to the floor actually. Perfect way to blend in." Her tone was laced with self-loathing.

"I hate him," Gabe muttered as they all stared at his retreating form.

"Who is he exactly?" Sawyer asked as they all resumed their seats.

"He's a Norwood," Ella explained, "and Norwoods believe they own everything."

"His father is the mayor of Willow Oak. Though around here, the official title is Lord Mayor. I know," Gabe said at Sawyer's raised brows. "It's just the way it is. It's not like where you're from."

"From where we're from?" Kira glanced to her brother before she said, "You do realize we all live in the same country, don't you?"

This time it was Ella and Gabe who exchanged a meaningful glance. Sawyer noticed, and it set his already frayed nerves on edge. "What?" The question was asked through gritted teeth.

"See," Ella said, her eyes focused in on the food she was absently pushing around on her tray, "here…we don't…it's not like we're really part of the Non-Magical World."

Once again, Sawyer glanced to his sister. She shrugged, her way of telling him she didn't understand either. His brow knitted as he tried to make sense of it all. "So are you telling me you don't leave this place?"

"No," Gabe said, but then he quickly amended, "Wait...I'm not explaining this right."

Sawyer cut him off with a shake of his head. "Ella's dad mentioned some sport or something. How can you have that if you don't leave this place?"

"That's why I said I wasn't explaining it correctly. We do, but most of us only travel to other places like this."

"There's other, I don't know, magical towns?" Kira asked. Her tone held a healthy dose of skepticism.

"Oh, yeah." Ella was looking up now, a genuine smile lighting up her features. "There are towns all over this country just like Willow Oak. Actually, they're all over the world. Obviously, the ones over in Europe, Asia, and Africa, are older than ours are, but they're everywhere. Though the magic here dates back thousands of years."

"So what you're saying is that this magic stuff...it's bigger than just here?" Sawyer needed this clarified. But the feeling of dread running down the base of his spine already told him the answer before it was vocalized.

"Yeah, we're all connected together—there's a governing council with members from all over the world—but there's so much more than just here." Gabe explained, his fork in his hand, all but forgotten. "You'll both learn all about it in the History of Magical Culture class. Usually, that's introduced in lower levels and gets more advanced with each year, so it might take you a bit to get caught up to where we are. Let me see your schedule."

Wordlessly, Sawyer handed it over.

"You have Magical Life Skills. That's where you'll get most of it. We had Professor Kemp when we were younger. You'll love her. Some of the stuff though will come from just living in this world. This year after we get our powers, we'll have Professor Lee. I've heard he's annoying."

It was all converging on him too fast. Sawyer had really hoped he'd go to school and find out that Michail Hopewell was a crazy loon. He didn't want any of this to be true, but that sinking feeling in the pit of his stomach told him that nothing was ever going to be the same again for them, ever.

Kira leaned forward in her chair and pushed her tray out of the way, so she could rest her arms on the table. "So let me get this straight. These places are all filled with people who can do magic?"

"Not everyone can do magic." Ella looked at Sawyer once before focusing in on his sister. "Sure there are healthy numbers of witches and wizards in these towns, but there are also vampires, werewolves, shapeshifters, and to a lesser extent fairies. The crystal cough hit them years ago. They almost died out. They're just now starting to rebound from it."

"Fairies?" Sawyer couldn't let that one pass. "So you're telling me that the Tooth Fairy is real?" He couldn't keep the skepticism from his voice. "Next thing you'll tell me is to watch out for Santa Claus coming down the chimney."

Gabe tried to bite back his chuckle but failed, so he smoothed it over into a cough when Ella shot them both an annoyed glare and turned her focus back on Kira. "Those are the ones that, for the most part, live in towns and are members of society…well, their societies."

Sawyer leaned forward to listen in spite of himself.

"Vampires? Werewolves? Those are monsters in stories people read about," Kira said, shaking her head in disbelief.

Sawyer glanced around the cafeteria. There was still a good number of the student population focused on their table. Lucien Norwood was one of those people. The dark-haired boy smirked when Sawyer glanced to him. With an annoyed shake of his head, Sawyer turned back to the occupants of his table. "Are there any here?" he found himself asking. He would almost bet that Norwood was a vampire.

"Here, yes, but only a couple," Gabe answered, finally taking a bite of his previously forgotten pasta. "But other places, there's a healthy population of them. Fairies live either in their own communities or around Magical people. But the others tend to stay with their own kind. There's not a lot of intermingling, though not to say that there's not any, but it's not common. One of the schools we play has quite a few vampires. Werewolves tend to form close packs, and vampires, well, most magical people tend to stay away from them. There's not a lot of trust there."

"What's a shapeshifter?" Kira ended on a whisper and with a glance over her shoulder as if expecting an attack from behind.

"Don't worry." Ella was quick to reassure. "Shapeshifters can only change from their human form into an animal. They can't make themselves be other people."

"Well, I guess that's something." Kira didn't sound convinced.

Sawyer knew he wasn't. He'd be worried later when he had time to think about it. However, right now, he didn't know what to believe. Was it true? Were all the monsters he had heard about as a kid real? There was only one way to know for sure, he'd just ask them.

"So if I walk out in the woods here, am I going to run into Big Foot?"

Gabe snorted.

Ella sent him a quelling look when she realized the question was a serious one. "No," she reassured them both. "Big Foot is a legend Nons made up probably from an actual encounter they couldn't explain, but there are other creatures. Some live among us or as much as they can, like mermaids, centaurs, nymphs, and even goblins. But there are other things out there that, well, you should fear."

"Like what?" Kira whispered.

Gabe opened his mouth to explain, but the ringing of the bell cut him off. There was a mass scrape of chairs as the students started milling out, ready for their afternoon classes.

"We'll have to finish this later," he said right before he stuffed the last bit of food in his mouth.

Sawyer nodded, but his mind was too busy trying to process everything he had just learned.

Vampires, werewolves, goblins, mermaids.

They were fiction; monsters that belonged in the dark corners of a child's imagination. They couldn't be real. But as he glanced to his sister and saw the horror displayed in her own eyes, he had the sinking feeling that they were.

Life was never going to be the same again.

V. A. Risby

6

She was scared, terrified. Her mind was racing as she tried to make sense of everything she had learned.

The mantra of vampires, werewolves, shapeshifters, and fairies came echoing in her brain, causing an almost near state of panic.

Once again, she glanced around the room of her last class of the day, Magical Life Skills. She had chosen a seat in the back of the room. The rest of the room was composed of empty tables. She didn't understand why she was the only person so far; there was ten minutes between classes, which was nice, not the rushed, sometimes near frantic five she was used to. But as she checked the clock, those minutes were quickly dwindling down. Surely, at least one other person wouldn't want to skid in at the last moment. If she hadn't double-checked the number on the room, she'd be afraid she was in the wrong place. But she wasn't. She was just the only person who apparently had decided to arrive to class early.

She shifted uncomfortably in her chair. She just wanted this final hour over, and then she could go home and pretend none of this had ever happened. That was the only way any of this would make sense.

She was seated in the far corner of the room, an empty chair to her right, a bank of windows to her left. Absently, she watched a few people scurrying around outside, gripping backpacks tightly as they hurried to their classes. Perhaps there was another building. That Gabe Meyer had said this was typically a lower level class. From what she knew, those were housed in separate buildings.

Was she in the wrong place?

With a sigh, she leaned back in the hard, wooden chair. Honestly, she didn't care if she was or not. She was tired and ready to go home. The rest of the day, while bizarre, had been bearable after this morning's mishap. Ella Hopewell had kept up a steady stream of chatter—not about anything supernatural—unless Kira had asked her a question. It had been a normal conversation, and it had made Kira believe, for at least a few moments, that everything was going to be all right. She'd forgotten about this strange world she was now living in and could pretend she was a normal teenager again.

But she would admit it was unnerving the way she would sometimes catch Ella watching her. Finally, the girl had sheepishly explained that since they had used to be best friends, she wondered if perhaps she would say something, and Kira's memory would come rushing back. After that explanation, at least the looks made sense, and it put Kira more at ease around the other girl.

However, Ella was not in this class since it was beneath her grade level; she was actually in a class learning about the Non-Magical World. And as Kira sat there, listening for the bell, waiting for the teacher, she had a horrible feeling that her brother wouldn't be there either.

With a loud bang, someone hit the door while struggling through it, carrying an armful of books.

Her heart stopped until the person finally made it through the doorway.

It was Sawyer.

He made a grab to catch his bag before it fell. Once he had it secured, he glanced up, his eyes widening at the empty classroom before his gaze fell on her. He stopped abruptly. "What?"

She quirked a brow. Then added, "Don't know. I thought I was going to be the only one in here."

He glanced back to the door he had just come through. "Are we in the right place?"

She nodded, propping her elbow on the desk so she could rest her chin in her hand. "Yeah, I double checked."

With his brow furrowed in confusion, he made his way through the rolls of empty tables. "This is weird."

"After everything we've seen and heard in the last few days, *this* is one of the most normal things that's happened."

His lips turned up at that. He dumped his books in the empty space behind the table and tossed his bag down in the empty space behind the chair. He grabbed out a notebook and pen and then took the seat next to her. "I doubt everyone is waiting until the last minute to come in at a mad rush."

Kira nodded. She'd had the same thought. "I agree. We're either in the wrong place or…"

"We're the only two in here," he finished for her. He glanced around the stark classroom with its plain gray walls. "Yeah, this isn't going to be awkward at all."

She snorted at his droll comment and rolled her eyes. "At least we won't be in this class with young kids. That's what I was afraid of ever since that Gabe said it was for primary grades. Can you imagine?"

Sawyer's own relieved look said he felt the same way.

She gestured toward the pile of books. "What's with all of that?"

He shrugged his broad shoulders. "None of my classes made any sense. I want to catch up. Or at least know what in the world they are talking about."

Kira made a face. She hadn't thought of that. All she wanted was to pretend this day had never happened.

With another glance toward the window, she saw there weren't any other students on the grounds. She turned to tell her brother that they had to be in the wrong place, but she was halted when the door opened.

She was tall, the woman that breezed in the room. She appeared to be in her mid-twenties with a slender frame and long, nearly white blonde hair spilling down her back in a riot of chunky curls. She unceremoniously dumped the books in her arms down on the sturdy wooden table, and then she turned to face them.

She was pretty and had an easy smile, which she bestowed upon them. And then her beautiful Caribbean colored gaze narrowed on them for a moment. Then the pale brow quirked up in amusement.

Her hand swept out before her to encompass the room. "You two are the only students in the class, and you're seriously going to sit in the very back?"

Kira darted a hasty gaze over to her brother. His expression was just as hesitant and sheepish as she figured hers was.

However, before they could move, the teacher strode forward. She took a seat on the table two rows in front of them, her booted feet landing in one of the chairs. "We'll do it this way then," she said with an easy smile. "I'm Risa Kemp. The school is going to tell you to address me as Professor Kemp." She leaned forward slightly. "But you see, us three, we're going to become good friends, so I insist you call me Risa."

Kira could feel her brow furrowing. She didn't know what to make of this woman in front of her. A month ago, she would have thought the teacher was friendly, if, perhaps trying a bit too hard to fit in with her students. But now…

With things no longer being what she had always thought they should be, she had no idea of what to make of this woman. Was she genuinely a nice person, or did she, too, want something from them like it seemed many people did?

The woman must have known them before, or at the very least knew of them. Heck, for all she knew, this woman had once babysat her. And that thought made her uncomfortable. She didn't like the feeling that people knew her when she couldn't recall their first encounter.

"Now as I was appraised of your situation before, I'd still rather talk to you both openly about what is going on. Is it true that you have no memory of your previous time here?"

Kira darted a quick glance to her twin before she turned her wary silver gaze back to the woman sitting before them. "It's true. We don't remember." She couldn't keep the suspicion from her voice, didn't even know if she wanted to mask it.

Risa Kemp seemed unfazed by the borderline frosty tone. She nodded as if she was mulling something over in her mind. "All right. That gives me a place to start with."

Sawyer leaned forward in his seat. "And where would that be."

The teacher's smile was warm. "At the very beginning."

"Not that d…" Sawyer caught himself. After a moment's pause he added, "Prophecy again. That's all I've heard about all day."

If the near cursing bothered her, Risa Kemp didn't let it show. In fact, she waved away his explanation. "No, I should have worded it better. We'll start with the basics about this world, about magic. And if you have *any* questions, please, ask. This is all new to me, too. I typically teach Magical Life Skills to younger children. But for you, we'll have to do something different as you know nothing of our world."

Kira sighed. "Okay, fine. Here's my first question, so there's magic here. I get it—though I really don't—but let's say I'm fine with all of this, why does everyone keep acting as if we're in some far-off country? We *drove* here from Chicago. We are still in America, the good old U.S. of A. The President is still in charge of the entire country. Why does everyone keep acting like that's not true?"

The older woman's gaze softened. It caused Kira to stiffen. She didn't want to be placated. She wanted the truth, no matter how harsh or cold it was. Everything she had ever thought was apparently a lie. She didn't want to add more to it.

"Technically, we are attached to the continent of North America. We're in America, but not really."

As far as Kira was concerned *that* explained absolutely nothing.

The teacher must have realized that as she rushed to explain. "You both were told about the protective charm on Willow Oak, correct?"

"Yes, but it still doesn't make any sense." When Sawyer spoke, his voice was filled with frustration. It was the same emotion Kira felt coursing through her veins. It seemed as if everything was a puzzle with half-truths and whispered secrets given out only sporadically. Just enough to exasperate a person but make them think this was real, but never enough to actually explain what was going on. Why couldn't someone just spit it out?

"The United States government has no jurisdiction over this place or the other places like it spread throughout the country because they do not know we exist."

"How?" Kira ran her hands through her chocolate colored hair. She barely resisted the urge to tug on the waves. Her mind could not comprehend what the woman in front of her was saying. "I mean…can't they just drive up like we did? Yes," she rushed to continue when the older woman opened her mouth, "the Hopewells said something about reading the letter would only let us enter, but I don't understand. Not at all. Not even a little bit."

Risa leaned forward. "Just…just be patient with me, and I'll try to explain."

Kira sighed and glanced once more toward her brother. At his nod, she sighed again but remained quiet.

"All right." Risa smiled. "Good. So…let's start with that letter and why the U.S. government doesn't have any control over this place, but we're still left alone. It all started back before the Salem Witch Trials, before there was even that large a population of European settlers in North America. You see people with magical abilities never lived out in the open. Sure, they weren't hidden as they are now, but they weren't brazen about their abilities. As with all things, those without magic did see things. Sometimes it was fluffed off as a trick of the eye, or they just completely doubted what they had seen. Other times, it was accepted without question. Yet, as time moved on, and society became more scientific, more things were doubted and said to be impossible.

"And with this changing of beliefs, Non-Magical people became more skeptical of things they couldn't understand or find a scientific explanation for. Sometimes…usually…that leads to unnecessary fear. Magical people started to become more secluded. It wasn't mandated. It just naturally seemed to happen over time. The more isolated, the less worry of having their abilities questioned and discovered."

Risa leaned forward, resting her elbows on her knees.

She was so unlike any teacher Kira had ever known, and she'd had some wonderful ones, some she'd adored. But this woman before her and Sawyer seemed so earnest. She wanted them to understand; she wanted to explain. However, she wasn't being patronizing. It was as if they were talking with a friend. It wasn't like when Michail Hopewell had tried to explain things to them. This was different. And this easy way Risa Kemp had about her started to make Kira believe, believe what she had been told; believe in this strange, new existence she now found herself in.

"Some Magical people," Risa said, "did not like the life they now found themselves living. They didn't like the secrecy. They felt they deserved to live openly no matter what Non-Magic people thought. It caused fighting amongst the Magical community. Others wanted things to remain as they were. Sure, they weren't free to be obvious with their powers, but they still liked their lives. They had friends who were Non-Magic.

"There were also completely magical communities springing up all over the world at this time. There these people were content, happy. They were free to be who they were. But for some, it wasn't enough. There were many debates, lots of infighting. There were threats of actual fights, the cursing of some Non-Magic people. But calm heads prevailed.

"Then the Salem Witch Trials began. Magical people paid it no heed as it was Non-Magic giving into mass hysteria. But then an actual witch was burned at the stake."

"Mr. Hopewell told us that was because she fell in love with a normal guy and told him about being a witch," Sawyer said when the teacher had paused.

Risa nodded. "He's correct. After her death, the side that wanted to fight the Non-Magic became more vocal. They wanted all-out war. They wanted to take over and subjugate those that didn't have any magical abilities. They said it was what they were owed for the years of forced secrecy. Really, they just wanted power, and they have always, *always*, viewed Non-Magical people not as good as those with magic. There was fighting between those on either side of the debate. It was bloody and costly. The uprising was put down, but before one of the most powerful wizards of the time was killed, he set the curse. However, the curse didn't put the barriers in place.

"After everything that had happened, Magical people retreated further. Before, there was no planning of entire magical communities. That was no longer to be the case. After what had happened, they didn't want to risk another war. Every person and creature with magical abilities had to relocate to certain areas. That's when the magical barriers were invoked. These magical communities were protected from Non-Magic entering."

Kira shook her head. "I still don't understand that. People move everywhere. Even if it's a wooded area, they would go there." She couldn't grasp how no one had stumbled upon the place. It had to have been seen.

Risa didn't seem annoyed by the interruption at all; in fact, she smiled as she sat up straighter. "Magic is a powerful force that has nearly no limitations. The barrier that surrounds this town, and other towns all over the world, is powerful. When someone Non-Magic approaches the area on foot, car, even air, they are—for lack of a better word— zapped immediately to the other side of the barrier. It doesn't repel as it doesn't push them back, but it rushes them through so fast that they don't even realize it happened."

Sawyer's brows drew together. "So you mean that when we drove into this town…"

"Yes, you all were allowed to pass through, where as another vehicle that traveled on that same road would have basically been spit out on the other side of the area."

"Does someone feel…something…when they are shoved through the other side?"

"I've never experienced that feeling, so I don't know for certain. I don't know any Non-Magical people to ask. Some people, their entire job is to keep tabs on the 'normal' world and see if anything occurs there that shouldn't. But still they can't reveal the Magical World to them."

"So we were only allowed through because of the letter?" It was the only question Kira could articulate enough to ask. Too many were running rampant through her head at the moment.

"No."

"But that's what Mr. Hopewell said." Kira rubbed at her forehead. She could feel the beginnings of a headache starting. "He said reading the letter allowed the four of us in."

"He's right to an extent."

Kira opened her mouth to say something, but the patient smile on the teacher's face stopped her. Instead, Kira abruptly sat back in her hard, wooden seat. She'd allow the woman to continue unhindered. She had a feeling Risa Kemp would explain everything if she would only give the woman a chance.

She wasn't disappointed.

"You both possess magical abilities. If you had come upon the barrier yourselves, naturally, you would have been allowed in. It was your parents that needed to read that letter. They had to be invited in to cross the barrier. Likewise, since they are Non-Magic, they can leave anytime they want."

"Wait." Sawyer glanced to his sister, a hint of trepidation growing in his marbled colored eyes. "Does that mean we can't leave here?"

Risa sucked in a deep breath. "Technically, no. You can leave, but only to travel to other Magical communities. After the war, the Non-Magical world was deemed The Forbidden. As such, magical travel was banned. Through the years, though, there have been changes made. There's a permit one can apply for to travel outside the barrier, but there has to be a good, documented reason for such travel. A person can't decide they want to see New York City and take off for a vacation. It's impossible. You can't cross the barrier without a token."

Kira had a feeling she knew when that was. "It was because of us, wasn't it, that changes were made?"

Risa's bright blue eyes dimmed with a hint of sadness. "Yes. When your parents…" Her voice trailed off. She cleared her throat before she continued. "When you both were missing, people knew they had to find you. It took work and a powerful spell to break through the barrier. It had been created from old magic that no one knew any longer. No one had been outside of it since its creation. Once it was finally breached, only two people are allowed out at once, such as the permit states. And the only way to go is with the tokens. Michail Hopewell was allowed more frequent movement after you both were found. He was Lord Mayor at the time."

Kira glanced to Sawyer. His own gaze was narrowed, as he seemed to be working out something in his mind. She wondered if it was the same as hers. The only way to find out was to just ask. "Then how did Sawyer and I get out of here? If it was only with a spell and now tokens that others can leave, how did we end up far from here in a Non-Magical area?"

"And there lies the question that many people want answers to. How did two seven-year-olds break through a barrier that has been impassable for nearly three hundred years?"

The silence was unnerving.

Sawyer couldn't handle it apparently, as he broke it. "And what's the answer?"

"No one knows." Risa sat forward again, seeming to study them. "Did someone find a way to cross the barrier and keep it a secret? Did that person or persons take you two out of here that night? Or, as The Prophecy says, you both will have powers that no one has seen before. Did those powers manage to get you across the barrier when it was vitally important that you get away?"

Kira's hand went up to gently massage her temples. Yes, the headache was getting worse. She shut her eyes for a moment as she sought to collect her thoughts. "Everyone keeps talking about our magical abilities." She gritted that out through clenched teeth. She gestured between herself and her brother. "We don't have magical abilities. I've never turned someone into a toad or something."

Now it was Risa's turn to look confused. "I thought Michail had explained about the binding of power."

"He said something." Sawyer explained. "But, honestly, we didn't really listen as we didn't believe a word he was saying. It all sounded so ludicrous. We thought he was insane."

Risa was nodding before he finished speaking. "It would be hard to take in," she agreed. "First, magical people don't turn people into toads…well at least not typically. I'm sure some have, but there's really no reason to. At birth, a child's power is automatically bound. Children are so impetuous. And then comes teenage years with hormones and all, making the power unstable. At the age of seventeen, though, one should have learned some self-control—at least somewhat. That is when the bind is broken. In the seventeenth year that child receives his or her full power."

Apprehensively, Kira glanced to her twin again. His gaze met hers, and she knew he was thinking what she was. She wanted an explanation, but she was afraid to get it. She didn't know if she should trust this woman before them. She seemed genuinely sincere, but that could all be an act.

But as she looked at Risa Kemp, Kira couldn't believe for one moment that the woman before her was some power-mad megalomaniac who wanted to take over the entire world and enslave everyone.

The words tumbled out before Kira could rethink them. "I made a lamp explode."

Those bright blue eyes blinked once, twice. "Excuse me?"

"The other night…" Kira's hands tightened into fists. "I waved my hands and…it just exploded." The last word ended on a whisper.

Risa leaned forward. Her own voice was quiet when she spoke. "Actually exploded?"

Sawyer nodded when Kira found she couldn't—or didn't want to—answer the question.

The other woman blew out a measured breath of air as she leaned back. Her hands came up to cup her mouth, as she seemed to be thinking. The silence stretched before she leaned forward again. "It's not unheard of for there to be a spark of magic before someone comes of age. Typically, that's moving something…or making it wobble. Nothing big. You need a wand to do real, powerful magic. Only a few learn even the simplest wandless spells. It takes much time and control, not to mention magical ability."

"Will it happen again?" Before the teacher answered, Kira shook her own head. "That's not…I know you can't answer that for sure. You just said it happens sometimes, but I…I don't want to wave my hand and blow up someone. I don't even have my full powers. I turn seventeen next week apparently. I don't know how I even did this, and that wasn't even really my supposed powers. I could…What if I…" Kira shut her eyes and tried to bite back her rising hysteria. What if when she was talking to Sawyer she waved her hand and hurt him? Or her parents? She wouldn't be able to handle that. She could kill someone, or at the very least hurt them horribly.

The warmth of a hand enclosed her own. Kira started not having sensed the coming contact as her mind was too occupied with thoughts of the pain and horror she could accidently inflict. When she glanced up, she expected to find that it was Sawyer who was offering her reassurance. And he was, with his concerned-though-trying-to-be-boisterous expression, but it was the teacher Risa Kemp whose hand was covering her own.

The young woman gave her a warm, compassion-filled smile. "I wish I could reassure you that it wouldn't happen again, but I can't." Then her expression took on a decidedly determined glint. "But I can tell you that we will work together to control this new power that you're both experiencing. Magic is a wonderful, beautiful thing. But it can be scary, and it can be downright dangerous in the wrong hands."

They were simple words, but the determination, the resolve behind them touched something in Kira. She knew, just *knew*, that Risa Kemp was right. That she'd help her and her brother; together they would navigate through the vast unknown they were stepping into.

She'd get through this strange, new world.

She could do it.

She had to.

V. A. Risby

7

"So, uh, how was school today?"

Sawyer glanced up from the pizza before him to find his mother's curious, concerned gaze. She'd went out of her way to make their first day of school bearable by making one of their favorite meals. She'd made individual pizzas tailored to each of their own likings. His was loaded with different meats, though some looked not what he was used to, while his sister's, who was sitting across from him, was filled with vegetables. His father's was typically a barbeque chicken but it looked different tonight, too, while their mother went supreme. But the true splurge for the evening meal was dessert. As soon as Sawyer had walked through the door, the smell of fresh baked pumpkin pie had wafted through the air and assailed his senses. Not only had she made his favorite dessert, but alongside that mouth-watering aroma was that of Kira's favorite sweet, peanut butter chocolate chip brownies. Sawyer had been practically salivating.

He'd known it had been for a reason. His mother was trying to do everything within her power to make this right for them, but as he looked up and studied her, noticed the pinched lines around her eyes that he didn't recall being there a week ago, he realized that this wasn't all about him and Kira. No, this was happening to his parents, too. Granted, they didn't have to worry about magical powers suddenly shooting out of them or whatever was supposed to happen, but they were going through their own life-altering changes.

If he glossed over how much his head was spinning with all the revelations, if he ignored his nearly over whelming confusion, and that somehow made it better for his mom and dad, he'd do that. He *needed* to do that. If he could relieve their burden of worry, his parents could be the strong, pillars of support they'd always been. Then he knew he would be all right. He needed them normal for him to feel normal. And he wanted that; he wanted it desperately.

With that thought firmly in mind, he chose his words carefully. "It was a day. Honestly, it was a lot more normal than I expected."

As he watched, his parents seemed to almost sigh in relief at that admission. It cemented in his mind that this was the right thing to do.

He cast a quick glance to his sister to get her on the same page. As soon as he met her gaze, she nodded a barely perceptible movement.

"Well it was embarrassing," Kira said, pulling part of her pizza away from the whole.

His parents tensed.

"I wasn't watching where I was going. I ran right into the doorframe of a classroom. Knocked a guy to the floor. I mean we actually went all the way down." She shook her head at the memory. "I definitely made a first impression."

It was said with such self-deprecating humor, that Sawyer felt the tension drop another notch. His father quickly took a sip of his water to hide the grin that was threatening to turn up the corners of his lips, while their mother fought to keep hers at bay as she asked a question.

"Was he nice about it?"

Sawyer felt his own tension kick up at the thought of Lucien Norwood and the conversation in the cafeteria. Thankfully, though, he didn't have to answer.

"Yeah, he was. Still embarrassing though." She took a bite of her pizza. Her eyes closed as she savored the taste. She gave a little sigh of pleasure. "This is so good, Mom." Then she met her mother's pleased gaze. "Even after all this craziness, this still tastes the same."

That compliment seemed to break through the last of their parents' tension. Their mother seemed to sag with relief. "Good. I know they all seemed insane, but...that Constance Hopewell dropped by this morning. I went to the market with her. Everything is so different. No boxed or canned food here. Everything is fresh. Though, there's this little Non-Magical goods shop where they sell items from...well what we're used to. Thank goodness, I had her, as they don't use normal money here. It's all coins. There's gold, silver, copper, and bronze. She took me to the bank first and helped me exchange money. She seems...she seems nice enough."

Sawyer took a long look at his sister. He noticed her barely perceptible nod. She agreed. Neither of them wanted to leave their parents out of what was happening. Trying to be secretive and hide it would only push their parents away. He didn't want to alienate them, and he knew his sister didn't either.

What was happening to them all wasn't normal; it was as far from normal as one could get. But sadly, it was their new *normal*, and he didn't want his mom and dad to feel as if they were being left in the dark. To do that would hurt them more.

"We met their daughter, Ella, today. She seemed nice." Sawyer said that as he pretended to study his pizza before he took a healthy bite. In reality, he was watching his parents, trying to gauge their reaction to this news.

Before they could respond, Kira spoke up. "I spent most of the day with her. We have all but one class together. She is nice. She…she knew us from before." She said in a rush.

Their parents tensed.

Kira forged ahead. "She said she was my best friend." Her words were coming fast now, seeming to try to get it all out before she could change her mind. "I don't remember her, but she still seemed familiar, and she was so nice, and she made this day seem less weird than it already was, or at least how I thought it would be, but it wasn't that bad, nothing came flying at us, no one shot spells at us like I was convinced they would and…" She sucked in a deep gulp of air, her wide-eyed, near frantic gaze darting between their parents. "I don't want you to be frightened because I'm frightened, and I'm worried I'm going to hurt someone, and I need you to tell me it's all going to be okay even though I know you don't think it will be. I just need it all to be all right. It has to be all right. It all—"

"Breathe," their father said, his hand coming to cover Kira's.

She immediately fell silent, her gaze still darting back and forth between their parents. Their mom and dad glanced to each other for a minute before their mother's gaze fixed on Kira. "Everything *is* going to be all right. We just don't understand everything about this place yet. But when we do, things won't seem so strange. You'll see."

Sawyer wanted that to be true. "You really believe that?"

"Yes." His mother gave him a genuine smile. "I do."

He didn't. He realized that deep down, but for the moment, he was going to take whatever small measure of comfort could be found in his mother's words and hold to them. He was going to pretend they were the truth.

V. A. Risby

8

"So I've been trying to decide how best to approach everything I need to teach you. Some of it is vitally important, so it might seem a bit disjointed as I try to catch you up." Risa exhaled a deep breath. "Let's start with the basics. That way you'll know how the magical world works and functions. Each magical community has a governing board, which is called the Council. Each Council is comprised of seven members. The head of the council is the head of the town. That title is Lord Mayor. Here in Willow Oak, Kenrick Norwood is the leader. Each magical community from all over the world elects one representative to be a member of the Grand Council. That is the council that governs the entire Magical World. There's no capital city as there is in Non-Magical countries. Every six months—unless an emergency meeting is called—the Council meets in a different community. This way no one place gets too much power.

Every three years, the Council elects the Grand Chairman from its appointed members. The Chairman can be reelected up to four times. After the fourth term, that member can no longer be Chairman, nor can that person be a member of the Grand Council. And in that way, no one person can get too much power. At least in theory."

It felt wrong to be taking notes, but Kira banked that thought and furiously scribbled down every detail, for no other reason than to share it with her parents later. They were getting their own introduction to the Magical World via the Hopewells, but Kira wanted to make sure that what they were all told meshed up. A glance to her twin showed that Sawyer wasn't of the same mind. He was just raptly studying their teacher, seeming to hang on her every word.

"For a vast change in topic, currency in the Magical World is simpler than what you're used to. Here money is all in coins. We have gold, silver, copper, and bronze. The big difference here is that no matter where you go in the magical world, the currency is the same. Be it here, or in Europe, Africa, or Asia. It has that cohesiveness. It's the same with our educational system. Same curriculum and courses no matter where a person is. The only variation is how much time is spent on magical creatures. While everyone covers them, obviously, places where those creatures are found spend more time on them."

Kira's pencil stilled over the paper in which she had been furiously writing.

Before she could, her brother asked, "Creatures? You mean like vampires, werewolves, shapeshifters, and fairies, right?"

She could hear it in his voice, the hopeful note that had crept in that there were no more surprises. She hoped so, too.

"Not exactly. Those are not considered magical creatures. But you've heard of them?"

"Yes, Ella Hopewell and Gabe Meyer mentioned them." Kira glanced down at her paper. "What makes something a creature?"

"You see as I said before, the Magical World and the Non-Magical used to basically co-exist. When they separated, magical beings and creatures were regulated into myths and legends in the Non-Magical world. It wasn't until you both went missing that travel to the Non-Magical world occurred. We had no idea about the Nons. About how many of them there were. About their inventions. About the place that magic had fallen to in their society. We knew nothing."

Kira's brow furrowed. It made no sense. She glanced down at herself. Her school uniform could have come from any private school. There was nothing about it that stood out; that screamed that it was from some other world. She even had a locker.

"When people were sent out to look for you, they also brought back books, and what you call pictures to us. While some were devoted to finding you, in other communities, witches and wizards gathered all the information they could on the Non-Magical world. The Nons are ingenious. The things they have discovered and created without the use of magic…It's incredible. We've taken the things that work and are useful and implemented them here. Food is one such thing. We're trying to incorporate more of their choices and varieties here. Another is clothing styles. I can't tell you how happy I am that change has happened. Before, we were dressed as people in your old history books showed from the sixteen hundreds."

She glanced down at her long black skirt and long-sleeved white shirt. "Yes, this is much better. Though there still are those that rigidly hold on to the old ways. But I digress." She waved a hand in the air. "We've veered off topic. I know this really seems to be going in no order, but you needed to know how the government works. And you need to know about what dangers you can come upon in our world."

Kira felt the hair prick on the back of her neck. The nearly over-whelming urge to glance behind her was great, but she fought against it. She didn't want to look silly or worse, like a coward, in front of this woman.

"Dangers?" Sawyer asked. His voice was steady as he said that one word. Kira envied that about him. Sawyer had always had a strength that she was sorely lacking.

"Yes. You've already said they mentioned a few things. I'm sure they told you, that typically, most magical beings like to live in their own communities. Though that's not the case with everyone. There are seven members on the Council. There is also a Special Emissary, Ginette Moondust. She is a fairy, and it's her responsibility to be a voice for those living in this community who are not witches or wizards. Well, half-fairy I should say. Her mother was a fairy and her father a wizard. She inherited the fairy wings and magical abilities. But in this community, we also have a couple of vampires and one witch is married to a werewolf."

"Isn't that dangerous?" The question left Kira before she could halt it. But in all honesty, she didn't even know if she would given the opportunity. Married to a werewolf? Seemed like that could get a bit precarious whenever there was a full moon. Or did werewolves even change at a full moon? Was that one of the myths that had taken shape in their old world? Was that not even the truth?

Their teacher, though, didn't act as if it was a stupid or judgmental question. "It could be, if they didn't take the proper precautions. But they do. They had to agree to construct a room for her husband, to use during his transformations before they were allowed to move here. The werewolf you've heard of in the Non-Magical world is mostly based in fact. They do transform at full moons. You become a werewolf if you've been bitten by one. There's no cure, and when they are in wolf form, they have no memory or thoughts of the life they lead when they are not transformed. They are dangerous to anyone, even those they love. And to be perfectly honest, most people in the Magical World do not trust them. There's a tonic he takes every day, which minimizes the effects of his transformation. His body might transform, but his mind does not. Yet, even knowing this, they still sometimes face…difficulties here. Most werewolves do, which is why most tend to live among their own kind. They don't want to deal with the prejudices that run rampant in the Magical World.

"The same can be said for vampires, shapeshifters, and to an extent, fairies. Think of the Magical World as you would the Victorian time period in the Non-Magical. The Victorian era was a time of a strict class system. There was no real chance of mobility within the classes. Many witches and wizards hold that same opinion. Some even believe that any magical person or being who is not a witch or wizard is beneath them. They want nothing to do with them. But I want to save that discussion for another time.

"No, what I want to go over with you are the different creatures and magical beings you might come across in the surrounding area. Now, I wouldn't recommend venturing into the woods until you become more familiar with this new way of life. But I'm sure you're both anxious to explore, so I need you to be somewhat prepared for what or who you might come across."

Kira had the distinct feeling that after this class she was going to stay locked in her house. Perhaps even locked in her room to hide from all these strange things she was learning. It couldn't be real. It just couldn't. A fairy on a council? A werewolf husband? It was insane. No freaking way was any of it true.

"In our area, one might find a troll, ogre, or a wendigo."

"A what?" Sawyer asked, his gray eyes wide.

Kira's fingers tightened around the pencil she still held. Yes, she was definitely going to go home, lock herself in her room, and never come out.

"Trolls are typically not the most quick-witted of creatures. They need to live in rocky areas, usually in a group. They like to collect things, anything really. If you have something they want, they won't stop until they take it from you, even if it means killing you."

Never going outside again.

"An ogre is taller than a human, hairier, and destructive. What an ogre wants, it takes. If you get in an ogre's way, it will kill you."

She didn't want to hear anymore. She wanted Risa Kemp to just shut up and let her go back to thinking that magic was just something that was pretty and sparkly, not this horror she was describing.

"The worst is a wendigo. It's a tall, skinny creature with haunting yellow eyes that seem to glow. It has an insatiable need for flesh, any kind, though it prefers humans. A wendigo actively hunts its victims. And if someone is unfortunate enough to be caught by one, a wendigo will devour you alive."

She was going to faint, dead away, right here.

"I'm never going into the woods. Ever," Sawyer said at her side.

Kira couldn't form her own reply. She didn't know if she would ever be able to speak again.

Risa leaned forward and placed her hands over theirs. "I didn't tell you this to scare you. It's just something you need to know. I don't know of any reported sightings of any of these creatures in years. And the forest, it doesn't hold just dangers. A person can come upon wondrous, beautiful creatures there like the phoenix, unicorns, and talogoes, which are flying horses," she explained before either of them could ask her.

When Kira turned to look at her brother, she found him staring at her, his eyes wide with the same disbelief and bafflement she knew was apparent on her own expression.

"I know it seems too fantastical to believe, but I just want you both to be prepared. I'm not telling you that you walk into the forest and all of these creatures are going to come up to meet you. In fact, most people go their entire life with never seeing any of them. Unicorns are very independent creatures. They are distrustful of Magical people. To see a unicorn is rare, to be close enough to touch one is unheard of. A unicorn is pure magic and has more power than any of us can ever hope to understand. Back in the first war, the side of darkness wanted to try to harness that power for their own use. It didn't work. Unicorns can sense true intentions, so those people went after unicorn blood. And while the blood of a unicorn does have healing properties, taken against their will, it will not help a person. It will actually harm them."

It was too much converging on her all at once, but at the same time, something Risa just said stood out. "Against their will? So a unicorn will gladly give a 'good' person their blood?"

Risa sat back on the tabletop, her long white-blonde hair floating around her as if it was a cloud. "No, but a witch or wizard that a unicorn has connected with will have that unicorn's unwavering support. A unicorn will sacrifice itself for that person."

It was all too much.

"I know this is a lot to take in. I don't want to overwhelm you, but I feel we need to at least begin to discuss what will happen on Monday."

Next week? Was it some kind of festival she didn't know about? Some holiday in this freak show world she apparently now lived in?

The teacher must have realized that as she added. "Your birthdays, when you get your powers."

Oh, crap, how had she forgotten about that? Something she'd wanted to know for her entire life—or at least the part she remembered—and she'd already forgotten it. Monday apparently flames would start shooting out of her, or whatever was supposed to happen.

"Yeah, I've decided I don't want them. So keep them bound." Kira sat back in her chair. She wanted no part of this. Enough was enough of this freaking carnival ride of a life.

Risa sighed. "It's not that easy. Once a witch or wizard reaches the age of seventeen, one's powers cannot be bound. There's only one-way to take someone's power and that's with their consent. And even then—"

"Didn't you just hear me? I'm giving consent. Take them and let me out of this insane place."

The older woman was shaking her head before she had even finished. "Kira, you mustn't say things like that."

"Why not?" Sawyer asked. "It would save us a lot of grief. We could go back to our normal lives in the normal world and pretend this is all just some horrible bad dream."

"No." Risa shook her head for added emphasis. "You mustn't say things like that, especially around certain people. They will take you seriously."

"We are serious," they said at the same time.

Abruptly, Risa lunged forward, startling them both. "If you were to have someone take your powers, that might put your mind at peace, but it could prove catastrophic. Since you have to have a witch or wizard's consent, the person who is given that consent gets that person's powers. For you two to relinquish your powers, for you to say that to the wrong person, there could be disastrous consequences."

"So the fate of the world rests on our shoulders? That's great, no pressure at all there," came Sawyer's sarcastic voice.

"I just want you to be aware that a decision like that will have consequences."

Kira exhaled a slow, deep breath. She needed time to make sense of all of this, but she didn't feel as if she was going to get that, at least not at that moment. Especially when she needed to know something. "When you're older, and someone takes your powers, can you ever get them back?"

The teacher seemed to relax a bit at the question. "Yes, one can, but either the one who took the powers gives them back freely or on the death of the person who received the powers."

"So if this prophecy is correct, then someone who might want to start a war would like our powers?" Sawyer asked, his brow furrowed as he tried to piece together all the information they were receiving.

"Exactly."

"But again, what powers? We don't have any powers." Kira thought it was necessary to point that out. When Risa opened her mouth, Kira rushed on. "I know we're supposed to get them on our birthday. I know that, but it all still seems so crazy, especially with the talk of monsters."

"And I think it will until you do come into your powers. It's not some, bam you wake up that morning, and you have your powers. What happens is at the exact time of a witch or wizard's birth that is when he or she receives their powers."

For the first time during that hour, Sawyer mouth twisted up in a grin. "Looks like we'll finally know who's the oldest."

Kira couldn't help it. Her own lips lifted at the thought. For years, that had been a point of contention between them. Now, they'd finally know. But on the heels of that, another thought hit her. "Wait, we have no idea what time we were born, do you know?"

The teacher shook her head, but then explained. "Since you both were the first twin birth in over three hundred years—as twins were rare before in the Magical World—the exact time of your birth was kept hidden except to your immediate family."

"So we could just be at school, and all of a sudden we get these powers?" A note of near hysteria had crept into her voice at the images that caused.

"No, on a witch or wizard's seventeenth birthday, it is customary for that individual to stay at home. It is an excused absence from your classes."

The relief was almost instantaneous. At least there was one thing to be relieved about.

"That's not the only thing. At the time they receive their powers, every witch or wizard meets his or her familiar."

"Familiar? What is that? We get a black cat or a toad? That's what you see in movies or TV shows all the time."

"It's not like what Non-Magical people think of. They associate familiars with demons, and like you said, more often than not, a toad or cat. A familiar is a companion animal, the most loyal one a person could have. As long as the familiar is with their person, they do not age like a typical animal. That doesn't mean they can't be hurt or killed. They can. When their person dies, the familiar then ages as the typical animal of their species, or as close as possible to it."

"What type of animals are we talking about here?" Sawyer glanced to his sister, still grinning. "We get to find out who's older, plus I might get the dog I always wanted."

The teacher couldn't help but share their smiles. "Basically, any type. Some can be the same type of animals that people in the Non-Magical world have as pets. Others can be more… On her seventeenth birthday, one witch's familiar was a Finnish dragon."

The pencil fell out of Kira's hand and rolled over the side of the table to land in the floor. "What?" She managed to sputter. She couldn't picture it. First, that dragons were actually real, living, breathing creatures. And second that in less than a week, she could be faced with the very real and terrifying possibility that she might have one show up at her home unexpectedly.

"Don't worry." Risa rushed to reassure them. "That rarely happens. Most familiars are not wildly exotic animals. Mine is what is termed a Siamese cat in the Non-Magical world."

Siamese cat? That sounded all right. She could handle that.

"So you don't get an option for this familiar?" Sawyer asked. His tone held a slight hint of disappointment.

"No, you don't get to pick your familiar. The animal that comes to you is the one best suited for you. No one knows where they come from. They just appear. When they arrive, a familiar will also have in its possession your wand."

"Wand?" Kira managed to ask, even though she was still recovering from the thought of a dragon.

"Like a magic wand? We're supposed to say 'hocus pocus' and make stuff disappear?" This time Sawyer's tone told clearly that he didn't believe a word of this.

The teacher laughed; it was almost musical. "No, wands are not used like that. To do magic a witch or wizard needs a wand. With lots of practice and patience, some simple spells can be performed without one. Say I wanted that book on the shelf." She inclined her head toward the front of the room behind the desk where a shelf loaded with all types of books resided.

Kira and Sawyer automatically glanced toward her. Once they were looking, Risa waved her hand in an almost careless motion. A red, leather-bound book freed itself from the shelf and came flying across the room, landing softly on the table where the teacher sat.

It took a long moment before Kira could form a thought. It had been the first magic they had seen since Michail Hopewell had made that door appear out of thin air, well that and when the movers floated their furniture into the house. But they had used wands for that. "Making something blow up seems to be like something you should need a wand for. It would be kinda rude to blow someone into a million pieces. That seems evil."

"Kira," Risa said, her tone soft and understanding, "what you did was accidental magic. It's not uncommon for it to happen. Perhaps not to that degree." She rushed to explain when Kira opened her mouth to refute those claims. "But the closer one gets to seventeen, the more the magic is eager to get out. We see more and more little bits of magic, but typically, it's like a flower growing and usually only comes in times of high emotional stress. When the mind is unfocused, magic can be very unpredictable. That's why, I know you're both worried and scared, but I need you both to try to remain as calm as possible. And magic, it's not good or evil. It's what a person does with it. Magic is just a thing."

Kira didn't know if she could give the teacher that reassurance. She felt anything but calm. In fact, she was basically scared to death.

"There's one more thing about coming into your magic. At that moment, a mark will appear on the underside of your left arm. It's an indication that you're of age." She sat forward again, but this time she raised the sleeve of her white blouse. Sawyer and Kira both leaned forward. Starting just under Risa's left wrist and running to about halfway to her elbow were swirling black lines.

Kira studied the curves and lines. Then, her brow furrowed. "That looks like a woman's face." She glanced up.

Risa smiled. "I've always thought so, too."

Now it was Sawyer's brow that was knit. "Thought so? You don't know?"

She shrugged. "No, not for certain. Every witch or wizard has a different mark. In its own way, that mark represents that witch or wizard."

Sawyer leaned back in his chair. "So I have to go home tonight and tell my parents that not only am I getting a pet that could be anything, maybe even a dragon, but I'm also getting a tattoo." He glanced back to his sister. "Yeah, they are not going to be thrilled about this."

Risa nodded. "Yes, it will be very hard for them to understand."

"Them?" Kira couldn't help but ask. "Of course it will be! I can't even wrap my head around any of it. It all sounds so ludicrous. I know you just had a book float in the air to you. I *know* I saw that, but at the same time I can't even comprehend it."

Again, came the understanding nod and patient smile. "I know, and if there was anything I could do or say to make this easier on both of you, I would do it." Her shoulders dipped. "But there's not. I feel the only thing that will help is when you get your powers. I think that will be what will make you realize that all of this is real."

"You're right." Sawyer agreed. "Right now this is all just insane." He sat back in his chair. "Take our classes, Metamorphosis, Potions and Elixirs...and what in the world is Maleficium Armor? I've sat in that class for basically an hour and a half, and I still have no clue about what is going on in there." When Risa opened her mouth to explain, he shook his head. "It doesn't even matter. My point is that not a single one of these classes is going to help us. I'm sure this school is not going to send a transcript to the college of our choice, so what are we supposed to do then? How can we get into college once we leave here?"

"Sawyer." Risa reached out a hand as if to touch him, but she didn't. It hovered over his before it fell back onto her lap. "I thought you realized...you now fall under the rules of the Magical world. Magical beings cannot cross back and forth between the Magical world and the Non-Magical world without special permission, and even then, it wouldn't be for a reason like for you to attend the Non-Magical higher education."

They were prisoners then, stuck in this crazy, insane place.

"And what about our parents?" Sawyer demanded, his voice hard and filled with an underlying anger.

The teacher didn't seem taken aback; in fact, she ignored the tone to answer the question. "Your parents are not bound here. They may leave at any time."

"Yeah," Kira said, "but can they come back? Or was it just a one-time thing? Lure us all here, then kick them out to separate us?"

Risa was already shaking her head before Kira had finished speaking. "No, it's not like that at all. Your parents may come and go as they please. I know your father is going to be a special liaison for the magical communities. Your parents just have to be careful. So far, any vehicles that approach the barrier are driven by Non-Magical people, so when they pass through they are all there when they reappear on the opposite side of the barrier. Your parent's vehicle would not, so that would be unsettling for a non-magical person to have a car in front of them and then for it to suddenly seem to vanish. The barrier is strong and can't be breached, but we don't want to draw unwanted attention. That would cause those that want to enslave the Non-Magical population and live out in the open an even greater desire to achieve that goal. We can't have that."

Did she believe that? That was the question Kira was asking herself as she stared at the woman before her. This teacher seemed friendly enough, pleasant, and patient, but was that the truth or was it all just an act. For all they knew this woman was to gain their trust and give them a false sense of security, making them easy prey for whoever had murdered their biological parents. And in that vein, how could they ever trust anyone here? The answer was they couldn't. No one here could be trusted unless...

"Isn't there something you can do to make us remember?" Kira blurted the question out, and once she had, she was glad for it. This would tell her if the woman before them could be trusted. If she could, she would help them, if not...

"Yes," the older woman said hesitantly, "there is a spell to recall memories but it's only for those that have been taken away by magical means. It can't restore memories that have been forgotten because they are too painful to remember or memories that are hidden as they were too traumatizing to relive."

"Well, we have to try." This time Sawyer's voice was determined. "We have to know one way or the other, so do it."

"I—"

"It's simple, either you want to help us, or you don't." The words were designed to be manipulative and to force a response. And this would tell them all they needed to know about where Risa Kemp stood. They'd at least have the answer to that one question.

"All right, I'll do it, but I do believe you both are wasting your time. What happened to you, to your parents, it was traumatic, especially for young children."

Sawyer shrugged. "Still one way or the other we'd at least have one question answered."

Almost reluctantly, she nodded. Her hand came up to touch the charm at the end of the silver chain that hung around her neck. The charm seemed to disappear before their eyes as it transformed into a long, white hued wooden wand.

"What?"

"How?"

She smiled at them. "On your birthday, when you receive your powers, your familiar will bring you your wand. It will be inside the trinket on their own collar. This way you can always have your wand with you. It will become your wand only with your touch and the incantation *Amplifico*. To return your wand to its charmed size, again, your touch, and the incantation *Mazevo*." And once again, the wand resumed its place on the silver chain. "Each wand is designed for one owner. A wand will truly only work for that witch or wizard it belongs to. It knows its master."

Kira shook her head as the teacher withdrew her wand again. She would never understand this place.

Risa seemed apprehensive as she looked at them both. "If no memory spell has been put on you, you won't feel anything," she told them. "But if it has, you should remember almost instantly."

Kira let out a long, soft breath. She glanced to her brother. She did not want that wand pointed at her. She didn't want any magic performed on her, but at the same time, she knew this was the only way. With a barely perceptible nod to her brother, she gave her consent.

Reluctantly, his gaze left hers as he faced the teacher. "All right. We're ready."

V. A. Risby

9

Once more Risa touched the charm to claim her wand. Then she raised it, pointed it at Sawyer, and whispered the incantation, "*Thymamai.*"

Sawyer thought it would feel as if he was being zapped by an electric charge. A few years back when he had helped his dad hang the Christmas lights, he had plugged in the white icicle lights to test them, never noticing the broken bulb until he had touched it. He had felt the jolt from the tip of this finger all the way down his legs. It had taken about an hour before the charged sensation had left him. He hadn't told anyone, as he hadn't wanted them to worry. That's what he had been expecting, something similar to that sensation. That wasn't the case.

This felt odd, almost like a warm shower, but from the inside out. He felt bathed in a comforting heat, and then it was gone. And he was left with no new memories.

That was his last hope.

It was with great reluctance that he met his sister's nearly identical gaze. He saw the disappointment waft across her features before she seemed to stiffen her spine and sit up straighter. She turned to the teacher.

"I know it's not likely, but we should try anyway. Perform the spell on me."

For one wild and crazy moment, Sawyer had to fight down the urge to burst out in laughter. On a list of things he'd thought he'd never hear his sister say that would have to rank right up there. It sounded insane coming from her mouth. But as absurd as it sounded, he now realized this insanity was his life. He lived in a world where magic could be performed, and strange, terrifying creatures roamed the surrounding woods.

He watched as the soft white light came from the tip of the wand and entered into his sister's head. It was one of the most bizarre things he had ever seen—no, scratch that, the most bizarre thing he had ever seen.

The need for oxygen was nearly overwhelming; it was then that he realized he was holding his breath. He sucked in a much-needed gulp of air. He hoped beyond all hope that this would be the answer to their prayers. If only they could remember what had driven them from their home, how they had gotten through some supposedly impenetrable barrier and ended up in Boston. If only they could remember what had happened to their parents.

However, he knew this wasn't going to be the answer as no look of recollection dawned on his twin's face. And when she glanced to him, her silver colored eyes were shaded with disappointment.

"Nothing," Kira said her tone full of frustration and bitterness.

"It will come back, when you're ready and able to handle it," Risa said, the compassion all but bleeding from her voice.

Logically, Sawyer knew she was correct, but still, that didn't make it any easier to handle. He didn't want to have patience and wait; he wanted all the answers now. What he wanted to know was if he had been in contact with the people responsible for his parents' deaths since his return to this mad world. But he didn't say that, and he wouldn't, not yet. Risa Kemp seemed like a nice enough person. She seemed to be a teacher who genuinely cared about her students, but he couldn't risk that she knew who was involved in the murders of their parents.

If this barrier kept everyone in, then it made sense that the person or people responsible were still in this town unless they had died. Until either he or Kira remembered, they couldn't trust anyone, no matter how nice they seemed, no matter if they said they had been their previous best friend or not.

He nodded in response to the teacher's comfort, and then glanced to his sister. He forced his voice to be lighter than he was feeling. "Guess we'll just have to wait."

Kira regarded him quizzically for only a moment before understanding dawned in her own gaze. She sighed. "Yeah, it was too much to hope for. But still it would have been nice to have all the answers now." She glanced to the teacher. "I've never been any good at waiting."

Risa nodded. She cut a quick look to the clock that hung on the wall at the front of the room. "Class is almost over for today. With Monday your birthdays, we only have one other class, and there's no way we can get everything covered tomorrow. Since you don't really know what to expect, nor do your parents, and it's not something you can really describe would you like for me to come over and spend the day there? I don't want you both to be worried or frightened. I can find someone to cover my classes." She added that since they both regarded her in silence.

Have his teacher come to his house to hang out for the day? Yeah, he really couldn't think of much else that he wouldn't want to happen instead of that. It might be one thing if he knew he could trust the woman, but since he couldn't, he didn't want her around anymore than necessary, especially when both he and his sister were going to be vulnerable, as he knew they'd be nearly insane that day. No, locked in the house seemed the way to go.

He should have realized this possibility sooner. He blamed himself for his preoccupation, but too much had been converging on him all at once. He was too overwhelmed with this strange, new world to take the time to truly think about all that had been revealed to them.

His parents had been murdered. He didn't remember, couldn't even recall the vaguest of images of them, but it had happened all the same. Someone had killed them to try to separate him and Kira from their influence. If they weren't careful, that same thing could happen to their parents now. That was something he wouldn't recover from. He refused to allow it to happen. He didn't even want to think about it; their safety was his number one priority.

He didn't glance to his sister to even address that comment. "No, we'll be okay, but thanks."

Risa nodded, her features still drawn into those of worry. She looked as if she wanted to say something more to probably convince them to accept her help, but the sound of the bell saved them from that.

Never in his life had Sawyer been happier for the end of class. He had to refrain from jumping up and running from the room. Instead, he forced himself to gather his belongings at what he hoped was a reasonable pace. As he lifted his backpack to his shoulder, Risa Kemp slid from her position on the table before them. A quick glance at her showed she was all but wringing her hands. She appeared really worried.

Silently, he urged his sister to hurry before the woman made another appeal to be with them on their birthday. If he turned her down much more, it would look suspicious rather than going for the brave front as he hoped she mistook his earlier denial.

Finally, Kira hefted her own bag to her shoulder. He couldn't wait any longer. He felt as if he was about to come out of his skin. He headed for the door and was out in the hallway without a backward glance.

Automatically, he went to his locker. He felt as if he were on autopilot as he methodically placed the books he would need in his bag. He'd need his book for History of Magical Culture as he had an essay due over magic and mythology in Greek culture. Then there was the reading in Magical Creatures over sprites, and in Potions and Elixirs, he had to explain the benefits and weaknesses of the various types of cauldrons on Tuesday.

Even though he didn't understand even half of what the topics and assignments were, he gathered the needed materials.

He wasn't surprised when his sister appeared at his elbow. She opened her mouth to say something, but he forestalled her with, "Not here."

She looked annoyed and like she wanted to say something to argue the point, but after a moment, she nodded. Quickly. But still she stood at his side.

"Go get your stuff." The directive was all but whispered as he kept his head in his locker, digging for his last book.

In a moment, he heard her move away. Finally, he felt as if he could breathe a little. He didn't know why exactly—perhaps it was only from the thoughts running rampant in his head—but he felt as if he was being watched, which probably was happening. Everywhere he went he drew more than the typical new student curiosity.

He dropped the last book in his bag. After closing his locker, he swung the bag on his shoulder once more. He preceded other students out the main door, keeping his eyes focused straight ahead to avoid any stares or attempts at conversation.

It wasn't a long wait at the bottom of the wide staircase for his sister. Automatically, he fell in step beside her, and they started across the large, manicured lawn. They remained silent, and for the umpteenth time, he was glad they always seemed to know what the other was thinking. He didn't want to talk about his suspicions or concerns right here, when they could easily be overheard.

"Hey, Sawyer. Kira. Wait up."

Automatically, they both stopped and turned. Inwardly, Sawyer cringed as he saw Gabe Meyer making his way toward them. The guy seemed nice enough. And previous best friend or not, at least he hadn't hounded Sawyer to remember a past that he didn't. Instead, he seemed content to get to know him again, but after the thoughts that had just popped into Sawyer's mind, he didn't trust the other boy. He didn't trust any of these people.

True, there's no way Gabe Meyer would have been old enough to have a hand in whatever happened to his and Kira's parents, but that didn't matter. His family could have. Sawyer didn't know them. He felt the same about the Hopewells for that matter. As far as he was concerned, everyone was a suspect.

Yet, he knew he couldn't let anyone know he was suspicious. If he did, that might tip off the people who were truly responsible. Guilty people were dangerous and unpredictable, so instead, he forced his features into one of friendliness.

"So up for some exploring this weekend?" Gabe asked as soon as he joined them. "I can take you both around and show you where everything is."

"Yeah, that would be great," Kira answered automatically.

It would be good, as they needed to familiarize themselves with this place, especially if they needed to make a mad escape in the middle of the night. And Sawyer wouldn't rule that out; it felt like something that just might happen.

"Ella," Gabe yelled over his shoulder at the other girl as she exited the building.

The petite brunette waved at a girl with blue streaks in her hair and headed in their direction.

There was no denying it; the Hopewells' daughter was pretty, very pretty. If this would have been his life before, Sawyer would have been nervous, but he still wouldn't have hesitated to ask her out on a date. But now…Put aside the fact that he didn't know if people dated in this world, he didn't know if her parents were murdering psychopaths with her following in their footsteps. Definitely, the best course of action was to be friendly so as not to arouse suspicion but keep it there. It didn't matter how cute she was.

"Hi," she said in way of greeting when she joined them.

Sawyer nodded in her direction while doing his best not to notice the hint of berries that seemed to waft in the air from her direction. He shampoo perhaps?

"We were making plans for this weekend." Gabe informed her. "I thought we could show them around."

"What do you all do around here? Do you go to the movies?" Kira asked.

Ella and Gabe's brows knotted in confusion.

"What's a movie?" Gabe finally asked into the silence.

Sawyer glanced to his sister. Surely, they weren't serious. But one more look at the boy and girl before them showed they seemed just as perplexed as the original question sounded.

"You don't have movies?" Sawyer asked his tone more than a little doubtful.

Apparently, it set Ella's own nerves. She drew herself up to her full height. "Again, I don't know. Perhaps we do if we knew what a movie was. We might have it but call it something different."

There was no getting around it; she sounded more than a little peeved. Sawyer opened his mouth to explain it to her, as it was obvious they were very serious, but just as quickly, he snapped it shut. How in the world was he supposed to explain how a movie worked to them?

"A movie," Kira said, her words coming slow as she tried to pick ones, so she could explain it correctly, "it's like moving pictures that tell a story." At the still confused expressions, she added. "It's with actors, someone who plays a part…like Shakespeare. Instead of a theatre, you watch them on a big screen."

"We've actually read Shakespeare. But we haven't seen anyone perform it."

Finally, a question dawned in Sawyer's mind. "Do you all even have TVs?"

"No," Gabe said, "but we know what they are from our Non-Magical world class. But we were told that's where you get your news. That and an internet."

Sawyer tried to stop it; he really did, but he felt his jaw go slack in shock. Too much had been going on for him to pull out his laptop. In fact, he hadn't even touched his phone since he'd arrived in Willow Oak. He'd been in too much shock with all the revelations. He'd just assumed when it came time to write his essay, he would use the internet for his information. Now, he had the horrible realization that that wasn't the case. They were truly cut off from the normal world by more than physical proximity.

"Wait. So you're telling us there's no TV or internet here?"

"Well, no, but then again we're not really sure what internet is." Ella hoisted her bag a little higher on her shoulder.

"Computer?" Sawyer asked in a croaked whisper, dreading the answer.

Gabe replied, "We've seen pictures of those, but, no, we don't use them here. And from what I've understood in class they run on something called electricity."

Sawyer knew his eyes must be nearly bugged-out from his head; Kira's nearly were. But on the heels of that came another thought, and this one led his voice to take a suspicious tone. "You all know what electricity is. We turn on the lights in our house."

Ella was already shaking her head. "My dad had it fixed that way. He's spent more time in the Non-Magical world than anyone else here. He's mentioned computers and the internet as he's used them, but it was hard to follow without actually seeing it. He has a good understanding of electricity, so he had your house fixed so it would run in a similar fashion. Typically, a charm is put on a room. When you enter the room, it becomes lit. When you leave the room it goes dark."

"How about sleeping? Your bedroom would be lit because you're in it. Do you all sleep with it bright?"

His sister's tone told exactly how crazy she thought all of this sounded.

Neither of the two people before them seemed to take offense. "It's a charm. Charms are different than spells really," Gabe explained. "You see most simple charms don't require the person to have magical ability because there's enough magic here, in this town, in this place, for the charm to work. And even if a person hasn't reached the age of seventeen, magical ability is still inside them. That's the reason a person who is underage can make them work."

"It's the same as with other simple tasks when the charm is already in place. A person just needs to activate it." Ella added. "So no matter the age, as long as a person has magical ability, they only need to say *Kleino* and the lights will go off. Likewise, if you need them on, a person needs to say *Anavo*."

Sawyer resisted the urge to shake his head. There was just too much in this new world, and most of it didn't make any sense. And he knew what he wanted to ask would only confuse himself further, but Sawyer still found the words coming forth of their own volition. "How about just out in the world?" At everyone's—even his twin's— puzzled expressions, he scanned the area. Then, finding what he wanted, he gestured toward the nearby tree-lined area that looked as if it led into the woods. "So out there, say I'm exploring the woods and—"

"No one is going to go out and explore the woods," Ella said with a shudder.

With that comment and the nearly horrified look that accompanied it, Sawyer decided that he was going to explore the surrounding woods. It might not be the smartest decision he'd ever made—in fact, it would probably turn out to be downright stupid—but it would happen. He had to know what exactly was out there. Yet, they didn't need to know that. "It's just an example. I mean if I'm out somewhere, there's no fixtures, no anything, I take it you all don't have flashlights." At their perplexed expressions he added, "Yeah, didn't think so. That leads me back to my original question. Say you're some place where there isn't anything, is there something you can do to create light, besides, you know, use a match and build a fire." He did his best to ignore the puzzled looks at the word 'match.'

"Yeah, there is, but you need a wand for that spell."

Sawyer whipped around at the sound of that matter-of-fact comment from his far side. Standing behind his equally stunned sister was Lucien Norwood. Once again, a petite raven-haired girl was at his side. As Norwood's icy blue gaze swept to Kira, the black-haired girl laced her arm possessively through his. He paid her no heed.

"And tomorrow, I'll be getting mine. Actually." The word was drawn out as he brushed a non-visible piece of lint from his cobalt blue jacket. "My parents are throwing a party to mark the occasion."

"It will be the party of the year." The dark-headed girl's hold on Norwood's arm tightened as she gazed up at him, all but batting her eyelashes. "The Norwood's parties are always the most fabulous."

Sawyer's gaze cut to Gabe. The other boy shot Sawyer a glance, shaking his head, his lips compressed in a line of suppressed laughter.

"I wanted you both to be aware." His gaze lingered on Kira a bit longer. "It's at seven. You're both welcome. Feel free to bring your parents."

"It's a Norwood party." The girl at his side simpered. "Make sure you dress appropriately."

Lucien shot her a quelling glare, which immediately had her mouth snapping shut.

And in that split instant, Sawyer realized he had gotten the other boy wrong. Perhaps he wasn't as bad as his first impression of him had led him to believe. Maybe he'd been too quick to judge.

Then Lucien added, "This way you can see how real witches and wizards live."

Before Sawyer could react—as he was completely blindsided by that comment—both Norwood and the girl were already walking away, leaving Sawyer and his sister staring after them.

"Was that against our parents?" Kira asked at his side, completely as confused sounding as he felt.

"Probably more against me," Ella said, drawing their attention to her. "Lucien's father does not like mine at all. My father's on the Council now," she explained. "They disagree on most everything."

"Or mine. Kenrick Norwood and my father were in the same section at school. Apparently, they've never gotten along at all. It's been worse as they've gotten older. They hate each other now, plus my mom and his don't have a nice word to say about each other. Lucien's mom especially can't stand that my mom's on the Council. Apparently, she doesn't feel that's the appropriate place for a woman." He accompanied that look with a roll of his eyes.

Sawyer decided he'd go back to his previous opinion of the boy, definite jerk. How could he not be when it seemed to be a family trait?

"But that girl with him, Regina Townshed, she was correct," Ella said with a glance toward the departing pair. "Norwood parties are formal affairs, and Lucien's birthday…his mother treats it like a lavish holiday. When my father started going out into the Non-Magical world, he would bring back books, history, literature, that sort of thing. Cerise Norwood fell in love with something called the Victorian Era. Since then, what she deems Victorian attire is demanded at Lucien's birthday ball, which she holds every year. And this year, since he'll be getting his powers, I'm sure it will be even more spectacular."

Gabe snorted in disgust at her side. "It's demanded at every function they host, though only a select few are actually invited to those. Those people…" He shook his head; he couldn't even finish the sentence. "Since her husband is Lord Mayor, she had him pass an ordinance that every empty home be re-magiced in the Victorian style."

Sawyer's brows furrowed. "So our grandparents' home?"

He didn't have to ask the entire question as Ella seemed to follow the direction of his thoughts immediately. "It didn't always look as it does now, though the furniture inside was theirs. It wasn't changed, well except the kitchen. When Kenrick Norwood was elected to Lord Mayor five years ago, his wife Cerise had him enact the rule. It was also *suggested* the rest of us change our houses, too."

It irritated him. He didn't remember his grandparents at all, but Sawyer did *not* like the idea of their home being changed on the whims of a selfish, self-centered woman. "That's the first thing I'm going to learn."

He hadn't meant to say it aloud, but he realized he had when Gabe asked, "What's that?"

Sawyer glanced at them and saw that even his sister looked perplexed.

He glanced in the direction Lucien Norwood had headed. "I'm going to learn how to change the house back."

"That would be nice," Ella said, her tone trying to be encouraging.

"Problem is," Gabe added into the lull, "she had a sticking charm added to the handy work."

"What's that?" Kira asked at his side.

Gabe turned to her. "It's a charm that can be placed on a spell to hold it in place. She had the same problem, so she wanted to annoy everyone else just as much." Now at the confused looks thrown his way, he explained. "When old Kenrick was elected Lord Mayor, they had to take up residence in the estate that goes with the title. Problem was the Ivywood Estate couldn't be re-magiced to look like whatever era someone wants. It stays as it's always been. As you can imagine, that did not sit well with Mrs. Norwood. On all abandoned homes, she had a sticking charm placed on them."

Sawyer glanced to his sister. "No, I will find a way to remove the charm."

Gabe laughed. Before Sawyer could get annoyed, the other boy clapped him on the shoulder. "And I'll do whatever I can to help you. Norwoods need to learn they can't have that much power. They can't control everything and everyone."

It hit him then, a wave of familiarity. It felt right, him and Gabe, banding together, them against a common enemy. It felt like something they had done before. And maybe they had; maybe back in a time that he couldn't remember, it had been as Gabe had said, best friends.

He wanted to remember.

The thought hit him, made something tighten in his chest. With everything he had discovered and learned in the last few days, he'd had the fleeting thought it would be nice to remember, but it hadn't seemed that important.

But it was.

He wanted to remember and know if he had been good friends with this boy, if he was someone he could trust. And he wanted the memories of the grandparents whose house he was going to restore. And more than anything, he wanted to know his parents. He wanted to know what they were like, if he took after them in any way.

Yet how was he going to figure that out? The spell hadn't worked. Neither he nor Kira had remembered anything. So what was left? Patience and time?

He almost snorted at the thought. Yeah, he had next to no patience, and he now had this feeling, it wasn't prominent or even urgent, but it was there, lodged in him, that said he was going to have to remember; that it was imperative that he did. But he couldn't force it, he knew that much.

There was silence for a moment before Kira asked, "So are you both going to this party?"

Gabe's face screwed up in annoyance. "Yes, sadly, I have to go, with my mom on the Council." He offered that as explanation. "It's kinda mandatory that we attend."

"Basically, if the Norwoods invite you, you're expected to show up."

And that right there was reason enough not to go Sawyer decided. His lips turned up in a smug expression. "Well, they won't be seeing us there. We don't happen to have Victorian Era clothing lying around nor do we plan to go get any just to impress his mommy." He couldn't help the unchecked discursion that swept into his tone. The more he heard of these people, the less he liked them.

He could feel his sister's gaze on him. Slowly, he met it. She was annoyed with him; he could tell. Her look was long, hard, and told she'd have plenty to say about it later. He didn't care. Just because she wanted to attend did not mean they had to bow down to him.

Finally, with a roll of her eyes, she turned to the others. "Unfortunately, Sawyer is right. We don't have anything that they would deem appropriate for the occasion."

"Oh, that's no problem at all," Ella said, her voice tinged in excitement. "I do. My mom is amazing at altering clothing. Some people have an aptitude for it, and she does." Ella looked Kira up and down. "You're taller than me, but that won't be a problem for her. She can lengthen something of mine, change color and fix anything you don't like."

"I…" Kira glanced to him, not seeming to know what to say.

It was a nice offer, and it seemed genuine. And the other girl looked truly happy to do it. And to his horror, Sawyer realized Ella was even prettier when she was excited and happy. He shook his head in a sign of inward disgust. He hadn't needed to notice that. This was just great, especially since her family could be murderers and all.

However, how was he supposed to piece together everything that had happened if he didn't spend more time around these people? Even if he did, that didn't mean that he had to trust them. He just needed to figure out if they knew anything about his parents' deaths.

Sawyer shrugged and tried for a nonchalant attitude. "That's up to you. But since I don't think I'd look that good in one of Ella's outfits, I'll leave it to you to represent the family."

The two girls exchanged an eye roll at that comment, and just when Sawyer was feeling quite pleased with himself, Gabe offered, "No, one of Ella's probably wouldn't work, but you're more than welcome to use one of mine."

Sawyer shot a glare in the other boy's direction. Gabe's lips lifted at one end along with a shrug of his shoulders. Then he added, "If we're all going to suffer, no reason you shouldn't join us."

Sawyer glanced around at all their smug faces. He knew a losing battle when he saw it. Besides, he didn't really want to throw his sister to the wolves, but that didn't mean he was happy about any of it. "Fine," he said, shrugging his backpack higher on his shoulder, "I'll go." Then he turned to Gabe. "Thanks." He couldn't help it; the comment came out on a grouch.

Gabe laughed. "No problem."

"Great!" Ella said, her smile nearly blinding. "Let's get outfits sorted tonight as we won't have time after school tomorrow. Kira, you come home with me, and we'll start looking through my stuff. Gabe, take Sawyer to your house and find him something. Then bring it over to my house, and my mom can handle the alterations."

Divide and conquer. Sawyer glanced toward his sister. Her look said she understood him. "Yeah, okay. We'll need to tell our parents where we're going first and then we should be good to go."

"Great, then it's all settled." Ella's smile was near blinding. He felt it then, this slow warmth seeping through his extremities. He needed to be careful because if a stupid smile could cause this type of reaction, he was headed for some serious trouble.

His "Let's go" came out gruffer than he intended. It caused them all to look at him strangely, but he ignored it. Instead, he turned on his heel and started in the direction toward his house, the others falling in step with him.

10

"It's beautiful." Kira breathed the words out as she stared up at Ella's home from the front walk.

An embarrassed smile stole up the other girl's features. "Thanks." She shuffled her feet, and then breathed out a sigh as she tucked a stray chestnut tendril behind her ear. "I liked it better before."

Kira turned toward her, but Ella's attention was focused on her home.

"It used to be simple. I liked it that way. When my dad was elected to the Council... It had to match with what Cerise Norwood wanted. The other way...it felt more like home."

Kira turned back to the house and studied it with a critical eye. It was magnificent. The house was a cornflower blue for the most part, though hints of navy and cream dotted the trim around the windows and decorative accents. The wrap-around porch's rails were in navy while the spindles were a cream hued. Two sets of stair cases led up to the porch, separating them was a cream-colored three-quarter circle inlaid in the railing of the porch. On one side of the house was a turret, complete with what looked like round, portal windows circling the top level.

Looking at this house, simple definitely wasn't what came to mind. All of these homes were vastly different from what she was used to in Chicago. Her mom had always talked about moving to the suburbs, but they never had. Instead, they had stayed in their modern, downtown condominium, which was close to her father's work—or fake work apparently. Every house she'd seen in this town was as far removed from that as possible.

Kira didn't know what to say to that, so she didn't say anything. The silence lasted for only a moment before Ella seemed to shake herself. "Come on. I'll give you the tour and then it will be time to get down to business."

The petite brunette started down one path and up a set of stairs. Kira followed closely, her gaze scanning her surroundings. "You sure your mom's not going to mind doing this?"

Ella glanced over her shoulder and offered her a reassuring smile. "Seriously, this won't take her long at all. She loves this type of stuff."

Kira could only nod. What was she supposed to say, that she was apprehensive being around this woman who had apparently known her parents well? She was, more than she could even put into words.

As she crossed the threshold, she sucked in a quick gasp of air and waited. She was met with silence. No monster came out to attack her. It was like entering any other home.

The entryway was painted white, which lightened up the room as the ceiling was slightly lower when you came inside, but it opened up to a large foyer. A large, pointed arch was on each side, leading off to other rooms. As Kira stepped further in, she saw the reason for the low ceiling. The curved staircase angled over the double-door entryway. In the center of the foyer hung what looked to be a white wrought-iron chandelier. Tiny crystals hung from the bottom of it. It wasn't overly large; it didn't dwarf the entry space. It just seemed to fit it perfectly.

"Mom?" Ella called into the silent house.

"In the kitchen," a voice answered back from the left.

Ella turned to Kira and smiled. "Okay, living room first." She led Kira to the right and through the pointed arch. The room had the same white walls, and the same light hardwood floors carried through from the foyer. A white marble fireplace dominated one wall; opposite was a white brocade sofa with two matching armchairs in the room. One of the chairs set in front of a bay window complete with a plush white cushion. The pop of color came from a cobalt blue rug that set under a white coffee table. The room appeared elegant, pristine, but at the same time completely warm and inviting. It was easy to picture lounging in a window seat reading a book from one of the two large, white bookcases that stood on either side of another bay window.

As Kira's gaze surveyed the room, she found Ella standing by another larger, pointed archway, watching her.

"I really like your house," Kira said.

As soon as the words left her mouth, the grin on Ella's face slipped a bit. Kira's brow furrowed at that. The other girl hadn't liked the compliment. That seemed odd, and it set Kira's nerves on edge. How much did she really know about these people, and yet, here she was, in their house. For all she knew, they could have had something to do with her biological parents' death all those years ago. Caution edged down the base of her spine. She had to come up with a way to leave that didn't seem completely suspicious.

Just when her mind was working feverously on her excuse, Ella said, "I have to admit…" She glanced down, seemingly embarrassed. "I hoped that when you saw this room, you'd remember me. I'm sorry. I know we're getting to know each other again, it just…we would move the chairs closer to this window." She pointed to the one furthest in the room. "We'd drape sheets over them, saying it was our secret room. We'd stay in there for hours, playing or hiding from your brother and Gabe."

Kira felt the apprehension drain from her body. She realized she wanted that, too, desperately. She actually hated telling the other girl that she didn't recall it. She'd had no memory jog, nothing like Sawyer had experienced on their first day here.

She was shaking her head before she even started to speak. "Sorry, but I don't remember anything."

The petite girl looked crestfallen, but then she shook it off and stood a little straighter. Her hand came up to indicate the room. "Well, from what I've learned in my Non-Magical World class, this is called the living room or front room to be very informal."

She smiled, and Kira couldn't help but return it. The moment of uncomfortableness was gone.

"In here is the dining room." Ella stood off to the side and let Kira survey the room.

More white walls but that's where the similarities to the front room ended. This room was formal with its Victorian Era sideboard, dining table with matching chairs, and cabinetry. All the pieces were a powder blue, with gold trim, even down to the cushions on the dining chairs.

"Before people ventured out in the Non-Magical world, the furniture here hadn't changed much. It was the same dark wood and not very comfortable at all. But once some had ventured out and brought back books and flimsy books called magazines, people wanted to try many of the Non-Magical inventions and furniture. My mom, she loved the colors." She glanced around the room. "I have to say in this case I do like this better. Before it was so dark, but now everything seems so light and airy. It even brought new occupations as now some witches and wizards perfect making furniture into the new, modern styles we've been shown."

The confusion came rushing back. "But couldn't anyone just make something? You know look at the picture and then make what it is?"

Ella was shaking her head before Kira even finished asking her question. Then she explained. "No, you can't make something from nothing. In our Metamorphosis class, we'll learn how to change things into another form, but the thing is that's not permanent if it completely changes the form. Colors and such are all right on non-living things. But you can't change even a non-living object completely and have the change last. Like I couldn't change an apple into a chair."

"What about if you use one of those sticking charms Gabe mentioned?"

"Those can only be performed by someone with advanced magical abilities, and witches and wizards actually specialize in certain types of spells such as those. It's almost as if that's their occupation. It costs a lot to have it done. That's why they typically can't be removed. But in the case of furniture and such, you can permanently change it by using magic to cut pieces off or carve it. Sort of like how in your books it talked about woodworking. We have people that specialize in that now. Just like with the countertops for cabinets or the installations they use for lighting." She pointed up at the chandelier that hung over the table."

It was impressive with its decorative bronze pendent panel connecting it to the ceiling. Tiny crystals cascaded in a line down from the top, ending in the bottom in a bowl like shape. Surrounding that was a gold hoop that ringed right about the crystal bowl. Along the gold ring stood twelve lit white candles. Kira's brow knitted. Even though they were lit, they didn't seem to be burning. The candle wax seemed to be frozen in place.

"Certain people have developed that into their trade. It started here, and people from all over the Magical world come here to study the books and all the information that has been collected from the Non-Magical world. Of course, the Council shared everything with the Grand Council. Others have now ventured out in other places, but it's just as restricted as it is here. Since we made it out first, Willow Oak is further along than other areas."

The slight throb of dull pain hit behind Kira's eyes. It was all too much to take in. Every answer just brought more questions, but she wanted to understand. "So you have to study to know how to do that?"

This time it was Ella's brow that knitted in confusion. "Isn't that how it works in the Non-Magical world? Can everyone just make something like, for example, furniture? Does everyone know how?"

Put that way, Kira realized how ludicrous her question sounded. She supposed it did make sense that some people were better at certain spells than others were, which led to more questions once again. "No, you're right. Definitely not everyone can. I wouldn't even know where to start."

Ella's smile reemerged. She appeared relieved. "Oh, good. I thought I had a good understanding of it from my Non-Magical world class. I was afraid I was completely confused."

Kira's smile was more forced. She felt like an idiot. She didn't know anything of this world she had been thrust into, and the more she learned, the more she realized she would never understand it. However, since Ella was being so patient with her, she thought she should take the time to ask questions.

She gestured up to the impressive chandelier. "How does the fire not melt the candles?" Then she glanced up again. "Or does it? Do you have to change candles often?"

"No, it's not a real fire. The candles have a spell placed on them, *Selumina*. That's the spell that makes them capable to light. Then we use *Anavo* or charm them to light when someone enters, like these are."

Again, that brought on more questions. "So it's not really fire?"

"No, that's the only way we have of lighting rooms and would get really messy with dripping candle wax. Besides, a person can't create fire with a wand."

"You can't?" Kira barely stopped herself from saying that's the way it always worked in movies. She didn't want to have to get into trying to explain all of that again. "How do you start a fire?"

"Well, if you're talking about a fire to keep warm type thing, it's not really any different than I figure the Non-Magical world does. When we want one in the fireplace, we have to set the wood and then usually some kindling in the form of this fibrous papyrus used for it. Then, with a wand you can create a spark with the enchantment *Arde*."

"So you can't just like create a fire with magic?"

"Well, you can."

This time Kira couldn't help but rub her forehead. The confusion and runaround answers were giving her a headache.

Ella's smile was all patient understanding. "I know, and I'm sorry. It does seem like I'm talking in circles, but I'm really not. See a witch or a wizard can start a fire, but you have to make a potion for one."

"A potion?" They had that class today, Potions and Elixirs. She hadn't understood even half of what was being said, and the teacher had completely lost her when he had mentioned a cauldron. He'd spent the rest of class time expounding on the merits and disadvantages of cauldrons made of cast iron, copper, stone, and the newest creation from a witch in Spain made of copper and cast iron, castiropper, which was apparently something new that was the rage in England.

"Yes, and it's kept in bottles like those lining the shelves in Professor Topsfield's classroom. When you throw the bottle and it breaks, that's when you get fire."

All right, she could follow that, and she realized she would have to go out of her way to make sure she never dropped anything with a liquid inside it because who knew what in the world it would be.

She nodded to Ella as if what she was saying was making perfect sense. It probably was if she had grown up in this freak-show of a world, but she hadn't. It actually all sounded insane. Ella's smile brightened. Then she turned and headed through another pointed archway. Kira followed, taking one last look at the dining room.

The kitchen was bright with white cabinets. The sink was large and white with a copper faucet. The light fixtures seemed to be of a like theme, made of copper with an ever-present candle—a single in each fixture—to light the room. Three, evenly spaced lights hung over an immense blueish gray tinged island, complete with what looked to be a white marble countertop with shots of blue and gray running through it. The same countertop ran along the cabinetry. But what held Kira in place was not the sight of the modern, stainless steel refrigerator and oven, but the woman standing at the island cutting up an onion into fine, evenly sized pieces.

She was humming a tune under her breath. Then she picked up her wand and turned slightly, pointing it at the pot that set on the stovetop, a spoon rhythmically turned whatever was inside it as a gentle steam bellowed out from the top. Her flame red hair was piled atop her head in a careless bun.

A movement from the side drew Kira's attention. Laying on the rug in front of the glass double doors was a tan and white Cocker Spaniel. The dog raised its head and tilted it in their direction. It almost seemed to nod at them before it laid its head back down on its paws and closed its eyes, seeming to be napping in the bright light streaming through the doors.

When she glanced back, Constance Hopewell's hazel-eyed gaze was on her. Her lips were turned up into a warm, tentative smile.

And Kira returned it. It was instinctual. They hadn't had a chance to discuss it, but she knew exactly what her brother was thinking: divide and conquer. Find out what they could about these people and what had happened before, but do it all without rousing suspicion.

She could do that; she could pretend.

"Hi," she offered the older woman, careful to keep her tone light but letting a little of her unease bleed into it.

"Mom," Ella said, dumping her book bag on one of the blue cushioned barstools on one side of the island, "Lucien asked Kira, Sawyer, and their parents to come to his birthday *party* tomorrow night."

The older woman's eyes widened in surprise.

Ella nodded as if in understanding. "I told Kira she could borrow one of my dresses. Will you have time to fix it for her?"

The question seemed to pry her from her momentary stupor. "Oh, yes, it shouldn't take any time at all. You're both relatively the same size."

"Thank you very much," Kira said and meant whole-heartedly.

Ella grinned. "Thanks."

Constance stared at her daughter a moment longer before she finally raised a red brow in question.

Ella's smile widened as her fingers tapped against the marble countertop in feigned innocence. "Do you think you might have time to help Sawyer out too?"

Her mother just shook her head and chuckled lightly. "Yes, I can do that. Do I need to see about some of your father's clothes for him?"

"No!" The word burst out from the petite brunette in horror.

Up went the red brow again.

"Gabe's finding him something at his house right now. And then I sort of told them to come over here with it."

Constance resumed cutting the rest of her onions. "Yes, that will be fine." The slicing stopped, as she seemed deep in thought. Finally, she said, "I should look through my things and your father's for Kira's parents. We all know how strict Cerise Norwood is about her dress code."

Before Kira could respond, Constance continued.

"I know. We'll have them over for dinner."

She went to a small desk tucked over to the side of the room. She pulled out the center drawer, grabbed a piece of paper, along with a bottle of dark liquid, and what looked to be a fountain pen.

Kira felt the hair stand up along her neck and arms. Was that a potion? Were they going to all be engulfed in flames? Had she been foolish to even stand here?

Constance set the objects on the island countertop. She removed the cork from the top of the bottle, and Kira froze.

Nothing happened except Constance took the pen and dipped it in the bottle. In flowery strokes, she penned a short letter. Then she reached over and grabbed the wand that rested by her cutting board. It was long with a green hue that appeared to have different layers. She pointed it at the paper and said *Adsicco*.

Kira waited, but she didn't notice anything. The woman folded the paper in thirds and then tucked it into an envelope that came soaring to her with a wave of her wand and the words *Seface*. She placed the folded paper in the envelope, inserting the flap in the body of it to close it. Then she laid the tip of her wand in the corner where a stamp would go and said *Sigiliu*. Instantly, the outline of a tree with large, leafy branches appeared. Then the letter was gone from sight.

"What?" Kira rapidly looked back and forth between them. "How? Where did that go?"

Constance's smile was filled with patient understanding. "I sent my husband a note to have him ask your father if they would all join us here for dinner tonight."

Kira shook her head. "But how? I don't understand?"

"It's how we send letters here," Ella said. She walked over to the desk and pulled out what looked to be a wooden stamper. She brought it to Kira and held it out.

Hesitantly, Kira reached out her hand and took the proffered object. Carefully, she turned it over. On the bottom of the stamp was a red circle with the image of the same tree she had just seen on the now vanished letter.

"Before a person can use magic," Constance said, "they use the stamp to send letters. Every family has one. We can still use it, or we can use the wand to make the image appear with the word *Sigiliu*."

Kira looked to the wand still in the woman's hand. "And it just goes?"

"Yes." And then Constance held out the wand that Kira's gaze was still fixed on.

She didn't want to take it; she was afraid to even touch it. Yet, at the same time, something seemed to be pulling her to pick it up. Tentatively, she reached out and slowly her fingers wrapped around the long, thin wood.

She was right; it was textured. It felt delicate and yet sturdy at the same time. But that observation fell to what she was feeling. It was as if an invisible force was humming through her body. It was...power, strength. She could feel it where the wand was grasped in her hand as if it was something tangible. She wanted to point the wand at something, say some random word or just think it, and see what happened.

Still looking down at the object she said, "Risa told us a wand will only work for the one it belongs to."

"Well, a person can use another's wand, but it won't work well for them. If the wand has completely bonded with its master, it won't work at all." Constance agreed. Then she glanced down at the countertop as an envelope appeared out of nowhere.

It was enough to break Kira's momentary fascination. Quickly, before she gave in to the almost overwhelming urge, she set the wand back on the countertop. She brushed a hand through her hair, something mundane to try to control her rapidly beating heart. It took her a moment before she was composed enough to ask, "Did he talk to my dad?"

"Yes, he and your mother will be coming for dinner." Constance's smile was genuine. "You girls go up and start looking at gowns while I get busy in here."

"Thanks, mom," Ella said as she snagged a bunch of plump, green grapes from a bowl on the counter. She turned to Kira. "Come on. Let me finish giving you the grand tour."

After heading back to the foyer through the eat-in area of the kitchen, Ella led her up a curved staircase. She pointed out the door that led to her parents' bedroom, then showed her two other guest rooms each with their own ensuite, and the staircase, that led to the third floor where her dad's study and library were, before finally leading her to the round, circular torrent she had seen from outside.

"And this is my room," Ella said as she pushed open the door.

Kira paused in the center of the room to take it all in. Three-fourths of the room—the part that faced out—was lined with narrow rectangular windows that allowed for natural light to bathe the room. Once again, the prevailing color was white, though pink and wood accents gave the room character from what could be a sterile appearance without it. The centerpiece of the room was the dark wood stained bed. It could be called a four-poster except the four columns ended in an elaborate curve before they connected to the decorative top. White marble was inlaid through the headboard and the legs. A pale pink duvet marked the top, along with pink and white throw pillows. There were two doors on either side from where they had just entered the room. Tucked off out of the way was a dark wood stained spiral staircase.

Ella caught her gaze. "That's where I have my desk and some chairs and such for just hanging around." She started toward them, and automatically, Kira fell in step behind her.

The walls in the room at the top were painted a pale pink. This is where the round port windows were. They ringed the entire room. A white rug set on the dark, hardwood floors. An antique dark wood desk was tucked into a corner, while a comfortable looking white sofa and matching chairs dominated the rest of the loft.

It was warm and inviting. "This is amazing." Kira breathed out.

Ella's smile was positively blinding. "I'm glad you like it." She dumped her book bag down on her desk. She held out her hand and Kira automatically handed her own to her. It quickly joined Ella's. She gave Kira a handful of the grapes.

"Come on," Ella said, starting down the stairs again. "Let's look at my dresses and see what you like."

Again, Kira followed. This time they went to the door that stood to the left of the entrance. This room was actually built out in the main part of the house though it was only accessible through Ella's room. Inside was a large closet. An assortment of what appeared to be "normal" looking clothing hung on one side, a long plush bench ran down the length of the room.

Ella saw her gaze and said, "Once books started coming in most everyone really liked the new clothing choices. It was so much more comfortable. Of course, some of the more set-in-their-ways people have not conformed at all. And they definitely haven't taken to the idea of females wearing trousers. The school has still not let up on that. That's why we have to wear skirts and the boys get pants. Typical, but at least they have decided that girls can be on the Sloignis team, and they do get to wear the standard uniform for that."

Kira had turned toward the other wall that was lined with what looked like ball gowns and long formal dresses, but that comment had her turning back around. "slogoes?" The word tripped out on her tongue.

"Sloignis." Ella came to stand beside her. Her hands went up and started going through the dresses. "Yeah, it's the sport we have here. Are you interested in sports?"

Kira popped a grape into her mouth and chewed it before she answered. "No, sports are really not my thing."

"Not mine either." Ella pulled out a light green dress. "How about this one?"

Kira was still running the strange word over in her head, but she shook it off to focus on the clothing Ella was holding up. "It's beautiful," she breathed out. And it was. It had a full skirt and fitted bodice. She hesitantly reached out a hand to touch it. "I don't want to mess it up." It looked as if it belonged in some museum.

Ella waved off the concern. "What's your favorite color?"

"Blue," Kira answered automatically.

"Great! I'm sure that will be no problem for my mom." Ella beamed.

"What won't be?" Constance asked from the doorway.

Ella held out the dress before her. "Mom, do you think you can make it blue? It's Kira's favorite color."

"Still," Constance said with a smile. "It will be no problem at all."

It was then Kira realized what the older woman meant. Her favorite color had been blue from when she knew her before, from a time that she herself could no longer remember. It would have made her uncomfortable if she'd had time to dwell on it.

Instead, Constance said, "Try it on so I'll know how much length to add and what needs adjusted."

Before she could respond, Ella hung the dress on a hook at the end of the room, and then she and her mother started to leave, but not before Ella said, "Once you get it on, I'll help you with the back of it." And then she was gone.

Kira watched the now closed door for a moment longer then she turned toward the dress. It looked like something she had seen in books that queens wore. It was beautiful. She reached out her hand, and her fingers glided over the satin material. Hesitantly, she shrugged out of her school jacket and laid it over the bench seat; the rest of her clothes quickly followed. And then she was stepping into the dress. She slid her arms into the sleeves to find them a bit tight. They were fitted to her elbows and then belled out. The skirt of the dress was big and voluminous, but it just hung. Surely, there was something missing. And there was no way she could fasten the back of the dress. It was a corset top with the matching laces to tie it up. No wonder Ella had offered to help her.

Lifting up the skirt, she made her way back out into the main room. Ella was sitting on her bed, while Constance had taken up residence in a white plush chair by a window.

Ella glanced up as soon as she appeared. "Oh I forgot!" She rushed back toward the closet and then emerged holding something that looked like a wire cage. "It goes under the skirt." She explained that to Kira's wide-eyed expression.

"Oh, okay." She didn't understand at all. Her face must have shown that as Ella offered to help her. They went back into the closet, and after much struggling, reemerged. It wasn't tight at the top, as she'd had Ella not lace it too snugly. With the wire cage, the skirt of the gown now swirled around her. It also showed that it was too short.

Constance was on her feet, slowly circling Kira, her finger thoughtfully tapping her chin. "We'll need to lengthen it." She waved her wand and a cloth tape measure came flying into the room. From the movements of her wand, it flew around the dress, taking measurements. "How about a powder blue."

"That...that would be very pretty," Kira finally managed to stammer out as she continued to watch the tape measure.

Abruptly, it finished. With a neat little twist, it rolled itself up and landed quietly on an end table next to Ella's bed.

"After school tomorrow, come home with me, and we can get ready together." Once again, Ella's smile was wide and sincere.

Kira felt like an imposter. How could she believe this girl was anything other than what she portrayed herself as, yet at the same time, how could she just blindly trust her? "That would be great...if it's okay with your mom."

"Sure, it's no problem at all. We might as well just all go together as a group."

These people seemed genuinely nice; they had to be just what they said they were. But flying on the heels of that thought came the realization that apparently now, anything *was* possible. Magic and monsters truly existed in this world, which meant there was no limit to what could happen, no limit to what people could be capable of by a wave of a wand.

She forced a smile. "Sounds like a plan."

11

He felt like he belonged in a circus. As he stared at his reflection in the full-length mirror, Sawyer fiddled with the vest or *waistcoat* as he was told was the proper term. All he knew was that standing here in one of the Hopewell's guestrooms, he felt like a complete idiot. He could think of many things he'd rather do than go to Lucien Norwood's birthday *gala*.

Even alone, Sawyer couldn't help but roll his eyes. It sounded like something a girl would want. And, yes, he knew that was stereotypical, but he also knew his own twin would love something like that. Well, she would have, before their lives had been turned up on end.

Now, he couldn't see her wanting anything that was remotely like this. To have a party of this magnitude in one's honor…no, all eyes would be focused on the birthday boy or girl. No way would Kira want something like that now.

And as for him, well Sawyer would be happy to skip the whole birthday thing. He didn't want whatever was going to happen to him. But since the fear of the unknown was worse than the actual knowing, that's the reason he had consented to go to this stupid party for a guy that he didn't even like.

It would help his parents, too. They hadn't said anything, but he knew they were anxious over what was coming— how could they not be. This might help relieve their minds somehow. Anything he could do to help them, he'd do.

Really, he just wanted the entire thing over. He just wanted to get these stupid powers, or whatever they were supposed to be, and move on with his life.

The rapping on the door ended his musings, and instead had him calling, "You can come in."

He thought it would be one of his parents, but instead found it was Gabe who quickly stepped inside, shutting the door behind him. The blond boy was tugging on the necktie that completed his authentic Victorian look.

He glanced up and met Sawyer's gaze. "I *really* don't want to go to this."

He couldn't help it. Sawyer's own lips lifted in a grin. Finally, someone who felt the same way he did. His sister sure didn't. Even though she was nervous about their own upcoming birthday, she was looking forward to Lucien Norwood's. Not that she knew the boy to even really care, but the amount of production going into it had her intrigued. And then with the meticulous attention to the dress code... No, Kira was excited. All Sawyer wanted to do was throw on his jeans and tee shirt.

And that thought sent another horrid one to him, and it had him eyeing Gabe suspiciously.

The other boy noticed as one eyebrow lifted in question. And if that wasn't getting his point across, he also asked, "What?"

Sawyer took a step back. "What type of clothes do you wear?"

This had Gabe's brow furrowing. "Excuse me?"

Sawyer took another step back. This thought was more disturbing than any other detail he had learned since moving to this freak show. And he knew that was an over exaggeration, but he didn't care. This would push him over the edge. "I hadn't even thought to ask." Sawyer shook his head in disbelief. "It just never occurred to me that you wouldn't, but now…What type of clothes do you wear." At Gabe's continued wide-eyed expression, Sawyer tried to clarify. "I mean I know the school uniform, but I'm talking everyday clothes. Do you all wear clothes like this? Or clothes like in the sixteen hundreds—I don't even know what those would be. Or do you wear normal clothes? Please tell me they're normal."

"We don't dress as I remember us dressing when I was younger," Gabe said as he leaned against the wall, once again tugging on his necktie. "They brought in magazines and such with clothing. I have to tell you, some of that stuff was just plain odd." He shook his head at the thought. "I don't know how anyone could move in some of that, and then other things, well, you could see right through them. No one I know wears anything like that."

Yeah, Sawyer himself didn't understand some things that passed for fashion in his own normal world, so he figured it was really strange for someone who had never grown up around that. However, he didn't want to debate fashion trends and whatnot. He had more pressing matters causing him worry. "But do you wear jeans? Tee shirts? You know *normal* everyday things. Not stuff like this." He gestured toward the outfit he had donned for tonight.

"No," Gabe shook his head. "This is definitely not standard attire."

Sawyer knew a moment of instant relief.

"But I don't know if it's exactly what you're used to either."

That wasn't reassuring at all. He had to know one way or the other. Since they had come to the Hopewell's right after school, all he had was his school uniform, so he couldn't even show Gabe what he meant. "Tomorrow you come over to my house, and I'll show you my clothes." It was Sawyer's turn to shake his head as Gabe just grinned. "Yeah, those are words I never thought I would say." He felt like his sister must have when she and her friends in Chicago would trade clothes.

Gabe stepped further into the room. "I can't even imagine how this must feel. I don't know how I would adjust being thrown into some other place. It's strange enough when we have to go to another town."

"Wait. What? Why do you…Where do you?" Sawyer didn't know which question he wanted answered first. Risa said they couldn't. Had she been wrong? Had he not understood her correctly? She said only two people could go out at once. Could they really travel wherever? Did they visit *Disney World?*

To his credit, Gabe didn't seem bothered by all the questions coming at him. In fact, he seemed incredibly patient, something Sawyer didn't know if he would be if the circumstances were switched.

"Well, with my mom a member of the Council, sometimes she has to go to other towns for meetings if something important enough comes up or if it's for the Grand Meeting, which happens every six months. We went with her the last time. And then when we were in the Championship game we went. It was in Romania."

Sawyer didn't know which part of that he should ask about first. But then his curiosity over the thought of some sort of sport won out. Back at his old school, he'd played baseball and basketball. He couldn't believe they'd have anything as mundane as that here. "Championship game?"

"Oh, yeah. We ended up losing, but it was the first time we had made it that far in longer than anyone could remember."

Apparently, he was going to have to come right out and ask. "And what sport is it?"

"It's Sloignis."

That sounded like some sort of contagious disease. He didn't want to even hazard a guess on how one would play it. "Is that the only sport you have here?"

"Well, we have Vralatechni, which is using magic to produce shapes and colors. You're judged on artistic ability. But that's not my thing."

Sawyer didn't know if he had ever heard of anything that sounded more boring. "Okay, so what is this sloing?"

"Sloignis." Gabe corrected without being condescending. "The name represents the fire and ice walls that surround the field. Only fourth and fifth years are allowed to play on the school team."

"Wait. Hold up. Granted I don't know what's going on in this sport. But walls of fire and ice don't sound good, and fourth and fifth graders play?" What type of world was this? Apparently, they hated young children, or at the very least, felt they were expendable.

"What's a fourth grader?"

Sawyer's eyes nearly bugged out of his head. "It's what you just said. A fourth grader. Like a kid that's nine or ten."

Gabe was shaking his head before Sawyer finished. "No way do they let anyone that young play. You have to be in either fourth or fifth year."

Something was not making any sense to him at all. "Okay, what in the world is a fourth or fifth year?"

"We're fourth years." Gabe must have seen his confused expression as he went on to explain further. "Here in the Magical world school is divided into three parts. You have primary, middle, and finishing. We're in finishing. The finishing then is divided by years. There's five years. After the completion of our fourth-year term, we'll be in our fifth and final year."

"So then to play this…Slo…ig…nis…," he said carefully trying to get the word out. When Gabe nodded, Sawyer figured he must have been right or close enough. "Anyway, you have to have magic to play?"

"Yeah, or at least you'll come into your powers during that school term. You can be on the team without having your powers. You can practice, but you can't play in a game until you have them."

He didn't like the sound of a fire and ice wall, but at the same time, he wanted to participate in something. No, that wasn't right. He wanted to play baseball and basketball. He wanted to play something normal, not take part in something that seemed like a spectator sport to watch kids die by torture.

"So is it hard to get on this team?" Sawyer couldn't see a bunch of people fighting for the chance to be set on fire.

"We have tryouts. There are ten players on a team with six substitutes, and the team is made up of both males and females."

Sixteen spots. Sawyer still hadn't heard anything that made him want to run to join this.

"I'm going for the team. Tryouts are Tuesday. Captains are always fifth years since they've typically had the previous year's experience."

Sawyer had to ask as so far, Gabe had seemed normal—or as normal as anyone in this strange world could be. He didn't seem as if he had a death wish, but apparently, he'd been wrong. "Let me get this straight." Sawyer crossed his arms over his chest. "You want to try out, so you can be set on fire?"

A deep chuckle escaped Gabe. "You're not set on fire."

Sawyer didn't say anything. It still sounded dangerous and a stupid idea to participate in.

"The flames surround the field. They sort of chase each other. You have your blue-white flames for ice and then of course your fire. Other players can hit you into the flames. Once in there you're trapped inside for ten minutes. They don't actually burn or freeze you, but they do make you extremely uncomfortable with either heat or cold and so dizzy. When you're released, you're disoriented. The other team will hit you in, as you can't have a sub for that. And they want less people on the field. Subs are only for actual injuries. But the more times a person is hit in, the more effects they feel. So in that way, you can get hurt from them."

Well, it sounded a bit better since he now knew they actually weren't setting kids on fire, but it sounded somewhat pointless. "So what? Then whoever has the less players is the loser?" It honestly sounded next to no fun at all.

"Oh, no. See there are hoops on the field. They're not in a fixed position. They all move and rotate. There are three different sizes. The biggest is only worth one point, while the smallest is worth fifty. First team to three hundred is the winner."

That seemed more interesting, and if it was the only thing here... "I might have to check it out."

"You have to." Then Gabe cocked his head to one side as he studied him. "Did you play any sports at your old school?"

"Yeah, baseball and basketball." At the other boy's confused expression, Sawyer added, "I'll show you tomorrow when I show you the clothes."

Gabe's smile came easily. "Sounds good." He glanced toward the door. "I guess we should head down. We don't want the girl's beating us. We'll never hear the end of it."

Sawyer nodded. Then with one last glance in the mirror, which produced another disgusted shake of his head at his attire, he followed the other boy out the door.

As he stepped off the last step that placed them in the foyer, Sawyer thought to ask, "What vehicle are we taking?" Yet, as soon as the words left his mouth, another thought occurred to him. "Do you even have cars, SUVs, or trucks here?" The only one he'd seen was his parents. His eyes widened as a horrible thought came to him. "Are we flying on brooms?"

Gabe's mouth hung open, but then just as quickly, he snapped it shut as he started to chuckle. Shaking his head, he said, "In my Non-Magical World class, we talked about how the Nons said witches rode on brooms. I didn't really believe it, but now...Why would anyone..." Still laughing, he managed to get out. "No, we only use brooms for sweeping. About vehicles, only a few people have ones that look like the one your parents have."

"What do you all drive?"

Gabe shoved his hands into the pockets on his black dress pants. "Well most people don't drive. Either you walk around town or you take the trolley. Once you get powers, you can Alsaafaro. But that doesn't work for long distances, plus you need to practice it. If it's visiting another town, it depends on where it is. In this country or any other that is connected to it, you take the train. If it's traveling to overseas, you take the bus."

Sawyer froze; his eyes went wide. Surely, he hadn't heard that correctly. There was no way one could take a bus across the ocean. That wasn't possible. Yeah, he knew magic and all of that, but it made no sense. He needed clarification. "You take a bus over water?" He couldn't help it, his tone held disbelief.

Gabe appeared confused. "Yeah. Up at the station, you can either catch a train or the bus, depending on where you need to go."

Right behind his left eye, Sawyer felt the dull throb of an impending headache coming on. No other word for it, this place was freaking insane. He rubbed a hand over his face. "These buses don't sink as they go over the water?"

"You're just thinking the Non-Magical world, Sawyer," Michail Hopewell said as he came into the foyer.

Subconsciously, Sawyer's hands tightened into fists. Of course, he was; he was still part of the normal world no matter what these people said. He didn't trust any of them, especially Michail Hopewell. And he resented the man for his condescending comment now.

"Which is entirely understandable," the older man added, even accompanied by a slight smile.

Sawyer relaxed just the tiniest of bits. All right, so he had been wrong once again. He was going to have to stop rushing to judgement. He glanced to the side and saw his mother and father had filed in, along with Constance Hopewell and both of Gabe's parents.

"Our buses are more in line with what you would call a monorail or what you would call the 'L' in Chicago." Michail continued. "When people came here from Europe and other countries, they traveled on boats. The Magical community decided that mode of travel took too long. Honestly, I think it was probably a case of seasickness that caused it. Anyway, elevated platforms were developed that spanned the seas. They can take a person all over the world. At first, they looked like a horseless wagon, but they've greatly improved in design since then. They're very comfortable now, plus with the added bonus of it being enclosed, weather is no longer bothersome.

"It's the same for our trains; they're much better than they used to be. And Gabe is right." He glanced over to the blond boy. "In town most people walk or take the trolley. It's only recently that we've begun to develop vehicles that look like what are on your roads in The Non-Magical world. Only a few people have them."

With a quick glance to his parents, Sawyer could see they, too, were trying to digest all those revelations.

It was his mother who asked into the silence, "But these trains and…buses?" At Michail's nod she continued. "Do Non-Magical people see them?"

"It's the same as the barrier that surrounds this town. Non-Magical people can pass through them without any issue. But unless they've been invited into the Magical world, they won't see them."

And then a thought hit Sawyer. "Wait, Risa told us that you all cannot cross the barrier into The Non-Magical world, so how can you travel all over the country and overseas?"

"Risa?" That question came at him from more than one direction.

He waved it aside. "Risa Kemp, my teacher for my Magical Life Skills class. Anyway, how does that work? Can people with magic…" He paused, those words sounding ridiculous to him. He shook it off though to continue. "No, she said they can't travel freely so how?"

"You see," Cornelius Meyer, Gabe's father, explained, "the lines the buses and the trains run on, they are all connected within the magical barrier. They only have certain places they can stop, and those are within Magical communities."

"But if there's a problem or a breakdown on one of the lines, what happens?"

"They don't breakdown since they're run on magic. They don't operate the same as the vehicles you are used to."

Sawyer glanced to his parents. They appeared just as shell-shocked as he felt. This place kept getting stranger by the day.

"But tonight we won't use any of those means." He went to the hall closet and opened the door.

Or Sawyer thought it was a hall closet. From his position, he could see there wasn't anything inside, not a single coat or jacket, just emptiness, like the one in their house where they'd stored things they didn't know what to do with.

"Houses and businesses have these," Michail said, holding open the door.

Sawyer resisted the urge to do a slow clap. It was nice to know that the Magical world liked to be tidy and hang up their stuff.

"It can only be activated by a person who has received their magical powers. In the case of a home, only the people who live there can activate it. As with a business, a shop, or a governmental building, only an authorized person may activate it."

Yeah, he still didn't know what *it* was. Only people who had magic were allowed to hang up their coats in the closet. Sounded odd to say the least. Perhaps it washed them when stuff was hung up in there. Either way, it didn't really seem all that fascinating to be in someone's house, staring at an empty coat closet.

"What are we doing?"

That question was asked by Ella as she descended the stairs.

Sawyer turned to tell her 'thank you' as it was insane, but the words died in his throat. She was in pale pink. The neckline and the edge of the belled sleeves had white lace, along with the hem at the bottom and two pieces that draped on either side of her gown. The only other adornment was a strip of lace that circled each sleeve right before it flared out below her elbows. Around her throat was a choker necklace of pearls. Around the front, other strings of pearls connected from that centerline and hung around her neck. Her shoulder length chestnut hair was arranged in intricate braids and fastened atop her head.

She was pretty, really pretty.

Suddenly, a sharp pain radiated in his side. Quickly, he glanced to the spot to find that Gabe was beside him, the ache was from the blond's elbow where he'd landed the hit.

Sawyer thought to say something, but then realized that in fact he owed the other boy. He'd been gawking, open-mouthed, at Ella Hopewell as she had descended the stairs. Belatedly, he realized his twin was behind her. One of Kira's eyebrows was raised in amusement as she stared at him. Yeah, he'd been caught.

"Thanks," he muttered to the boy at his side, careful to keep his voice low. No reason to draw anymore unwanted attention to himself.

"No problem." But Gabe's focus wasn't on him. No, Gabe was staring up the stairs now that Kira had come into view. Her dress was a very light blue. It looked more elaborate than Ella's, as the blue one had more lace and something that looked to be beading along the front. Sawyer supposed his sister looked all right.

Apparently, Gabe thought she did, as he was gawking up at her with the same fascination Sawyer had looked at Ella with. It was only fair that he returned the favor. He nudged the boy at his side with a well-placed elbow. It broke him out of his stupor. His grin was sheepish as he hastily looked away, but not before his own mumbled, "Thank you," drifted to Sawyer's ears.

"You're welcome." The words came automatically, along with a grin. And it was then that Sawyer realized that this was the first time he'd felt normal since arriving in Willow Oak. Well, as normal as one could be dressed up as if he was going trick-or-treating and standing around staring into an empty closet.

"I was just about to explain to Mr. and Mrs. Randal and Sawyer about the speculo. Kira will want to hear this, too."

His sister shot him a look accompanied by one raised brow. His response was a barely perceptible shrug of his shoulders. Michail Hopewell could call it whatever he wanted, it was still a coat closet.

Once the two girls had managed to clear the stairs without incident from their outlandish costumes, the older man continued. "This," he said, gesturing to the still open closet, "is a speculo."

Sawyer resisted the urge to burst out laughing, but it was hard. There he was, standing in someone's front hallway with a group of people, and they were staring into an empty closet. It was insane. However, that seemed on par with this world so far. Everything about it was crazy from the special names for closets to throwing your teens into walls of fire and ice.

"As I was saying before, around town a few people use cars, though it's more common to use one of the trolleys. But there is another way. Each house and most businesses, especially the governmental buildings also have a speculo. Now a person who has magical abilities has to turn the speculo on and off. If it is on, after you shut the door, you say the name of the place you wish to travel. You are then transported to that place nearly instantly."

Sawyer's eyes widened as he stared at the closet more closely. It didn't appear to have anywhere to hang a coat or a jacket, no shelving at all. He hadn't realized he had even moved closer until he could see right inside. It was bigger than any elevator he had ever been inside.

"In the case of a home, only a family member is allowed to open and close the speculo. At a business, the owner will set authorized people who may close and open it. To open you say *traversare* and to close it, you use *inchide*. Once open, as long as there is someone inside with powers, the speculo will work. If no one has his or her powers, it won't go anywhere, as you need a wand. This is a case though, where you don't have to have your wand out. You can touch the charm to make it work." His hand went to the chain around his neck. "What you need to remember." His steady gaze drifted back and forth from Sawyer to Kira. "That when it is not in use, you must disable it. Do not leave it open or it would be an invitation for anyone that possesses magical powers."

The chill ran down to the very base of his spine. It was a cautionary warning, but a part of Sawyer wondered if it was something more. Was that what had happened to his parents? Had they left this speculo open, and that's how the intruders that murdered them got inside?

"But I have a question." Kira's voice broke through his musings. "So I take it that's how we're going to this party tonight..."

"Yes," Michail said. "Typically, for something like a party, the host will open the speculo to allow for easy entrance."

"Okay, so how do you close it? I mean, we're all going to be gone, so how do you keep someone from coming in when you're not here and robbing you blind?"

"That's a good question. When there is no one left in the house with magical abilities, the speculo becomes dormant. It will not admit anyone unless they are from that family in regards to a home." Cornelius explained.

"So once Kira and Sawyer have their powers, and say they both leave, will it then become deactivated?" Diana asked.

"Yes," Constance was the first to reply. "Since neither you nor Gary possesses powers, it will become dormant if they are both out of the house."

Sawyer's mother looked relieved. "That's nice to know. I wouldn't want someone popping in at random."

Adalia Meyer gave a soft laugh. "No, you won't have to worry about that." Then she glanced around the group. "With these dresses, I think we should at least make a couple of trips or we'll be hopelessly wrinkled."

"And we definitely wouldn't want that," Cornelius said, his arm going through hers.

"We'll do three groups." Constance stepped forward. "That should save all our clothing. Adalia, Diana, and I will go first. Then Cornelius, you can bring Ella and Kira, and Michail will accompany Gary, Sawyer, and Gabe."

Everyone nodded. Sawyer glanced to Kira. He had a lump of dread lodged in the pit of his stomach. He honestly thought he might be sick.

However, before he could, Michail had his wand and pointed it at the door with the murmured word *Traversare*. Without any hesitation, Adalia Meyer stepped inside. With a smile meant to be encouraging, Diana proceeded Constance Hopewell inside the speculo. Once the door was shut, a flash of light could be seen from around the edges of the door.

Sawyer couldn't move; he was frozen though everything inside of him was screaming at him to run for the door and yank it open to make sure his mother was all right. But he was terrified to find out that she might not be.

Then Michail opened the door.

It was empty. She was gone. It was like some magician in a Vegas show with a box to make someone disappear. Except, to his horror, this was real.

Ella stepped in next, and then with a slightly distrustful look, Kira hesitantly followed. Cornelius was the last to walk inside, and once again, after the door was shut, there was a flash of light around the edges.

Too soon, Sawyer was staring into the empty recesses within. Gabe went in immediately, but Sawyer found he couldn't make his feet move until his father place a reassuring hand on his back. With a slight nod, Sawyer sucked up his courage and entered the speculo. What he noticed now, that he hadn't noticed before was that it wasn't pitch dark, as it had been when he had looked inside before it was activated. Now it was bathed with a soft glow.

His father stepped beside him, followed by Michail, who shut the door behind him.

"The Ivywood Estate," Michail's voice said in a clear and precise tone.

The glow brightened, and then there was a loud roaring in Sawyer's ears. He had the sensation he was falling. And just as quickly as it started, it stopped, leaving him dragging in a deep breath of air as Michail opened the door.

"We're here."

V. A. Risby

12

He didn't want to be here. He was annoyed by the spectacle even though it was all for him.

Lucien Norwood didn't understand why his parents insisted on such a grand display every year. No, that wasn't right, he knew why. He was just tired of being a part of it. He didn't care for half the people in attendance, and his parents liked even less than that.

Glancing over the balcony railing, he looked down into the formal sitting room. All of the Victorian furniture was pushed up against the walls, leaving plenty of space for people to move around. It was a good thing as it was fairly packed below, even with people spilling out into the grand ballroom, other attached rooms, and even more taking advantage of the pleasant September air and surveying the verandah and gardens.

He'd yet to make his appearance. Not because he wanted to make some magnificent entrance, but more because he couldn't be bothered.

Tugging on the tie of the authentic Victorian Era clothing his mother insisted he wear, he resisted the urge to roll his eyes. It was his birthday; one would have thought he might have been able to have some say in what he did to mark the occasion. But no, his birthday was used as a means to posture and pose and, in his mother's case, force people to dress the way she wanted.

Some barely put up with it, and then others acted as if they loved it only because they wanted to stay in the good graces of Cerise Norwood. Lucien wanted to tell them good luck. He'd been trying to get in her good graces for years, but to no avail.

Whereas his father had been happy their one child had been a boy—a continuation of the Norwood name—his mother had been less than thrilled. She doted on him, gave him everything he wanted, except the birthday he desired, but he still knew she held part of herself back from him. But perhaps that had nothing to do with him being born a boy. His mother was aloof. No one ever knew exactly what she was thinking unless she chose to make it obvious. That's why some people seemed to fall at their feet to please her. One never knew what was going on behind her cool blue gaze.

His father on the other hand, Lucien could read him easily. Kenrick Norwood had a quick temper, which he wasn't afraid to let anyone see. Acquaintances were intimidated by his unpredictability. Lucien wouldn't say his friends as he honestly didn't believe his father had any friends. Kenrick had people he would turn to if he needed something, or even people he was polite to if he thought it was in his best interest.

That's how he had been elected Lord Mayor. A little schmoozing, some promises, a little intimidation, and some downright threatening had managed to guarantee the office for him. And while he was in his final term in the office, he was still on his best behavior. He had his eyes set on the position of Grand Chairman. For tonight, he'd even invited oversea visitors from the Grand Council. No expense had been spared. He couldn't allow anyone to see his true nature or there would be no attaining that lofty aspiration.

No, Kenrick saved that for Lucien and his mother. They were the only ones who truly knew what a cold, arrogant, and cruel individual he was. Lucien would never admit it to anyone—he even refused to admit it to himself most of the time—but he was one of the people intimidated by his father.

That wasn't to say Lucien didn't know he had his own faults. Or at least he thought he must. He wouldn't say he was arrogant. It wasn't his fault that he was better than everyone else was. That's just the way it was. He couldn't help that he excelled at his studies without even trying, or that he had a ridiculous number of people who claimed to be his friend. It just was the way things were.

His sigh was long and loud. Slowly, he moved further to the right. It was easier to see those arriving, with the added bonus of it being darker, so that he blended into the shadows better in his all black attire.

With a rueful shake of his head, he glanced down at the Victorian suit. His mother had been annoyed when he'd had his entire outfit made black, but she hadn't said any more than an irritated tsk of her displeasure. Just once, he'd like to get a true reaction from her. Perhaps she didn't indulge in such things since her husband took them to the extreme.

However, tonight, eliciting an emotion was really the last thing on his mind. No, he was nervous, and he could admit it to himself, he was scared of getting his powers. The thought of 9:12 p.m. was actually quite terrifying, even though he would never say that aloud. He wondered what it would feel like, having his powers running through his body. Would it hurt? Would he even feel it at all? He wanted to be alone to experience it, not on display for the entire town.

A slight squeal of excitement drifted up to his place in the shadows. He glanced down to find that Regina had arrived with her family. She was already in a tight circle with her group of friends, Nona Vandear, Susette St. James, and Flora.

Since he was shrouded in darkness, he gave into his desire to roll his eyes. For as long as he could remember, Regina had been by his side. They had consistently been thrown together as Melantha Townshed was truly the only woman Cerise Norwood considered a friend. The two women had grown up together. Melantha had married a wizard at eighteen, but he had tragically died from an overdose of Night Tonic. A month later, Melantha was married to the much older and wealthier Osric Townshed. If her first husband's death had seemed suspicious, no one said anything about it.

A few years after their marriage, she'd given birth to Regina. Lucien's own mother had given birth to him a few months prior. He didn't remember a time in which Regina hadn't been around. Any parties or gatherings, no matter how small, she was always there, right at his side. As a child, he'd done his best to ignore her. He didn't want some girl always hanging around.

He leaned forward, his elbows resting on the banister.

His mother and Melantha spoke as if it were a forgone conclusion that their children would marry once they were out of school, and Regina acted as if she had proprietary access to him. They'd all decided his fate for him, though his father wasn't of the same mind.

Regina was pretty enough. She actually looked quite lovely in her red and black ball gown. The deep, rich colors accentuated her pale complexion. But pretty or not, Lucien didn't know if he even liked her. She was annoying most of the time with her catty gossip and never ceasing talk of fashion. He would have told her a long time ago to stay as far away from him as possible, but he hadn't, just to irritate his father. Yeah, Lucien knew he wasn't great either, leading someone on just to annoy someone else. But still he did it. He supposed that was his one flaw.

Kenrick Norwood barely tolerated Melantha, and only then, it was because of her husband's influence, not out of any affection for his wife's dear friend.

No, his father had designs on someone else for his son and heir. He had since before they were a year old. And because it meant so much to his father, Lucien was predisposed to not want anything to do with her. Too bad for him she had turned out pretty.

He hadn't done a good job of ignoring her existence so far. In fact, she'd all but bowled him over. Well, actually, she had. He'd felt it, a jolt when their hands touched. He'd like to forget it.

He straightened a bit, his hands going to the banister railing. He knew he'd have to go down soon, but he just couldn't force himself to move.

"There is such a thing to be said for punctuality."

Lucien didn't visibly start at his father's sudden appearance, but it was close. The only indication he gave of the unwanted intrusion was the slight tightening of his fingers on the banister. He didn't reply, didn't have a comment for his father's words. Lucien knew he wouldn't have to; his father would continue soon enough.

"You did remember to invite them, didn't you?" The question was biting.

Lucien thought to pretend he didn't know what in the world his father was talking about, but prudence took over. Instead, he sighed. "Yes, father. I invited them and their parents yesterday."

"Their parents?" Kenrick turned to him. "Why would you invite those plebeians?"

Finally, Lucien rose to his full height, putting him and his father on an even playing field. "I thought it was the polite thing to do."

"The polite thing?" Kenrick shook his head in disgust. "That doesn't go along with the plan. What has gotten into you?" Kenrick hissed.

"All the years of mother's ingrained good manners," was Lucien's flippant reply.

Kenrick tensed, his features like a thundercloud. Yeah, Lucien knew he'd pay for that remark later. But at the moment, he really didn't care. "Look, I thought they would be more apt to show if their parents were invited, too. Come on, they've only been here for a couple of days. That isn't time for them to get to know anyone enough that they would feel comfortable without them."

Glancing down at the guests spilling around his estate, Kenrick asked in a deceptively quiet tone, "They haven't had enough time to get close to anyone?"

Lucien thought to reiterate what he had just said, but something about the barely controlled menace in his father's voice caused him to pause and look down at the people milling about. He saw them then. Well first, he saw Adalia Meyer and Constance Hopewell with a woman who appeared to be around their same age. Before he could even wonder about who she was Cornelius Meyer stepped in leading Ella and the girl he knew to be Kira Randal.

Following in behind them were Ella's father, another man whom he didn't know, Gabe, and Kira's twin brother Sawyer. They hadn't exactly gotten off to a friendly start. Lucien wondered what his father would say about that.

"Well, at least they know how to dress correctly."

And they did. The twin's mother was clothed in a red and gold gown that went perfectly with the theme Lucien's mother had insisted upon, as did their father's attire. Sawyer was tugging at his tie as Gabe said something beside him. Kira was in between her brother and Ella. Kira's gaze was moving over the surroundings as the other girl said something at her side.

"Come, it's time to greet our guests." Kenrick didn't wait to see if his son followed him.

Lucien thought to stay put. Everything inside of him was bulking at doing what his father asked—no demanded. But years of unnecessary pain had taught him to curb his rebellion, at least a little bit. But it did have him all but dragging his feet, and when he appeared in front of the new arrivals, he knew his expression was downright mulish. He supposed it was the same expression that Sawyer and Gabe were giving back to him. Lucien was hard pressed not to sneer, well that was until his gaze moved on to Kira.

It annoyed him that he found her fascinating, but she was. She looked pretty, really pretty in the ice blue gown. She looked well put together and polished, as if she belonged at this party, not at all how he thought someone who had lived her entire life in the Non-Magical world would appear.

His gaze briefly slid to her mother. She fit right in, too. He figured the two women at her side had something to do with it. In fact, he could almost hear his father's silent fuming about how the Hopewells and the Meyers had already fallen in with them. He'd never hear the end of it how he hadn't befriended them first.

"Diana, Gary," Michail Hopewell said, "this is Kenrick Norwood, Lord Mayor of Willow Oak and his son Lucien." He then turned. "Kenrick, Lucien, this is Diana and Gary Randal, and their children Sawyer and Kira."

"It's a pleasure *all* of you could join us for my son's celebration." Kenrick's voice sounded stiff and formal. It offered no warmth what so ever.

"Thank you for having your son extend the invitation," Diana Randal said. Her tone was friendly enough and calm, though at the same time there was an unmistakable note in there. That along with the pointed look, and Lucien knew immediately that this woman had already guessed she and her husband had not been wanted at this gathering, at least by the host that had just greeted them. She was polite enough, but it was obvious from her tone that she was no fool.

His father must have noted it, too, as he stood a bit straighter. Lucien recognized the stance; it was the one his father used to intimidate people into doing his bidding. However, with one glance at Diana and Gary Randal, Lucien knew it would be a futile attempt. They didn't appear to be the type of people who could be easily cowed.

The silence that stretched was awkward, almost bordering on painful until Adalia said, "Well, we're going to introduce them around."

"I can't believe the Rowleys are actually here. I thought they'd have the decency to not show up," Cerise Norwood said, her tone cool and dismissive, as she came to stand at her husband's side. "At least Valene had enough sense to leave that thing she calls a husband at home."

Lucien's gaze darted over to see how the two newcomers took that comment from his mother. He could read the confusion and disbelief on their faces. Yes, his family was doing a wonderful job ingratiating themselves to them.

With an annoyed shake of his head, Gabe looked to the twins and Ella. "Come on," he said, moving off, away from their group and further into the receiving room.

Sawyer followed immediately. Ella glanced to Kira. As one, the two girls took a step after them, but Kira darted one quick glance to Lucien before she took another. As her gaze caught his, he felt as if she was searching for something. He didn't know what it was. All he felt was the jolt go through him at her appraisal. Then, with a slight shake of her head, she went with Ella as they followed the two boys.

He didn't know why, but Lucien wanted to follow them. In fact, he took a step to do just that, but a hand snaked through his arm holding him in place.

"There you are. I've been looking everywhere for you." Regina's words came out like a purr as she tightened her grip the tiniest of bits.

He wanted to tell her, that no, she hadn't been; she'd been gossiping with her group of friends, but he held his tongue. It wouldn't do to say that here, in front of his parents, where it would bring him rapid disapproval. No scene was the rule.

Instead, he allowed her to lead him off, anything to be away from the condemnation of his family. He was just glad that he saw a couple of his friends in the direction she was heading them. Well, perhaps, not friends. He wasn't really close enough to call anyone that. But he could at least converse with them. It didn't hurt that they were of his same station.

"I can't believe they had the nerve to show up here," Regina said, all but fuming as soon as she was in the protective circle of her friends.

"I know." Nona all but simpered that comment.

"That dress she was wearing is hideous." Flora added with a glance in the direction the foursome had disappeared. "She thinks she's so wonderful because of the prophecy. I was so glad to be rid of her the other day. She's very rude."

Lucien shook his head. He didn't even have to be there to know that's not what happened. Flora always did like revisionist history.

"Really?" Brenton Mayfair questioned. His hand ran through the spikes of his black hair. "I thought she looked really pretty."

"What!" his girlfriend Nona all but screeched.

As was typical, Brenton gave a casual shrug of his shoulders.

Aghast and furious all at once, she stormed off.

"Was it something I said?" he asked the group at large, his grin saying adequately enough he knew what he had done but just didn't care.

Dalen laughed. "Look all you want, but don't say anything about it when the girlfriend's around."

The rest of the girls gave them both scathing looks.

"You didn't think she was pretty, did you?" Susette asked her boyfriend, Eamon Malford, her hand tucking into the crook of his elbow.

He smiled down at her, his teeth stark white against his dark complexion. "Of course not."

Her smug smile told of the satisfaction of his answer.

"What did you think of her, Lucien?" Regina said at his side.

The guys in the group turned to look at him. Dalen even accompanied his by a raised brow.

Honestly, he didn't know Kira Randal enough to really form any type of opinion of her, but he'd learned over the years to not let anyone know his true feelings. He'd learned that lesson with having favorite toys and possessions destroyed by his father when he felt as if Lucien had disappointed him. He'd realized that it was best to keep his feelings, no matter how minor, to himself. "She's pretty I suppose, but I'm not interested." And he wasn't, not in anyone either of his parents deemed a worthy match. With that in mind, he disentangled his arm from Regina's cloying grasp.

"Well, I think I am." Dalen looked in their direction again, even though they could no longer see them.

"That's what my father had planned," Flora said, her smile smug. "That's why their schedules match perfectly with ours. He had this vision of us becoming close friends." She laughed then as if that was the most absurd thing ever. "I've been hearing of nothing but his displeasure since I didn't become friends with her on that first day." She shrugged her slender shoulders unconcerned. "But I don't like her at all. She seems very struck on herself." Flora reached up to gently pat at her artfully arranged dirty blonde hair.

Lucien resisted the urge to roll his eyes. If anyone had an abundance of self-importance, it was the headmaster's daughter.

"Sawyer's not friendly at all. Then he ditched me. Can you believe that?" Dalen looked around at the group.

Yes, Lucien could believe it. Dalen wasn't the sharpest of individuals, but his family was of old money and had a long, impressive lineage. It was the reason Dalen was always included in this circle. These were the people—minus Nona who was still off pouting somewhere—that his family saw fit for him to associate with.

There were a few more his parents approved of, but these were his fellow fourth years in his same section.

"All right, enough. Who cares," Regina huffed, still at his side even though he had pulled away from her. "Let's get to more pressing matters." She turned to face him. "Let's hope your familiar is more in line with your station." She glanced to the others, her hand going to her chest in a dramatic fashion. "You all know I love Beck, but his dog." She gave a little shiver in apparent revulsion. Quickly she turned back to him. "Lucien, your familiar must be better than that...that rat he got." She grabbed his arm. "Won't it be wonderful if our familiar's match? It will be fate."

This time, Lucien did give in to the temptation and roll his eyes. However, Regina didn't notice as she had already turned back to Susette and was discussing matching colors of animals.

Brenton caught his gaze and smirked. Lucien just shook his head. There was no way he wanted to have matching familiars with Regina. In fact, he hoped their familiars hated each other.

"Well, I thought he was adorable," Flora said. "He makes Beck look even more handsome."

Brenton rolled his eyes that time, along with Eamon and Dalen.

Beck Thoren was in fifth year. Tall, blond, and muscular, most every girl fawned all over him. He was certain to be captain of this year's Sloignis team. He'd excelled at the sport last year. That's why it was so shocking when his familiar had come to him on his birthday. It was a tiny sandy colored pug dog with the name of Bert. Beck's parents had been horrified, and he suffered a great deal of ribbing from his friends.

However, Beck had taken to the animal immediately. Now, no one said a word against Bert, well that was until Regina.

"Lucien, I need a word with you."

Once again, his father had caught him unawares. With a barely perceptible nod, he turned, but he couldn't resist adding, "Father, you know my friends." His hand swept out to accompany the group.

"Yes," came the clipped reply.

Kenrick moved forward, and Lucien had no choice but to follow. He'd only taken a couple of steps when he felt Regina slip her arm in his again. Before he had a chance to try to untangle himself, his father stopped and drew himself up to his full height.

"Alone, Regina. Contrary to your opinion, you are *not* part of this family." Kenrick turned abruptly, dismissing her instantly.

She froze at his side. Her chin wobbled. Lucien actually felt a pang of compassion for her. He knew that remark had cut Regina deeply. It was on the tip of his tongue to say something to comfort her, but all that would do was bring more of his father's unwanted and cruel attention. The kindest thing he could do for her was to follow his father.

With that thought in mind, he carefully unwound her arm from his and gave her what he hoped was a reassuring smile. Then, he drew himself up and with determined steps followed his father in the direction of his study. Something had set his father off this time, and Lucien dreaded the consequences from that.

13

She felt out of place. Oh, sure, her outfit fit right in; Ella and her mother had seen to that. But everything else… And it wasn't just because she hadn't grown up here. No, she didn't fit in with most of these people. That was readily apparent when the *Lord* Mayor had been introduced to them.

If he wasn't the most condescending person she'd ever met, Kira didn't know who could even run a close race. He hadn't wanted their parents there; that had been apparent. It was no wonder that Lucien Norwood had been as smug as he was in some of their previous encounters. She was happy when Gabe led them off.

But she couldn't help but cast a glance over her shoulder to Lucien one more time just to see…she really didn't know what. Perhaps some sign that he wasn't as big of a jerk as his father seemed to be. But he was still standing there, right at that man's side. And he was staring at her, watching her move away.

The jolt of awareness shot right through her, but she brushed it off as nerves. With a shake of her head, she fell in step beside Ella.

Carefully, they weaved their way through the crowd, following in Gabe and Sawyer's wake.

It was crowded in the mayor's home. Their murmured "excuse mes" drew attention. Some gave a merely cursory glance, while others openly stared. She felt like some sort of oddity, something in one of those old carnivals that advertised freaks.

Thankfully, the next room they entered wasn't as suffocatingly crowded. It seemed most people hadn't managed to move further than the first room where they had arrived.

The room they were now in was beautiful; there was no other word to describe it. The few walls and the high ceiling were white with countless gold etchings. The room was a long, wide rectangle. With the two narrower ends having a matching bank of windows that allowed unobstructed views of the other rooms of the house. The same was for one of the long walls, windows that displayed other parts of the home. But the last wall's windows showed unobstructed views of the outside, the perfectly manicured lawn, what looked to be a hedge, which seemed to be part of a maze, and a large, fantastic fountain that shot water high in the air.

In the center of the high ceiling hung a large, dazzling chandelier. The lights inside of it seem to glint of what appeared to be diamonds, distributing a warm glow. On either end of the room were matching chandeliers in a smaller size.

Along one end and off to the corner, appeared to be an orchestra, or at least there were instruments. In front of them, stood an older, very plump man. In his hand was his wand. He waved it in front of him, pointing in the direction of certain instruments in turn.

Kira stopped abruptly. That couldn't be right. Instruments played by themselves? But that had to be it. There were no people at any of the different ones, yet the soft sounds of the different instruments were filtering throughout the ballroom.

Of all the things she had recently seen, she couldn't say why this was the most shocking to her, but it was. It actually had her coming to a complete stop. Thankfully, Gabe had steered them around the edge of the grand ballroom, so she wasn't in the way of any of the few dancing couples.

"Come on," Ella said with a laugh. She had noticed Kira was no longer with her and had come back to get her. She looped their arms and guided them around the other people milling about.

Gabe had stopped in a far corner. He and Sawyer were standing unobtrusively away from the edge of the marbled dance floor. From their vintage point they could see, not only the entire ballroom, but it also gave an excellent view of one of the wide double arched openings that led to the receiving area they had just come from. Also, it displayed a view of the bank of windows, which Kira could now see led to what appeared to be a living room of sorts as people were sitting on gold brocade sofas.

"What is his problem?" Sawyer asked that question as Kira and Ella joined them.

Gabe shrugged his broad shoulders. "I don't know exactly. Personally, I think he's just an egotistical snob who thinks he's better than anyone else."

Ella made a tsking sound of disapproval.

One corner of Gabe's lips raised in an amused gesture. He glanced toward Ella. "She thinks we should give Norwood the benefit of the doubt and overlook his ogre like tendencies."

Sawyer snorted, his look telling well enough he didn't think Lucien had any redeeming qualities.

Kira couldn't help but glance toward the archways. She could make him out. He was standing with a group of people who looked to be around their age. Once again, that girl from the other afternoon was at his side.

Yes, Lucien Norwood seemed arrogant and slightly struck on himself, but then again, she didn't know him well enough to form any definitive opinions about him. On her initial encounter with him, he had stunned her; he was that good looking. Subsequent times, he'd been almost openly antagonistic toward her brother and Gabe. But then, after the brief meeting with his parents tonight, she was surprised he was even bearable.

However, thinking of his parents brought something else to her mind. She turned to Gabe and Ella. "Who are the Rowleys and why does Mrs. Norwood apparently not like them?"

"First," Gabe said, leaning closer to her, so close in fact that she could see that the eyes she assumed before were just green, actually had a ring of amber around his pupils.

It was fascinating really, so much so in fact, that it took her a moment to realize he was still talking. She felt heat rush up her face, more so by the smile that turned up the corners of his lips.

Instead, he all but whispered in her ear, "Don't let her hear you call her *Mrs.* Norwood. It's *Lady* Norwood, and he's always *Lord* Mayor."

She couldn't help it. Kira felt her own lips turn up at the sound of his exasperation with the Norwoods.

Then Gabe straightened a bit to address the group as a whole, but his words were for Kira and Sawyer. "The Rowleys are Valene and Nadir Rowley. They have a daughter, Almira, who's in our year. She's over there. You've noticed her in class I'm sure." He indicated the direction with a tilt of his head.

Just coming through the archway were a mother and daughter. The mother's long black hair was in a single braid down her back. And her gown, which was a deep, rich purple, with a pale pink running from the bodice down through the front opening, looked like something one might see at a Renaissance fair. She was not adhering to the dress code. The daughter's reddish-brown hair was fastened in intricate braids around her head. Her gown was of the Victorian period. It had dark, emerald green outer part and sleeves, while black was at the bodice and down the opening of the long skirt.

She had seen her before. They had Potions and Elixirs and Maleficium Armor together, but she'd never spoken to her.

"Mrs. Rowley's husband, Nadir, was not invited tonight. He never is." Ella's tone told blatantly of her disgust at the situation.

"Why isn't he?" Sawyer asked.

It was a valid question. Looking at the great number of people in attendance, it was hard to believe they had excluded anyone.

"He's a werewolf," Gabe said. "He faces a lot of prejudices here."

"They all do." Ella added.

Both of their tones spoke eloquently enough that they felt the situation was wrong. Kira did her best to stamp down her rising panic. So far, Gabe and Ella had seemed pretty normal, well as normal as someone from this screwy world could be. She didn't want her own fears based on horror movies to form some snap judgements of people. Besides, Risa said it was perfectly safe. Yet if she knew she could actually trust these people, then what they said might hold more weight.

But the honest truth of the matter was that someone in this town knew what happened to her biological parents; someone had a hand in it. And until someone confessed or either, she or Sawyer remembered, no one, no matter if she was starting to like them, could be trusted one hundred percent.

On the chance that neither of their memories ever came back, Kira realized she couldn't risk alienating anyone. She had to understand what was going on around here. She could be civil; she could push her fears aside. But she wouldn't forget them either.

"Are you all friends with her?" Sawyer asked as he studied the girl across the room.

"Yes, she's very nice." Ella shot Gabe a look.

Just when Kira was starting to grow suspicious of the two of them, Gabe shuffled his feet. He ran a hand through his short blond hair, sending it sticking out in haphazard spikes. He looked decidedly uncomfortable. When he spoke, his words were hesitant.

"Actually…there are some people who want to meet you both. Everyone's wanted to give you space. They didn't want to crowd you all before. You know, give you all a little time to adjust. But perhaps tonight might be good. We're all here, and it might be nice to have more than a couple of friendly faces around."

"Who wants to meet us?" Kira asked before her brother could. She had visions of people just coming up and staring at them, or worse something like a celebrity since they had said they were famous in this world. She was *not* signing anything.

"We know you don't remember from before," Ella said.

This time it was Kira and Sawyer who exchanged a look. That fact made them decidedly uncomfortable. Kira shifted, and her arms automatically came up to cross over her belly in a protective gesture.

"No." Gabe stepped forward and pried one of her hands loose, taking it in both of his. "It's not like that. Since they know you don't, they didn't want to overwhelm you. They didn't want to come up on the first day of school and say 'Hey, we all used to be friends.' They wanted to give you both some space, to get the feel of this place first. But maybe meeting them would help."

His words were meant to reassure her, but instead they had the opposite effect. It was as if they had hidden something from her. She knew they knew her old life better than she did, but she didn't want details purposely kept under the guise of sparing her feelings. She pulled her hand from his grasp. Her gaze went from him to Ella and then back again. "So you all were sent in to get us comfortable, befriend us, and then report back to everyone." It wasn't a question.

Ella was shaking her head before she even finished. "No, that's not it at all."

Kira held up her hands to ward them off. "I just…I need a moment." She turned and started off. She knew without looking her brother was behind her. "Give me a minute, Sawyer, and you take one, too. Then we can decide what we want to do with this information."

"All right."

She glanced over her shoulder and saw him disappear out a door that led to the verandah. Squaring her shoulders, Kira turned in the opposite direction. She ignored the looks in her direction and edged her way around the other guests. She finally made it to a set of open doors that led into a hallway. There were less people out here, but still too many for her liking. She kept going, moving down another hallway, stopping when she came to a room, but after hearing voices, continuing on.

Finally, she turned another corner and was met with emptiness. She felt as if she could breathe. A glance told her there were two doors on either side of the hallway, with a final door at the very end.

She moved further into the dimly lit corridor. With a quick glance behind her to make certain she was still alone, she felt herself relax a little bit. She leaned against the wall, her mind swimming.

Granted it was nice to have not been bombarded on their first day with people running up to them and telling them that they had used to be friends, but at the same time, what Gabe and Ella did seemed devious and calculating. It was as if they had been sent ahead to find out information on them, and then report back to this group of people.

Perhaps, their early assumptions were correct. Maybe none of these people could be trusted.

"For just once can you do as I ask?"

That growled comment drifted up the hallway. Kira froze. Slowly, she looked in the direction it came. It was from the door at the end. Further away, she'd assumed the door had been closed, but from her new vantage point, she could see it was slightly ajar, a faint glow spilled out from it. She thought to leave the way she had entered. She didn't want to eavesdrop on someone's private conversation. However, when she moved, she found herself getting closer to the door.

"And what was I supposed to do, Father? Show up on their doorstep and beg for their friendship?" That flippant remark was proceeded by the sound of glass shattering.

Her hand flew up to her mouth to muffle her gasp of surprise. She recognized the voice now, even though she had only heard him speak a handful of times, Lucien Norwood.

"You were supposed to do as I say. *Don't* disobey me again. For once, make yourself useful." Then a muffled word followed by a crash. The door was yanked open.

Kira knew she only had a split second, but she couldn't be caught standing outside, listening to their conversation. Quickly, she ducked into the room nearest to her. She'd just pressed herself against the wall by the door, when she heard the angry footsteps of Kenrick Norwood stalk away.

She hadn't realized she'd been holding her breath until it came out in a low hiss. She found she couldn't move. Her heart felt as if it was about ready to pound out of her chest. She hadn't meant to hear any of that. She'd only wanted time to think on the revelations from Gabe and Ella, but now...

Show up on their doorstep and beg for their friendship?

Instinctively, she knew that was about her and Sawyer. The question was what did they matter to the Mayor? Something else was going on here, but she couldn't reason out what it could be, not when other things were weighing so heavily on her mind.

The sound of shattering glass brought her quickly back to reality. It came from the room at the end of the hall. She knew she hadn't missed the Mayor's return.

Hesitantly, but as if it wasn't of her own volition, she found herself making her way down the hall. She faltered for just a moment, but then she raised her hand and pushed the door open.

She was met with chaos.

Her silver eyes widened as she took in the destruction of the room. Shards of what looked to have once been a sculpture dotted the floor around the sofa. Slivers of glass sparkled on the dark wood floor and around his feet.

Lucien Norwood stood in the center of the room, facing the massive desk and the portrait of his father that hung on the wall behind it. His hands were balled into fists at his sides. The ridged lines of his shoulders told how tense he was.

"How much of that did you hear?" His voice was hard and cold.

Kira flinched. She hadn't realized he knew she was there. She bit her lower lip in indecision as she carefully weighed her words. She finally settled on the vague, "Not much."

If anything, he tensed more at her words. She didn't understand that until he spoke again.

"I thought you were Regina."

She stamped down the small kernel of disappointment his words caused. Of course, he would have assumed it was his girlfriend, not some virtual stranger, which probably made this all the worse for him.

Kira didn't want that, so she offered, "I can go get her if you want. She was the girl with you yesterday at school, right?"

Silence met her. It stretched between them, feeling uncomfortable and oppressive. She thought to suggest it again, or just go find her. She'd just started to move when his words stopped her.

"Soon I'll have a wand and be able to have this entire mess cleaned up almost instantly. I'll like that. It will save me grief later." Then with a sigh, he bent at the knees, crouched down, and started collecting the pieces of glass, placing them in his empty hand until he could dispose of them.

Slowly, Kira edged forward. She tried to bend to help with the cleanup, but the cut of the dress would barely allow it. She made a snort of disgust. "Sorry," she said when she almost tipped over on him as she reached for a shard.

In silence, he waved away her concern as he continued his cleaning, though he did point in the direction of a tall waste bin that stood in the corner. She went and retrieved it. She brought it to him, and wordlessly, he let the fragments fall inside it.

For long moments, she watched him in silence, from his bowed head to the now resigned lines of his body. He didn't look like a boy ready to celebrate his birthday. Instead, he looked almost defeated. She glanced at the antique grandfather clock that set in the corner. It was after eight. She wondered what time his birth had been. Surely, this party wouldn't go into the late hours of the night. Either way, it had to be closer to time. But after what he'd just been through, she figured celebrating was probably the last thing on his mind.

"Are...are you nervous?" The question seemed to just come from her with no real thought.

For the first time since she entered, he raised his head. His ice blue gaze met hers. He didn't pretend to not know what she was talking about. "I'm terrified." The admission nearly echoed in the otherwise silent room.

She felt as if some of her own apprehension had left her body. This boy who had grown up in this world was scared of what was coming, and he knew what he was facing. It made her feel better about her own situation.

"Are you looking forward to it at all?" The question was a near whisper.

One corner of his lips lifted. "Definitely." He glanced around the room. "It would make things like this easier."

She wanted to ask him if this happened often, but she held her tongue. That was too personal. She didn't know him well enough to get into the dynamics of his home life. Besides, if the roles were reversed, she wouldn't want anyone to know. She'd respect his privacy on this.

He moved to gather up more glass. Silently, she followed. She wanted to ask him something more, something else about magic. She couldn't explain why she felt as if she could, especially after what she had overheard. Or perhaps it was because of that. She'd unknowingly witnessed something she knew he'd rather she hadn't, and for some reason, that made her feel like she could now talk to him.

"You might as well say it."

The words startled her. She'd been too inside her own thoughts that she hadn't realized he was studying her. It would have unnerved her if she had.

The question came out in a rush. "Have you had any…Any unintentional bursts of magic?"

His eyes widened in what she assumed was from the personal nature of her question. She opened her mouth to apologize, but he stopped her first.

"That wasn't what I was expecting. I thought it would be about what you heard." He shook his head as if to clear his thoughts. Slowly, he rose to his feet, tossing the remaining glass from his hand into the trash bin; he brushed them off on his black pants. "Nothing big, but it's like sometimes, especially, if I get angry, I can feel it. You know it's like there's something inside of me."

That sounded terrifying.

He considered her for a moment before he asked. "Have you?"

Kira glanced down at the floor. "Well, I just…I—"

Abruptly, he reached for her hand, cutting off her words. Her gaze flew up to his.

Before she could question it, he said, "Not here." Then, with her hand firmly gripped in his, he led her from the room; she barely managed to let go of the trashcan. When they reached the end of the hallway, he turned in the opposite direction from which she'd come.

She got the distinct impression he was leading her away from the throng of party guests. She didn't question him, and not once did she try to pull her hand from his grasp. Instead, she blindly followed him down hallways, through empty rooms until they came to a set of glass double doors.

Without releasing her hand, he pulled open one of the doors.

The heat hit her first. It was so muggy. She felt as if she was in some tropical jungle. Then she glanced around and saw that it appeared she was. They were in the middle of a large, completely glass enclosed room. Vibrant flowers in shocking pink, brilliant red, burnt orange, silky teal, dandelion yellow, and even soft white, filled the entire space, lining the winding paths through what had to be a greenhouse.

The smell hit her then, not cloying, as she would have assumed with as many varieties of flowers that abounded inside the glass enclosure. It was actually sweet and soothing, seeming to relax her.

"This is so beautiful." The words whispered out as she mutely followed in his wake.

He smiled at her over his shoulder. She felt her stomach lurch, her pulse quicken. Now, she was all too aware of her hand trapped in his larger one, of knowing she was suddenly alone with him, a boy she didn't know really in the slightest.

"We shouldn't be overheard here."

She felt a chill sweep down her spine. That sounded ominous. She glanced around nervously. "It's so beautiful out here. I can't believe anyone else from the party won't want to enjoy this." She fought to keep the nervous chatter from her tone. She must not have succeeded completely as one of his black brows rose in question.

However, instead of asking about it, he explained. "No, they won't. This is our private garden. The only way someone can enter is if they are a member of my family or with a member."

It took a moment for the words to reach her. When they did, they caused more questions than fear. "Private? Isn't this your home? It's all yours."

"No, see, the Lord Mayor of the town must live in the mayoral residence. It's the Ivywood Estate. The estate has its own gardens, which can be accessed from the ballroom. This is my family's private garden. Each Lord Mayor contributes their own garden to the estate. Once that person is no longer Mayor, those family gardens are then part of the estate."

"They just kind of fuse together?" She didn't understand that at all.

He nodded. "Once my father no longer holds the office, we will go back to our own home."

She had so many questions she didn't know which one to ask first. Both ended up spilling out at nearly the same time. "How much longer does he have in office? Where is your actual home?"

His grin widened. "My father is on his last year as Lord Mayor. The term began in July. As far as my real home, I actually live right next door to where you used to live. The back of both of our grounds bordered each other."

There was no mistaking the ice that ran down her spine now. He'd known her before.

Of course, he had!

She called herself all types of stupid. She should have realized. It wasn't as if he was new to town like she and her family were. He'd been here all along, so of course he knew that she had no memory of her previous life. She tried to pull her hand from his grasp, but he stayed firm.

The look she shot him told of her annoyance. It should have given him at least a small measure of pause. It didn't. In fact, his grin widened a little.

"You don't like people to bring up that they knew you before, do you?"

She didn't try to keep the irritation from her voice this time. "Surprised you figured that out, Einstein." Once again, she tried to pull her hand away. He didn't budge.

"Though we've covered Albert Einstein in the Non-Magical World class, I don't really understand that reference but that much disdain is hard to miss."

"Yeah, you're sharp." Kira rolled her eyes. When all he did was continue to smirk at her, she glanced away. Finally, she huffed, "Why did you drag me all the way out here?"

His hold on her loosened immediately, but he didn't release her fully. He still glanced around the otherwise empty area before he said, "I didn't want to talk in my father's study. I didn't want us to be overheard."

That comment told her a lot. Since no one was waiting in the hallway for them as they made their way out, it had to be that his father's study was bugged. But why? And for whom? Did the man really record his own family's conversations?

"You were going to tell me about your involuntary magic." Lucien prompted.

Abruptly, Kira's gaze swung back to him. As she studied him, she realized she didn't know if she wanted to tell him any longer. That moment of vulnerability he had back in the ruined study was gone.

He must have sensed that. "You don't have to tell me. I just…if you wanted to, I wanted you to do it somewhere safe." Slowly, his hold on her hand eased until he released her completely. His now empty hand dropped to his side, where he balled it into a fist.

Immediately, she felt bereft. It was a strange feeling to have. But nevertheless, it was still there. And that feeling caused the words to tumble out. "I made a lamp explode."

His mesmerizing ice blue eyes widened as his mouth fell open. He stared at her for so long and so silently that she shuffled uncomfortably under the scrutiny.

For the second time that night, she wrapped her arms protectively around her waist. Her movement seemed to jar him as he quickly snapped his mouth shut.

"Who have you told this to?" There was an urgency to his tone that she didn't understand.

"Well, obviously, my parents and brother know. And then I told Risa." At his blank look, she added, "Risa Kemp, the teacher at school."

Lucien's eyes widened in understanding. He moved closer to her. Without preamble, he pulled her hands from her protective position. His grip was filled with resolve. "Don't tell anyone else."

That was *not* what she had been expecting. "Risa said the same thing, too. I don't understand."

"Exactly, there are things…just…I know you don't know me…We don't have the time to get into it all tonight but trust me on this. Please."

He looked so earnest, as if he truly did only have her best interests at heart. But on the heels of that thought came his words from the disagreement with his father.

Show up on their doorstep and beg for their friendship?

She'd made a terrible mistake. She shouldn't have told him anything. *He* couldn't be trusted. All she wanted was to take it back, to pull her hands away, and get as far from him as humanly possible. But she couldn't. She didn't want to tip him off to the thoughts clashing inside her head.

Instead, she forced herself to give a slight nod as if she was taking his caution under advisement.

He relaxed a bit at that. Then his expression turned repentant. "I don't want to, but I know it's getting close to my birth time. Both my parents will have fits if I'm not in the ballroom."

She nodded in seeming understanding. Anything to be away from him for a moment so she could have time to think. But still he didn't release her.

He cleared his throat, once, before he spoke. When he did, his tone was filled with a sense of urgency. "Look, I know this won't make any sense, but, please, we have to pretend like we really don't know each other. It will be better for you if no one knows that we've talked."

Bright red flags.

They were basically hitting her over the head. She'd like to think that everyone was good and meant what they said, but the reality was, that wasn't the case. In fact, the murderer or murderers of her biological parents could be in attendance at this party at that very minute.

Reality was she couldn't trust any of these people. But Lucien didn't need to know that she'd come to that realization. In fact, the more she kept everyone in the dark, the safer it would be for her parents and brother. So she nodded in agreement to his suggestion.

He breathed a sigh of relief. "Good. All right let's go back."

Wordlessly, she walked with him through the twists and turns of the corridors. When he finally came to a stop, in the distant she could hear others' voices.

"I don't want us to walk in together. You go on ahead. I'll follow soon."

She nodded, ready to be away from him so she could think on all the things she had seen and heard tonight. But something stopped her after she had taken only a few steps and had her turning back to him. He was watching her intently.

Her head tilted to one side. "Try not to be nervous out there." She didn't know why she was offering reassurances to someone who might want to cause her harm, but she felt as if something was compelling her to do it.

He tried for a reassuring smile. "I'll see you out there."

With one last smile of her own, she forced herself to turn back around and make her way to the ballroom to rejoin the party.

V. A. Risby

14

Well, he'd royally frinxed everything up. And just in case he hadn't realized that, Ella drove the point home.

"I don't think that went as planned," the petite brunette said dryly as they watched Kira and Sawyer walk away.

"Definite understatement," Gabe muttered. He didn't know what had come over him. No, that wasn't right. He knew what his problem was.

He could clearly remember the last time he had seen them before they had disappeared. It was the afternoon of the night their parents had been murdered.

It had been a cool, crisp October day. The leaves were a kaleidoscope of different hues of red, orange, and gold. He and Sawyer had spent the morning at the Sayer's home—that was Kira and Sawyer's real last name. He hadn't mentioned it to them as they hadn't asked, and he hadn't wanted them to think he only saw them as the friends he'd once known, not as the people he was getting to know now.

Their mother, Fay, who had been like a second mother to him as he'd been at their home so much, had made them chococanes—their favorite treat—and had even brought them out to the fort they had built in Sawyer's backyard.

Even though they'd had to deal with Lucien and Brenton yelling at them from the backyard of the Norwood's—it was rotten luck that their properties had bordered each other—and Kira trying to join them in their fort, it had still been a great morning.

It had been late afternoon when Gabe had finally gone home. His dad had been out of town for a week. As part of the Magical Beast Containment Squad, he was sometimes gone for weeks at a time on assignment. This had been one of those times. Typically, he would have spent the night with Sawyer, but he hadn't wanted his mom to be alone. Sawyer's father Castor had opened the speculo and sent word to Gabe's mother. After she'd had the cup of tea, he and Sawyer had begged her to have, just so they could play longer, she and Gabe had gone home.

That had been almost ten years ago. And while he knew that Kira and Sawyer were now vastly different people, a part of him still hoped they would remember and things could go back to how they should have been.

When he'd been talking with Sawyer at the Hopewell's house before the party, a piece of Gabe couldn't help but be resentful that he was having to explain things—Sloignis for cripes sake—that Sawyer should already know. And as soon as that thought even crossed his mind, the guilt was nearly over-whelming. Neither Sawyer nor Kira had wanted what had happened to happen. It wasn't their fault, and he knew he was a horrible person for even having such thoughts.

He and Ella hadn't set out to get information from them or mislead them at all. True Sawyer had always been Gabe's best friend, and Kira and Ella had been inseparable. However, that wasn't to say they hadn't played with other kids, too. They had. And those were still people that Gabe called his friends today.

When he and Ella had found out that Kira and Sawyer were returning, their first thoughts had been to show up on their doorsteps immediately. Thankfully, though, the calmer heads of their parents had prevailed. Not only did the twins have no memory of their previous lives, but they also had yet to learn of the existence of magic.

Gabe couldn't even pretend to know what they were thinking or feeling. He'd talked it over with Ella and then with the rest of their group of friends. They all had thought it would be less over-whelming to be approached by a couple of them, not a crowd. Since he and Ella had been closest to them, it made the most sense for it to be them. And, honestly, Gabe would have insisted it was him. Sawyer might not remember him, but he remembered Sawyer, and he'd missed him greatly.

Gabe wasn't as friendly and open as he typically was, as he didn't want to put pressure on Sawyer, to make him think he was just remembering him from their past and not trying to get to know the person he had become. It was a hard line not to cross, to constantly have to censure himself so he didn't bring up something from their past that they didn't want to know yet. It was stressing him out and wearing on his last nerve.

But he needed to do better. He'd been so careful, trying to make sure he didn't say or do anything to upset them that he had ended up upsetting them anyway.

"I feel like we've went about this the wrong way, but I don't know how else to have done it differently. There's so much going on that even we don't understand with what happened that night. There are so many unanswered questions."

Ella laid a sympathetic hand on his shoulder. "It will be all right, Gabe. I know you were just trying to help them. They just have so much to deal with."

He shook his head. He didn't deserve her comfort when he had so many conflicting feelings warring inside of him. "I know I don't know him. I don't know either of them." He turned to face her. "But I'm angry, Ella. I know that we were only seven, but he was my best friend, and I resent like Hades that we didn't grow up together. I've missed him, and I know I shouldn't." He glanced away. He couldn't look at her to say the rest. "This isn't about me. It's about them. It's about how to make this right for my friends to make this as easy as possible. But I resent him for not missing me. And I can't say any of this to him, as I shouldn't feel this way. It's not fair that I do."

"Oh, Gabe."

He shook off her overtures of any more comfort. He was a truly horrible person. He needed air. He turned to head out the doors leading to the verandah to get that, but the sight of Sawyer standing behind him drew him up short. By the look on his face, he'd heard everything.

Cripes.

He'd really stuck his foot in it this time. There was no way Sawyer would ever hear him out now, but he had to try. "Look, I'm—"

"No, I heard everything." Sawyer took a step closer.

And here it came. Gabe braced himself for the worst of it.

"I'm sorry. I shouldn't have stormed off without giving you both a chance to explain. This is hard on Kira and me, but it hasn't been easy on you both either. It's all just a mess."

Gabe couldn't help it. He figured he was standing there like a madman with his mouth hanging open, but he'd never known such relief in his entire life. And it wasn't because

Sawyer had apologized. No, it was because his onetime best friend had heard everything, every selfish word, and still was going to give him a second chance. It was more than he could have hoped for under the circumstances.

Ella came up and stuck her arm through Gabe's, and then, after a moment of hesitation, she did the same to Sawyer. She glanced around. "Where did Kira go?"

Sawyer scanned the crowded ballroom, too. "She went the opposite direction of me. I know her, she'll have realized the same thing I did and be back here before too long."

After Sawyer's easy understanding, Gabe was optimistic for the first time in days. "Hopefully, she gets back soon." He glanced to a large, gold clock that was floating over their heads. "It won't be too much longer until it's Lucien's actual birthday."

Sawyer leaned in closer and bent a bit, so he could include Ella, who was still in between them, in the conversation. "What happens? Does everyone just stand around and watch?"

He looked horrified at the very thought as he was probably thinking of his impending birthday.

Gabe sought to reassure him. "Typically, no. These are the Norwoods, and we weren't kidding. Lucien's birthday is treated as a holiday. A lot of people tend to stay home and have only family on their birthday." Gabe glanced around the room again, taking in the vast number of attendees. "I almost feel sorry for Lucien that his is going to be such a spectacle."

Ella rolled her eyes. "He's not *that* bad."

Gabe actually couldn't believe she'd really said that. "We'll debate his supposed good points later." Over her head he mouthed to Sawyer, "He doesn't have any."

The other boy bit back his laughter. The movement caused Ella to glance up. One look between the two of them, and she glared. They all remained silent for a bit, until Sawyer cleared his throat. When he did it a second time, they both looked at him.

He glanced around the room at anything but them. His words were quiet when he finally spoke. "I know I should already know this, but when are your birthdays?"

Gabe had to lean forward to hear the end of that, and when he did, he felt awful. He didn't want Sawyer feeling guilty because he didn't remember. It wasn't his fault he couldn't. It was just a cruel twist of fate.

"Don't feel bad because you don't." Ella reassured the other boy before Gabe could. "You're not to blame and we don't expect it of you. And to answer your question, my birthday is October third."

"And I'm September eighteenth, so we're both after you and Kira."

"I was hoping you could tell me what to expect, especially without all this fuss."

"At least the particulars will still be the same. No matter how big a party the Norwoods throw, nothing can change that."

Ella loosened her grip on Gabe's arm to wave at someone across the room. "I'm going to go talk to Mari." She started to walk away, when she stopped. She seemed to be weighing something in her mind, before she blurted out to Sawyer, "Do you mind if I have her come over and introduce herself?"

He gave her the ghost of a grin. "It's fine, really," he added when she didn't appear too convinced.

They both watched her walk away, Sawyer's gaze still on her departing form when he asked, "Are you nervous? You know, about getting your powers?"

Gabe sighed and ran his hand through his blond hair, tousling it. "Yeah, I'm nervous. I mean my dad and mom have both said it doesn't hurt or anything like that, but still…It's just…"

"Nerve-racking," Sawyer finished for him.

Nodding in agreement, Gabe glanced to him. He wanted to say more but didn't know if he should. It seemed easier now between them, and he didn't want to jeopardize that, but at the same time, if he could be of help, he wanted to do that. He thought he better start off slowly though. "What has anyone told you?" At the other boy's look, Gabe added, "About your birthday?"

Sawyer's brow knitted. "You mean about what happens?"

Gabe was already shaking his head. "No, I figure this spectacle of Lucien's will answer some of those questions. But I'm talking about your actual birthday."

"Nothing." That one word was tinged in bitterness.

The compulsion to help was nearly overwhelming now. "Do you…want to know something? I don't want to pressure you or…"

When Sawyer's gray marbled gaze came to him, the look could only be described as desperate. "Yes, please."

"All right. I just didn't want…if you didn't want to know I didn't want to say anything."

"I want to know."

Gabe felt better about it now. He wasn't forcing the past on him. He hadn't broken his word to his mother than, for she had told him the memories would come at their own pace and to not try to force them out. "Well, no one knows the exact time of your birthday. Your parents…" He let that thought drift off. No need to remind him of the mother and father he had lost.

Again, Sawyer nodded. "Okay, but what I don't understand is why."

"I can only tell you what I assume as no one ever came out and told me anything. With you and Kira being the only siblings in all that time, the only reason I can think it was secret was for your own protection. Your parents knew you told me everything, so when you were seven, you still didn't even know the exact time. But I know it was later in the afternoon. You told me that."

He couldn't read all the conflicting emotions washing over the other boy's face. But there was still one more thing. "I know it's a lot but there's something else."

Sawyer appeared nearly overwhelmed, but Gabe had come this far. He figured he might as well get the rest of it out.

"Do you want to know who's older?"

For a moment, confusion clouded Sawyer's eyes, and then the understanding dawned. It was replaced by excitement and incredulousness. "You know who was born first?"

"Yeah." Gabe's lips lifted in a grin. "I do."

"Who is it?"

The question was asked from his side. Both boys whirled in that direction. Kira was standing behind them. She'd crept up quietly.

Inwardly, Gabe cringed. He quickly glanced around, hoping she was the only person to overhear them. Granted they hadn't spoke of anything too secretive, but Gabe didn't want his suspicions to be known, especially before he figured out if they were true or not.

She was staring up at him, a question in her liquid silver eyes, and he completely forgot what he was about to say.

When he'd known her before, she'd been a pest, an annoyance. Both Kira and Ella had bugged them mercilessly. It was either demanding they play what they wanted, ordering them around, and ingratiating themselves in his and Sawyer's games. She'd been irritating. She was as much of a sister to him as she was to her own brother.

However, that had been ten years ago. A lot had changed since then. She was no longer the little girl he remembered who had always wore her long, brown hair in two braids down her back. And standing before him in her icy blue gown, she didn't look anything like the little girl who used to love to play in the mud—well, except that one time. She was no longer Sawyer's annoying sister. Now, she was just pretty enough to make Gabe completely tongue-tied.

But she was staring up at him, waiting for him to say something. For the life of him, he couldn't remember what that could be.

Then Sawyer prompted. "Who was born first?"

Thank goodness for his once best friend; now Gabe didn't have to stand around like a complete imbecile any longer. He had planned to ease into it, but the words came out in a blurted rush. "You are, Sawyer. You always held that over her head."

The two siblings glanced to each other. There was something in their eyes, a knowledge now that neither had ever expected to receive. Gabe felt as if he was intruding on some private moment. He knew they need time to digest what he had just told them.

He thought to do just that, when a voice boomed out, "Ladies and gentlemen may I have your attention please."

Gabe glanced to his group then turned his full attention on Kenrick Norwood who was now standing in the center of the ballroom. They'd all been too intent on their own conversation; they hadn't even noticed the music had stopped. At the Mayor's side was Lucien, looking every bit the arrogant, cocky prick he always was. This wasn't the best time for Lucien's birthday reveal. Kira and Sawyer needed time to process what Gabe had just so thoughtlessly blurted out. But apparently, they weren't going to get that.

No, now was time for the show. "Here we go," Gabe muttered under his breath.

15

He was older.

Something Sawyer had always longed to know, and now he did. He didn't know how he felt. Wait, no, that wasn't right. He was elated, but on the heels of that came this deep chasm of irritation. He hated that he couldn't remember. He shouldn't have had to have someone tell him he was older than Kira; he should know. But he didn't. He couldn't remember anything. He hated that, hated this feeling that there was something wrong with him, that there was some hole inside him that needed filled up.

He couldn't process it. He'd wished he'd told Gabe to hold off on the telling until they were out of the stupid party. Here they were smack dab in the middle of it, and Sawyer was reeling. A glance to his sister showed Kira wasn't fairing much better.

He exhaled a deep breath. He told himself to calm down. Now was not the time to lose his mind. He was in the corner of a very crowded ballroom where the most condescending man he'd ever met was giving some sort of speech. He tuned out when the Mayor spoke of the joy Lucien had brought to their home.

Sawyer cast a quick glance over to Gabe, and the other boy rolled his eyes. It was such a typical friend thing to do that, for just one moment, Sawyer forgot he was some freak living in some freak town in some freak world. He was normal.

He'd missed that.

But on the heels of that revelation came one thought running back into his mind.

He was older.

He'd wanted to know that for so long. While he and Kira had waited in foster care, crowded in homes where all anyone did was fight, including them as they were so terrified and scared, he'd wanted to hold it over her that she had to do what he said because he was older. He'd never dreamed that they would actually find it out, at least he hadn't until they had come here.

And while this place was freaking strange and crazy, one good thing had come of it. And on the heels of that came more questions that he wanted answers to. His gaze flew to Gabe again, but the other boy was watching the spectacle in the center of the room. It was hard not to.

Gabe would tell him. Instinctively, Sawyer knew that if he asked a question, Gabe would do his best to answer it truthfully.

But did he really want to know that way?

He could have asked before, and he hadn't. Why was that? As soon as he asked that of himself, he knew the answer. He was afraid to know, because to know was to open himself up. It meant he was going to have to deal with the realization that his birth parents were not only dead but murdered. And while he might not remember them, he knew—*knew*—that he'd loved them and that they'd loved him. And to know that, to know about them, would open up a void in him that he could never fill. Memories or not, he couldn't get them back.

He didn't want to have to deal with that. He didn't want to have to miss them. Just the thought of it caused a slow ache over the center of his heart. Absently, his hand came up to rub the spot.

Quickly, he exhaled another breath. Now was definitely not the time. Later, he'd deal with it all later.

"Hey," Ella said, appearing at his side.

He started. For the second time in a matter of minutes, someone had snuck up on him. He was really becoming unaware of his surroundings.

She glanced around him to his sister. Ella's voice was a whisper. "Kira, Sawyer, this is Mari Cutler. Mari, Kira and Sawyer Randal."

Sawyer couldn't help the warm smile that turned up his lips. Ella had introduced them as if they were all meeting for the first time. He appreciated that more than he could say.

"Hi," he said to the other girl in the same quiet tone that Ella had used. Neither of them wanted to draw attention from the Mayor who was still speaking in the center of the room.

"Hi," Mari said to him and in turn to his sister.

The girl was taller than Kira. She had a mass of black and purple curls that tumbled down her back in disarray and a friendly, outgoing face. She was dressed in Victorian attire with a teal and black gown.

He waited for some spark, some rush of recognition, but nothing came.

She opened her mouth to say something more, but immediately snapped it shut as the Mayor's voice boomed throughout the room.

"It is time." With a wave of his hand, the lights dimmed. The man stepped back and left his son standing, alone, in the center of the now vacated dance floor.

If Lucien hadn't been such a prick, Sawyer would have felt sorry for him as he stood there waiting, with every guest at this horrendous party gawking at him. To his credit, Lucien seemed to be ignoring the rapt attention. And then he absently glanced around. His gaze locked in on Kira. It was only for a brief moment, but it was long enough for Sawyer to glance to his sister and see that she had been staring at Lucien, too. Sawyer would have thought nothing of it, since everyone was looking in Lucien's direction. But there was something different there. If Sawyer didn't know better, Kira had been giving the birthday boy a nod of encouragement.

However, before Sawyer could dwell on it too much, the golden clock that hung in the air gave a chime.

Instantly, a soft white glow seemed to come from inside the boy in the center of the room. From the direction of the sitting room from where they had entered came an answering glow. The people in that direction gave a little exclamation of surprise or shock. They moved back almost parting in a smooth, synchronized order as if they had planned it.

Just when Sawyer was trying to figure out what was going on, the light grew brighter. The last person moved, and he saw what was making the commotion. A large, pure white dog—no it was too big for a dog; it had to be a wolf—had stepped into the ballroom.

It was a beautiful animal. And amazingly, it didn't seem concerned with the numerous people staring at it. Instead, it walked forward as if no one was around. It stopped a couple of feet from the boy. For a moment, Sawyer wondered if it was going to attack Lucien as the wolf's tail didn't move and every line of its body seemed tense and poised, as if waiting for something.

Just when he thought he might be right, the wolf's back legs folded as the animal sat at attention.

While everyone else couldn't help but stare at the beautiful animal, Sawyer darted a glance at the apparent owner. A look of smug satisfaction and if he were honest, actual happiness, were openly displayed on Lucien Norwood's features.

With purposeful steps, he crossed the distance between them. He actually bent down before the animal, going to his knees.

Off to the side the prissy woman dressed all in white who he'd learned was Lucien's mother made a sound of distress.

Sawyer bit the inside of his cheek to keep from laughing. She looked put upon by her son kneeling on the floor. She probably didn't think it was dignified enough.

With his left hand, Lucien petted the wolf's head. Then his fingers went to the charm on the animal's collar. For a moment, he studied it. His lips moved, and then the wolf, as if reacting to whatever Lucien said, raised one paw and put it on his leg.

A loud, almost swooning sigh came from the opposite side of the room. Quickly, Sawyer found the reason for it. It was the black-haired girl who had been with Lucien yesterday at school. She was fanning herself as if she was going to faint as she watched him.

"Overly dramatic much." Sawyer heard Ella whisper that to Kira and Mari as she stood in between them as the other two girls tried not to laugh.

It was one of the more bizarre things he had seen since arriving in this town, and that was saying something. But he pushed that thought to the side. Right now, he watched as Lucien opened the charm on the wolf's collar. From inside, he removed a silver chain with its own pendant attached to it. He placed it over his head.

With one last affectionate pat to the wolf's head, Lucien rose to his feet. His right hand came up to the charm. The word *Amplifico* echoed out into the otherwise stillness of the room.

Instantly, a wand appeared in his hand.

As Sawyer stood there watching this, unbidden came the thought that now was the time Lucien turned that new wand on all the party guests and blew them all up. He raised the wand, and Sawyer's thought was here it came.

Instead, the word *Selumina* now reverberated in the ballroom. A nearly blinding jet of light shot out of the tip of Lucien's wand, which he had thankfully pointed at the ceiling.

It seemed as if it was the cue that everyone needed. The resounding applause started then. That black haired girl and the group she was standing with rushed out to meet him in the center of the room. Other guests started chattering excitedly as they now moved freely about the room.

Sawyer glanced first to his sister, then to Gabe, Ella, and Mari in turn. All of their eyes were just as wide as he knew his were.

"Well that was terrifying." As soon as the words left his mouth, Sawyer wanted to call them back. He didn't want to give name to his fears, especially, in front of everyone. But it was already out.

For a moment, they all stared at him in stunned silence. Then Ella laughed. She raised her hand to cover her mouth to try to hold it in, but it didn't work.

Sawyer's spine stiffened. She was laughing at him.

But before he could completely close himself off, her words gave him pause. "Oh, thank goodness, I thought I was the only one who thought so."

Gabe apparently agreed. "And to have to do that in front of all these people." He shook his head. "I'm telling you all right now. I'm going to be home alone on my birthday, in my room."

Mari gave a sigh of agreement. "Yeah, locked in my room. I probably won't be able to even get my wand. I'll probably say the wrong thing or something. That would be so embarrassing."

"I'm more worried if my familiar hates me." Ella's dark emerald eyes were large with fear. "Seriously, I can picture it. My mom and my dad's barely tolerate me. I'm awful with dogs, so I know I'll get one."

Then without conscious thought, her hand flew to Sawyer's arm. He felt his skin jump at the contact. If she noticed, she didn't let on, as the next words out of her mouth were, "What if I get a dragon? It would literally burn down the house."

"I'm afraid I'll burn down the house," Kira said, her words quiet as if she didn't want to voice them aloud.

Sawyer thought to reassure her, but before he could, Gabe groaned. "I hadn't thought of that. I'd only assumed I wouldn't be able to work my wand. Maybe locked in my room by myself isn't such a good idea."

"Especially if your familiar can't even fit in your room." Ella's voice had rose a bit in her panic.

"What are you saying, out in an open field?" Mari's already pale skin seemed to be almost translucent.

"I am *not* doing that. I can tell you all right now."

As a whole, the group turned. The girl who had said that touched a hand to her hair liberally streaked with strands of dark and pale blue piled high atop her head. Again, she was dressed appropriately. Her pale white gown with tiny pale blue flowers set off the cocoa color of her skin. She stuck out her hand, first to Kira who she was nearer to, then to him. Automatically, Sawyer shook it.

"Carra Radnor. My father and grandfather own the furniture shop here in town. They can make anything you might happen to need. They're amazing at it. Me, I'd probably chop off my own arm instead of actually creating something. Oh, and by the way, I'm not doing that." She pointed to the center of the floor where Lucien was surrounded by even more people now.

"How about we go outside before we get crushed in here." The boy at her side said that. He was shorter than Sawyer's own height but only by a couple of inches. Then he stuck out his hand. "Landen Thomas."

Sawyer shook it with a grin.

"Come on." Gabe didn't wait for anyone; instead, he turned and headed outside. Quickly, they all followed him out into the twilight. The verandah was deserted. It seemed everyone else was inside, offering the birthday boy congratulations.

Once they were well away from the door leading to the ballroom, Sawyer turned and found more people than he had originally thought had followed them outside. Apparently, this must have been the group of people who had wanted to meet them earlier.

Noticing his gaze, Ella said, "Sawyer, Kira, I would like to introduce you to Chinira Hedley." She indicated a petite redhead with a pixie cut. "Almira Rowley." She gestured to the girl they had pointed out earlier whose father was a werewolf. "This is Dante Alverz."

A boy with a head full of short black curls said, "Hello."

"And this," she said with a gesture to a tall boy with dark auburn curly hair and a face full of freckles, "is Devlin McManuse." She paused for just a moment then said, "Everyone, this is Kira and Sawyer Randal." And then to break the ice further plus share information with them that they didn't have, she added, "the next to get their powers."

And just like that, Ella had told them useful information without revealing it as if she was trying to teach them something. She was different than he had expected. After meeting her father, he thought she'd be overbearing and slightly pushy. But she wasn't any of those things. She was the type of person his sister would readily become friends with and the kind he'd want to date.

He froze. He'd been thinking way too much about dating her. This wouldn't do, not in the very least. He had to get his mind on something else, and quickly.

He blurted out the first thought he had. "What type of familiars do your parents have?"

Everyone, even his own sister, looked to him at the abruptness of that comment. He shifted uneasily. "Well, I know that Ella and Gabe's have dogs. Is that like a normal thing? Are most familiars some sort of dog? Or wolf?" He added that thinking of Lucien.

To their credit, no one acted as if this was something he should already know.

"Both my parents have dogs," Dante said. "My mom's is a Chihuahua. Cripes, she is *never* quiet. Mom says she's talking to her. I think she just likes to be annoying."

"Cripes?" Kira asked. "Is that her name?"

Not a single person laughed, though a few looked confused for a moment. Then apparently understanding dawned as Dante explained. "No, cripes is a swear word in the Magical world. That and frinx are probably what you never want your folks to hear you say. And well, depending on the parent, you might want to add Hades in there, too."

It was then, with the ready explanation that didn't make them seem as if they were stupid for not knowing, Sawyer decided he was going to go on and like them all. They seemed like good people. And even if he was friends with them before, but no longer remembered them, he realized that he wouldn't mind getting to know them now. He'd just have to be careful about it.

"Oh, okay, thanks." A faint red stained Kira's cheeks.

To spare Kira any further embarrassment, Landen steered the conversation back to the previous topic. "My mom's familiar is a coyote, and my dad's is a cheetah."

Sawyer thought his eyes were going to bug from his head. Surely, he hadn't heard that right. "A cheetah? Like an actual cheetah? One of those cats that is super-fast?" He'd thought a dragon was all he had to worry about, but apparently not.

"Yeah," Landen said. "And let me tell you, he has an attitude. I accidently stepped on his tail once. It's kind of hard not to as he likes to flop down in the floor right in front of you as you're walking. He's annoying that way. Anyway, I stepped on his tail, and I just knew. I took off.

He chased me, just to knock me down. Then he walked off as calm as you please."

"You weren't terrified?" Kira asked.

Sawyer wondered the same thing. If some cheetah decided he was their next toy, he'd be scared out of his wits. Right then and there, even if they became good friends or not, he decided there was no way he was ever visiting Landen's home.

"I was at first." Landen assured them. "But the thing about a familiar is that it's incredibly loyal. Sure they'd fight back to defend themselves or their person, but they are also loyal to the entire family. So while Yafeu, that's his name, is all big and intimidating, he wouldn't hurt me."

Well that was a bit more reassuring, especially if in a few days' time a dragon showed up on his doorstep.

"My parents both have cats," Carra offered. "Just normal cats. When they started venturing into the Non-Magical world and brought back books, we checked out a few from the library. One was all about pet breeds. My mom's is what they call a British shorthair and my dad's is a Siberian. They tolerate each other at best. The cats, not my mom and dad," she added quickly.

Sawyer couldn't help but grin at her.

"My dad was a bit disappointed when he first saw his animal," Chinira said. "It's an Arctic Hare, named Alby. But now, they are inseparable. Alby has a fit when my dad goes somewhere he can't, like Council meetings. It's cute but ridiculous. My mom has a Boston terrier named Button. Sweetest little dog you will ever meet."

"My mum," said Devlin, "has a dog termed a Scottish terrier. My da, he has a cat. It's a Scottish Fold. Funny thing. It's like he has na ears." He paused for a moment then grinned at them both. "I'm Scottish if ye couldn't tell. We moved here after I was born."

Sawyer hadn't even considered something like that. It seemed so *normal*. He didn't picture that happening in this world, but it had to. The boy had a very thick Scottish brogue. Sawyer had a feeling he was slowing down his speech for them. He figured once the boy got going it would be hard to keep up with what he was saying.

"My dad," Mari offered, "has a cat. It's a Bengal named Zora. She thinks she's this huge, tough animal."

"She's chased Yafeu before." Landen chuckled. "It was funny."

When Mari didn't say anything more, it was on the tip of Sawyer's tongue to ask about her mother. But he bit it back. He didn't know if that was something the seven-year-old him knew or not.

"My dad doesn't have an animal. He's not a wizard. He's actually..." Almira glanced out to the empty pathways below their position that led to the gardens. "He's a werewolf." Quickly, her gaze darted back to them to see how they had taken this revelation.

Sawyer still didn't know how he felt about this. A werewolf? All he knew of them was what he'd seen in horror movies. All that was replaying in his head was that chilling scene in *American Werewolf in London* in the subway—or tube station. He'd been in sixth grade when he'd watched it at a friend's house. There'd been a group of boys, and they'd decided to watch one of those movies their parents had told them not to. That scene was the one that had kept Sawyer up the entire night and given him many sleepless nights after.

He felt the hair stand up on the back of his neck. He felt as if he was being watched from somewhere in the dark grounds below. He had to fight against the urge to turn around and look to make sure nothing was there.

This wasn't the movies, but apparently, werewolves were very real and alive. And he'd be lying if he said that thought didn't terrify him. Too much about this strange world freaked him out. He hoped his familiar was a dragon. He wanted something to protect him.

As soon as that thought came, he cursed at himself. He was an idiot. He hadn't acted like a scared baby when he'd been living in an abusive foster home, so he wasn't going to start now. He could handle this, just as he'd always handled everything else.

Yet, he didn't know what the correct response to that statement should be. He didn't think he should tell her that he was happy for her. That made no sense. Instead, he remained silent, as did Kira.

Apparently, Almira took their quietness as acceptance as she continued. "My mom has a cat. It's a sand cat, named Bahira. That means sparkle."

"What's a sand cat?" Kira asked.

At Almira's smile, Sawyer realized she was happy that was the only question they had posed to her.

"We didn't know that's what she was called until my father read up about her in those Non-Magical books. She's a tiny little thing, but she thinks she's the boss of our house. Actually, she probably is. She came to my mom when she got her powers, but she loves my dad, too. She typically goes to work with him."

"Almira's dad owns the *Familiar Realm,* the best shop in town to get anything you happen to need for your animal, no matter what type you have," Gabe said.

Almira blushed at the praise. "He loves animals." She shrugged her shoulders. "He was so excited to get his familiar on his birthday. But he was bit by a werewolf a few days before. He always hated that he went out exploring." She looked at both Sawyer and Kira in turn. "You see, if a witch or wizard gets bit by a werewolf, they lose their magical powers. My dad still got his mark on his seventeenth birthday, but that was it."

And now Sawyer felt sorry for the man. He wondered if he had known this all before. They'd only been seven, and it seemed a little deep and complicated for them to understand. But he wondered if his biological parents had been friends with the Rowleys? Had they known all of this?

"Did this happen around here?" Sawyer found himself asking.

She shook her head. "No, we're originally from Egypt. We moved to Willow Oak when I was three." She looked as if she wanted to say something further, but instead, she snapped her mouth shut.

Sawyer leaned back against the verandah railing. It was a lot to take in all at once. He felt as if he was almost on overload. They all fell silent.

Inside, he could hear the music still hadn't started back.

Suddenly, from the open doorway of the ballroom, a dull thump of what sounded like a gong could be heard.

At his side, Devlin groaned.

Sawyer glanced to his sister, his raised brow asking the question he knew she didn't have an answer for; it was Dante that explained. "That means it's time for dinner."

He was a bit hungry, so he didn't know why the rest of them acted as if they were going to be marching to their deaths.

"You haven't seen anything until you've had a Norwood dinner." Landen shivered at the thought.

Sawyer felt his apprehension kick up another notch.

Kira was suddenly at his side. "I don't know about this."

Ella tried for a boisterous smile. "It will be fine."

Over her head, Gabe shook his in disagreement. Then the blond expelled a deep breath. "Just stick with us and you'll be fine."

"Really, you will." Ella threaded her hand through Sawyer and his sister's arms in what was to be a comforting gesture. And it would have been if he hadn't felt the slight shiver pass through her.

With impending dread, Sawyer slowly fell in step with the rest of the group. He didn't know how dinner could change the mood of everyone so quickly, but it had. It made him afraid of what they were going to find.

V. A. Risby

16

She'd never thought of herself as pushy or even a take-charge type person, so for the life of her, Ella Hopewell couldn't figure out why she was doing it now.

No, that wasn't true. After ten years, even before they knew Kira and Sawyer were still alive, she'd always still thought of Kira as her best friend. Call it being young and naïve, but she'd always had faith that they would find her again. She'd thought of her as a sister. She'd missed her. And she knew she couldn't just snap her fingers and make them best friends again, but she did want to get to know this new person.

When they were young, they had been together almost every day. They played together, looked out for each other, protected each other from the torment of Sawyer and Gabe, and from the viciousness that was Flora and her group of friends.

It pained Ella to admit that when she had first seen Kira in the hallway at school, walking with Flora, she'd felt a pang of jealousy. But she wouldn't say anything. She was a virtual stranger to her once best friend, and to that end, she knew she couldn't say anything to cloud her judgement. She had to leave it up to Kira to make her own decisions about the other people in their class, in the town.

Ella had immediately gone to her when Kira had fallen in the hallway that first day. She had to; it was as if some unseen force had compelled her to her side. And for it to be with Lucien Norwood, too.

Lucien had never gotten along with Sawyer and Gabe. They'd always been pitted against each other in school. And as antagonistic as Lucien had seemed to Sawyer in the dining hall the other day, it didn't seem that Lucien cared if Sawyer could remember their past or not. He was apparently still holding the same grudge.

But none of that mattered. The only thing Ella wanted was to get to know her friend again, to see if they could actually become the best friends she had envisioned in her head that they'd always be. She knew she couldn't push; that things had to progress naturally. However, she couldn't help herself for looking out for both of them.

They hadn't said anything at all to each other. It had been natural when she had approached Kira and it seemed to have been the same for Gabe with Sawyer.

Everyone else had just stayed back. But what Kira and Sawyer didn't remember was how close they had all been.

Their parents had been suspicious of anyone who tried to have their children befriend theirs if they hadn't known them before their birth. Too much was riding on Kira and Sawyer's young shoulders with the prophecy, and then to have to deal with those that thought power might come to them by association. Their parents had tried to shield them.

It had been a lot for young children to understand. And for that reason, Ella had always felt as if she was sort of Kira's protector. She knew her best friend was important. She didn't know how exactly, but she knew something was going to happen and her friend was going to be right in the middle of it. And even at a young age, Ella knew it was her job to have Kira's back. No one had told her that; it hadn't even been insinuated. She just knew.

And all of those old protective instincts were jumping to the foreground again. She was having a hard time keeping them in check.

She glanced up to her left. And then there was Sawyer. She'd never been particularly close to him. Sure, she thought of him as her own brother as they were always around each other. But, being children, they'd been more intent on tormenting each other. It had been fun, and she'd enjoyed their childhood.

But whereas her mind held fast to the idea that Kira was still her best friend, Sawyer was a completely different matter. He was like a stranger, so completely different from the small boy she remembered. Tall and muscular, Ella wondered if he had left a girlfriend behind in his old life.

A blush stole up her cheeks, and she tried to shake off the thought. She had no business thinking of him that way. He was dealing with too many changes in his life to worry about her fawning all over him. It was Sawyer, the boy who had teased her and pulled her hair. She needed to keep that firmly in mind.

Focus.

Her mind screamed that to herself. For as long as she could remember, whenever she had to be in the presence of the Norwoods, she'd always felt it best to be on her guard. Just because they were in a crowd of people, she didn't want to change that now.

Gabe was in the lead. His back was rigid and tense as if he was walking them all to their deaths. Landen was at his side. Sawyer and Kira kept glancing at the two boys, to Ella, then to the rest of the group behind them, trying to piece together what had everyone so nervous. Ella didn't even want to think about it. She knew she should try to prepare them, but Ella couldn't even put into words what everyone's concerns were. It was too horrible to even think about.

They moved through the ballroom and out a set of glass doors. Inside was a room, larger than the immense ballroom they had just passed through. A few round tables were out, guests sitting in the chairs. Gabe moved them to join the line, and that's when Kira nearly stumbled, and Sawyer froze. If Ella hadn't had a hold of them, she was worried one or both of them might have bolted.

Up at the head of the line was a nearly translucent man. What the twins had just noticed was that his feet were hovering above the floor as he floated.

"What?" came the stuttered question from them both.

Ella tried for a reassuring smile. "Since this is the Lord Mayor's estate...well, see back when Willow Oak was founded, and the position of Lord Mayor came to be, the Mayor needed a staff. Those witches and wizards were very devoted. You see while everyone who is a witch or a wizard has magic, some people can't control it, or are not very good at it. Their power turns weak, almost nonexistent. These are the people who were in the servant class."

They both looked horrified.

"Is there still a servant class?" Sawyer asked.

"No, with more progress there are other occupations for those people, as there are people who aren't very good at magic or have little to no magic at all."

"I didn't know that could happen," Kira said, more to herself though they could still hear her. "I just assumed that there wouldn't be an issue with getting these powers." Her eyes widened. "You mean that they had this party in front of everyone, and yet Lucien might not have had any magical ability at all?"

"Yes," Chinira said from behind them, "but it would have been rare. Things like that typically occur in a family."

"It isn't so bad now if it happens. There are so many more options for employment," Mari added. "My family runs a market here in town. One of our clerks really can't do magic, but it's because of a trauma."

Ella sent her a quelling look. The last thing she wanted was for either Kira or Sawyer to think they might not be able to have their magical powers because of what had happened in their past. Mari must have thought the same thing as she blanched then tried to turn it into a smile, which came out rather like a grimace.

"Anyway." Ella rushed to continue. "Back to what I was saying. These people in the servant class took their devotion to the Ivywood Estate to the extreme. When they died, they didn't completely move on. Their ghosts remained here, performing their same duties as if nothing had happened. I don't know if they even realize they aren't among the living any longer."

"He's a...he's a real ghost?" Kira looked from the translucent man and back to them all, her silver eyes wide.

"It's okay," Gabe said. He and Landen had turned back to the group as they waited in the line. Automatically, his hand reached out and took Kira's free one. He gave it a reassuring squeeze. "It's all right. The only thing to know is that they still take their job seriously. They are very stiff and formal."

"Wait. There's more than one?" This came from Sawyer.

Since Gabe had hold of her best friend, Ella relinquished her grip on her, so she could turn to the boy on her left. "Yes, you will find that the wait staff tonight is made up entirely of ghosts."

The tan Sawyer had from sun exposure seemed to pale. He breathed out a sigh and then seemed to draw himself up. He nodded in acceptance.

He'd always been the brave one; it was comforting to Ella to know that some things hadn't changed.

There were only two other groups in front of them now.

"All right," Gabe said, his grin now firmly back in place, trying to bring the levity back to the group. "Get ready."

17

All Kira wanted to do was dig her feet in and not move another step forward. No, that wasn't true. What she really wanted was to flee, to escape this house of horrors. She wanted to run and keep running until she was back in her old home in Chicago. That's what she wanted.

Instead, in a few more steps, she was going to be standing right beside a ghost.

A ghost!

Frantically, she looked around, trying to spy her parents. She found them with the Hopewells and the Meyers, along with the woman that had been identified as Almira's mother. There were other couples sitting at the same table. Her parents looked wide-eyed and astonished, but not scared. They appeared to be taking it all in.

It calmed her a bit, gave her a piece of her sanity back. Well, that was until her gaze darted to the translucent figure that was now nearer to her. He appeared older—could a ghost even have an age? He was dressed in what she assumed were formal clothes. He had a tie and a jacket. It was just very hard to focus when she could see right through him.

She didn't want to look any longer. She wanted to scream and run. Subconsciously, her hand tightened around Gabe's. She hadn't released him when he'd first offered his reassurance, and now she had his hand in a near death grip.

Death?

Oh no.

Deep breath. She fought for some small measure of composure. She told herself to relax her hold and let him go. She still didn't know what to think of all these people. He and Ella had probably been right. It would have been overwhelming to have their forgotten friends introduce themselves at once. What she'd seen so far, she found she genuinely liked them.

However, she didn't know Gabe well enough to cut off the circulation to his hand. She told herself to relax her grip and let him go. To her horror, she found it tightened even more.

To give him credit, he didn't even flinch. Then, suddenly, she was moving. She was taken so by surprise, she lost her grip. Before she could recover, he had her other hand firmly in his own, and to her amazement, she found she was now on his left, which put him between her and the ghost.

She almost sank to the floor in relief.

"How many, sir?" came the gravelly voice of the ghost.

The voice startled her. She hadn't expected him to speak. She cast a glance over her shoulder to find Sawyer watching in stunned curiosity.

"Eleven please."

As soon as the words were out of Gabe's mouth a table came flying from a far corner of the room, the white tablecloth draped over it, flapping as it zoomed into its position. Eleven high-backed dining chairs followed.

With a reassuring grin, he gently pulled her in the direction of the table. She had no choice but to follow, her eyes wide as she took everything in. More ghosts were gliding soundlessly through the room, carrying overburdened trays as tables and chairs sailed over seated guests.

The dining room mirrored the ballroom as it was all in white with gold etching, complete with large, sparkling chandeliers.

As they approached the table, she debated on where she should sit. She wanted her back to a wall. She felt as if too much was converging on her all at once. She didn't want to have to deal with the thought that someone, or *something*, was sneaking up behind her.

Thankfully, Gabe led her in that direction. Before she could reach for a chair to pull it out, it slid back on its own.

"It's not a ghost chair, is it?" The question came out in a whisper, so that only the blond heard.

"No, it's just charmed." He gave her a reassuring grin.

Sucking in a deep breath, she straightened her spine. She felt as if she was going to her execution. Gingerly, she eased herself down in the chair. She'd no sooner gotten situated then it pushed up to the table.

She froze, afraid to move again in case it decided to do something else. When nothing more happened, she dared to dart a glance around the table. Everyone else was settling into seats. Gabe was on her left, with Sawyer to her right. Everyone who had been out on the verandah had been seated together. She realized then that's what Gabe's eleven meant. He had given their number as if being seated in a restaurant.

Quickly, she glanced around the large room. She realized that there was no set number of seats at a table. For that matter, the tables were of varying sizes, though all were round. In the very center of the room sat the Mayor and his wife. At their table were four other couples. One, Kira noticed, included the headmaster from the school.

Lucien was at the table next to them along with thirteen other people that all looked to be about the same age. Right beside him was the girl from yesterday. She must be the Regina he had mistaken her for earlier. He had ignored her remark to get her. And he never brought her up again, but she had to be his girlfriend. She was always at his side.

Belatedly, Kira realized that most of the occupants at that table were looking in their direction. She started to glance away—she didn't want to be caught staring—and then Lucien caught her attention. He winked.

She could feel the blush steal up her cheeks. Hastily, her gaze shot away and landed on Ella. The lift of a brown brow told Kira the other girl had seen the exchange. But Kira wouldn't talk to her about it. How could she?

So far, all these people did seem nice. If things were different, if they had just started a normal school in a new town, she could see herself being friends with them. But this wasn't normal, nothing about it was. So that left her trusting no one but her family.

Her gaze darted over to where her mother and father sat. They still seemed a bit shell-shocked, but at the same time, they seemed to be taking all of this in their stride. Perhaps they were in shock.

Either way in a few days' time, she and Sawyer were going to be completely different from them. They weren't going to be able to understand what they were going through. That left her with Sawyer.

Man, she really missed her old friends. She couldn't pick up a phone and chat with them. She couldn't even send a text. She'd tried her phone the other day after getting home from the Hopewells. She'd had no service, which was understandable since she was living in some sort of bizarre nightmare.

"Drinks?" a soft, monotone voice asked.

Kira's gaze darted immediately in the direction, and she jumped. Her hand found Gabe's.

She hadn't heard the person—No, not a person, ghost—approach. It was a woman this time. She appeared younger than the man did, but she had fine lines along her forehead and the corners of her mouth. Her hair was neatly kept back under a linen bonnet. Her long dress was in pristine condition.

As her gaze went to her brother, Kira couldn't help but notice the table across where Lucien sat. The dark-haired girl at his side was laughing along with Flora who was at her right. They were looking in Kira's direction. She knew they were making fun of her. She felt the red heat creeping up her face again. Lucien's attention was also on their table, but his countenance was stony.

Kira pushed the group from her mind and turned to her brother, her hand still gripping tightly to Gabe's where they rested on the table. Sawyer's focus was on the female ghost, and Kira felt her own gaze go to her again. It hit her then, what was bothering her.

"That poor woman is dead." The words slipped out in a whisper.

Her brother heard her though. "I know. I just keep thinking she's stuck here, serving people. Is it forever? Is there no way out?"

"I can't imagine. Surely, there's something someone can do."

"A ghost will move on when it's ready." Gabe leaned closer to them to say that. "There's not as many here as there used to be. When they find peace, that's when they go. Or at least they can on All Hallows' Eve. That's the time when spirits can leave this realm."

She felt the prick of tears at the back of her eyes. "That's so horrible."

"It is." He agreed. "We keep thinking if they feel they've done a really good job perhaps that will be what they need."

Kira's gaze darted up to the ghost figure again. "She looks so sad. She's not happy. It's almost as if she's being forced to do this."

"I guess she is."

Her gaze cut to her brother at that comment.

He continued. "I mean if it's because they were so dutiful to their role as servant, I suppose that duty is still keeping them chained here." He sat up straighter, seeming to think of something. "Can they leave this estate?"

"No, a ghost is tethered to the place where they died. The ghosts that are here cannot leave the grounds." Gabe explained.

Kira quickly surveyed the room. There were over twenty of the translucent figures hovering around the dining room. She met her brother's gaze and knew he was thinking the same thing. That was an awful lot of people to have died on these grounds to just be of normal circumstances.

And then the most horrific thought hit her. She couldn't breathe, and her grip on Gabe tightened enough for him to look to her. Her voice was barely above a whisper when she spoke. "Our parents...are they..." She couldn't bring herself to finish as the sting of tears gathered in her eyes.

His features soften, and he leaned closer to her. "No, your parents aren't ghosts. They moved on."

She gave him a watery smile. She didn't know if she was happy or sad about that. She didn't want them stuck, but she wanted to see them, to know what they looked like since she couldn't remember.

He switched hands with her. His left now held hers firmly, while his right arm went around her shoulders to give her a half hug. It felt comforting; it felt right, like something he had done before.

"Drinks?" The question came again.

"I don't suppose you have a *Dr. Pepper,* do you?" Sawyer asked with an uneasy laugh, still affected by what his sister had asked.

The ghost stared at him unblinking.

"I guess not," he said more to himself than anyone else.

"Three Dragon Breaths," Gabe said.

The ghost glided off.

Kira glanced around the table; she needed to think of something else. "Did the rest of you order?"

"Yeah," Almira said, "I ordered a Mint Bubble." At their quizzical look, she explained. "It has a minty, creamy flavor. I like it because of the bubbles, though. They continuously blow and pop until it's all gone."

That sounded bizarre.

No further explanations were forth coming as their ghost server glided back to their table with an overloaded tray. Each drink was set down in a precise, orderly manner. The drink she set before Kira was in a glass that looked like it came from the pint set her mother had given their father for Christmas a few years back. The liquid inside was a dark, vibrant blue with a white foaming froth on top. But what was alarming was the smoke coming up from the glass. It rolled like a Halloween prop of dry ice at a party.

A quick glance around the table showed that she, Sawyer, Gabe, Carra, Dante, and Landen had the same drinks. Chinira and Almira's Mint Bubbles were in the same type of glass. The liquid was a pale green with a frothy top from which a continuous explosion of tiny bubbles kept popping. Devlin's beverage was in a clear tankard. His drink was clear, too, but little burst of what appeared to be a lightning storm kept going off inside it.

He noticed her attention as he said, "It's a Lightning Bolt. Tastes lemony, but no too much. What I like is if ye take a drink when one of the bolts goes, it sends a wee jolt of heat in it."

Kira nodded as if she understood when in fact she was doing everything possible to keep her head above water. It was all so strange.

Mari and Ella's beverages were in the same tankard as Devlin's. But while his was clear, theirs was a pale orange. Again, a frothy top, but it was continuously moving. As Kira looked at it closer, it seemed as if it was waves on an ocean, rolling into the shoreline.

"It's a Mango Monsoon. It has a light mango and cream taste. With the continuous rolling, it makes it fizzy," Ella explained.

Kira and Sawyer both nodded. They didn't know what to say to anything really that had been set on the table.

But she shook it off to stare at the concoction sitting in front of her. She started to look to Gabe for an explanation, but she was stopped by Sawyer.

"What is he doing?"

Her brother sounded genuinely perplexed. Kira looked in the direction he was staring and saw Lucien at his table. In his hand was a glass like theirs. Even from across the room, she could see the ruby red color of the liquid and the flames. It would have been hard to miss the fire coming from the top of his glass. He was pointing his glass in their direction like in a toast.

"Show off," Gabe muttered under his breath at her side.

"What's that drink?" Sawyer asked as he watched the dark headed boy take a sip. Then with one last look to them, Lucien turned back to his dining companions.

"That's a Dragon Blood." Landen explained. "Once a witch or wizard receives their powers, they are of age, which means they can drink the stronger spirits."

For a horrifying moment, Kira thought of the ghosts in reference to spirits, but then calm realization dawned. Apparently, seventeen was the legal drinking age in the Magical world. Since she was no longer worried that people might be drinking the souls of poor, unfortunate people, she turned back to her own beverage.

"And what's this? It's a Dragon Breath, right?"

"Right," Gabe said. "It steams like the fire of a dragon's breath, but the drink is always cold, no matter if you leave it setting for a long while."

She didn't know what else to do but nod. She glanced to Sawyer, and with a shrug of his shoulders, he picked up the glass and hesitantly, took a sip.

His eyes widened. "That's actually really good. It tastes like a cream soda with a hint of blueberry and something else."

Kira raised her own glass.

"What's cream soda?" Ella asked as she sipped her own beverage.

As Kira listened to her brother explain sodas to the table, she took a drink of her own. He'd been right. It did taste similar to cream soda, but with a hint of blueberries and…hibiscus. It went really well together. But what made it perfect was the ice-cold temperature of the drink. Finally, a part of this crazy world she could get completely behind.

"Roasted beets and onion sandwich," the monotone voice said from her side.

She almost dropped her glass, but thankfully managed to save it as the ghost set down a small, china plate before her. With quick efficiency, every member of the table had an identical plate. On it set two delicate looking little sandwiches cut into precise rectangles.

Once the ghost had floated off again Sawyer looked to her. "Beets and onion? Sounds like your kind of thing." He looked to Kira.

"It will be a seven-course dinner tonight," Dante told them.

"Seven courses of this?" Sawyer's tone told adequately enough that he didn't want to be here that long.

"Each course is different," Carra said. "It usually goes in a certain order, a cold hors d'oeuvre, a soup, a hot hors d'oeuvre, then typically a pasta or a salad, first main course, second main course, and then dessert."

"That's a lot of food."

Kira looked up and noticed that Almira's hand was white as it gripped her fork. "Are you alright?"

The other girl glanced up, startled. She nodded but looked as if she might be ill.

Ella leaned forward to whisper around Sawyer. "It's the reason none of us wanted to come in for dinner. You never know what you're going to be served. At the last party, the main dishes were centaur loin and flank of a...of a werewolf."

Kira felt her own stomach drop. She was going to be sick. "But a werewolf...isn't a werewolf a person most of the time, right?"

"And a centaur is one of those half human half horse things?" Sawyer asked.

Ella nodded. "Ghosts are the cooks here. Some have been here for hundreds upon hundreds of years, back in a time when werewolves and centaurs were looked down upon as less than. They were viewed as mindless, mad creatures."

"Thankfully, I wasn't in attendance," Almira said, her voice barely above a whisper. She darted a glance over her shoulder at the table where Lucien and his friends sat. "But some of them made sure to let me know all about it." She glanced down at her plate. In her lap, her hands twisted her napkin. "I'm scared of what they'll bring out."

"It will be alright." Chinira put her arm around the other girl's shoulders.

"But the ghosts don't like it if you don't eat what they give you." Almira's voice was so low Kira could barely hear her.

"What do they do?" Sawyer asked.

"They shriek," Landen said. "And it's not some little noise. It's a flat out wail and it just goes on and on and on."

Gabe's words were bitter. "Which, of course, doesn't make the illustrious *Lord* Mayor happy. The last person who interrupted one of his dinner parties that way..."

"He lost his shop in town," Devlin added. "An then he was gone." He shrugged his broad shoulders.

Kira stared down at the beets and onion sandwich, seeming to wait for it to attack her. The table fell into a tense silence after that, wondering what the next dish would bring. Once finished, that plate was removed, and a cup of peas and mushroom bisque was placed before them. So far, the two dishes were fine, if a little odd in their pairings. But they tasted all right; the bisque was actually quite tasty without a hint of seafood.

She was just starting to think they'd make it through the dinner unscathed when the ghost set down the third course.

"Pickled cucumber and lemon tuna."

Kira blanched at the fish in front of her. The words came out automatically. "I don't eat meat."

The ghost stared at her, unblinking. Then she opened her mouth.

"She's kidding," Gabe rushed out. "She likes to joke. She loves fish."

Immediately, Kira realized her mistake. There was no way she was putting that in her mouth, but with that ghost standing there, mouth frozen in a scream, she quickly agreed. "Yes, I love fish." And she did. She just liked hers out in the water, alive and swimming.

It was as if the entire table was holding their breaths as the ghost continued to stare at them. Then, finally, she resumed setting down the last two plates and then glided away.

Kira slumped down in her chair with a relieved sigh.

"You don't eat fish?" Dante asked, right before he took a bite of his.

Shaking her head, Kira said, "No, I'm a vegetarian. I don't eat any meat." She added that in case they didn't know the word. "I have been since I was twelve."

"She won't like it if she comes back and it hasn't been touched." Mari took a tiny bite of her own tuna.

"I'll eat it," Gabe offered. "Anything to keep her from screeching." He ate half of his, and then quickly switched their plates, taking Kira's.

It was such a ridiculously goofy and thoughtful thing to do that Kira couldn't help but smile warmly at him, which he returned. Perhaps these people weren't the monsters she was worried about them being. Perhaps they were truly who they said they were. "Thank you."

He actually blushed a bit as red stole up his face. "It's just tuna." He tried to play it off, but his own grin was equally pleased.

Beside her, Sawyer cleared his throat and shook his head, a knowing smirk tugging up his lips. She kicked her brother under the table.

The next course of parsnip and pear linguine was another odd flavor choice. In fact, it made her feel a bit nauseous with the sweetness of the pear. But when the ghost set down the first main course of dried apricots and honey bear flank, it was then that she thought she might actually disgrace herself by throwing up on the table.

"Oh, poor Cian," Carra murmured with a glance at table that was two over from them.

Kira had to think of something other than the fact that there was a piece of a poor bear setting on a plate in front of her. "Who's Cian?"

"He's over there," Devlin said, indicating the table where a very tan, muscular boy sat with a group of apparently his friends. Every single person at the table was staring at their plates in something akin to shock and horror.

The only thing Kira could think of was that they all must really like bears.

"He's a fifth year. His familiar is a sun bear," Almira said, staring down at her own plate. "Sun bears are also called honey bears."

At her side, Sawyer set his fork down. "Do we seriously have to eat everything on this plate, because I'm not touching this?"

"No," Ella said, looking at her own food as if it might attack her.

"I only ate half of that tuna," Gabe said. He took his fork; then taking a deep breath, he cut into the meat. But he didn't raise his fork to his mouth. Instead, he moved the food around enough on his plate that it appeared as if he had eaten some. Without a word, he once again switched his plate with Kira's and repeated the process.

Taking their cue from him, the rest of the table did the same, not a single person took a bite. When the ghost removed those plates, she didn't screech or howl. Apparently, they were safe; only two more courses to go.

Kira darted a glanced over to the other table. The boy Cian looked extremely pale, but his face was set in a grim line of determination as the ghost that served his table took away his plate.

"Pan-fried garlic and lime griffin leg."

Kira gagged. She could feel the bile burn the back of her throat as she tried to force it down. Thankfully, the ghost didn't notice as Ella, Almira, and Mari were having their own difficulties. With that many people gagging, she ignored them to continue placing plates.

"Isn't a griffin one of those half horse, half eagle things?" Sawyer had paled drastically as he stared down at the beautifully arranged plate before him.

"And there's not too many left." Landen looked down at his plate in disgust. "I cannot believe they would serve this."

"I can't wait to get out of this place." Sawyer glared over at the table where Lucien sat. The birthday boy was laughing with his friends, seemingly having a grand time. "I don't care what he invites me to. I don't care if it's mandatory in this insane place; I'm not coming here again. Ever. And I want him and his entire freaking family to stay as far away from mine as possible."

The entire table was silent for a long moment, and then Gabe laughed. He sounded almost relieved. It took only a moment then Landen, Dante, and Devlin joined in. The other girls smiled, even Almira who was still alarmingly pale.

Kira didn't know what to make of this. Apparently, neither did her brother as his expression darkened.

"What?" The question came out as a near growl.

"We didn't want to say anything." Gabe managed to get that out around a chuckle.

It did nothing to help her brother's disposition. "Now would be a good time to say it."

"It has to do with when you were here before, the parts that you and Kira don't remember. We don't want to force that on you." Ella tried to explain.

"You've got a minute to tell me what it is, or I'm leaving here, and that ghost can scream her head off. I won't care."

Gabe's laughter died down, but he continued to grin. It was as if he was seeing Sawyer for the first time. "We didn't want to say anything as we wanted you to form your own opinions, but before, when you were here, you hated Lucien Norwood. You two didn't get along."

"Not at all," Dante added.

If anything, Sawyer looked relieved. "I imagine he was the same prick as he seems to be now, probably just a younger version."

"Most definitely," Gabe agreed.

Then the two boys looked at each other. Kira could see, the moment her brother let his guard down just a bit. She was happy for him. Gabe seemed nice, and apparently, they had been best friends before. It was good, and maybe, having that friendship back, perhaps, Sawyer would start to remember something from their past. One of them needed to.

As soon as she thought that, Kira's gaze darted over to Lucien's table. He was only halfway paying attention to what was going on with his own group. He was keeping an eye on them, too. With Sawyer's declaration, Kira felt it, as if a line in the sand had been drawn. If she mentioned anything to her brother about what had happened with Lucien earlier or if she told him she'd confided in Lucien about the lamp, Sawyer would never let her hear the end of it.

Her brother was as stubborn as they came, and now that he'd made up his mind about Lucien, there would be no changing it, not without some monumental action or discovery.

Gabe reaching for her plate pulled Kira's attention away from the ice blue gaze she only just realized was focused on her. Lucien was glaring at them, or more specifically in Gabe's direction.

She didn't know what had ever transpired between the boys that they seemed to hate each other so much, but she didn't want to be stuck in the middle of them. And honestly, she didn't know if she even wanted to be marginally friendly to someone who ate werewolves and bears or thought that was appropriate dinner food.

No, the best thing she could do was pretend she'd never had a conversation with Lucien Norwood. While she'd thought he might be a misunderstood boy, making the best of living with a tyrannical father, that wasn't enough for her to be dragged in the middle between him and her brother. Sawyer was the one person here—besides her parents—that she could trust completely. No matter how vulnerable Lucien seemed, it could all be an act.

And what was I supposed to do, Father? Show up on their doorstep and beg for their friendship?"

Unbidden the words she had overheard came back to her. The Mayor and his son were up to something. She didn't know what she and Sawyer had that would make the Mayor want his son to get close to them.

A set of two will be born, each with a power never known before. Their birth can mark the end to the hidden lives of cowards.

Was that it? Did it have something to do with their powers? With magic?

Her frantic silver gaze darted toward the table where the Mayor and his wife sat. To her horror, she found his coolly assessing gaze staring right back at her. She couldn't look away; she couldn't break the contact. It was true. He wanted something from her and Sawyer. What, she didn't know. But she knew whatever it was she couldn't give it to him. A cold shiver of fear ran down to the base of her spine. The man was dangerous. Instinctively, she knew that.

The ghost appearing to remove her plate finally forced her to break the gaze. She refused to look in his direction again. But she didn't have to as an 'aww' from the next table drew all of their attention.

Ghosts were moving about the room, each carrying a two-tiered cake that seemed to be floating on the serving platters they held. They were a variety of pale, pastel colors. But each one seemed to be shimmering as if it really were flying.

"They're fairy cakes," Ella explained. "Typically, they float about a room at parties. Once cut, that piece won't float anymore."

"You have to watch the fairywings," Mari added. "Those cookies will totally fly off if you don't keep a hold of them. But they are so good."

"*Sugar Bliss* the confectionery in town makes the absolute best ones." Chinira's eyes closed at the thought.

"I like their frozen kisses," Carra added with a contented sigh.

Suddenly, Almira sat forward as large slices of cake were set before them. "Tomorrow's Saturday, how about we meet in town and show you around?"

She looked so eager and so hopeful that Kira couldn't bring herself to say no to the other girl. She was finally starting to get some of her color back now that the meal was nearing completion. She darted a quick glance to her brother. She caught his barely perceptible nod.

She had his agreement. "Sure, that would be great." As soon as the words were out of Kira's mouth, she realized she meant it. It sounded normal, and she desperately needed that after all that she had learned tonight.

"Gabe's coming over tomorrow," Sawyer said.

Kira glanced back and forth between them, catching Gabe's nod of agreement.

"How about in the morning?" he asked the blond.

"Yeah, that would work."

"All right," Sawyer said. "Then what time do you all want to meet?"

"How about noon?" Landen offered.

"But wait. If it won't be too much, we all know where you live since it used to be your grandparents' place. How about at noon we all come over, then walk to town, and give you the tour?" Mari offered up that suggestion.

"Yeah," Kira said. "That sounds good." They smiled at their ready agreement, and Kira realized it didn't give her a sense of foreboding. In fact, for the first time, she felt as if she had something to look forward to.

But right now, all she wanted was to go home and take the time to think about everything she had seen and learned tonight. She'd taken in so much information, she hadn't even had a chance to process the fact that she now knew her brother was older than her. It had been a very interesting night to say the least.

With everyone around the table now more at ease, happily chatting and eating the cake, it was almost as if it were normal. Perhaps she was wrong about the Norwoods. Perhaps the Mayor just wasn't a nice person, which there were plenty of in the Non-Magical world. And perhaps his son was a snobby jerk, which again, her previous high school had been full of them. If that were the case, she could deal with it. It wouldn't be anything huge; it would be typical. And if that were how things truly were, then maybe, just maybe, it wouldn't be so bad living here.

V. A. Risby

18

He felt as if he wanted to come out of his skin. The tense lines of his muscles, the dull throb behind his right eye that was becoming more insistent, all of it was making Sawyer feel as if he was climbing the walls. But who knew, perhaps before the day was out, he would be able to do that.

It was vastly different from the last couple of days. After that disastrous party, the weekend had actually turned out to be enjoyable.

From Gabe, he'd found that their clothing wasn't horribly different, but the boy hadn't owned a pair of jeans—he did now. With them being the same size, he'd given him a pair, plus tee shirt of his favorite band Gabe had liked even though he didn't know who they were nor, could Sawyer play him any of their music. Gabe had worn them that day as Sawyer expected it was so that he and Kira didn't feel or look too different from the others.

After the exclamations over his, Kira's, and now Gabe's clothing, they'd all been hungry. For lunch they'd went to *The Plain Duck*, which had reminded Sawyer of one of the English pubs in Chicago. They'd actually had pretty normal food, no griffins or bears on the menu there. But they hadn't eaten a lot as they'd saved room for the bakery. The food there had been amazing. He'd been near to bursting by the time they'd left, as he'd wanted to try everything.

Sugar Bliss was run by a plump, older woman who introduced herself as Matilda Bennett. At first, he had been uncomfortable as she was near to fawning all over them. But after she'd relaxed a bit and didn't seem as nervous, he'd found she was a pleasant, cheerful woman. Once she realized they wanted to try a bite of everything, she was in her element. She'd given them sample after sample refusing to take any money in return.

The fairywings were light, airy cookies in vibrant colors. They were in a glass container by themselves, floating around, bumping into the sides of the lid. The taste reminded him of a sugar cookie, though whatever color they were, they had that flavor. Yellow had the hint of banana, green lime, and so many more. The entertainment had come when Kira had set her cookie down after taking a bite as she reached for a napkin. It took off as soon as her hand was away and shot all around the pristine shop. If anyone would have entered, they'd thought they were all insane as they were all running around, trying to corral the cookie. In the mad scramble to get it, a few others had gotten loose.

But at the same time, it had been fun. Sawyer couldn't remember a time he'd laughed so hard, and definitely not since he'd moved here.

It had only stopped when the smiling Matilda had said *Ingheta*. With a wave of her wand, the fairywings were frozen in place. It had been amazing.

After that, they had all settled down, and this time Kira kept a firm hold on her food. They talked, laughed, and gotten to know each other as they'd ate frozen kisses, which were ice cold squares of chocolate that once bitten into warmed, almost tasting like cocoa; crumblies, which were apple cookies that tasted like apple crisp but in cookie form. After a bite was taken out of them, if the person waited too long for another, they would dissolve into a pile of crumbles. The nudgefudge was amusing to watch. Pieces set next to each other would continuously knock—or nudge—the piece next to them, sometimes colliding so hard as to break bits off. His favorite was the chococanes, which tasted like a brownie but thin and in the shape of a candy cane.

They'd been so full when they'd left, and they hadn't even managed to try all the wonderfully colored candy.

They'd walked off all the sweets with a tour of the town. They'd been shown where each of their new friends lived and, in some cases, the shops their families ran. They'd met Carra's father Jabin who was working in the furniture shop. He'd been very friendly and had even asked Sawyer and Kira's opinion on some furniture he was creating from the styles in some magazines brought back from the Non-Magical World. At the market, they'd met Mari's father Berwyn, who had tried to give them all sweet treats he'd purchased earlier from *Sugar Bliss*. Being too full, they'd begged off.

Their last stop had been the *Familiar Realm*. It was the shop run by Almira's father. To put it mildly, Sawyer had been apprehensive about meeting the man; however, Nadir Rowley had been a surprise. Tall and lean, with his thick black hair falling to his shoulders, he was a quiet, unassuming man. At first, he was friendly, but very reserved, probably from facing the prejudice he had in town. Yet, after they had spoken to him for a bit, he'd started to warm up. He showed them around his shop. He sold a wide variety of products for a witch or wizard's familiar, but also for other pets, which Sawyer learned people did have in the Magical world.

At the moment, there were three cats and a dog in his shop. The cats were laying on various shelves looking bored by the interest they were garnering. The dog, a sleek black lab, would wander over to someone to be petted then go back to his previous spot on the rug before the empty fireplace. Nadir had explained those animals happened to have been previous familiars of witches and wizards who were now deceased. They had shown up on his doorstep, each in turn, and he'd taken them in.

Watching him, Sawyer had realized the man had a way with animals, almost as if he could understand them. They left the shop, only after promising to return when they received their animals, so he could meet them.

She hadn't said it, but Sawyer had noticed how relieved and happy Almira had been by the ready acceptance of her father.

Finally, they'd all returned to Sawyer and Kira's house. While Kira had taken the girls upstairs to show them the clothes they were so curious about, Sawyer had grabbed his basketball from his room and then taught the guys how to play in the front driveway.

It had been fun and seemed so normal that he'd forgotten where they now were. It was no surprise that on Sunday they had all turned up. They'd spent the day playing basketball and baseball—he'd gotten around to showing them that. His mother, who always had to feed everyone, had introduced them to chocolate chip cookies and fudge brownies in the afternoon. And at dinner that night, Gabe and Landen were ready to move in after they had homemade pizza for the first time.

It had been a perfect weekend.

But that was then.

Now, Sawyer was anxious. He should have gone to school. Gabe had said his birthday was late afternoon, but since he hadn't known an exact time, Sawyer hadn't wanted to risk it. Instead, he'd spent a restless night, tossing and turning, only to be wide awake early enough to watch the sunrise.

And then there was nothing to do but wait. He'd tried to concentrate on something else, anything, but it was no use. Kira was just as bad, pacing from room to room. Both his parents were home. For a while, everyone had sat in the living room. But with no television, no computer, no *Netflix* to distract them, it was maddening.

After an hour, Sawyer couldn't handle it anymore. He'd went back to his room, thrown himself down on his bed, and waited.

And there was still nothing.

He glanced over at the clock that hung on his wall.

It was nearing five. It could happen any time now.

"Sawyer!"

He sat up so abruptly he fell off his bed at his sister's panicked voice. Quickly, he stumbled to his feet then took the stairs two at a time. It couldn't be her first. Gabe said he was older.

When Sawyer got near the bottom, he jumped the remaining few, and then skidded to a stop when he noticed she was standing by the open front door. He glanced from his sister to his parents that were standing in the archway that led to the living room. He didn't know what was going on, nor the reason for their surprised and shocked expressions.

The clock in the living room chimed signaling it was now five.

Then it moved, crossing the threshold of the door and walking into the house as if it belonged. The it in question was a cat, a typical, normal sized everyday cat. It was gray with black and brown liberally sprinkled in its long fur. The tail swished back and forth, long and full, reminding Sawyer of the bushy tail of a squirrel.

"What is that?" the question popped out before he could stop it.

"It's a cat," his mother said.

Quickly, his marbled color gaze shot to see if she was being flippant with her obvious answer, but instead, her focus was on the cat that was now standing in the center of the foyer staring up at him with large, unblinking pale lime eyes that were streaked with brown.

"I heard a noise, so I went to the door," Kira said, watching the animal as if expecting it to do something. "It was just sitting there." She was quiet for a moment before she finally asked, "Do you think it's one of our familiars?" Then her eyes widened. "What if it's a shapeshifter?"

The cat turned and looked at her with a baleful glare.

He didn't know how he knew but he was certain that it wasn't. The cat resumed its focus on him; its large eyes watched him intently. As he stared back at it, he noticed the collar. Hesitantly, he bent down. He waited a moment, his hand out before he touched it, waiting to see if it would swipe at him.

Instead, the cat tilted its head slightly to give him better access. With a quick glance to his family, he looked at the collar. It had a small circular golden pendant on the forest green collar. With a trembling hand, he touched it, but it wouldn't open. As his fingers skimmed across the engraving, he leaned closer to read the name.

"Flower?"

The cat gave a soft, dignified mew as if telling him he was correct.

"Has to be a female with a name like that," Gary said.

Hesitantly, Sawyer's hand came out to gently pet her head. He glanced up. "I think she was someone's familiar. I wonder if it's like Almira's father said about how some have shown up at his shop and house."

"But why here? And why today?" Even though the words were said aloud, it seemed as if Kira didn't really expect an answer. Instead, she shut the door then cautiously approached the cat.

Those large, lime green eyes stared at her for a moment; then the cat turned and moved between their parents to enter the living room.

With a glance to his sister, Sawyer quickly followed after the animal. They all watched as the cat effortlessly jumped onto one of the high-backed chairs. She sat on her back hunches and surveyed the room, her gaze eerily intent.

"What are we supposed to do with her?" Diana asked that as they all watched the cat from the doorway. "She looks a little skinny. Should we feed her?"

"Feed her what, dear? I don't think they sell cat food around this place." Gary looked as perplexed as they all felt.

"Should we get Almira's father? He might know what to do." Even as she said it, Kira went to the fireplace mantel. The stamper the Hopewells had given them yesterday— along with a stack of pristine white paper and envelopes— still sat there. "We'll write him and ask him what we should do."

It was as good a plan as any. She went in search of a pen.

Carefully, Sawyer approached the cat. He still wasn't sure it wouldn't bolt and run, even though she looked perfectly content, sitting there, watching him.

The cat looked as though she knew what was going on. She also didn't appear disturbed at all by the four strangers she found herself with. It gave him an eerie feeling, as if he was in some horror movie.

"I found one," Kira said as she reentered the room. "Okay so let's see…" She sat down on the sofa in front of the coffee table and rested her paper on it. Her neat precise handwriting started appearing.

Sawyer glanced back at the cat to find it was still watching him as intently as ever. It was making him uncomfortable. He plucked at the neck of his tee shirt. His discomfort was making him warm. He started to ask if they could turn on the air conditioning when he stopped, wondering if there even was air conditioning in this world.

The heat was becoming nearly unbearable. It felt as if it was encompassing his extremities then slowly moving up his body in a rolling wave.

"Sawyer?"

He heard his mother's voice, but he couldn't answer her. Instead, his gaze shot to the cat, who was watching him unnervingly.

It was overwhelming; he felt as if he was being burnt alive from the inside. Then just as quickly, it was gone. But he could feel it, feel something that was hovering just under the surface, centering on his left arm.

"Sawyer?" Then his sister gasped, as did their mother.

"What?" His father's question died off.

Slowly, Sawyer turned. At the entrance of the living room stood a tall, lean, German Shepherd. With slow steps, truly not believing this wasn't some sort of hallucination, he approached the animal. It seemed the most natural thing in the world to crouch down before the dog. A bright, red collar with a silver pendant encircled its neck. On it was what appeared to be the image of a flame and the name emblazoned across it. He opened the charm. Inside was a silver chain with what appeared to be a tiny silver and red object shaped like a tiny wand.

He tilted the dog's pendant, so the necklace fell into his open palm. As he shut the charm on the Shepard's collar, a little flash of light came from it, fusing it into a solid. Automatically, he placed the necklace over his head. He felt it again, the flow of warmth as it settled into place. He reached out a hand and scratched the dog, which was watching him solemnly, behind the ears. She perked up then, her tail wagging up and down rapidly.

"Hey, Molly." He turned on his heel, his hand still on the dog as he faced the occupants in the room.

His family was all looking at him in varying degrees of shock and horror. Well, except for the cat. If he could describe her look, it would be satisfied. Gracefully, she hopped down from the chair and approached him. But she didn't look at him. Instead, she turned to the dog. She made a series of high and low trills, as she stood right in front of the Shepherd. Then Molly barked a series of short woofs. It was as if they were having a conversation.

"Sawyer?"

He glanced back to his family. It was his mother who had said his name. "I'm okay." He wanted to reassure them, tell them he was all right, but he didn't know how to convey that. He felt…different. It felt as if there was something inside him, a deep hum of something, some force, coursing through his veins.

Slowly, he rose to his feet as the two animals continued to seemingly communicate with each other. For the first time, he looked down at his arm, rotating it slowly so he could see the underside. Halfway between his elbow and wrist was the image of some sort of bird with a long, flowing tail and wide, curving wings. The outline of the graphic was in black, but along the wings and tail red and gold shot out giving the impression the bird was on fire. No, wait; it was fire.

"What is that?" Hesitantly, Kira approached him. Her hand still clutched the now forgotten pen.

The name came to him, suddenly, and without real thought. "It's a phoenix."

"I think I need to sit down." Diana Randal slid into the chair the cat had recently vacated.

She was pale, her eyes dazed. Gary went to her side, his hand patting her shoulder soothingly.

"I'm really okay, mom." Sawyer sought to reassure her.

She tried to give him a smile, but it came out more like a grimace. "I know. I just didn't think my baby would get a tattoo so soon." She was trying for levity, and he appreciated it. His thoughts were still too chaotic to really form anything coherent.

Automatically, his hand went to the charm on the chain that now rested around his neck. For some reason, he glanced down to the cat and dog. Molly was watching him intently, as was Flower, but then it seemed as if the cat nodded, as if trying to reassure him, to tell him it was alright. It descended on him then, peace.

"*Amplifico*." The word tumbled out of his mouth without thought.

Instantly, the charm in his hand expanded into a wand. It was long, probably a bit over twelve inches. It had a square barrel that eventually tapered off in a round end. The shaft of the wand was a dark brown wood. Lines ran down the wand's entire length, like the veins on a tree in varying colors of black and red. Near the broader end were three rings that encircled it, red, black shot through with gold, and then red. Carefully, he held it in his hand.

It felt right. He felt as if he'd been missing something all this time, until right now, when he'd finally found it.

"How did you remember the word?" Kira asked, her voice a near whisper as she stared at the wand.

Sawyer couldn't pull his gaze from it either. "I don't know. It just came out."

Finally, her gaze darted up to him. "How do you feel?"

"Hot."

Her eyes bugged for a moment, and then her mouth clamped down as she pressed her lips into a firm line. Her shoulders shook as she tried valiantly, but the first giggle broke through and then another until she was laughing unhindered.

For a moment, he looked at her as if she was nuts. Finally, it dawned on him. The scowl he sent her only caused her to laugh louder. "Not like that. I meant warm."

A short burst of giggles came from his mother; then another until her and his father had joined in with Kira. Sawyer wanted to roll his eyes, but instead, he felt any remaining tension drain from his body. It was okay; they were going to be all right.

"*Mazevo,*" he murmured, and the wand resumed its place on the silver chain. With a shake of his head and a grin, Sawyer said, "Let's send that letter to Mr. Rowley." He glanced back at the cat, who though sitting peacefully by the dog, now had her attention on Kira. There was definitely more to the cat than met the eye, and he wanted to know what it was.

19

She fought against the urge to bite her nails. But it was hard, especially with that cat just staring at her, watching her with her wide, unblinking eyes. It wasn't behaving as a typical cat would, or at least how she assumed a typical cat acted. She didn't lick herself, no grooming, and no scratching. She hadn't even dozed off. All she did was now sit on the table in front of Kira, staring. It was enough to make her want to run from the room screaming.

She'd been this watchful, this intent on Sawyer before he'd gotten his powers. Now that he had his, Kira expected hers would come quickly, though she didn't know how long twins were typically born apart. But it couldn't be a coincidence that this cat showed up today of all days. No, this had to have something to do with their birthday.

Forcing her gaze away from the cat, she found Sawyer. He was sitting on the floor, his back against the wall. The dog, Molly, was sitting in front of him, looking up at him. She was a big dog. Her face and back were black, while from tan to light brown shot through the rest of her coat, very pretty. And funny enough, her brother had always wanted a German Shepherd growing up. They'd never had a pet before, but he always said that was his favorite breed of dog. Sawyer was scratching the Shepherd behind her ear again; apparently, she liked that as she flopped down, her head resting on his leg.

Yesterday, Mr. Rowley had told them that familiars weren't that much different from regular animals, except in the sense of their loyalty. Some witches and wizards said they could communicate with theirs, but more in the sense that they just seemed in tune to each other. While a close relationship with one's familiar helped the witch or wizard's power to be more focused, they still needed to be taken care of as if they were a regular pet. They could understand their person, or so he had said. Whether they chose to listen was another story entirely. He'd said there had been cases of familiars abandoning their owners if they didn't agree with them. He'd told them back before the curse had been enacted, when there was a clear line of good and evil, some familiars had abandoned their people from differences in beliefs. It could happen, though it was rare.

But looking at her brother and his dog at that moment, Kira couldn't ever imagine it for them. Yet, who could tell. Everything was different now. Her brother had actual magical powers, though he hadn't done anything yet. He hadn't shot off a shower of light, or whatever Lucien had done. In fact, all Sawyer had done was enlarge his wand then shrink it back. Actually, when she thought about it, it was pretty anticlimactic. But that was typical Sawyer, laidback and just easy going.

At this moment, he didn't look any different from normal. However, when it had happened, he'd actually glowed, red. It wasn't like at Lucien's birthday when that white light had seemed to come from within him. No, Sawyer had a red cast about him. It had been creepy and looked really warm, almost as if he'd been on fire. He'd even said he'd been hot.

She hated that. Give her winter and snow any day of the week. She didn't like heat at all. Well that wasn't true, she liked it that time they had went on vacation to the beach.

That had been nice. But, typically, no, she liked it cool. That's why she didn't even like the color red; it brought visions of heat. No, blue and coolness all the way.

Sawyer was the exact opposite. Hot summers and red everything. Even the dog's collar was red along with his tattoo and wand. It was odd.

Or was it?

Their mother had gone into the kitchen to fix supper. Typically, either one or both Kira and Sawyer helped, but tonight, she didn't feel as if she could move. She was afraid if she were to try to cut anything, she'd slice off her finger in her inattention. Besides, at any moment, she could start going all glowy, and then who knew what was going to happen. Sawyer and their father had offered her help, but Diana had waved them all off with a reassurance that she had it handled. Really, Kira thought their mom just wanted a moment to herself. She hadn't heard any noise from the kitchen, not pots and pans banging or the clanging of dishes. She wouldn't be surprised if her mother wasn't just taking a moment to regroup. It wasn't every day that a person's kids turned into freaks before one's very eyes, plus two pets joined the household, with a third on the way.

Out of the corner of her eye, Kira looked at the cat. It was still watching her. She'd be glad when Almira's father arrived. Perhaps he could figure out what was going on with the animal. A few days ago, Kira had never thought she'd willingly invite a werewolf into her home. She'd been apprehensive about meeting the man, but he'd turned out to be nothing as she had expected. He was warm and friendly, and listening to him talk, she could tell that he truly loved animals, all types. And the animals must sense that, too, what with how they showed up on his doorstep. Perhaps this cat would go with him.

There was another shop, *Growls and Howls*, in town that specialized in familiars' needs, but instinctively Kira knew it wouldn't be anywhere near as good as Mr. Rowley. Almira had admitted to them that some people in town refused to set foot in her father's shop because of his condition. It bothered her, Kira could tell that as the other girl told the story. Kira had kept to herself her own reluctance at first meeting the man, but after speaking with him, she couldn't think of a better person to explain this cat's sudden appearance.

Plus, after watching Sawyer with his dog, she had some other questions. She knew these animals were familiars, but Molly didn't seem like the ordinary pet. It was confusing, but she was sure he'd be able to explain it all once he arrived.

It would be a while, or so the letter they'd received back from Almira had said. She'd wrote it for her dad as he'd been busy as their Astronomy and Meteorology teacher Celestria Blakeley's familiar was injured and he was trying to help it.

Surreptitiously, Kira tried to glance at the cat again without being seen. It didn't matter. The cat was still watching her. She couldn't imagine anything getting the best of this animal.

Hesitantly, Kira reached out a hand. She paused with an inch separating her from the cat. They regarded each other curiously before Kira closed the distance. Her finger made contact with the fuzzy softness of the cat's head. For a moment, Flower did nothing, and then she turned, just slightly and leaned into the touch.

A slow smile turned up the corners of Kira's mouth. A chill swept over her. She shivered and glanced to the clock over the mantle, almost six.

Stay with Flower.

Unbidden an urgent, feminine voice floated into her mind, tugging at the back of Kira's memory. Her forehead furrowed as she tried to hold on to it. There was something else there, something more. She was remembering!

She glanced up, opened her mouth to call to her father and brother, but another shiver swept her, and her hand jerked away from the cat. It felt as if it came from inside her, growing getting stronger, rushing around her body, then just as suddenly, it sped up and ended in a rush at her left arm.

Flower was on her feet at the same time that Sawyer and her father both jumped to theirs. Kira's gaze shot to where they were all looking at the archway of the living room.

It was a cat, but not like any other she had seen before. It was big, whatever it was, standing about two feet tall and almost four feet long. It was all black but seemed to have tufts of brown throughout its fur, along with what appeared to be the occasional gray hair. Its tail was long and bushy. One ear stood straight and tall, while the left one was bent. It stood straight at attention, watching her with unwavering lime green eyes.

It was hers; instinctively, Kira knew it. It was all she could do not to rush to the animal. Once she was before it, she dropped to her knees. Around its wide neck was a brilliant, sapphire collar. It, too, had a silver pendant. Before she reached for it, her hand came up and stroked the bent, velvety ear. Deep in its throat, the big cat made a sound like a purr. Then it moved its head, seeming to nudge her fingers toward its collar.

On the charm was the outline of something that seemed to be an ocean wave.

"Pepper," she said the name engraved on it.

The cat made a sound that sounded put upon as if it hated its own name. Kira smiled as her fingers opened the pendant. A delicate silver chain fell out into her waiting hand. Once she closed the charm, a faint glow radiated from the crack of the two pieces; then it was gone as it fused itself into one.

She strung out the chain, holding it between her fingers. Its wand-shaped charm was gray with blue shooting through it. Carefully she placed it over her head. As it fell into place, her right hand came up to touch it.

As Sawyer before her, the word, "*Amplifico,*" whispered passed her lips. She hadn't had to think about it; it had just come. The wand grew in her hand. It was long and slender with a tapered end. The larger end of the wand was round and circular. In front of it were two other round circular parts, almost as if it formed a sure place to grasp it. Two of the circular parts were blue with the center one being a silvery white. It was then that she glanced down at her left arm.

Again, like her brother, the tattoo was midway between her elbow and wrist on the underside of her arm. But while his had been a black, red, and gold fire phoenix, her image was in cool, muted tones. It almost looked like pictures she had seen in a book of dragons. She could make out the scales. It had long wings that spread out over its body. At the tips of them white, then turning to a light blue that got progressively darker until it reached the end. It had a long tale whipped around itself, with scales that seemed to shimmer between blues and silver. Around it where varying shades of blue water droplets.

A soft trill brought her focus away from her arm. Beside her, Flower looked tiny in comparison to the black cat. Yet the gray and black fluff was letting out a serious of mews and trills in various tones. The amazing thing was that Pepper's head was tilted as if listening to every sound.

With a whispered "*Mazevo,*" Kira turned her wand back into a charm. She turned to find her brother and father staring at her, wide-eyed. Molly moved from Sawyer's side and approached the two cats. She stood off to the side quietly as Flower continued, then added her own series of yips as Pepper answered back in deep trills. It was as if they were all communicating with each other.

"So what does everyone feel like eating tonight?" Diana's question ended on an abrupt squeal as she took notice of the large black cat standing in the front room. She gripped the archway frame, her knuckles turning white. "Wha—what is that?"

"This is Pepper." Kira turned to look at the cat, which was regarding her mother with curiosity. "I actually don't know what he is. Perhaps, Mr. Rowley can tell us."

Her mother could only nod.

"Well," Gary said, clearing his throat, "perhaps we should start with cake. Everyone does love dessert." His slight chuckle was forced.

No one moved.

The knock sounded on the door. As one, the animals turned to stare at it. It was what they all needed to break them from their frozen positions. Since Kira was closest, she went to the door, not at all surprised to see Almira and her father there.

Both their smiles were quick and easy.

"Hello, sorry it took…" Nadir's words trailed off as he noted the chain around her neck. "You received your powers?"

Kira nodded. "Just a few moments ago. Sawyer got his first." Then seeming to remember her manners, she moved back to allow them to enter. "Please, come in."

"How do you…" Again, his words trailed off, but this time, it was because his gaze had become snared by the trio of animals in the archway.

Or at least she thought that was the reason he was rooted to his spot, his gaze unwavering.

But then Nadir said, "Flower?"

The cat gave a guttural trill and then bolted. She was at the man's legs almost instantly, winding her way around them, high-pitched mews and purrs coming from her. Nadir bent, crouching down, his hand going to pet her ear and then her chin in turn.

"I can't believe it."

Sawyer and Gary had joined them in the foyer now, too. Diana had moved further into the living room but was still keeping a watchful eye on the big cat.

When Nadir glanced up, Kira thought she saw a hint of moisture in the corner of his dark eyes. She didn't understand it. She cast a quick glance to Almira, but she looked just as confused as Kira felt.

Nadir was still petting the cat when he finally darted a look to her and then Sawyer. "I can't believe it. This cat…she was your mother's."

20

He'd rather be anywhere than at school, which was insane as yesterday, Sawyer would have given almost anything to have been there than sitting at home, waiting with impending dread. Now, he felt on edge, and he had the sneaking suspicion that everyone would be staring at him. There was too much to try to wrap his mind around to be able to deal with that well.

And while getting his powers was huge, that wasn't where his mind was focused. No, that was the cat, Flower. His biological mother's familiar was alive and had found them, on their birthday no less. But with this strange world, he wouldn't have even thought that was too unusual if not for Almira's father.

Nadir Rowley had been shocked; the disbelief had all but rolled off him in waves. But it was his departing words to them, for them to keep her reappearance quiet for now that stuck with Sawyer the most. The older man had seemed as if he had wanted to say something more to them, but at the same time, he hadn't seemed to know what that was. He was that at a loss.

What Sawyer needed now was time to think. But he didn't have that luxury. Instead, he had school, and he knew he needed to focus. He needed to learn all he could about his powers, how to use them, how to control them. Even right now, he could feel a hum reverberating through his body. He wanted to know about it; he wanted to understand.

He'd thought—hoped—that once he got them, he'd feel more self-assured in this crazy, mixed-up world, but instead, he felt even more out of place.

The one thing having powers had to recommend it was his familiar. Already, he loved his dog. Perhaps that was still the kid in him who had always wanted to have one, but never could because it wouldn't have been fair living in an apartment in the city. Plus with school and sports, he'd never have the time he wanted to devote to a pet. Now, though, he didn't have an option. Powers came with a familiar, end of discussion.

His poor mother was trying to deal with it all, but he knew it was rough on her. Her children had magical powers that none of them understood; she had three animals in the house, one that needed to remain a secret; plus said children had been tattooed almost instantly, when she was vehemently against all forms of body art.

Glancing down at the phoenix on his arm, uncovered by the rolled-up sleeves of his shirt and school jacket, Sawyer noticed that when the sun hit it, it seemed to shimmer. He'd never really given much thought to tattoos, had never really wanted one. However, like the pet, there had been no choice in the matter. It just was.

"I don't want to go in. Do you think we can ditch?" Kira asked.

He glanced up. He'd forgotten his sister was even there. They were outside the brick and stone school, partially hidden by some towering trees. Other kids were milling outside the old building. He pulled down the sleeve of his jacket. He didn't feel like advertising the mark.

"Where would we go?" Even as he asked that, he was running through scenarios in his mind of places to hide.

"I don't know. I just don't want everyone staring at me. I'm tired of it. I just want out of here."

That would be nice; he just didn't think it was an option, not anymore. "I don't know how we can leave, with the barrier and all."

She was silent for a moment, digging the tip of her black patent shoe into the dirt. Then she darted a glance at him. "I've been thinking about that. How did we get out of here as kids? I think…"

She didn't finish her thought; she didn't have to. He knew what she was thinking. "You think we should try. See if we can make it through on our own."

Kira nodded, seeming to not want to agree to it aloud.

They both mulled it over for a bit before she said, "But we should find out about it, don't you think?"

He could follow the wave of her thoughts. "Find out what happens if a person tries to cross it without permission."

"Exactly. But who do we ask?"

"I don't think it should be Risa. I think she would be on to us. No, someone who won't think that much about it, or who would just think we're curious." He paused for a moment. "I'll ask Gabe. I have first period with him."

Nodding, she agreed with him, though she was looking up at the building again. "I don't want to go in, but I also don't want to be the last person getting to class. Thursday, I hated it. I didn't know anyone first period. It was horrible. But it won't be so bad today. I'll have someone to sit with."

"What do you have first period?"

"Light and Spells," she answered. "Professor Edwards said last week we'd really start working today."

"She told that to us, too."

Neither of them moved.

"It's like I need something to force myself to go." She glanced up and waved her hand at the sky. "If it was raining or something, we'd have no choice."

No sooner had the words left her mouth, did a crack of thunder sound in what had been a cloudless, sunny morning. They both stared up, shocked; then the rain began. No gentle little sprinkle but a full-on downpour that cut like razors it stung so hard.

They bolted, running for the building as everyone else on the lawn was now doing, too. They skidded to a stop to keep from knocking into people as they all rushed to get into the protection of the school. He could feel the gazes on him, of people staring. It must have gotten around that they'd had their birthdays yesterday. Either that or people already knew since they seemed to know so much about them. He did his best to ignore them.

They arrived at his locker first, damp. "I'll see you at lunch."

She nodded, brushing back her wet hair. "Don't forget to ask him."

"I won't." He sent a glare in the direction of the few guys who glanced as she walked away, one being Lucien Norwood as Kira passed him. The black-headed boy just smirked then resumed his appraisal.

Feeling his annoyance building, Sawyer yanked out his textbook, *Metamorphosis: The Change, Volume I*. He shoved it in his backpack along with his *Guide to Transformation*. He'd already taken more than a few steps in the direction of his classroom, when he realized he hadn't shut his locker door. The irritation kicked up another notch as a quick glance showed him that Lucien and his crew had noticed the same thing and were chuckling.

Aggravated, Sawyer turned to stalk back to his locker, but before he could take a step, he waved his hand in frustration. The locker door slammed shut with enough force to shake the entire wall of them. Some younger students shrieked in surprise.

Sawyer knew his own eyes were wide, that he looked just as shocked as everyone else did, but thankfully, sanity took hold. He schooled his features and resumed his glare. This time when he turned back to walk up the hallway, some in Lucien's group looked wary, which as far as Sawyer was concerned was good. The only one who didn't was Lucien; he was watching him with a hint of curiosity now.

Without another look in their direction, Sawyer made his way down the hall and into his first class of the day, Metamorphosis. He paused as soon as he crossed the threshold. The layout of the room was entirely different than it had been last Thursday. On that day, there had been individual small tables in a row. Now, the tables were larger, each one with two chairs behind it. He didn't even want to hazard a guess on what that meant.

Instead, he chose a seat in the back, on the opposite side from the girl who almost always seemed to hang on Lucien's arm. She was sitting with a pretty brunette with light blue eyes. They were whispering furiously back and forth to each other. In the front of the room sat a boy with a very tan complexion and wavy brownish blond hair. He was engrossed in the book before him, which Sawyer noted wasn't either of the two textbooks for this class.

He ignored them all and instead laid his backpack on the table.

"Hey," Gabe said as he slid into the seat beside him, sure of his welcome. "So?"

Sawyer looked to him. The other boy's expression was all earnest excitement, and it helped lift Sawyers sagging spirits a bit. In this, it was almost normal. Almost like someone wanting to know about that great present he had received for his birthday, only in this case it was magical powers.

Crazy.

The corners of his own lips lifted into a grin as he pulled the chain free from his buttoned, crisp, white shirt. He held out the pendent for the other boy.

"Yours looks so cool. Let's see your mark."

"Oh, I want to see," Ella said, appearing at his side.

The hand that had been pushing back the sleeve of Sawyer's cobalt jacket jerked at her sudden appearance. He hated when she caught him off guard. After spending most of the weekend with her, he realized what it was about her. She unnerved him, and right now, she was slightly leaning over him, peering at his arm, waiting, and he was at a loss as to what she was waiting for.

"Oh, good, I want to see it. Come on then." Dante dumped his bag on the table in front of them and turned around.

Mari perched in the other seat. "Oh, how pretty. Your wand has red through it." She was looking at the chain that still hung uncovered.

"I've already seen his mark." As soon as Almira made that comment, four sets of eyes glanced in her direction.

"What? When?" Ella asked that, looking between the two of them.

Almira smiled. "Last night, not long after it happened. They both had some questions about how to take care of their familiars."

That started another barrage of questions as everyone wanted to know what animals he and Kira had received. But Sawyer glanced at Almira and nodded a silent thank you to her. She'd effortlessly glossed over the true reason she had been to his house. As she smiled back at him, and then he took note of how excited the rest of them were, he realized that without even trying he'd actually become friends with them all. It was more than he had first thought when he arrived in this town, and definitely more than he'd hoped for after finding out about the town's craziness.

They were actually all right, which was good as he had a feeling he was going to need a few friends with the little bits and pieces of things he was discovering. Something was going on here, and he just had to figure out who was involved in it.

But at the moment, they were still urging him, so as he described Molly, he rolled up the left sleeve of his jacket. A chorus of exclamations followed. Then Ella grabbed his arm and turned it back and forth. Sawyer felt the contact burn throughout him.

"Look," she said, still twisting his arm, "when his arm moves, it almost looks as if the phoenix is moving, too."

Another round of exclamations drowned out the ringing of the class bell.

The loud clearing of a throat finally broke through the noise. With sheepish expressions, Ella and Almira quickly slid into seats at the vacant table beside Gabe, while everyone else quieted. It was only then that Sawyer noticed the envious stares of some of the other students, namely Dalen.

Their teacher for this class, Professor Hawtrey, was the one who had cleared his throat. He was a strange man, tall and thin, with long blond hair parted in the middle that fell in waves down to his waist. His wide almond-shaped eyes were an unusual color of violet with hints of pale pink. He seemed quiet and unassuming, but his voice was loud and booming when he spoke. He was a little frightening actually.

"Yes," he said, as he laid a stack of books on his desk, "I know we've had a bit of excitement over the weekend. And that has a reason to do with our switch. If you all have not noticed, our seats have changed. As I'm sure you were told yesterday in your classes, the same thing is happening in all your classes today."

Sawyer darted a quick glance to Gabe, his brow raised in question, as he had no idea what had happened yesterday in school.

"Yes, Mr. Randal, I realize you are probably unaware, so I'll help you catch up. In each class, you will be assigned a partner. This will be your partner if you have a group task or project. Sometimes you will not, but the table with your partner is your assigned seat until further notice."

Sawyer's gaze cut quickly to Dalen. There was no way he wanted him for a partner.

"Now at first, we partner students by birthdates, so that the students have their powers at nearly the same time. Once everyone receives their powers, we might change up the partners by magical ability, as we should have some sense of where everyone falls."

Sawyer could do no more than nod.

"Everyone up and to the side." They all did as told. With a wave of his wand, Professor Hawtrey had the tables and chairs moving about the room. Three tables in the front with two behind them in the empty space between the tables. "Mr. Randal and Mr. Meyer, up here please." He pointed to the table at the front of the room.

It took Sawyer a moment to realize who his partner was as he was too busy thinking of having to sit in the very front of the room. But once he did, he relaxed a bit and took his new seat, right by the door.

"Mr. Alverz and Miss Vandear." They grudgingly took the table in the middle on Gabe's left. "And Miss Hopewell and Miss Rowley." Ella and Almira sank into their seats with a relieved sigh. "Mr. Langley and Miss Cutler." They took their seats at the table at an angle behind Sawyer and Gabe. Neither Mari nor Dalen looked extremely happy about the situation. "And finally, Miss Townshed and Mr. Barnett."

With a satisfied smile, Professor Hawtrey went behind his desk and selected one of the many books. "Now if you will please take out your book *Metamorphosis: The Change, Volume 1*, we will start with the preface before we delve into the wonderful world of change."

~~*~*~*

"I'll show you mine, if you show me yours."

Kira's startled gaze flew up. "Excuse me." She hadn't been prepared for Lucien Norwood to whisper that in her ear. They had just gotten their new seating arrangement from Professor Edwards. Kira had been more intent on seeing where her new friends were at, then the boy she'd been paired with.

Oh, who was she kidding.

She'd been doing her best to pretend he wasn't there, but his presence was hard to ignore, especially when he was seated right at her side, staring at her now with those icy blue eyes, a slight smirk turning up one corner of his lips.

When the smirk turned into a full out grin, she realized she was staring shamelessly. She shook her head to clear her thoughts and looked at her bag that was still setting on the tabletop. She'd completely forgotten what he had said. "Excuse me?"

If it was possible, his grin grew even wider. "I said I'll show you my mark if you show me yours."

His voice was low, deep, and what should have been an innocent request sounded like something dangerous and too tempting to her ears. Her teeth came down to chew mercilessly on her bottom lip. She didn't notice that his gaze followed the movement.

"Alright," she finally breathed out. She started to push up the sleeve of her jacket, but he had his already rolled up. She looked at his first. It was the very distinct image of a wolf's head with the black lines of its fur going out to almost form a half circle around it. It reminded her of his familiar.

"You're turn," he whispered.

Shyly, she pushed up the sleeve of her jacket.

"Wow!" He reached for her arm, his fingers barely grazing her before he asked, "May I?"

She nodded, and he took her arm, turning it slightly back and forth, studying her tattoo intently.

"It looks as if it's moving. The way the colors shimmer...I've never seen anything like that before." Suddenly, he seemed to remember he still had a hold of her. Hesitantly, he released his grip.

"You haven't?" She'd really only seen Risa's mark before his, and both of theirs were black outlines.

"Haven't what?" He was still looking at her arm.

The uncomfortableness came back in full force. She quickly pulled her sleeve back into place. It took him a moment, but then he shook it off and turned his attention back to her.

"I'm sorry. I didn't hear you." He smiled then, fully.

She realized then he probably broke that smile out when he wanted something or someone to capitulate to his will. Right at this moment, he was all cocky arrogance, nothing like the withdrawn boy she had found in his father's study amid the broken glass. She hadn't liked seeing him like that at all, but this person in front of her, she didn't know if she could take anything he said seriously, or if it would all just be a ploy to get something from her. Because he did want something, or at the very least his father did, and what that was she still hadn't found out.

"Are tryouts today?" the boy seated at the next table to her left leaned over to ask of Lucien.

For one long moment, he continued to look at her. Finally, Lucien said by way of introduction, "Eamon Malford, Kira Randal."

Eamon gave her a look that could only markedly be considered friendly, before he turned his gaze back toward Lucien, waiting for the answer to his question.

"Yeah, at five."

"Why so late? Most of us have free period starting at three, and you get out of class at four. We could do it then. Fifth years are free then, too."

"I think Coach Chatham wanted to make sure Kira and her brother had a chance to tryout, too." His voice sounded as if the idea was the most amusing thing he'd ever heard. Then Lucien turned his icy gaze back to her. His tone was patronizing at best. "Do you know if he plans on it? Are you?"

It made her grit her teeth. "Try out for what?"

"I take it that's a no then. Just as well," Eamon said. "Sloignis is difficult. I wouldn't want either of you to hurt yourselves. It will be funny enough watching Meyer fall on his face, though. Perhaps you should all go out for vralatechni."

He didn't sound concerned; he sounded condescending. She didn't know what in the world this sport was exactly— and she'd never have a desire to play it anyway—but she'd make sure Sawyer did. He loved anything even the slightest bit athletic. He'd thrived on it back in Chicago.

"Oh, did I tell you the good news?" Lucien leaned in to whisper in her ear.

She didn't look at him. Instead, she kept her teeth locked firmly together so that she didn't say anything rude.

He didn't wait for an answer. "I don't know if you've noticed before, but we have all the same classes on Monday, Wednesday, and Friday, and we've been partnered up in all of them."

He was aggravating her. Being pompous one minute and then trying to be all flirty the next. No, thank you. "I just heard Professor Edwards say it was only until everyone got their powers, then we'll be partnered by magical ability."

Elbow on desk, Lucien rested his head in his hand, so he could stare at her. "Oh, you think we'll have to change up partners then?" Once again, that look was back, saying he agreed but because he assumed he'd be so much better than she was.

He was getting on her last nerve this morning being nothing like he was the other night at his birthday party. It was almost as if he were two different people, and this boy before her, she didn't really like. And now she hated the fact that she had told him anything about her powers. She'd plead a moment of temporary insanity to anyone who asked. Her smile was all false sweetness to go with her syrupy tone. "But of course." The smile dropped then. "You won't be able to keep up with me."

His eyes widened in surprise, then, to her horror, he burst out laughing.

She could feel it then, the barely simmering rage inside her. He could get under her skin so easily. Probably because everything he brought up was something she was already concerned and worried over. He didn't help her confidence in the least.

"Today we are going to start with our book *A Guidebook of Spellcasting*," Professor Edwards said as she took her place in the front of the room behind her dark wood podium.

Silently seething, Kira took out her book, studiously trying to ignore the smirking boy at her side. She opened up her notebook and grabbed a blue fountain pen. She had to push him from her mind. Come January, she was getting a new partner. She was leaving Lucien Norwood and his condescending attitude in the dust.

V. A. Risby

21

Rubbing his head, Sawyer set his tray down on the table in the cafeteria, or refectory, as he'd heard some students call it. At the moment, he didn't care. All he had was a powerful headache, and he could blame its cause at one person's feet.

That person entered the cafeteria—Sawyer was always going to call it that—surrounded by his group of minions. When Lucien Norwood walked, he strutted, everywhere, and when he talked, it was like nails on a chalkboard. And he talked, a lot. Sawyer figured it was because Lucien liked the sound of his own voice.

When Sawyer had entered Potions and Elixirs and been paired with the condescending jerk, he'd thought his day couldn't get any worse. Well it had, as Lucien Norwood was also his partner for Maleficium Armor. The only good thing Sawyer could come up with in that class was that on Thursday, he and Lucien would start counter spells since they were the only two with their powers. Now he just needed someone to teach him some curses to cast on the other boy, or perhaps he could make something in potions, cause painful boils to break out on Norwood's hands or something. Actually, Sawyer would settle for Lucien to lose his voice. That would be a nice moment of peace.

Sawyer plopped down in a vacant seat. It was different from last week when only Gabe and Ella had sat with them. He'd actually entered the cafeteria with Dante; their lockers were near each other. Carra and Chinira hadn't been far behind as they'd all come from the same class. It had seemed natural for them all to sit together.

Taking a sip of Lime Nectar, which was a slightly sweet juice that tasted like a lemon lime soda, Sawyer tried to think of something else. Anything else to ease his pounding headache. He glanced down at his tray, suspiciously regarding the meat smothered in some type of gravy. He was going to be wary of food from now on, thanks to the Norwoods' freak show of a party.

The slamming of a tray down on the table caused him, and his three friends to jump. He glanced up to find his sister, her face stony. Gabe and Ella were at her side, with Almira, Mari, Landen, and Devlin right behind them.

Sawyer glanced to the others for an explanation.

Gabe shrugged his shoulders. And if that wasn't enough of an answer, he added, "I got partnered with her in Maleficium Armor and Potions and Elixirs, I've asked, but she hasn't said a word. All she's been doing is furiously taking notes and having steam come out of her ears."

As the rest were taking seats, Ella looked around the table. "Oh, we need another chair." She moved to grab an extra one from another table.

Before she took two steps, Sawyer waved his hand and a free chair came effortlessly sailing over.

It didn't even register what he had done, until he noted the silence in the cafeteria. Everyone was staring in their direction. It hit him then. He hadn't even thought about it; it had just seemed to come naturally, like something he had always done before. When he noticed that some members of his own table were staring at him in open-mouthed amazement, he started to feel a bit self-conscious. "What?" he finally asked.

"It's just…Wow!" Carra managed to say.

Well, that didn't explain anything at all.

Carefully, Ella settled in the new chair beside him. She brushed her chestnut hair back from her face, tucking a bit of it behind her ear. "It's just that…well…" Her words trailed off, as she still seemed to be in shock.

Landen let out a long, slow, measured breath. "It typically takes years for a wizard or witch to learn enough concentration, have enough skill, to do wandless magic."

"It takes a lot of practice," Dante added, still looking at the chair that had just recently joined their table.

"And you did it so effortlessly." Chinira darted a glance around the room, taking in all the attention still focused in their direction. "I don't know if I would…I'd just be careful."

The hair on the back of Sawyer's neck rose. It sounded like the same warning Mr. Rowley had given them last night. A quick glance to Almira said as much.

What was going on here?

Apparently, though, Kira had something else on her mind entirely because she suddenly burst out with, "I don't know what this Slogoesit is but you're trying out for it. And you." She rounded on Gabe. "You better do well at tryouts. Don't fall or anything."

"Well, hello to you, too," Sawyer said, with a brow raised in question.

It was what they all needed to defuse the intense situation and move on from his burst of magic. The rest of the table broke out into amused laughter. That noise brought conversation back into the cafeteria. Hopefully, with the moment past, everyone would forget about what they had seen.

"Sloignis," Gabe automatically corrected. Then he said, "I hadn't planned on messing up, but thank you for the concern."

Kira leaned closer to him. "Well, don't. Lucien Norwood and that friend of his Eamon something or other are sure you'll fail spectacularly."

Gabe jerked up in indignation. "What? When did they say that? And why were they saying it to you?" He paused for a moment. "Why's he talking to you?"

"In first period where I'm stuck partnered with Lucien. I'm stuck with him every class on Monday, Wednesday, and Friday apparently." She raised her glass and peered into it. "What is this?"

"It's gingerroot punch," Mari said. "You grabbed it up before I could tell you what it was."

Eyeing the glass as if it would bite her, Kira took a tiny sip. Then another. "It tastes almost like ginger ale," she told Sawyer. Then she got back to her previous concern. "They don't think you're going to try out because they don't believe you can handle it. They said you and Sawyer should join the Valatechi or whatever it was."

That had Sawyer sitting up straighter in his chair. "What?" True, he hadn't really planned to try out. No matter what Gabe said, playing with a wall of fire didn't sound like Sawyer's idea of a fun time, but to hear that…

"They said they don't want you to hurt yourself."

Red, bright red haze. Sawyer glanced over his shoulder to where Lucien and his crew were sitting. Once again, that brunette was at his side, but at his right was another boy, Eamon Malford, Sawyer had learned his name from Potions and Elixirs. Lucien was looking in their direction. He nudged the boy beside him, and he glanced up, too. After a bit, all the occupants of that table were talking and looking in their direction, Lucien with a smug smirk while the others laughed.

Sawyer turned around and speared the meat on his plate with a fork. He almost took a bite before he set it back down. "I'm definitely trying out."

Devlin and Gabe gave a whoop of excitement.

Sawyer couldn't help his own grin from forming, but then a thought hit him, causing his brow to furrow. "When are tryouts?"

"Today at five."

"At five? I don't get out of class until four thirty."

Gabe waved aside the concern. "You're with Professor Kemp then. If you tell her, she'll let you out."

Sawyer very seriously doubted that, especially since this would be the first time he and Kira would see her since they had received their powers. But he supposed it was worth a shot. "Okay, so what do I need to know?"

"I've already explained the basics of the game." Gabe told the table.

"Good," Devlin said, "so he's already got a starting point. Let's see, ye have tae throw the orbs intae the rings. Ye cannot kick them in, or it's a penalty."

"Four penalties and you're out of the game. Plus on a penalty, the other team gets a free shot. They can shoot for any ring they want, plus the rings don't spin and the other team can't defend." Gabe added.

"If ye fall through a ring, it spits ye out on some random part of the field, sometimes intae the fire or ice." Devlin finished.

"Excuse me," Kira said. She looked back and forth between them. "Fire and ice? What type of sport is this?"

"Only the best sport ever," was Devlin's excited answer. "I've been waiting for years tae play this." He glanced around then indicated a table that was three over from where they were sitting. "See that broad blond guy over there?"

"Yeah," Sawyer said, looking in the direction he was pointing. It was a group of kids he didn't have any classes with.

"Those are fifth years. An that blond is Beck Thoren. He's a sure in fur captain this year. He's amazing at Sloignis. We had a pretty good team but if it weren't for him, we never would've made it tae the playoff. Coach Chatham is hoping our team is even better this year. She spoke to my da about it at the party the other night."

"I don't know," Gabe said, considering the table. "I really think Royal will be captain. He's an amazing defender."

Sawyer surveyed the table with interest. "So," he asked, his attention now taking in all the occupants of the cafeteria, seeing who he thought his competition might be, "how many positions did you say?"

"Sixteen in total. Ten on the field at a time," Dante answered after he finished chewing his bite. "Each team has three defenders who protect the rings. Three runners who are the ones shooting for the rings, and the four guardsmen that protect them or go after the other team's runners."

"Are you trying out?" Sawyer asked him. He was starving, but he still wasn't sure about that meat. No one else seemed to be eating it either. With a sigh, he picked up the large roll that came with it and tore off a big bite.

Dante shook his head. "No, it's not really my thing."

"Well, I want to put it out there right now," Chinira said, "that we *not* have to talk about this every day. I could use some other conversation as I eat sometimes. Besides, I'm going out for Vralatechni. We'll have to discuss that."

"After a while, constantly hearing about Sloignis does make you want to pull your hair out." Almira agreed.

"But it's such pretty hair," Gabe teased, "so we wouldn't want that."

Almira blushed a deep shade of pink.

"What is…what was it?" Kira asked.

"Vra…la…techni," Chinira explained. "It's beautiful. It's only for fourth years that have their powers and fifth years. It's a contest to see who can produce the most beautiful, colorful, artistic spells."

"Do you cast them at other people?" Kira exchanged a concerned glance with her brother.

"Oh, no." Mari took a sip of her own drink. "It's one person on the field. They use the same one where they play Sloignis."

"It's so pretty," Carra added. "It's just…it's beautiful. The colors and designs they can produce…I hope I can do it once I get my powers."

Sawyer still thought it sounded incredibly dull, and not something he would want to spend his time watching, let alone participate in. He turned back to Devlin and Gabe. "Anything else I should know?"

"Well," Gabe said, "it's going to be harder for you today. Since you—and Lucien—have your powers, you'll try out with the fifth years. Any of the rest of us that make it won't get to really practice or play until we get our powers. Thankfully, I only have to wait until Sunday."

Devlin looked disgusted. "I still have to wait two months."

Sawyer glanced back over his shoulder to find Norwood's gaze on him once again. He knew that Gabe had said they hadn't gotten along as children, but this seemed to be even a bit more than that. The guy didn't like him at all, and as far as Sawyer was concerned, the feeling was mutual. He shot Lucien a smirk of his own. After tryouts today, Lucien was going to hate him, as Sawyer planned on trouncing him once and for all.

~~*~*~*

"Never mind," Kira said, her voice high pitched to match her wide eyes. "I've changed my mind. No way you're playing this. None of you are. It's too dangerous. Let's go."

Gabe grinned unrepentantly. "Don't worry. It will be fine."

"Yes, it will." She agreed. "Because you're not trying out."

For once, Sawyer thought to agree with her. They were standing down on the field, which looked about the size of a football field. The stands that surrounded it were high. There was the nosebleed section and then more rows above that, which Sawyer supposed stood to reason, as there were no seats on the pitch.

But that wasn't what his sister was staring aghast at. No, that was the wall of fire and the wall of what looked like a sheet of ice, chasing each other around the outline of the field.

He made sure he kept his face impassive. It wouldn't do to show any concern and definitely any fear, especially when he had the distinct impression that he was being watched very closely.

"Well, what do you think?" Gabe asked, standing by his side.

They were dressed nearly identically. Gabe had given him a pair of the standard pants for the sport. They were black and made of some type of synthetic material, or at least that's how they felt. They tapered at the ankle, but you couldn't see that for the almost knee-high black boots. The end of them almost seemed like a sneaker, while the bottom had metal cleats or something like it. Sawyer had on black kneepads and pads at his elbows that ran down his wrist and over the top of his hand. A piece of fabric that went over his thumb kept it in place. For the moment, he had on one of Gabe's long-sleeved shirts. Again, of an almost synthetic fabric that Sawyer knew would keep a person cool. Apparently, the official uniform was a blue shirt that matched their school jacket's color along with the school emblem, which resembled the crest of the town tree, just as the stamper did.

What did he think?

Sawyer didn't want to tell Gabe that his first thought was to turn around and run for the hills. Screw the barrier, he'd find a way to break through it, as this wasn't normal at all. But he tramped down that desire. He refused to give into his fear even as he watched the fire and ice surround the entire field in a never-ending loop.

What crazy person thought this up?

Instead, Sawyer said aloud, "Should be interesting."

Gabe slapped him on the back. "You'll be a natural. Look, I didn't want to tell you before or anything because well…I didn't know if I should, but we used to play this all the time as kids."

Incredulously stunned to silence, Sawyer could do no more than stare at him.

Kira was more vocal. "Our parents let him play in *fire* when he was young?"

"Oh, no, but we practiced with the hoops. Your dad would make them spin for us then we'd practice shooting."

Well that made a bit more sense.

Apparently, though, not to Kira. "I really don't think you should do this. None of you. I'm serious."

Before Sawyer could reassure her, Lucien came up to them with three other boys they had noticed him with at his party. "So have you really thought about this, Randal? Are you sure you want to do it? Wouldn't want to scare your sister, would you?"

Sawyer tensed. He was really starting to hate this boy. But he was going to ignore him; Lucien Norwood didn't deserve to get a reaction out of him. He refused to give him one.

Kira gave the black-headed boy a tight smile. "I'll be sure to throw water on you when you get burnt alive."

Lucien's smile was genuine if slightly patronizing. "The fire won't burn you, love. Well at least not badly."

"Norwood, leave her alone." Gabe sidestepped so he was between the intruder and Kira.

Whatever warmth Lucien's expression held was gone as he turned to Gabe. "I'll be looking forward to watching you fail." With that, he and his friends turned and walked back toward some of the fifth years.

"What did I miss?" Devlin asked, running up from the changing room.

"Only the fact that you are all insane!" Kira's voice raised another notch.

Sawyer had to get her out of there if he was going to be able to concentrate at all. With his luck, she'd chase him onto the field to try to stop him. He was just about to say something, when Ella looped her arm through Kira's.

"It will be all right. Come on let's go get some seats so they can focus and get ready to kick Lucien's behind." She started pulling his sister off in the direction of the stands.

Sawyer gave Ella a grateful smile, which she returned, along with the slight beginnings of a blush. He watched her as she steered Kira over to a set of stairs and all but dragged her up them. The rest of their group not trying out joined them.

"Let's began."

Gabe elbowed him in the side to garner his attention.

Reluctantly, Sawyer turned to face the field. Standing before them was a tall, lean woman with short chopped blonde hair. She looked tough. Beside her was a man, short and stocky with a shock of red hair and a bulldog of a face. "All right, welcome to tryouts for this year's Sloignis team. I am Coach Chatham and this," she indicated the man, "is Coach Bloodworth. You all will have a lot to live up to after our successful season last year. As you know, all fourth and fifth years may tryout, though, even if selected for the team, you will only play once you have your powers. I want fourth years here." She indicated with a sweep of her hand. "And fifth years here."

They all shuffled to line up in their designated location. As Sawyer stepped up on the line to face her, he wondered what in the world he was doing. Only this morning he was planning on his escape, and now he was joining a sport's team? He had to be going insane.

"Now," she said, eyeing Sawyer, Lucien, and a couple of other students on the fourth-year line, "some of you will tryout with the fifth years since you already have your powers. Everyone will be put through the basics. You'll shoot and try to defend the rings. Those that have their powers will be put into the fire and ice walls. We have to see now how you handle it. Some people cannot, and we can't have that in a game. Even if you're picked for the team but do not yet have your powers, your continuation will depend on how you handle the walls." Withdrawing her wand, she turned to the field and said, "*Apotravimai*." Instantly, the walls of fire and ice seemed to disappear.

"Let's begin." She led the way onto the field; the students trying out followed.

As he neared, Sawyer got a good look at the suspended rings for the first time. There were two identical sets, one in red and the other in blue. In the blue, there were three large rings easily twice his height. Then there were two rings that looked as if he'd be able to step through without any trouble. The last ring was the smallest of the group, reminding him of a Hulu Hoop in size.

They stopped in front of the coaches still in their separated years. At their feet were six balls or orbs as his friends had told him. They reminded him of the size of a basketball. But that's where the similarity ended. They were all clear, with what looked to be swirls of fire and ice shooting through them. Nor were they perfectly round. On the sides, they each had long, flat areas, which Sawyer realized would make them easier to grip.

"First, we'll try something easy. We'll just throw. No point in you being out here if you can't hit the ring when it's not spinning. Fifth years up first."

The fourth years stepped back to give the older students room. Sawyer supposed she had a point. It was just very blunt.

From the sidelines, he watched. Apparently, the coach had been correct as a few of the students trying out couldn't even get it anywhere near the rings. Everyone received ten attempts, with the person trying out deciding which ring they wanted to try. Either all three or just concentrate on the smaller one.

As the students cycled through, the two coaches continued to whisper and take feverish notes.

"That's Royal," Gabe said at his side, pointing to a tall, dark headed boy who threw his ten shots into the smallest hoop with ease.

The boy pointed out as Beck, also concentrated on the smallest hoop, along with a tall, blonde girl.

"Worried yet?" Lucien asked, coming up on Sawyer's left side.

He couldn't stop from rolling his eyes. "Of throwing a ball into a hoop? I think I'll survive."

Gabe and Devlin laughed, while Lucien's face took on a stormy countenance. His friends looked furious.

"Why does this son of a pleb even think he can try out? Shouldn't there be restrictions." Eamon's words were for his friends, but Sawyer couldn't help but overhear them, he'd said them loud enough.

He didn't know what a pleb was, but he knew it was a slur against his parents. He straightened and stepped forward, getting right up in the other boy's face. "You have a problem, Malford?" The words came out gritted.

The other boy tried to smirk, but it didn't have the same effect as he had to look up to Sawyer, not being of the same height. "You heard me."

Sawyer nodded. "Yeah, I did." Everything in him wanted to punch the boy in his condescending face, but he knew he couldn't. His parents would be so disappointed in him, even if he was defending their honor. "Let's see how that goes once I kick your ass out there."

"Fourth years," Coach Chatham called out.

Sawyer drove his elbow into the other boy's shoulder as he moved passed him. "She saved you." Sawyer was seething. Oh, he wanted to hit him, maybe even knock out a tooth or two. But he didn't; instead, he channeled that thought into focus. He had to smoke both Lucien Norwood and Eamon Malford. There was no way either of them could beat him.

The other fourth years before him threw the ball into both the medium and the smaller sized ring, especially when they missed the smaller one they switched to the medium wanting to get some goals. Devlin was the first one to concentrate on the smaller one. He missed two shots; Gabe missed one.

Sawyer was getting ready to step up, but before he could Eamon did. He missed two. As he passed Sawyer, he gave him a smirk. Lucien was next, getting the ball through the ring all ten times.

Once it was his turn, Sawyer stepped up. He knew he couldn't miss. He had to beat them. His first nine shots sailed through easily. He turned to the side and saw the two boys laughing. Sawyer stepped back, not one but at least ten feet, moving back further than any of the others had shot before him. He noticed that Lucien and Eamon were now quiet. This was either going to work, or he was going to fail spectacularly.

Channeling his anger and annoyance, he let the ball go. He threw it with more force then he intended—he didn't know where that had come from. It went through the hoop and then kept going down the field.

He turned, his own smirk tugging up one corner of his lips as he went to rejoin Gabe and Devlin.

The rest of the tryouts progressed quickly. Once Coach Bloodworth activated the rings, they took turns trying to throw them through. It was harder on the moving targets, especially the smaller one, but Sawyer felt he managed a decent showing, definitely better than Eamon. Next, they each had a go as a defender. That was only passable. Sawyer definitely liked the position of runner better.

Just when it seemed as if tryouts were winding down, Coach Chatham stepped in front of them. "Good job today, students. Just one more matter. Fifth years and those fourth years that already have your powers, we need you to stay. The rest of you are dismissed."

"Good luck," Gabe and Devlin both told him in turn before they left the field. Instead of heading to the changing room as some of the other students did. They went to the stands and took a seat in front of Ella, Kira, and the rest of their friends.

"*Leumesiructe.*" As soon as the word left the coach's mouth, the walls of fire and ice appeared, enclosing them in the field.

Beck Thoren went first. He walked up to the wall and just stepped into it. Sawyer couldn't help but flinch as the red flames swirled around him, forming a sort of circular vortex that rose taller than his head. Beck had to be the bravest person he'd ever seen or the dumbest to willingly step into that. Five minutes went by before he was spit out of the flames on another part of the field. With just a bit of a shake, the boy then stepped into the ice wall.

Again, Beck was trapped inside a vortex. This time it appeared to have shards of ice churning around him. When it was finished with him, he was spit out once again, this time back to where he started. He paused for several minutes, seeming to try to catch his breath.

Sawyer tramped down his impending sense of fear. He couldn't do this. He really couldn't, especially after watching some of the students come out puking and gagging. One had even fainted and been taken off the field by Coach Bloodworth.

"It is not as bad as you imagine."

Startled, Sawyer turned. He hadn't heard anyone come up beside him. He had to strain to understand what the dark-headed boy said through his heavy French accent.

"Royal Aurand." The boy introduced himself. "It will be all right. Just remember to breathe. Dis is 'arder than it ever is in a game since it's so quickly from one to zee other. It is rare anyone would get 'it in zat fast."

Sawyer could barely nod at the reassurance as Coach Chatham was calling his name.

The older boy gave him a grin of encouragement. Sawyer nodded then straightened his shoulders. He ignored everyone else and walked up to the wall. It was ice. Letting out a deep breath, he willed himself to do this. Then he stepped forward.

It surrounded him instantly. For a moment, it was crazy cold, seeming to freeze him from the inside. The ice bit at his face and hands. Then came the heat, but he realized it seemed to be coming from inside of him not from the swirling storm surrounding him. The spinning was making him lightheaded, so he shut his eyes. Then it wasn't that bad. It seemed as if it were no time at all, before he was spit out across the field.

He paused for a moment, wondering why it hadn't been as bad as he was imagining. But then he shook off the thought. He couldn't think too much, or he wouldn't step into that wall of fire. He didn't have a death wish. He blocked it from his mind and moved.

For a moment, the heat was intense, burning his face and hands, along with the spinning, his stomach was queasy. He was going to be sick. But he refused. He closed his eyes to block out the whirling. And then he felt it, that power he'd had at the base of him since last night. Except now, it seemed to be bigger and growing.

He was spit from the flames. For a moment, he didn't move. He felt as if he threw that ball now, it would go further than he'd been able to do it before. He felt powerful.

Let's see Lucien beat that.

Slowly, his lips turned up in a grin and he jogged forward, feeling no negative effects at all from the walls.

Game on.

V. A. Risby

22

He'd never hear the end of this. Even worse, he knew this was eventually going to get back to his father. He'd actually sunk down on the field to his knees. He'd wanted to vomit, but he'd swallowed the bile back. He had no choice but to glare at Sawyer when he'd finally raised his head, as the other boy had stared at him with a self-satisfied smirk.

Groaning, Lucien leaned back in the wooden chair. At least he hadn't collapsed completely on the ground as Ean Corsten, another fourth year, had, but it had been close. The ice had been bad enough. Lucien had never been particularly fond of the cold, but it had seemed to invade his body and mind, make him sluggish. However, nothing could compare to that fire. He'd felt as if he was roasting on the inside. And that was just for five minutes. In a game, once a player was hit into a wall, they were trapped in the vortex for ten minutes.

The heat surrounding him, seeming to flay him alive, plus the constant spinning of the wall of fire had made him want to puke. And to have seen Sawyer come out of it and then *jog* back to the rest of them. It was enough to make Lucien want to tear his hair out. Or beat the smug look off Sawyer's face. He'd settle for the latter. It would make him feel better.

He couldn't help it; he hated Sawyer Sayer—or Randal as he was now called. Lucien always had and probably always would.

But, no, that wasn't quite right. He hadn't always felt that way. In fact, the first time he had met Sawyer, he'd liked him and wanted them to be friends. They'd been children then around five, and Sawyer's ball had bounced into their back lawn. Lucien, who had been playing on his own at the time, retrieved it and brought it back to the other boy. They'd played together then, tossing the ball back and forth to each other. They'd had fun.

Later, Sawyer was called in to eat, and Lucien had gone inside his home, excited to tell his family about the new friend he had met. At the time, he'd only had two others, Regina and Eamon.

As he, his mother, and father had sat down to a very formal dinner—as was their typical evening—he'd shared the details of his afternoon. His father, to his surprise and delight, had been inordinately pleased.

Then, that night, Lucien had learned why. He'd overheard his father telling his mother how disappointed he was that he'd only been given the one child, why he couldn't be a father to the twins. He just knew his own son would be lacking in power compared to them.

The days went on, and Lucien kept hearing more and more about Sawyer and his sister. His father wanted to know if he had seen the other boy outside. It got to the point that Lucien didn't want to hear about either of them anymore. He had resented even the sound of their names.

It had finally come to a head at the annual Autumn Festival. The entire town was gathered in the square. It was a day of fun, food, and games. It had rained the day before so there were patches of mud here and there that some of the kids had been playing in. Lucien hadn't. His mother would never allow such frivolity.

He had seen him then, Sawyer, who was with Gabe. Gabe, Lucien knew. His father couldn't stand Cornelius Meyer, so in turn Lucien had nothing to do with the man's son. They were both teasing Sawyer's sister about the mud they were playing in, and that she was trying her best to avoid because of her new dress.

Lucien had watched them for a long while, envious with how close they'd all seemed, until his father had spotted Sawyer. After giving Lucien a talk about how not to mess everything up and get him away from the Meyer peasant, he'd sent Lucien in their direction.

He'd resented that, resented the fascination that his father had with these twins, resented that he knew his father wished they were his children and not him, resented the fact that Sawyer was friends with Gabe Meyer. Friend or not, he didn't want anything to do with any of them. As he approached the group, Sawyer had given him a friendly greeting. In turn, Lucien had pushed Kira down into one of those mud puddles that they had been tormenting her with.

She'd started crying as she looked down at her now muddy new dress. In the face of her tears, Lucien had instantly felt awful. He'd tried to apologize, but then Sawyer had shoved him, told him to get away from his sister. Gabe had pulled the girl up and wrapped his arm around her shoulders, trying to comfort her.

Lucien had retreated, only to then be pulled to the side and berated by his father. He'd struck Lucien that night, with magic. It was stupid and ludicrous, but instead of blaming his father, Lucien had blamed Sawyer and Kira, and to an extent Gabe. He couldn't blame his own father. His five-year-old brain couldn't wrap around the thought of not liking his own father.

Over the years, he'd gotten over that though.

But apparently, he hadn't let go of his resentment toward Sawyer. If anything, it seemed to have grown. It had intensified as once Lucien had rejoined the rest of the students trying out, he noticed Sawyer had been talking and laughing with Royal. That had irritated Lucien even more. Royal was a fifth year, from a prominent family, who Kenrick was always courting favor from. Royal was another person that Kenrick wanted his son to get close to, just to ingratiate the Norwoods with the Aurands. For that reason alone, Lucien avoided the older boy. And to have Sawyer fall in with him so easily...

Everything had seemed to always come easily for Sawyer, at least what Lucien could remember from their younger years. And now, even after everything, Sawyer already had friends.

Cripes, he'd made a chair go sailing over to their table and had it land effortlessly, all without a wand.

Quickly, Lucien had glanced away before he had said or did something stupid. When he had, his gaze had caught on the stands. They were elevated enough so spectators could see the field of play. Lucien had been able to glance to Kira when Sawyer had gone into the flames. She'd actually buried her face in Gabe's back, while Ella had hidden against Kira's side. It would have been comical if she hadn't been pressed against Meyer. Though Lucien wondered if she had hidden when he'd went in to the walls.

Lucien didn't know exactly how he felt about the girl Sayer—Randal, he furiously reminded himself. He'd been hearing about them at home too much again. His father was bound and determined for him to befriend them this time. But why, Lucien didn't know. Anytime he asked, he would only get a vague 'it's for the best,' which told him next to nothing. But he'd gotten an earful and then some the night of his birthday for not sitting with the twins.

He'd made the mistake of telling his father that he'd invited them and that was good enough. He'd paid for that bit of defiance.

Years of his own built up resentment and the benefit of aggravating his father were why he was so antagonistic towards Sawyer. He wanted to be that way with Kira; he'd been set to do just that until she had run him over, quite literally.

Something about her blush and her utter embarrassment intrigued him. It hadn't hurt, her open perusal of him, until she'd realized what she was doing. It had all been endearing.

For some reason, he had kept his conversation with her at his birthday private. As far as his father was concerned, he'd never spoken to her more than a sentence. He didn't know why he wasn't sharing. The fact that she'd managed to blow something up before she'd even received her powers seemed like something his father would want to know, but Lucien had kept it to himself.

The girl taking up entirely too much of his thoughts entered the classroom with Ella, Devlin, and Dante. It was as if they were the old gang again. With a laugh, Kira slid into her seat beside Lucien. Ella went to the third table in the front row. He caught the slight roll of her eyes. She'd been paired with Regina and was none too happy about that fact. Neither was Regina as she'd been whining about it for days.

"Feeling better?"

Even though he was looking right at Kira, it took him a moment to realize she was talking to him. When he did, the question perplexed him.

"I feel fine."

"Oh, good," she said. She genuinely sounded like she meant it. Then she added, "I was worried, you looked like you might be sick yesterday on the field."

He'd walked right in to that one. He could feel the red heat creep up his face and neck. Two could play at this game. He cleared his throat and sought a bored, detached tone. "I happened to see you up in the *stands* turning all different shades of green."

Her silver colored eyes narrowed. "Hello, you all were walking into a circle of fire. What sane person does that?"

All?

His characteristic smirk jumped into place. "Were you worried about me, too?" That thought pleased him for some reason.

Quickly, she glanced away. Then she squared her shoulders and turned back to him. "Yes, of course. I was worried about your sanity."

Lucien couldn't help it; he chuckled. From across the room, he could hear Regina's gasp of outrage, but he didn't care.

Apparently, his readily apparent mirth flustered the girl at his side. Kira glanced away, her bottom lip snagging between her teeth. He wanted to take his thumb and pull it free as she mauled it mercilessly. He caught himself leaning forward to do just that. He gave himself an abrupt mental shake.

Before he could do anything else that might be construed as stupid, he grabbed his *Guide to Weather*

Phenomena out of his bag. But he couldn't resist adding, "I made the team by the way."

As she took her own book from her bag, she said, "Yes, I saw that posted this morning. You must be excited. I know Sawyer was."

Lucien would like to forget her brother and Meyer had been picked. Three other fourth-years had also: Devlin McManuse, who'd proved amazing at defense; Brenton; and Druina Lanza, who was in the rotation ahead of them, having had her seventeenth birthday in July.

Kira glanced over at Eamon who was once again on her left. Then she actually leaned toward Lucien to whisper, "I saw he didn't make it."

Her warm breath on his neck caused him to shiver. It took a moment to realize what she had said. To give her credit, Lucien thought she actually sounded sorry for Eamon even after he'd been a prick to her the day before. So Lucien actually answered her truthfully when he said, "Yeah, he's not speaking to me at the moment since I did, and he didn't."

"Well, that's not fair. You didn't pick the team."

This time Lucien's grin was completely genuine, as she got angry on his behalf. He couldn't remember anyone ever doing that for him before. He shrugged. "He'll eventually get over it, and things will go back the way they were."

"It's still not fair," she huffed. She pulled out her notebook and fountain pen.

He figured they were probably done with their conversation then, when suddenly she turned to him and leaned in closer.

"May I ask you something?" Her voice was a mere whisper.

Curious, he leaned nearer to her, their foreheads almost touching. "All right."

They were too close for her to maintain eye contact. It seemed entirely too intimate, so instead, she glanced down, her finger finding a miniscule thread on the edge of her skirt. "With your father the mayor and all, I figured you'd know."

Out of habit, Lucien almost corrected her with Lord Mayor, but he stamped down the urge. Instead, he leaned a bit closer. Her hair smelled like coconuts. "Try me."

She shuddered from his nearness, causing him to smile. Then she seemed to shake it off. "What happens if someone tries to cross the barrier?" She darted a quick glance up, but then her gaze fell back to her lap.

That had not been what Lucien was expecting. In fact, it was so far out of the realm, it hadn't even been a vague thought. It took him a moment. "Why? Planning on sneaking off into the forest to try to breach the barrier?" He'd meant it as a joke, but when her gaze darted up to his, something nagged at the back of his mind.

"No." She forced a laugh. "Of course not, I was just curious."

He studied her bent head for a moment longer. "Well, if it's just for your curiosity, when someone tries to breach the barrier not only do they receive a shock, but it also alerts the Magicstratus."

"What's that?"

"From what I've gathered in my Non-Magical World class, it would be sort of the same as your police officers, but here the Magicstratus includes them plus what they call judges. It's one governmental office. When the barrier is breached without authorization it shoots up a red spark at that location, plus sounds an alarm inside the Magicstratus office."

"Oh." She glanced up, appearing deep in thought. "What happens when someone goes through it with permission?"

"A white spark is sent up at that location, along with a different sound at the office." He studied her intently. "You aren't thinking of trying it are you? It will hurt when it shoots you back. Sometimes a person can get a mild burn if they try it more than once."

Another forced laugh. "No, I was just curious. I want to learn all I can about this place."

"Let us open our books to page fifteen. Today we're going to study how fog can fog one's mind." Their teacher, Professor Blakeley, stood at her podium. Her dark blue hair was piled atop her head in a haphazard bun.

Kira sat up straight and opened her book. Pen in hand, she was poised to take notes. Instead of listening to the teacher, Lucien studied the girl at his side. She was planning something, and he realized that he wanted to know what it was.

V. A. Risby

23

After watching her brother walk into a wall of fire, Kira knew they had to get the heck out of this town as quickly as possible. It would be hard, as Sawyer seemed to be fitting in quite well. He'd made the Sloignis—she knew the word well now as Sawyer and Gabe had been drilling it into her—team, he was becoming very friendly with everyone, even a couple fifth years. He didn't seem as set on going as he had been.

But she was. It had been horrifying watching him. Granted, he hadn't been hurt. In fact, he'd been the only one to bound away completely unscathed by the entire ordeal, but that didn't mean it was something a sane person should do.

No, the more she was in this place, the more she knew she wanted to leave. Her parents could come and go as they pleased. She didn't think it would be that big of a problem to convince them. There were still things they needed to do before they left. She wanted to learn a few spells; hopefully something that would allow them to disguise themselves from anyone who might come looking for them if that was even possible. But before she even needed to think about any of that, she had to know if it was even possible to sneak across the barrier.

As children, she and Sawyer either had made it through on their own or had help. She needed to know which it was.

She stretched out on her bed, her head at the end, *Fundamentals of Spellcasting* opened before her. On one side,

Pepper was stretched out against her. When his big paw would hit her hand, she would scratch him behind the ears. On her other side, lay Flower, sleeping peacefully.

She'd have no trouble taking Flower out in the normal world; she looked like a typical house cat. Pepper, on the other hand, would be a problem. He was big enough people would assume he was some sort of exotic animal. She'd have to find a way to keep him hidden, as she wasn't leaving him behind.

But if they couldn't make it out the barrier on their own, then there was really no point in planning. No, seeing if the barrier could be breached, that would be the first order of business. And to do that, she'd have to venture into the woods, or at least near them. The road into town was lined with dense foliage and trees.

She hadn't counted on Lucien being suspicious of her question. That had thrown her a bit. But she'd had to ask him as Sawyer had never asked Gabe. Hopefully, Lucien would just let it go, put it off on her trying to learn all she could about this world. She didn't need him telling his father she'd been questioning the barrier. Who knew what that man would do with that information.

All right, so woods—or near woods if she stuck to the road—at night. She needed to come up with some way to have a light; and seeing as how she didn't think that she could go to one of the shops in town and pick up a flashlight, she was going to need a spell.

Pouring through the pages, she ignored the ones to warm or cool food and the one for darkness. And then she found it. Or she thought she had. She studied the diagrams that told of the slight wand movement needed to make the spell work and the broken-up words of the spell to make the pronunciation easier.

"Di…a…fot…izo." She rolled the word over and over on her tongue until she thought she had it mastered. "A…ver…tee." She tried the word to extinguish the light. She'd have to know the counter spell; it just made good sense. She tried out the rest of the words in the entry. "Mag…is." That wasn't too hard at all. "*Fara*" was even easier.

As she sat up, the big cat at her side grumbled at the disruption. Another pet to his large head, and Kira got to her feet. Flower opened one eye to look at her, then promptly went back to sleep.

Kira's hand went up to her charm. The word *Amplifico* came without any real thought; it seemed natural. She didn't understand that, how without even trying the word would just come. Was it a part of receiving one's powers? But that was something she could worry about later. Right now, she had other things that were more important.

She raised her wand, ready to try out the spell, when Molly came bounding into the room, Sawyer right behind her.

Pepper and Flower both raised their heads at the intrusion then promptly fell back into their positions on the bed, seemingly annoyed by the dog's always boundless energy.

Her brother got no further than the doorway as he froze when he saw her wand. With a raised brow, he folded his arms and rested his back against the frame. Just in case she didn't understand the unspoken question, he asked, "What are you doing?"

"I'm trying a spell." She really didn't want an audience for her first attempt, but she had a feeling he wouldn't go anywhere now.

Apparently, she was right, as he crossed the room and took a seat at her desk. Molly ignored them both and walked over to the bed to stare at Pepper. The big cat barely opened one eye.

"They are so lazy," Sawyer said, staring at the two cats on the bed.

"They're cats. They're supposed to sleep a lot." Her tone was defensive.

At his comment both Pepper and Flower opened their eyes and glared in his direction.

With a laugh, Sawyer shook his head. "All right let's see this spell."

She'd been hoping against hope he'd leave. Letting out a deep breath, she squared her shoulders and said, "*Diafotizo.*" Instantly a soft glow was emitted from the tip of her wand.

"Cool," Sawyer breathed out. "*Kleino.*"

As soon as he said the words, the light in her bedroom extinguished. The glow from her wand tip was too faint now in the pitch-black room. "*Magis.*" The tip of the wand grew brighter, illuminating the room. She had a feeling she would want something more than a seeming flashlight that needed its batteries changed if she was going traipsing through the woods.

Rising to his feet, Sawyer grasped his own wand. "What was the word again?"

"Di...a...fot...izo." She answered without hesitation. "Add a flick to your wrist for the movement."

He rolled the word over his tongue in the broken syllables a couple of times before he said it. Instantly, the tip of his wand was lit. He glanced over at her. She could see his excited features in the glow of the wands. "You know, magic isn't bad at all."

"It's not all good either," she muttered under her breath.

But he heard her anyway. "What do you mean?"

With a sigh, Kira said, "*Avertee.*" Instantly, her wand was extinguished, plunging the room in more darkness. "*Anavo.*" Her room was once again brilliantly illuminated. Kira went and flopped back down on her bed. Pepper gave an annoyed rumble at the disturbance. She ignored him to pick up her book and pretend to pour over it in hopes Sawyer would take the hint and leave. She wasn't ready to breach this with him yet.

"*Avertee.*" The light died from Sawyer's wand tip. He resumed his seat at her desk, while Molly nosed around the room. "Okay, spill it. What does that mean?"

She knew it was too hopeful to think he would just let it go. Another sigh. Tell him now or not? She'd rather be honest about this. "You walked into a wall of fire, Sawyer, for *fun*. How is that good?"

He shook his head. "I told you. I didn't even feel it."

"Whatever. It's not normal."

"Look around you. What about any of this is normal? These animals." He pointed to Pepper and Molly, who both looked at him. "They appeared out of nowhere. And that cat." Flower watched him with her large green eyes. "She was our birth mother's. She found us after all this time. What about any of this is normal?"

"That's my point. It's not. Look, I'm just going to say it. Our parents were apparently murdered here, but neither of us remembers anything about it. Now I know that Ella, Gabe, Almira, Dante, any of them didn't have anything to do with it. They were too young, but that doesn't mean that one of their parents doesn't know. Or that someone they knew knows what happened." Kira glanced around the room. Pepper and Flower were now sitting up, seeming on edge. From the floor, Molly watched her intently. "I just know that sometimes I get this uneasy feeling, like something is going on that I have no clue about." She had to tell him. He was her brother after all.

Exhaling a deep breath, she said, "The night of Lucien's birthday party, when Gabe and Ella first talked of meeting the others and how I stormed off."

Sawyer nodded, waiting for her to continue.

"I wandered around, looking for somewhere I could be alone to think. I overheard the Mayor yelling at Lucien. Lucien came back at him with am I supposed to 'show up on their doorstep and beg for their friendship?'" She didn't tell him about the broken glass or the subdued boy she had found. That almost felt like a betrayal of the boy she didn't even really like. She glanced up. Sawyer's face was a stony mask.

"Why didn't you tell me?"

She couldn't help it; she rolled her eyes. "Probably for this reason right here. You have an apparent dislike for Lucien Norwood. I didn't want that to cloud your judgement."

"Cloud my judgement?" Sawyer's voice rose. The dog ran to his side. Absently, he stroked her head. His voice lowered just the tiniest of bits. "He's plotting something with his father, something that apparently has to do with us."

"Now we don't know that for certain. I didn't hear our names."

"Don't be naïve. You know that's what he meant. Who else could it have been?"

"Look, he didn't tell me, but you're probably right. It's what I thought, but you're missing the key fact here." She had to make him see Lucien wasn't the problem.

"And what's that?"

"Lucien didn't befriend us. He hasn't tried to get all buddy-buddy with you. In fact, you and he clash horribly. He goes out of his way to be obnoxious to you, so how would that get him close to you?"

"I don't know." Sawyer's voice was now even more annoyed. "But I don't like him."

Kira rolled her eyes again. "Yes, I know that's apparent. But there's more. I told him…about the lamp."

"What!" he exploded.

"Sawyer, just—"

"After you heard that or before?"

She was loathed to admit the truth. "After."

His eyes bugged. He looked incredulous and furious, no easy feat. "I can't believe this! What were you thinking?"

"Look." She felt her own temper rise. "You can yell at me all you want later. Right now, don't focus on that, focus on that something is going on around here. What is it?"

Her brother expelled a pent-up breath. She could see him trying to ease some of his tension. "Fine, but I still hold that he's nothing but trouble."

She sighed in exasperation. "Duly noted. Now about the rest of it."

Sawyer leaned back in the chair and crossed his arms across his chest. Molly went and laid in front of the door as if blocking the room. "Let's go over what we know. I feel like with everything that's been going on we've lost sight of things. I know I keep getting so lost in some new experience or magic that I can't seem to concentrate on one thing for too long."

"Exactly." She agreed. "Let's start with that prophecy. *A set of two will be born, each with a power never known before. Their birth can mark the end to the hidden lives of cowards.*"

Slowly, Sawyer sat forward. "So because of us, the Magical World is going to come out of hiding? How is that possible?"

Her teeth began worrying her bottom lip. Surely that didn't mean what she thought. If it hadn't been her brother, she wouldn't have even voiced it aloud. "Does that mean we're going to all of sudden embrace this magic crap and go all nuts, trying to enslave normal people like they wanted to do before this curse was enacted?"

"Surely not." He didn't look too convinced. He shook his head. "It said it *can* end the hidden lives of the people who are content with the way things are. So someone wants to come out of hiding, to live openly and because of us that could happen."

"But there's no way we would do that. Can you imagine our friends back home? They'd freak out if we pulled out a wand, let alone moved stuff like you did with that chair. No, the normal world is not ready for full on magic."

His lips turned up at the corners. "You're right." He leaned forward, elbows going to his knees, resting his face in his hands. "But I get the distinct impression some people around here do not like people that don't have magic. At tryouts the other day, Eamon called me a son of a pleb. I had no idea what it meant but I know it was against mom and dad. Gabe told me later, it's what some witches and wizards call normal people. It's short for plebeians. I know in school we'd learned that's what the lower class in Rome was called, but Gabe told me here, it means peasant servants or slaves."

"So if someone like that wants an end to magical secrecy…"

"Stands to reason they probably want a class to rule over. And that would be people without magic."

She glanced toward the door. "So because of us…are mom and dad in danger?" Even as she asked the question, she knew the answer.

"Probably so. Our birth parents were killed. Thinking about it now. It was probably to get to us."

Beside her, Flower let out a deep, guttural yowl. Both of their gazes flew to her, as did Molly and Pepper's watchful scrutinies.

"I think she knows what we're talking about." As the words left her mouth, no matter how crazy they sounded, Kira knew she was right. "She came back to protect us."

The cat let out a little kitten mew.

And that cemented in Kira's mind what they had to do. "We can't stay here. We have to get mom and dad out of here. We have to leave. I want to try to breach the barrier."

24

He should have tried to talk her out of it. It would have been the logical thing to do, but a part of Sawyer was terribly afraid that his sister was right. He hadn't been able to concentrate on his classes for the remainder of the week. He'd been so unfocused that when learning defensive spells, he'd actually forgotten to block and allowed Lucien to knock him on his butt.

Lucien had been near giddy; Sawyer had not. In fact, he was still pissed thinking about it now. But he pushed that aside. He had other things to worry about at the moment. Ever since the conversation with his sister, Sawyer felt as if he was looking over his shoulder. He wanted to keep this just between them, as the more people who knew what they were going to try to do, the greater the risk of it getting out.

At first, they had thought about doing it during the day, figuring the spark sent up wouldn't show as brightly in the daylight, but they had discarded that idea, because it would still show up. Plus in the daytime, more people would be out moving around, which would mean if a spark did go off, someone could be there quicker.

That left them going at night. He wasn't looking forward to that, as it brought its own set of problems. They had to find a way out of the house so as not to worry their parents, and that left them in the woods—unless they stuck to the road, which in itself brought risks at night. Sadly, the woods would be the best option. If the alarm did sound, there would be more places to hide, and they'd be harder to find and reach.

However, this way involved them including others, as they needed a cover story. He could see nothing but trouble from this, but Sawyer really didn't see any other choice.

"So, it's our last weekend before we start with Sloignis practice every day, plus Sunday I get my powers, so what do you think we should do tomorrow?" Gabe asked that as he leaned against the closed locker by Sawyer.

Sawyer tossed his books inside then shut it before he turned to the other boy. Now was the time. "Actually, I need a favor tonight."

Gabe straightened, hoisting his bag on his shoulder. "Alright, sure. What is it?"

"I need you to cover for me just in case my parents ask, which I don't think they will."

The blond nodded, though his brow was still knit in confusion. "Alright. Cover for what?"

Sawyer glanced around at the numerous students still milling about the hallways. "Come on." He angled his head in the direction of the doors leading to the grounds. Gabe fell in step beside him. They didn't say another word until they were far away, almost at the edge of the school boundary.

"So tell me." Gabe said without preamble.

"I have something I need to do tonight. I need to tell my parents I'm going to your house."

The blond nodded. "But you're not, right? So what are you doing?"

"It's probably best if you don't know." Even as the words left his mouth, Sawyer felt bad saying them. "I'm sorry."

"Yeah, I'll do it. I just…I get the feeling this is dangerous."

And for some reason, even though he'd only known him for a little over a week, Sawyer didn't want to lie to the other boy.

Yet he was cut off from spilling everything by his sister's appearance. "Will he do it?"

Sawyer groaned. If that wasn't a tip off that something was wrong, he didn't know what was.

She realized her mistake as soon as she said it as she tried desperately to cover. "It's no big deal. We just want it to be a surprise for our folks."

Gabe's green eyes narrowed in consideration. Then, abruptly, he turned from them and yelled across the yard, "Ella! Come here!"

The petite brunette waved goodbye to Carra, then crossed the yard to where they were waiting.

He didn't give her time to say a greeting. "Did Kira ask you to cover for her tonight?"

Ella's brows rose. "Yeah, why is that your concern?" She seemed genuinely perplexed.

"Because Sawyer just asked me to do the same for him. Something is up, and I don't know. I don't have a good feeling about it."

As a unit, they turned toward him and his sister. Sawyer wanted to groan. If only Kira had kept her mouth shut. But what was done was done; now he just had to deal. He still didn't want to tell them the complete truth. It was better if they didn't know. "Look, we just need to do something. And we'd rather our parents not know what it is."

"Okay, fine, no problem. We'll cover for you, but you can tell us what it is," Ella said. "It's not like we'll tell your parents."

Sawyer shot a glance at his sister, his way of telling her that she was the cause of this.

Her huffed out breath told adequately enough of her annoyance with him and the entire situation. "Fine. Look," she said, lowering her voice, "we want to see what happens if we try to cross the barrier."

Gabe and Ella's eyes widened to the point Sawyer had some definite fear they would actually burst out of their heads.

"Why would you do that?" Gabe hissed, glancing around as if they were being watched.

That was a bit of an extreme reaction, or at least Sawyer thought. Hadn't anyone in this crazy place once thought about seeing the outside world? It wasn't as if he was planning a massive breakout. But perhaps to these people, that's what it seemed like. Apparently, everyone here just went with the status quo.

"Because Kira and I got out of here before. We want to know how. So we need to see if we can. Look, all we need is for you to cover for us. That's it."

They both looked pale at the thought. Then Gabe shook his head. "No, I'm going with you."

Seeing as how the very notion was making the other boy almost break out in a cold sweat, Sawyer didn't know if that was the best idea. "That's really not necessary."

"No, it is. Either you go by the road, which you could be seen, so why would we need to cover for you, or you're going into the woods. If you're going in the woods, I'm going with you. You all haven't lived here. You don't know what's out there."

"You told us," Kira said. "It sounds frightening, but we have to try. We just want to know."

Gabe's expression turned downright mulish. "I'm going. You need me."

"So am I," Ella said. She cleared her throat, trying to sound more self-assured.

This was definitely not turning out the way Sawyer had planned, but one look at their stubborn expressions, and he knew his entreaties would be ignored. "Fine," he said with complete ill grace. This was just a disaster waiting to happen.

~~*~*~*

"Are you sure you wouldn't want to spend the night over here?" his mother asked.

"We might come back and stay here after we hang out for a bit. It will just depend."

"All right. Have fun." She kissed them both on the forehead, careful to keep from touching them with her floury hands; then she resumed her place at the counter where she was kneading bread.

Both he and Kira nodded then quickly fled the kitchen. After telling their father bye, they hurried out the front door and down the steps, Molly and Pepper at their heels. They'd tried to leave the two animals, but the yowling and howling were too loud. Thankfully, Flower had taken their admonishments to stay, especially after they reminded her she really shouldn't be seen. It was with great loathing that she had walked from the room, taking refuge in Kira's bedroom.

Sawyer glanced up. He could see the cat's outline in the window. She was watching them. It warmed his heart, and yet at the same time made him think that what they were doing was incredibly stupid.

But he shook it off, and they started down the road. They had passed the next house and were nearing the corner when they saw Gabe and Ella shrouded in shadows, waiting for them. There was a slight nip in the air with the nights now getting cooler. They all had jackets. Sawyer was surprised to see that Gabe and Ella's seemed quite similar to their own.

"Copied from one of your fashion magazines. Easier to move in than our old long, flowing coats," Ella explained when she noticed his attention. She was all but burrowed into hers.

They all stood there for a long moment before Kira said, "Okay, if we're going to do it, let's go before we get spotted."

With a nod of affirmation, Sawyer turned and headed down the quiet lane. This would be the first time they had ventured by their old home. They'd thought it best to try to breach the barrier around the same spot they must have before.

"I wish it wasn't so clear. I feel like I'm being watched." No sooner had the words left Gabe's mouth than fog started to creep in.

They all stopped.

"How did that just happen?" Sawyer turned to ask that but really wasn't expecting an answer.

Then Pepper moved and bumped Kira with his large black head.

She looked down at the cat. "What?" she whispered.

The cat bumped her again.

This time she glanced to the rest of them. They appeared just as confused as she did. She surveyed their surroundings. She shivered. Then she asked, "Can a witch or wizard make fog?"

"You could make like a cloud of smoke with your wand," Ella said, "though I've never seen anyone do it."

"Yeah, they did that before when they were fighting." Gabe glanced around, nervously. "You know like to hide your escape."

Sawyer's brow knitted. None of that explained the fog that had taken over the entire area. It was creepy, really creepy. But something nagged at the back of his mind, though he couldn't for the life of him remember what it was. He pushed it away. He'd worry about it later.

"Whatever. Let's get a move on." He started again, and the rest fell in step with him. He, Gabe and Molly in the front. Kira, Ella, and Pepper in the back.

"That's the Bloodworth's house," Gabe said as they passed the last house on the lane. They rushed by it, so they wouldn't be seen. Once its lights faded from view they slowed their pace. On their left was what appeared to be a vacant field, on their right it almost seemed that way, too, until they got closer. Then they could make out the outlines of ruin and destruction.

"There's really nothing left." Kira's words whispered out.

Sawyer could do no more than stare. It was a pile of rubble. He had no clue how he, his sister, and even Flower had survived this. It looked as if a bomb had exploded.

"My father said it had to have come from the inside. I remember him telling my mom that when everyone was trying to figure out what had happened." Gabe's voice was hoarse when he spoke. "That was so long ago, but I still remember it. I was on the stairs, hiding, listening to them. I knew something was wrong, but they wouldn't tell me, not until later."

Sawyer had to clear his throat a couple of times before he could form any words. Finally, he asked, "Why would he say that?"

"When you and Kira were born, your parents put protective measures around your home and your grandparents' home. Unless someone had been invited, like through the open speculo, everyone in your home would have been alerted. There would have been time for your parents and you all to get out. No one could force their way inside."

Sawyer didn't know how to respond to Gabe's revelation. He glanced to his sister to see that she was watching him, too. He read her look; it was the same thought he had. It wasn't a freak accident or a mistake; someone had targeted them. And the only reason he could come up with was them.

Sawyer wanted to get to the barrier. Not to see if he could break through so he could make a run for it. No, he needed to know what type of powers he possessed because he had a feeling he was going to need them.

Suddenly, Molly issued a low growl, the hackles on the back of her neck raising as she bared her teeth. Instantly, Pepper had joined in, back up and tense as he moved to the front. The two sharp fangs in his mouth readily apparent. Without thought, Sawyer reached for his charm. Just as quickly, his wand was in his hand. Kira was at his side immediately, hers out, too.

"*Diafotizo*," Kira whispered the word. Light glowed from the tip of her wand.

Something shifted at the edge of the ruins. Then it separated, and the form of a person became distinguishable. At the person's side was the shape of a large dog.

Sawyer had a sense of foreboding and irritation drift down the back of his spine. It increased when the figure came into view. "What are you doing here, Norwood?"

The words came out like a snarl. They caused the wolf at his side to bare its teeth. Lucien put his hand on the large, white animal's head. It quieted instantly. "Call it curiosity, but after your sister questioned me, I knew something was up. And wouldn't you know it, I was right."

Sawyer glanced to Kira. She appeared downright furious. "That wasn't an invitation," she hissed.

The boy's smile grew as he approached them. "Might as well have been. Besides, you need me."

Sawyer couldn't hold it back, he laughed.

Gabe was more vocal, the incredulousness bleeding into his tone. "Why would we need you?"

"Because, unlike you, who's still worthless, I have my powers."

Even in the dark, Sawyer could see the red heat steal up Gabe's face. To diffuse the situation, Sawyer asked, "Why does that matter?"

"Because you're going in there." Lucien glanced over his shoulder at the line of trees in the distance. "Three wands and three familiars are better than two. You need me."

Sawyer didn't want him going with them. If they failed, Lucien would never let them hear the end of it. If they succeeded, he'd have something he could hold over them. He had no options.

"Look." The dark headed boy shrugged his shoulders and shoved his hands into the pockets of his fine, linen coat. "I'll make this easy. Either I go with you, quietly, I might add, or I turn right around and tell everyone what you four are up to. Choice is yours."

Sawyer glared. He wondered if he could manage what his sister had with the lamp and blow Lucien up. Sawyer doubted anyone would really miss the other boy. Even as the supremely satisfying thought crossed his mind, Sawyer knew he wouldn't try it. Instead, he rolled his eyes and said, "Let's go."

Quickly, they left the ruins of the house behind. Gabe was still at his side, muttering under his breath. The only change was that Lucien was bringing up the rear. For some reason, that thought was oddly comforting. Hopefully, it was just because he was as far away from Sawyer as possible, not that he was actually glad to have another person with a wand along, a person who had been around magic his entire life.

They all came to a stop at the tree line.

"Are you sure you want to do this?" Lucien asked as he stared up at the massive trees.

"I thought you said quiet," Sawyer growled over his shoulder. Lucien held up his hands in a gesture of defeat as he shook his head.

Sawyer didn't want to see it. It would give him doubts, and he was already having enough of those. He glanced to his sister who was now beside him. She straightened then gave him a nod.

"*Diafotizo.*" At once his wand lit, as did Lucien's. "We stick together. No matter what."

"Agreed," they all whispered. Then they stepped into the forest.

They formed a tight circle with Molly slightly out in front. Lucien's wolf that was named Arctic was slightly behind. In the center, Pepper's lime-colored eyes glowed.

It sounded like a typical forest; that was Sawyer's first thought. He could hear the chirps and buzzing of nocturnal birds and insects, the sound of the wind blowing the leaves of the trees. It was normal. Ever so slightly, he found himself relaxing. He held his wand a little higher to see further. "I figure this is the way we went."

"It is," Lucien agreed.

Sawyer stopped so suddenly, Ella ran into his back. His arms caught her to steady her. He made certain she had sure footing before he rounded on the other boy, but Sawyer still didn't release her. It seemed natural to keep her close. He kept her hand in his. "How do you know that?" All his suspicions were rising to the fore again.

"Because once your sister asked me, I had a feeling this is what she wanted to do. I didn't know she would bring the whole gang. I was going to help her. She didn't need to go into the woods alone."

"Wait." Gabe held up his hands to stop Sawyer from saying anything for a moment. "You mean you've been waiting for her each night out there?"

The red heat barely visible in the wand's light was answer enough. Kira stared at Lucien in openmouthed astonishment.

Sawyer would delve into Norwood staying as far away from his sister as humanly possible later. Right now, Sawyer had issues that are more pressing. "Go back. How do you know this is how we went?"

"Because I did research. You two are apparently important. Being as such there was a file on your parents' murders and your disappearances. My father is Lord Mayor, so I snuck in to read the files."

While that would have been an innocent explanation, Sawyer didn't like it. He didn't want Lucien knowing more about his past then he himself did. "What was in the files?"

Lucien glanced to Kira. His tone softened. "Just that when the Magicstratus arrived, the protective barriers your parents had put around your home were still functioning. They couldn't get inside. Your grandparents had to come and lower them. Which means…"

"That whoever did that had to have been invited into our house." Kira's voice was low and soft. Ella reached over and took her hand in her own, giving her a comforting squeeze, while Gabe's hand went to her shoulder.

Sawyer had to clear his voice twice before he could speak. "And we…we came this way?"

"Yeah." Lucien's arrogance was gone though he shot a glare at Gabe. "They followed your tracks into the woods and up to the barrier. Then it was like you both disappeared."

"Their tracks?" Gabe asked into the stillness.

"That much magic going off would have left a trace. But the barrier made them lose it. It took them too long to figure a way out of it. By the time they eventually did, you both were long gone."

It was too much. There was too much information being thrown at Sawyer all at once to process. He'd have to deal with it later when he had time to think. But now, out here in the woods, which were apparently home to monsters, he needed to keep his wits about him. "How do we know when we reach the barrier?" he asked, his voice quiet.

"It's colored now," Ella explained. "Sometimes people would accidently walk into it, so they colored it and made it shimmer on this side. You can't see it from the Non-Magical side."

Sawyer nodded. Taking a deep breath, he started them forward again. His mind frantically replaying everything Lucien had just said. He wasn't focusing on the task at hand. He didn't know if any of them really were, as it remained silent after that as they trekked through the woods. If it weren't for Gabe sticking his arm out in front of him, Sawyer would have kept walking.

Instead, he stopped so abruptly he almost tripped. The color didn't really show up in the dark, but that wavy shimmer did. It almost looked like some force field he had seen depicted in a movie once.

"Well." He breathed out a deep sigh. "This is it. *Mazevo*." Instantly, his wand was back as a charm on his chain. "All right. If any sparks go off, be ready to run. Go left. We'll get back to our house that way." He turned back to the barrier.

Kira's hand reached for his arm, stopping him. "No, this was my idea. Let me."

Sawyer was shaking his head before she finished. "Look, you said it would give off a shock. That's sort of like the fire and ice walls were in tryouts. That didn't affect me. Let me do this."

She stared at him a long moment, then finally she nodded. She took a couple of steps back.

"Molly, stay with Kira." The dog did not look happy about the command. If a dog could glare daggers, she was.

But she did as asked and went to stand on the other side of his sister, between her and Lucien.

Squaring his shoulders, Sawyer turned back to the barrier. He could do this. It was just like Sloignis. Taking a deep breath, he stepped forward until he was right before it. He held his breath and moved.

He waited for the zap, the little shock that Lucien had warned his sister about, but there was nothing.

No, that wasn't right. Sawyer had the sensation of walking through Jell-O. Then, just as quickly, it was gone, and he was on the other side. He whipped back around. Ella had been correct; the barrier was not distinguishable from this side. He'd made it. And since they were all standing there, staring at him in shock, he guessed no sparks went up.

He was more confident this time as he stepped forward and walked back through. He couldn't help it; he grinned at their stunned expressions.

"Frinx," Lucien breathed, mouth a gape.

"I can't believe that worked." Gabe was looking at Sawyer in shock.

Ella looked relieved. "I'm glad you're all right."

"*Mazevo.*" Kira's wand shrunk down. "I'm going to try. Pepper, wait here."

Before Sawyer could say anything to stop her, she was gone. He glanced up, looking for the spark, nothing, just his grinning sister on the other side.

She stepped back through.

"Cripes. I wonder if it will work for the rest of us." Even as Gabe asked that, Lucien was already shaking his head.

"No, you remember, not too long ago old Tom hit the barrier. He was out cold when they got to him."

"Old Tom?" Sawyer asked.

"He's this man, well, he's…"

"He's a drunk." Lucien finished for Ella.

She shot him a quelling look. Lucien just shrugged.

"Okay," Gabe agreed, "but what if one of us is with them? I wonder if it would work then."

Again, Lucien shrugged. "Worth a shot."

"I'm going."

Sawyer shook his head at the blond. "We don't know if it will work. I don't want to risk dragging you through there."

"How else are we going to find out?" Gabe asked. "We have to try."

"Take me."

Sawyer turned to Lucien, brow raised. He didn't want to. The less he had to do with Lucien Norwood the better. And taking him through the barrier…Sawyer was already putting too much trust in the boy keeping quiet about this. But he already knew enough to screw them all. Still, taking Norwood would be his very last option, but at the same time, it could work.

"No, you can't risk it—"

Sawyer cut off his sister. "All right. I'll take you."

"What?" That came from both Gabe and Kira.

Gabe added more to his. "How come you'll try with him and not me?"

"I would prefer if nothing happens to you. Him." Sawyer glanced to Lucien, "I really don't care."

"*Mazevo.*" Lucien stowed his wand. "Nice to know where I stand." He didn't seem bothered by the pronouncement at all. "Arctic, stay with Kira." The wolf pressed against her side. Molly shot him a disdainful glare.

Kira's fear was getting the best of her. "What am I, the animal whisperer?" The words were snapped.

Lucien grinned and petted the wolf on the head. Then he looked to her. "No, he just likes you." He touched her arm. "He has good taste." He turned to Sawyer. "Let's go."

With a nod, Sawyer turned toward the barrier. "Give me your hand."

"Aww, I didn't know you cared." Even as Lucien said that, he clasped his hand.

Sawyer ignored the comment. "Count of three. One…two…three." He stepped forward, his grip on the other boy tight. He might not like Lucien, but he didn't want him dying or frying or melting out here in the dark with them.

Once again, the slow-moving Jell-O feel hit Sawyer, then he was out, Lucien still at his side. They dropped hands immediately. Looking at the others on the opposite side of the barrier, they weren't moving or running. No spark.

"You know what this means," Lucien said, a smirk turning up the corners of his lips.

Sawyer glanced to him.

"We can now sneak out."

Sawyer rolled his eyes. There was no way in the world he was sneaking out with Lucien Norwood. They were not friends. Sawyer could think of better things to do with his time. He thought to tell him that, but Lucien stopped him.

"Something's wrong."

Sawyer glanced in the same direction he was, back to the other side of the barrier. At first, Sawyer didn't see anything to cause alarm, but then he did.

All three animals were turned towards the woods, their hackles raised.

"Can familiars cross the barrier?"

"Yeah," Lucien answered. "But it doesn't matter. Only witches and wizards supposedly can't. Anything else that lives in the forest can. Once the barrier was breached by the people looking for you all, everything else was free to move through it."

Kira now had her wand in her hand, Gabe and Ella at her sides as they all scanned the tree line.

"Let's go." Sawyer reached for Lucien's hand. With no hesitation, the other boy took it. No sooner had they both reemerged on the other side of the barrier, they had their wands out. They could hear it then, the low growl emanating from somewhere in the darkness.

He could feel it, watching them, studying their movements. It was close. Sawyer raised his wand higher.

"Definitely not a troll or an ogre," Gabe whispered.

"It sounds like it's coming from the direction we came." Ella pressed into Sawyer's side.

"If it's a wendigo, it's hunting us, and it has been for a while. We have to move." No one questioned Lucien. Pressed in a tight circle they went left, their pace brisk. The animals brought up the rear.

Sawyer pushed Ella in front of him. "I want you safe." Then he raised his voice, so everyone could hear. "We see anything, run." Then he dropped back beside Lucien. "Know any spells?"

"Just that one I used on you in class the other day to knock you back."

"That's all we got then. What was it? I wasn't paying attention."

"Great," Lucien snarled. He darted a glance behind them. "*Pulsatereto.*" Then he said, "Do that thing you did in the refectory the other day with the chair."

"I don't think we want whatever this is closer to us," Gabe said, as he'd fallen behind with them.

"Yeah, hadn't thought of that. What else do we have?" Lucien glanced to Kira.

Sawyer saw it, knew what the other boy was thinking. Sawyer didn't think his sister could blow up whatever it was. "How do they track?" Sawyer asked. If it was by sound, they were screwed, as they weren't exactly being quiet.

"Smell and sound," Gabe and Lucien said at the same time.

"Great." They needed something to muffle their footsteps. He didn't know how to get rid of their scent though. Then it hit him. "Thunderstorm would be good right about now. It could give us some cover, make us harder to track," Sawyer said as he heard another low growl. It sounded closer.

"I can't do that." Lucien darted a glance behind them. "Any suggestions of something we *might* be capable of?"

Suddenly, Pepper jumped ahead and butted into Kira's legs. "What?" She tried to muffle the squeal the unexpected bump caused. The large cat did it again. "You're going to trip me."

Just when Sawyer was getting ready to do his own yelling at the cat, as the last thing they needed was someone with a sprained ankle, it hit him. The fog, the rain the other day out of nowhere. His own experience in the Sloignis tryouts with the fire, his tattoo, Kira's. He stopped so suddenly Arctic and Molly had to skid around him to avoid hitting him.

He glanced out in the surrounding darkness. Behind him, he could see a pair of yellow eyes glowing. They needed something and now; it was getting steadily closer. "Kira," he said her name, not loud, but since they had all stopped when he had, she heard him.

"What?" Her gaze was darting around, wide and terrified, her wand out in front of her.

"We need a thunderstorm."

She looked at him as if he had gone insane. "Well that's all special and great but—"

Pepper head-butted her again.

She glanced down at the big cat and then back to Sawyer. He saw the understanding dawn.

The low growl came again, nearer. She glanced up at the sky, her face screwed up in intense concentration.

"I said a suggestion we could accomplish. We're wasting…" Lucien's words died with the first crash of thunder. Then the rain hit. Not a sprinkle but a downpour. His eyes widened in understanding.

"Let's go," Ella yelled. They took off at a run, darting and zigzagging through the trees.

With the storm, Sawyer could no longer hear the low growls, but he hoped that meant the creature couldn't hear them either. Since the animals continued to run at his heels, he just kept moving. He'd worry about it later. He grabbed Ella's hand to propel her along. Gabe and Lucien flanked Kira, neither touching her in case it interfered with her concentration.

Up ahead, Sawyer could see a clearing and what looked to be the faint glow of lights. They burst through as one, panting, but still moving, trying to get as far away from the edge of the woods as possible. They didn't slow until they got within sight of the first house.

"Kira, keep it up. The storm gives us cover." No one said anything to Sawyer's comment this time. They jogged in a group through the lanes until they hit a street. Finally, they stopped.

Kira half twisted her hand, and just as abruptly as it began, the storm stopped. Everyone was staring at her in shock. Belatedly, Sawyer realized even he was.

"How did you do that?" Lucien gasped as he caught his breath. Water dripped down his face.

She glanced down at her shoes as the big cat soothingly rubbed against her legs. "I don't know. I just…did."

"We'll worry about that later." Sawyer turned to the others. "Do those things in the woods come into town?"

Ella shivered in her wet clothing. "Sometimes, but it's rare."

That was too big of a chance to take as far as he was concerned. He kept hold of her hand. "Our house is closer, let's go."

As they started to move, Lucien stood in place. "I'll go back to my house."

"Don't be stupid. That thing could be out there. You can't go by yourself."

He turned to Kira. The smile he gave her was warm. "I'll be all right."

"She's right," Sawyer cut in. No matter how much of a prick he'd been, Lucien had just had their backs. Sawyer wasn't about to send him off on his own. "Look, I'm not inviting you over for us to be best friends. But there's a monster out there that was just stalking us. Come to our house. You can always use the speculo to get home."

Even as he fell in step with them, Lucien said, "I can't. I didn't use it to leave so it's not activated. It would have to be on at home for me to use yours."

As they walked up the front steps to his house, Sawyer was shaking his head. "No, I can get you in. I've done it before."

"What?" Gabe asked. "When have you?"

But Sawyer didn't hear him. He was frozen, hand on the doorknob as the memory assaulted him. He could see it happening. He could see the hallway, felt himself sneaking inside the speculo, then opening it and entering another house. He didn't know where it was. It wasn't familiar. He had been curious and looked around. Then he felt it, the terror. He couldn't see what it was just shapes and outlines, but he was so scared. It sent him running back into the speculo. He'd ran out at home and straight upstairs to hide. He was still cowering in a corner when he heard his mother's scream and a loud bang.

As quickly as it came, the memory fled, leaving him gasping, panting for air. He dropped to his knees on the porch. Instantly, Ella was in front of him as he'd still had a hold of her. She pushed back the damp hair from his face, saying his name, as Molly pressed against his side. Sawyer tried to shut his eyes to block out the images.

It was his fault.

He glanced up to his sister. "It's my fault." The words came out as a whisper, but they tore into his soul.

"What? Sawyer?" Kira's brow knitted in confusion. She glanced helplessly at those around them.

"It's okay," Ella told him. "We're all safe. Nothing happened."

He finally met her concerned gaze. She thought he was talking about what had almost happened tonight in the woods. If only that was it.

"That night." Sawyer glanced to Kira, the guilt and horror awash in his marbled colored eyes. "I was going to sneak to Gabe's house using the speculo. I had already figured out if I opened our end, I could go anywhere, even if someone else's was locked. That night...I don't know where I ended up. I can't really remember what I saw. It was just dark, but I was terrified. It was something horrible. I have never been so scared in my life. I ran up the stairs. I forgot to close it." He shut his eyes as he heard the scream all over again. "That's how they got in. It's my fault they're dead. I killed our parents."

V. A. Risby

V. A. Risby